GOING HOME

I'd counted on Sunrise being the same little hamlet it had been in my childhood and so far, thank God, I hadn't been disappointed.

I was on leave with no clock to punch, no one to account to. I was free (well, unmarried anyway), black (on the toasted almond end of the spectrum), and solvent (one gas card and one credit card for emergencies). I was here on a whim, just passing through, as it were, and one sure way of attracting attention, which I wanted to avoid, would be to drive around the residential sections of town at five-fifty-five in the morning. So I told myself I might as well have breakfast at Fred's Diner.

That's when the trouble started.

SUNRISE

Chassie West

HarperPaperbacks
A Division of HarperCollins*Publishers*

HarperPaperbacks   *A Division of* HarperCollins*Publishers*
                   10 East 53rd Street, New York, N.Y. 10022

Cover illustration by Linda Messier

First printing: October 1994

Printed in the United States of America

HarperPaperbacks and colophon are trademarks of
HarperCollins*Publishers*

❖ 10 9 8 7 6 5 4 3 2

ACKNOWLEDGMENTS

To Officer Carol Perry Blake of the Washington, D.C., Metropolitan Police Force, my sincere gratitude for her help and patience. Any errors in the descriptions of the setup and duties of that hard-pressed cadre of public servants are my lapses, not hers.

To the members of the Columbia Writers Workshop, especially Ruth Glick, our group's eternal flame—

And Linda Hayes of Columbia Literary Associates, agent extraordinaire and friend—

And Jean Elizabeth Morris Favors, bosom buddy/soul sister/crying towel of four decades—

And Maggie Sands and Farris Forsythe, priceless, loving friends—

And Carolyn Marino, an editor to die for—

And Bob, my husband, my rock—

My sincere thanks. I could not have done this book without you.

SUNRISE

Prologue

The kid was going to shoot me; that was a given. He had nothing to lose; he'd already shot one cop. Duck, fellow crimefighter, car pool partner, friend, sat slumped at the kid's feet, his back against the wall, a pool of blood widening around him. "Back in a sec," he'd said when he'd hopped out of the cruiser. "Got to leave my share of the money for Mom's present with Sis. The woman wants a monster TV, that's what she gets. Keep the engine running." And I, like a fool, had come barreling into the apartment building, a burr up my ass because in the time he'd been gone he could have put a TV together from scratch. How long could it take to run to the rear wing of the building, knock on the door, and cram two hundred dollars into his sister's hand?

It was after midnight. I'd been tired, evil, and I wanted to go home. With that on my mind, everything else was blocked out and for the first time my sixth sense for trouble brewing had failed me. So now here I was, my lungs pumping like bellows and sweat pooling between my breasts as I stared down the barrel of a ridiculously small nickel-plated revolver aimed right at my head.

I thought of all the things I'd meant to do and hadn't, like cleaning my oven and getting rid of the soap scum in my shower and seeing my hometown one last time. It was too late now. The headlines the *Washington Post* would use drifted before my eyes like words trailing along the sides of the Goodyear blimp: Off-Duty Police Killed in Late-Night Robbery. The kid held Duck's two hundred dollars in one hand, the gun in the other, and it was my turn to die.

1

I'd been humming "Carolina in the Morning" for the last fifty miles when it occurred to me I had no idea which Carolina the song referred to. North, I decided, and slapped the steering wheel to make it official. Hot damn. I'd made a decision, my third in three days. The first had been to get the hell out of town for a while, the second to turn in my badge the minute I got back. Now this one. *North* Carolina in the Morning. Why not? That's where I'd been for the past several days.

While at home in D.C., I'd cleaned the oven. Twice. Granted, I hadn't gotten to it until almost a month after I thought I was about to meet my Maker, but at least I'd done it. I'd honestly thought it might help. It hadn't. Neither had scouring the shower stall. The application of elbow grease to the grungier areas of one's life might be therapy for some, but it did absolutely nothing for me. I needed a change of scenery.

A friend's offer to use her condo on the Outer Banks had seemed a lifesaver; one more night of bad dreams and the screaming sweats and they'd have had to haul me off to the nearest ha-ha hostel. The prospect of the incessant murmur of the ocean to lull me to sleep had had me packed and out of D.C. in thirty minutes flat, barreling south like a late-leaving migratory bird with winter hard on its tail. For the most part, it had worked. I was rested but still restless, and after walking the beaches for three mornings had nothing more to show for it but a tan—which I didn't need, having been born with one—and sand under my toenails, which I also didn't need. In desperation I'd resorted to driving the highways at odd hours, which is how I'd wound up going westward ho, drawn by my memory of the sun rising behind Old Bluenose Mountain. Since I was in the area, I'd told myself, I might as well take a turn through Sunrise, my old stomping grounds, and have breakfast at Fred's Diner. Another decision made. Definitely on the mend.

Once there, I couldn't believe it. The diner was exactly as I remembered. A faux marble-topped counter running the length of the place, the stools alternately covered in bright orange and purple vinyl. Hand-lettered menu on a long board mounted on the wall, and booths along the opposite wall, purple banquettes flanking white Formica tables. The only difference I could see was that the plants hanging from the ceiling were now fabric rather than plastic, and the ripped upholstery on the second and sixth stools, which would goose you if you didn't mount them just so, had been replaced. It was incredible. I could well have been in high school again, stopping in at Fred's after the prom for a Superburger, fries, and a monster Pepsi. Fourteen years had passed and nothing had changed.

I'd counted on Sunrise being the same little hamlet it had been in my childhood and so far, thank God, I hadn't been disappointed. But then all I'd seen were the stores along Main Street. Several stood empty and desolated, but not nearly as many as I would have expected. The exteriors of those still in business were bright and clean, some featuring signs that warned of wet paint. The horse troughs along the curbs, weed gardens when I'd lived here, overflowed with recently planted flowers. There'd been a serious effort to spruce up things. Perhaps it wasn't as poor a town as it used to be.

The houses would tell the tale, but I hadn't dredged up the nerve to see my old neighborhood yet. There was plenty of time. I was on leave with no clock to punch, no one to account to. I was free (well, unmarried anyway), black (on the toasted almond end of the spectrum), and solvent (one gas card and one credit card, kept for emergencies). I was here on a whim, just passing through, as it were, and one sure way of attracting attention, which I wanted to avoid, would be to drive around the residential sections of town at five-fifty-five in the morning. Besides, I was ravenous. Except for the pecan roll I'd picked up at a Stuckey's on Route 85, I hadn't eaten anything substantial since the evening before.

I scanned the menu. The prices were higher—a double-dip of ice cream was fifty cents more—but I could swear that it featured the same selections I remembered, with the addition of a couple—and only a couple—of low-fat entries. The aroma of the coffee set up eruptions under my belt. I eyed the booths, then opted for a stool at the far end of the counter. It was where I had preferred to sit as a kid, and that was what this was all about, wasn't it? I was back home to wallow in my childhood. Getting shot will do that to you.

"Hold on, Caleb," a feminine voice called from the kitchen. "You eatin' or just drinkin'?"

"Both," I responded. "And it's not Caleb."

The kitchen door snapped open and an ash-blond head appeared from behind it. Azure blue eyes scrutinized me intently, reminding me of my status as an outsider. "Uh, sorry, ma'am. Be right out."

"No hurry." I settled down to wait, determined to relax and recapture the rhythm of my hometown. Life moved at a far more leisurely pace here, the high-tension, frenetic energy that charged my days occurring only if something was on fire, and depending on what it was, perhaps not then. Even the speed limit, a rip-snorting thirty miles per hour, was seldom exceeded, the tendency being to drift down the street at twenty in order not to miss waving at anyone you passed, whether driving or on foot. I doubted that had changed since I'd been gone and might never, probably because Sunrise was far enough from the nearest interstate to guarantee the continued disinterest of developers, suburbanites, and local politicians.

The waitress bustled out in less than a minute, tying a frilly lavender apron around the waist of her orange uniform. There was a lot of her. She was at least six-one, bordering on buxom and hippy, the kind of full figure that most women haunted spas to get rid of and most men probably overtipped to show their appreciation of. One long blond braid flapped almost to the small of her back, and her round, smooth face had the kind of fair skin that would scorch in a strong sun. She was vaguely familiar, but no more than that. About my age, give or take a year, I thought, with a face that was almost pretty if you ignored her expression, one of deep-seated boredom. I would decide later whether to take it personally.

"What'll it be?" she asked, notepad at the ready.

I rattled off a breakfast order worthy of a construction worker with a heavy day ahead of him. Her eyes never wavered from my features as she listened, nodding, but writing nothing on the pad.

"Butter or margarine on your toast?"

I spotted the Caswell Dairy logo on a carton of milk in the cooler, remembered the richness of their ice cream, and began to salivate. "Butter. And do you have any marmalade? Orange?" My gustatory memory had kicked into high gear.

She almost smiled. "You've been here before. Yes, ma'am, sure do. You want your juice or coffee first?"

"Juice, please."

"Comin' up." She left with a distracted air and a backward glance at me before disappearing into the kitchen and returning with what had to be a sixteen-ounce glass of orange juice. I sipped it and closed my eyes in ecstasy. Fresh-squeezed and loaded with pulp. After a decade of the supermarket's pasteurized, made-from-concentrate, I was in heaven.

The meal itself, when it arrived, fulfilled every nostalgia-crammed fantasy I'd ever had over the years. The bacon was thick, crisp, and lean, the scrambled eggs fluffed to the consistency of clouds. I'd chosen potatoes over grits and discovered that I'd completely forgotten how down-home home fries were supposed to taste. I was probably ingesting more cholesterol in this one meal than I usually ate in a month, but, after all, it was a special occasion. If I tumbled off the stool the next minute, dead of clogged arteries, I'd be leaving this world a happy woman.

I took my time, determined to enjoy every mouthful. A few customers popped in for coffee and doughnuts to go, acknowledging me with openly curious glances, a nod or a tip of the hat and a terse, "Mornin'." Otherwise they kept their distance, which was fine with me. I hadn't come to look up old friends.

The waitress monitored my progress from the porthole in the kitchen door, topping off my coffee whenever my cup reached a level she couldn't see from her vantage point. I was just finishing the last of the toast when she exploded from her sanctum sanctorum with more animation than she'd exhibited so far, even with her drop-in customers.

"I know you!" she announced. "Wait a minute, it's on the tip of my tongue. Uh, uh, Miss Nunna's girl!"

I stiffened, then relaxed. Getting my back up about being called a girl, especially in this regard, was unwarranted. From age seven, when I'd come to live with Nunnally Layton, until I'd left at seventeen, I was "Nunna's girl." In Sunrise, I would always be "Nunna's girl," and the fact that I was now thirty-one didn't matter worth a damn. Thirty-one years from now I'd be referred to the same way.

"Starts with an L," the waitress was saying, snapping her fingers. "Leigh Ann, something like that. Right?"

"Exactly like that. Leigh Ann Warren." It had been years since I'd heard my middle name attached to my first as if it were all one word and, to my astonishment, found myself close to tears. I wasn't sure which surprised me more, the fact that someone in Sunrise remembered me, or my reaction to it. This from a body who'd hoped to remain as anonymous as she could. Unfortunately, I still hadn't placed the waitress.

"Jesus, how long has it been?" she asked, wiping the counter out of habit. It was perfectly clean. "Your hair's a lot shorter, or I'd have known you right off. How come you never came back?"

"Once Nunna moved to Chicago, there was nothing to come back for."

"Ain't that the God's honest truth," she said, tossing the dish towel over her shoulder. "Sunrise's been—" The phone rang, cutting her off. She excused herself and moved to the front of the diner to answer it, giving me too much time to dwell on the fact that there was a second reason I hadn't returned before now. Sunrise held an IOU with my name on it. At graduation from high school, each scholarship student signed a pledge to render some sort of service to the town once they had a degree and were gainfully employed—Service to Sunrise or STS. It was viewed with deadly seriousness. I had yet to pay up.

The waitress came back and settled down to continue her conversation. "What was I saying? Oh, yeah. Sunrise's been a dead-end town if there ever was one. Still, I would have thought . . ." Whatever it was, she decided not to voice it. "I left in '82 and lived in Charleston until a couple of years ago," she said, with a trace of longing. "Had a really good job with the city. Then Mama took sick. With Daddy dead long since and Maurice—make that Brother Maurice—off recruiting souls for Jesus, I was the only one left to take care of her. So I had to come home."

"That's too bad," I commiserated, my mental wheels spinning. Maurice. The name rang a bell. If I could just make the connection . . . "I hope your mother's better." I also hoped I wasn't putting my foot in my mouth. The lady might be dead by now.

She wrinkled her nose. "She's poorly, but Mama was a Fletcher and married a Fletcher. Swear to God they've got the blood of Methuselah in their veins. She'll live to be a 103 and will still be doing poorly. Only reason Daddy died is that a tractor rolled over on him."

"Sorry to hear that," I murmured. Fletcher. Bingo! The elder Fletchers had been an embarrassment to the residents of the east side of Sunrise, their liquor-fueled weekend brawls legendary. Their kids, the only twins in town, must have hated Mondays at school, having to listen to their classmates rehash their parents' latest set-to. Maurice and . . . I took a stab at it. "Your name's Maude, isn't it?"

"Maudine." She seemed pleased that I was that close. "I'm surprise you remember. Maurice and I were two years ahead of you. He dropped out soon's he turned sixteen and I left the beginning of my senior year and went to work at the mill after a while. Didn't

take long for me to realize that if I didn't do something, come my sixty-fifth birthday all I'd have to show
for working all my life would be that dumb silverplate
tray they give you with 'Congratulations, Retiree, from
Sundler's Lumber Mill' engraved around the rim. I
went back to school and finished in '82."

All the pieces of the puzzle fell into place, especially the rumor that she'd gotten pregnant.
Something else stirred in the basement of my mind,
but it was stashed too far back for me to get to it. I
had no problem picturing her brother, however.
Really nice-looking. Really sweet. Really dim. "Your
brother's a priest? I didn't know there were any
Catholics in Sunrise."

"There aren't. He got mixed up with a bunch
called the Children of Hope. They renounce all
worldly goods and live in a commune out in
Colorado. Looks like a nice place." She removed a
picture postcard from the wall and showed it to
me.

Apparently the Children of Hope managed well,
despite the vow of poverty. Their residence resembled a mansion with a string of guest cottages on
each side. Elegantly rustic and rustic elegance, a
good trick.

"They travel around the country doing good works
and recruiting converts," Maudine elaborated. "I've
got postcards from him from all over. At least somebody in the family got to travel. So." She flipped her
long braid to one side and leaned, elbows on the
counter, giving a whole new dimension to the word
cleavage. "What have you been doing?"

I hesitated. Since the shooting, there'd been some
question in my mind about what I'd been doing and

how long I'd continue to do it. The matter was settled now but I framed my answer carefully. "Playing
cop."

She gawked at me. "No shit! Pardon my French.
Not that there's anything wrong with it," she added,
pink flooding her cheeks. "Being a cop, I mean.
Where at?"

"Washington, D.C."

Her eyes widened. "The murder capital of the
nation?"

I bristled, resenting the appellation. "It's no worse
than a lot of big cities and in some ways, a hell of a
lot better."

She cocked her head to one side. "You like it,
huh?"

"I guess I do. It's really a small town, just not nice
and quiet like Sunrise."

Maudine looked away. "Oh, Sunrise's quiet, all
right," she murmured. "So's a dead rat. The maggots
eating its innards don't make a lot of noise."

"What?" If she'd been trying to get my attention,
she'd succeeded. "What do you mean?"

She jerked out of her reverie, and gave me a
hard, closed glance, impossible to read. "Just that
sometimes the grass is greener on the other side
because they've spray-painted the shit, that's all.
Sunrise's got aplenty skeletons in its closets. You're
better off in Washington." Then a wistful expression
softened her features. "I went there once, in springtime. Got to see the cherry trees in bloom. They
were just glorious."

She refilled my cup again. If I drank much more
coffee, you could wire me for sound, but I wanted to
keep her talking. Not only had she aroused my

curiosity, it was a good way of passing the time and delaying the moment when I'd have no further excuse to stay.

"I'd give anything to get away from here," she said, her eyes bleak. "But, hell, at least nobody had to hunt me down for the reunion. Whether I'll go . . ." She shrugged.

I was disappointed that she'd changed the subject. "Got a big family wingding planned?" I asked, wondering how to reroute the conversation and follow up on her hints about the town. But the door opened. A tall, statuesque woman pushing a toddler along in front of her entered and waved at Maudine, snagging my interest because she seemed both familiar yet out of place. She wore the corporate uniform, a navy suit and soft white blouse, the combination looking as if it had cost more than I made in a month. I looked at her feet. Navy pumps that undoubtedly had an Italian name in them, and, as a shoe freak, I knew whereof I spoke. Short, fair hair, perfectly coiffed, and flawless makeup completed the picture.

"Oh, hell," Maudine muttered. "Miss Gotrocks, playing Lady Bountiful to the neighborhood urchins." She flushed. "I shouldn't say that. She was really nice to Maurice. Be right there, Mrs. Rowland," she called to the woman, but didn't move, eyeing me curiously. "I'm talkin' about the S.T. reunion. Didn't you get your invitation? I thought that was why you were here."

I wasn't about to explain my appearance in Sunrise. "'Fraid not. What invitation?"

"Jesus, I can't believe . . . 'Scuse me a minute." She hurried away to shove two doughnuts into a bag and ring up the sale. Holding the door open, she saw the woman out and returned, grabbing an empty cup from behind the counter and filling it for herself. "I'm not supposed to do this with customers in the place, but what the hell." She perched on the stool beside me. I'm five-seven and, even sitting, Maudine dwarfed me. "They're gonna tear down ol' S.T.," she began, "and build one of those outlet malls in its place. You wouldn't believe the trouble that's stirred up. Claire Rowland, the one who just left? Her husband designed the mall. He's a big shot with Waverly Associates, the builder. Anyhow, Miz Totton's going to retire, so—"

"What?" Estelle Totton had served as principal of Sunrise Township School since it had opened its doors. She had to be nudging eighty by now; she'd seemed older than God when I was a kid. If Sunrise were inclined toward a monarchy, she'd be queen, an educator who inspired kids and made a difference. "Man," I exclaimed, "I can't believe she's still alive and kicking."

"If she's not, a ghost just walked in," Maudine said, sotto voce, sliding from the stool and moving behind the counter again. "Mornin,' Miz Totton."

I stiffened and averted my gaze. This little woman was the last person I wanted to see. If I could just make it to the Ladies, she might not notice me.

"Good morning, Maudine." God, her voice sounded the same. "Pop one of your bran muffins in the microwave, please. I declare, you'd think a woman as intelligent as Claire could do better than feed a baby a doughnut for breakfast."

"Well, with none of her own, she maybe wasn't thinking," Maudine said, removing a muffin from beneath the bread tender. "This should only take about thirty seconds."

"Good. We're late already."

I eased from the stool, moving as casually as I could, and started toward the door with the female stick figure on it.

"Leigh Ann?"

Shit. I turned. What the hell else could I do? "Yes?" I frowned, playing the game. "Mrs. Totton! How nice to see you!"

She hadn't changed physically either, not one iota. She was a walking, talking caricature of a Norman Rockwell grandmother complete with granny glasses, fluffy white hair, cherubic and well-lined face, cabbage rose print dress, sensible shoes. There was a fragile air about Mrs. Totton that had deceived many an elementary and junior high school student at Sunrise Township School. But her eyes, a soft robin's-egg blue, could gaze upon you with the warmth of spring or turn you into an ice sculpture with a disapproving glare.

Estelle Totton could be as tough as a pit bull, and as persistent as a case of hives. Black or white, she rode you with no quarter given until you measured up to her expectations. As a result of her persistence, S.T. students arrived at Central High with more discipline, better study habits, and higher grades than the average kid. She'd been instrumental in helping the majority of Sunrise's kids get scholarships to college. Unless you wanted to stay and work in the mill the rest of your life, you toed this little woman's line. She was our ticket out of Sunrise.

"It's been a long time, hasn't it?" she said, patting

my hand. "What a lovely woman you've become. I can't tell you how much it means to see so many of my children again."

"Er, yes, it must be." I hadn't the slightest idea what she was talking about.

"Come by and visit, tell me what you've been up to, won't you? I mustn't keep Claire waiting. Maudine, is it ready?" she asked, hurrying back to the cash register.

It—the muffin—was. Plunking some coins on the counter, she took the bag. "Thank you, dear." She pushed open the door, then looked back over her shoulder at Maudine. "Will Maurice be coming to the reunion?"

"Yes, ma'am. He gets in on Saturday. You know him. He wouldn't want to miss the interfaith service."

"That's grand. Such a sweet boy." With a waggle of her fingers, she went out, chirping to me, "Come by anytime, Leigh Ann. I'm looking forward to it."

Maudine returned and took possession of her stool. Relieved that the encounter had been as abbreviated as it had, I sat down, too, and mopped my forehead. Thank God she'd been in a hurry. "So go on," I prompted Maudine. "They're finally closing the school?"

"Right. It's sort of the end of an era, so anyone who went to school there, teachers, too, will be coming back for one final reunion. There'll be an interfaith service on Sunday, class parties all week long, then a picnic on Saturday for everybody. The invitations went out a couple of months ago and the last I heard over seven hundred people had responded.

The whole town's been trying to fix itself up ever since."

Which explained the scrubbed face Main Street wore. I was silent, my emotions in a skirmish. Without Mrs. Totton's help, my going to college would have been difficult. Another time I might have stayed to participate, but I couldn't drum up the energy to do it. That I was here at all was an indication of the shape I was in.

The truth was that the shooting incident had really thrown me, hurling me into a chasm so deep that I'd developed a case of the bends trying to claw my way out of it. I had yet to reach the top. When I was sure I was about to die, I'd thought of Sunrise, yearned for it. Now I was here, even though without Nunna it wasn't really home any longer. This foray was simply an attempt to feel a connection with something, anything, a drive-through to remind me of what few roots I had in hopes that it might give me the grounding I needed to get my act together.

But I hadn't planned to ferret out old acquaintances. I'd hoped to be able to slip in and out of town without running into anyone I'd known, especially Mrs. Totton. And the Outer Banks were waiting. Besides, with an outlet mall going up, the Sunrise I'd known would cease to exist. I was hearing its death knell. I might as well change my will and leave instructions to have my ashes dumped in the Potomac.

I felt myself in the spotlight of someone's gaze and came out of my brown study to find Maudine's blue eyes fixed on me. "Sorry," I said. "Trying to make up my mind. I'll have to pass up the reunion, since I really didn't come to stay. I just want to see a few of the old haunts and then hit the road."

Maudine stirred her coffee, clearly trying to make up her own mind about something. "Looka here, I know it's not my business, and you have a perfect right to tell me to mind mine, but there's something I gotta say. Life's too short to bear grudges, Leigh Ann. Otherwise you couldn't have paid me to come back. Sometimes you just have to forget, even if you can't forgive, and you better believe I know that forgiving and forgetting ain't as easy as it sounds. Which means"—she sighed—"that I'll be going to the reunion. Gotta practice what I preach. What I'm saying is, whatever happened between you and Miss Nunna, you've got to put it behind you and go on."

I wondered if I'd missed something. "What are you talking about? Nunna and I were . . . are very close. Sure, I wish she hadn't gone so far away. I could have visited her in Chicago, but then she went to Africa, which isn't exactly around the corner. And she hasn't written all that often, but she's been going from one country to another and Lord knows where her letters might have wound up."

She gave me a smile edged with sadness. "I know how that feels. All I've gotten from Maurice is one stinkin'-ass postcard a year. I just thought you'd had a falling out with her. I mean, you don't show up for . . . what? Thirteen, fourteen years? And your first day back you come in here for breakfast instead of sitting down to eat at Miss Nunna's table. Good as that lady cooks?"

The impact of her words left me speechless for a couple of heartbeats. "Nunna's here?" My voice was a squeak. "She's back in Sunrise?"

"You didn't know? She got back . . . jeez, a couple of months ago. I'm sorry, Leigh Ann. I had no idea."

"Oh, my God." My fingers numb and shaking, I fumbled in my purse, found a five and a couple of singles and pressed them into her hand. "Gotta go. Thank you, Maudine. Thank you." I barreled out of the diner. I was going *home!*

2

By the time I neared Sunset Road, my euphoria was long gone, my nose so far out of joint I had to breathe through my mouth. She'd returned a year earlier than I'd expected, had moved back here instead of Chicago, which is where I'd assumed she'd go, and hadn't let me know. I was hurt and angry. But not just about this. Maudine had hit closer to the truth than she knew.

I'd understood when Nunna had pulled up stakes to move to Chicago my sophomore year in college. The home office of the missionary society she'd supported for years was based there. They'd been recruiting retired teachers to work in their equivalent of an urban Peace Corps and Nunna had fit the bill perfectly. From my point of view she was still accessible. Planes and trains left Washington, D.C., for Chicago umpteen times a day. But when, five years later, she'd called to say that she'd be going to Africa to teach, I'd felt abandoned, an echo of the

emotion that had consumed me after my parents'
death when I was five.

I admit my reaction when she left the country was
childish, especially since I was twenty-four at the
time and struggling to finish law school. She'd
already done more for me than I or anyone had a
right to ask, especially considering we weren't
related. She had rescued me when I was seven. I'd
been shunted from one distant cousin to the next for
the previous two years. Nunna, passing through
Baltimore, had stopped to visit the relatives with
whom I was living. Something about me had
touched her so deeply that she'd returned a week
later, and after a two-hour heart-to-heart with the
cousins, had packed my few belongings and had
taken me home with her. The cousins, with four kids
of their own to feed, had been only too glad to let
someone else shoulder the responsibility and finan-
cial burden of raising a child. Nunna had done all
that and more. So I had no reason to feel abandoned.

Another truth was that she and everyone else had
expected me to become a professional. I hadn't
wanted to teach and hadn't considered myself M.D.
or D.D.S. material. Law school had seemed the most
logical alternative, especially after I saw how proud
and delighted Nunna was at the prospect of a lawyer
in the family. I'd gone to law school primarily to
please her. It had not been easy. Then just as I was
about to graduate, she'd left and I'd never truly for-
given her for it. *That* was the problem. Now, adding
insult to injury, she hadn't even let me know that she
was back.

"Damn," I muttered. I should have asked Maudine
if Charlotte was here, too. Charlotte Reese, Nunna's

first foster daughter, had been married and living in Atlanta when I came to stay in Sunrise. She had a jealous streak the width of the Grand Canyon and had hopped the next flight north when she found out Nunna had taken me in.

Charlotte had tried her best to convince Nunna that at fifty-plus she was too old to raise another child. I remember hiding behind the door in the darkness, listening to that grating voice pose her arguments, terrified that Nunna would give in and send me away. If Charlotte was here with Nunna now, she'd be none too happy to see me. The thought cheered me. I was in a kick-ass frame of mind and if Charlotte so much as looked at me side-wise, I'd probably be in jail before the day was over. The closer I got to Nunna's, the angrier I became. Even seeing my old neighborhood had little effect on me.

The black population lived on the west side of Main, the white on the east. East or west, there were only two classes of residents: poor and poorer. There were no mansions in Sunrise, only small, weathered, clapboard houses, some no more than shacks on brick post foundations, most showing the effect of the years. Still, it was obvious that in the spirit of the coming reunion, they'd done the best they could. Their yards were immaculate, their gardens weed-free. And a new crop was sprouting along with the flowers and vegetables. Practically every other lot bore a sign at the end of the sidewalk. "Say No to Waverly." And "We Support the Mall." Maudine hadn't been exaggerating about the uproar the pro-posed mall was causing.

I was still fuming when I reached my destination,

but the sight of Nunna's house, at the end of Sunset, put the first dent in my anger. It appeared to have fared well over the intervening years; the renters had taken good care of it. One of the few on the street with three bedrooms, it sat back on its lot, protected from the sun by a host of pecan and sycamore trees. The awning over the deep front porch had faded, and the shutters were now a dull black instead of green. Otherwise, it looked much the same. The flowers lining the front walk were sparse, the window boxes empty, but Nunna's beloved garden was still a marvel of color.

The porch swing moved gently, pushed by a morning breeze, the same swing in which I'd spent many an evening listening to cricket symphonies. There was the walkway, poured when I was ten, which would bear my initials for all time. The front windows gleamed. They'd been decorated for each and every holiday, with snow, pumpkins and witches on brooms, Easter bunnies and tiny American flags made from construction paper. Home. The universe of my childhood. It was hello again and might well be good-bye again. But at least I'd seen it.

Nunna had no driveway and there were no curbs, so I pulled over as close to the end of the walkway as I could, cut the engine, and just sat, trying to slow my pulse. That turned out to be a waste of time, so I checked my image in the mirror and decided I looked as good as could be expected. I debated whether to run a comb through my hair and decided to hell with it. I'd worn it cropped since the night, years before, when I'd found myself between two prostitutes trying to kill one another and had learned the hard way that long hair, even confined by a barrette, was eminently yankable. I'd had it cut the very next day.

Since the shooting, however, I'd passed up my monthly clipping at the beauty salon, deciding to let it grow long enough to hide the half-inch welt in my scalp. Once it healed, it could have passed for an extrawide, off-center part but I had no interest in starting a new trend in African-American hairstyles. I'd opted for a curly perm. To be honest, I was ashamed of the scar. It was a flag hanging out there for everyone to see, a reminder that when the dreaded moment of decision had finally arrived—to shoot or not to shoot—I had wavered a second too long and had almost gotten my head blown off in the bargain. And when I did react . . .

I pushed that thought away. It would be back, in the middle of a sentence, in the middle of the night. Right now I had other unfinished business to deal with, so I got out, and started toward the long walk to the front porch.

A high-pitched squeal from some distance behind me, however, stopped me in my tracks. Wheeling around, I saw the source of the noise, and felt a surge of delight. Sheryl Anderson, schoolmate, confidante, and all-around bosom buddy of years before. There was no mistaking those eyes, as big and round as coasters, her bobbing ponytail, and her track-star form in tank top and running shorts. As glad as I was to see her, I wished this could have waited until later. The only thing I could do would be to keep things as brief as possible—if I survived it, because Sheryl came barreling at me full tilt from the house across the street, her cocoa-colored legs churning like a cartoon character's. At four-eleven-

and-a-half in high school, she'd had to make up for her lack of height with blinding speed and, even after fourteen years, she hadn't lost a step. I braced myself. She wasn't slowing down and, if I wasn't balanced, she would send me sprawling.

She skidded to a stop in front of me, propped her fists on her hips, and glared at me. "You bitch!" It was downhill from there. She launched into the most imaginative series of invectives I'd ever heard and for a cop that was going some. "Not a word from you in ten years! Not even a postcard saying, 'Hi, I'm alive. Up yours!' Where the hell have you been? Damn, it's good to see you!"

Then she hugged me, laughing, squealing, and I hugged her back, knowing that for all the godawful names she'd called me, nothing had changed between us. She was still the same irrepressible dingbat who could get out more in ten seconds than most could say in thirty. She was also smart, perceptive, fiercely independent, and took no shit from anyone.

Stepping back, she looked up at me, eyes narrowed. "You okay? I'm getting all sorts of weird vibrations here. I didn't mean all that stuff I just said. We are still friends, aren't we?"

"Of course, dummy."

"Good. But something's wrong. You aren't sick, are you?"

Smiling, I shook my head. "I'm fine."

"Liar."

"All right, I'm not a hundred percent, but ask me again after I've seen Nunna and I'll be a lot better. I didn't know she was here, Sheryl."

"You didn't?" Her eyes, always expressive, filled

with sympathy. "Oh, Leigh! No wonder you didn't come back sooner. Does she know you're here?"

"Not yet."

"Shit, and I'm holding you up. We can get together later and chew the fat. Oooh, girl! I can't believe it!" She gave me a quick hug and started away, backpedaling, then stopped. "Can you hang around for a while, Leigh Ann?" she asked, with uncharacteristic gravity.

"Maybe. Why?"

She came back. "Thing's have gotten really tense around here. There's been all sorts of trouble."

"I heard. Maudine said something really weird about maggots eating rats, and skeletons in closets. What's been going on?"

Sheryl snorted. "I don't know doodly-squat about any rats, but the skeletons ain't in no closets, that's for damn sure. They're in the cemetery where they belong and that's the problem. They want to put a mall on top of it."

"What? I don't get you."

"They want to wipe out New Bethel and the cemetery. It's tearing Sunrise apart. Whole families, on both sides of town, mind you, are battling among themselves, especially the younger generation against the old folks."

New Bethel Baptist, the only black church in Sunrise, the church I'd attended every Sunday morning the Lord had sent during the eleven years I'd lived with Nunna. And the cemetery. It was a piece of the town's history. Some of the first black residents were buried there, a few of them former slaves.

"Oh, hell," I muttered. This was bad news.

"We almost had a riot on Main Street the other

day, when a group of eastsiders ran into New Bethel's deacon board," Sheryl rattled on. "Accusations flying about westsiders—Miss Nunna's one of them—getting in the way of progress. The natives are up in arms, girl. Look, I've got to run—literally. We will get together before you leave, right? Like, soon? I live in Asheville now—husband, two kids, the whole bourgeois bit—but I'm coming back to Mom's with the crumbsnatchers day after tomorrow and we'll be here until the reunion's over."

"Great. Call me when you're free."

"Free? With two kids? Dream on. But hot damn! My ace-boon-coon is back!" Waving, she sprinted toward Main, running easily.

I watched her for a second, and wondered what I'd come back to. If Sheryl, the eternal optimist, felt that the situation was bad, then it must be truly dicey. But first things first. There was Nunna to confront.

The door was open, the screen unlocked. I could have followed local custom, called "Yoo-hoo! Company!" and gone on in, but I wanted to see who would answer, Nunna or Charlotte, so I rang the bell.

"Minnie, you touch that button again and so help me Jesus I'll skin you. You know how much it gets on my nerves." There it was, Nunna's voice, still strong, vital, full of life. "Come on in. The screen's unhooked."

In that instant, my anger dissolved, replaced this time by out-and-out panic. I, who in the course of my years in uniform had faced drug-crazed burglars, mean drunks, car thieves, and wife beaters who looked upon me as just another female to knock around, lost my nerve. I was a child again, terrified that I wouldn't be welcome. I rang the bell again.

"Dad-blast it, Minnie!" I heard a pan hit a hard surface. "What is your problem? Your hands full? I told you not to bring nothing. I'm whipping up a batch of cookies right now." She sailed into the living room from the kitchen, a black Valkyrie, seventy-four years old, tall, straight, her dark eyes snapping with annoyance. She wore flour up to her elbows. I broke out in a cold sweat.

Then she recognized me. Her full lips parted with shock. She stopped in her tracks, her mahogany face blazing with light. "Praise the Lord," she said softly. "My child's come home."

In one instant all the anxiety and uncertainty, the grief and anger were gone. I practically took the screen off the hinges to get into the strong arms that had rocked me back to sleep when dreams of fire had fueled my nightmares, the arms that had cradled me against her side on Sunday mornings as I dozed through the Reverend Breedmore's hour-long sermons. She grabbed me in a rib-cracking embrace and the mélange of familiar scents that were her signature—Dixie Peach hair pomade, Ivory soap, L'Aimant cologne, and cookie dough—filled me with joy.

I blubbered like a baby with pure relief and she pat-pat-patted and "there-there'd" me, rocking me gently until I'd geared down to hiccuping sniffles. Then Mother Nature reminded me that no matter how elated I was, a bladder can hold only so much. Maudine and her refills.

"Let me look at my child," she said, gripping me at arm's length. "My Lord, you're a mess, but you're still a beautiful sight to see."

"If I don't get to the bathroom this minute," I

informed her, "your child's gonna be an even bigger mess."

She laughed, a sound of rollicking hilarity. "Go on, then. You know where it is. And brush yourself off. I've got flour all over you."

That was the least of my concerns as I darted into the hallway to the john. Small framed prints decorated the walls—a couple by Degas, Van Gogh's *Sunflowers,* an unfamiliar Picasso. Nunna maintained that you might as well have something pleasant to look at if you were going to be in there any length of time.

I let myself out of the john to find Nunna waiting for me at the end of the hall. As we went back into the living room, she grabbed my elbow, spun me around and whacked me across the behind. It stung. Nunna had hands as wide and hard as breadboards.

"Where the hell have you been all this time?" she demanded, lightning flashing from her eyes. "I finally gave up calling."

"You called? When?"

"As soon as I put down on American soil. I tried at all hours. Couldn't you at least have an answering machine?"

I hated the things. So far I'd refused to get one, resisting the inevitable. "When did you get back?"

"Two months ago yesterday."

That explained it. She'd arrived the day after the shooting. I'd spent a couple of days in the hospital and a week with friends, who'd insisted on babying me through that first dark period. Even after I'd gone back to my apartment, I hadn't been there that much. The desk duty I'd been assigned was less demanding than I was used to, so I'd volunteered to work double shifts, anything to tire me enough so that I could sleep at night. Toward the last I'd been in such a funk that I hadn't bothered answering the phone. Even opening the mail had seemed more than I could handle. If I'd missed her call, I had only myself to blame.

"I was hoping you'd come down so we could open up the house together," she said. "I told Charlotte to let you know when I'd get into Asheville."

"Charlotte?" I might have known. "Where is she?"

"In Nairobi, married, again, to a Kenyan and working at the embassy. It's easy for her to call from there. She promised she'd get in touch with you to let you know I was coming home because of this business with the cemetery." Her face became very still. "She didn't, did she?"

"I haven't heard from Charlotte since she sent me the card with a dollar in it when I graduated from high school." The memory was a bitter one.

Nunna stared at me, through me, a human lie detector. She nodded. "It's past time I said it. That girl's part bitch. I'm so sorry, baby. And it's none of my business where you were all this time. Come on back. We've got a mess of catching up to do. Walter," she called, as we approached the kitchen. "My baby's come home."

"So I gather," a voice, dry with age, responded with humor.

I almost tripped over my feet. Had Nunna gotten married? He was struggling to rise as we entered, an elderly man with skin the color of Sunday morning biscuits, not a wrinkle in sight. Only his slightly stooped posture and snow-white hair betrayed his age.

"Miss Warren, I presume. I am purely tickled to meet you." He extended his hand.

I took it, and glanced at Nunna for a proper introduction.

"Leigh Ann, this is my . . . friend, Walter Sturgis," she said softly. "Sit. I'm going to fix you the best breakfast you ever had. I may even have an apple or two in the bin. Fry you up a batch in no time."

I had to waylay her. My stomach was only so big. "Thanks, Nunna, but I had breakfast not too long ago. Let's save the apples for tomorrow."

"You can stay then? We can have some time together?" The plea in her tone brought tears to my eyes.

I thought about the stuff I'd left at the beach. It could wait. "I can stay."

Mr. Sturgis reached behind his chair and retrieved a cane. "Then you won't be needing me for company," he said, and smiled with a gentleness that told me all I needed to know about the depth of his affection for my foster mother. This was interesting. "I'll see you at the meeting this evening. Welcome home, Miss Warren. You ladies enjoy your reunion."

Nunna excused herself to see him out, and I took a moment to pinch myself. I was indeed home, back in the roomy, pale green and yellow kitchen with its massive electric range and double oven, the worn kitchen table covered with oilcloth. The refrigerator was new, as was the green-eyed mouser on top of it, a black-and-gray tabby taking my measure, but everything else was the same—the captain's chairs, duck-decorated canisters, colonial spice rack, the little pots of herbs growing on the windowsill.

I ignored the cat, giving him time to make up his

mind about me, and opened the back door. The rear yard, deep and wide, was fenced in. A small vegetable garden, also fenced in, grew along one side; Nunna's tomatoes were coming up nicely. And directly opposite our door was the property in jeopardy, New Bethel Baptist Church and its cemetery. Accessed by a gate in Nunna's back fence, the grounds were a favorite old haunt of mine, as much park as graveyard, well tended, the grass mowed. I'd hate to see it go, but I wasn't sure there was anything that could be done about it. I smelled big business, in which case the cemetery was a goner.

I stepped out to check for the other feature of Nunna's backyard. It had to be here somewhere. I heard a stirring under the stoop and, shortly, a squat black dog of uncertain ancestry—part bassett, certainly—squirmed from under the steps and sat looking up at me, tongue lolling. Nunna had a dog; all was right with the world.

"That's Hannibal," she said, returning as I stepped back into the kitchen and another rib-cracker of an embrace from her before she released me to set the coffeepot on the stove. "He's been with me about five weeks now."

Nunna had always had a dog or three in residence, all acquired the same way: they'd wander by the house and she would open the side gate, lure them in with a tidbit, and with that, they became hers. No one had ever argued the point and no one had ever shown up to claim one as theirs.

"He's a nice old thing," she said, setting out cups and saucers, "but he's a digger. Took us a while to come to an understanding about my garden. I do not grow bones."

"What about your friend on top of the refrigerator?" The cat sat up, closed his eyes, and yawned.

"Name's Chester. He belonged to the people who were renting the house and stayed on after they moved over on Daybreak. Lazy as sin but he's hell on mice. Damn it, look at that." Nudging him aside, she reached up under his considerable girth, retrieved a bone, and tossed it into the trash can. "He and Hannibal have become such great buddies that the fool dog brings those to him. Chester plays with them like toys. I probably have bones all over the house. Sit, child. Coffee'll be ready directly."

I settled in the seat Mr. Sturgis had vacated, still trying to adjust to this new reality. Nunna at home in Sunrise, fretting about her animals, me here with her.

She sat down and reached across the table. "I'm truly sorry about leaving the country when I did, baby. That hurt you, I know. I could tell from your letters."

"It was the timing, that's all."

"I know. The opportunity to go arose," she said, "and I had to take advantage of it right then or they'd have had to find someone else. You can't believe how much I hated missing your graduation." Her eyes filled with tears.

We blew another few minutes being weepy all over each other. That lasted until I said, "Enough, Nunna. It's history. You're back."

She blotted her eyes with a napkin. "And so are you. My prayers have been answered."

"Mine, too." At least most of them. "So tell me, how was Africa?"

"I don't have the words. You know how badly I'd always wanted to see the motherland, Leigh Ann. And to be needed, to feel useful. I lost that after you grew up. They needed teachers and were grateful to get one with forty years of experience. They didn't care about my age. It was an education for me, too. Especially Africa. I saw so many places."

Her eyes were polished onyx, glowing with life now as she spoke of training teachers for their church schools, teaching a little herself. She had helped dig wells, had worked in rural clinics, wherever and whatever the need.

Rising, she removed the coffeepot from the stove and filled our cups. "I have to be honest, Leigh Ann. I wouldn't have missed those years for the world."

And if I were honest, I'd have to admit that I hadn't really grown up until after she'd left. With no one and no home base to fall back on, I'd had to rely on myself. I'd done that and was ashamed of the relapse I'd had this morning.

"Tell me everything," she said. "What about your young man, Mitchell? One of the reasons I told myself you'd get over my leaving was that I was so sure you would marry him. When you stopped mentioning him, I figured things had fallen through. What happened?"

"I wrote to you about it a dozen times and tore them up. It hurt too much. He was killed, Nunna. He was an undercover cop, remember? He walked in on a robbery in progress and was shot trying to stop it. We'd just gotten engaged the night before."

"Oh, my Lord." She smoothed my hand, depositing flour all over the back of it. "I'm so sorry, honey."

"Time has helped. Something else did, too." I had decidedly mixed feelings about relating the details of my life. Not that I had any qualms about what I'd done; I was just afraid that she'd be disappointed in the choices I had made. I took a deep breath. "I'm not a lawyer, Nunna."

She nodded. "I wondered. That's another thing you never mentioned in your letters. What have you been doing?"

"After Mitch was killed, I realized how much I wanted to be a police officer. Always had. I wanted to make the kind of difference he'd made."

"Leigh Ann Warren," she said, eyes snapping, "you never said anything about—"

"I know, I know. Aside from you and Mrs. Totton, the people I've admired the most were policemen. A beat cop saved my life. He ran into our apartment building to warn people that it was on fire. He found me in the stairwell full of smoke and carried me out. There was nothing he could do for Mom and Dad."

"Your cousins told me about that, but you never mentioned it."

"I couldn't talk about it. Survivor guilt, I guess. Then when I was living with Great-Aunt Zeenie in East Orange," I went on, "a policeman talked the acid-head next door out of tossing his baby off his balcony. The police have always been heroes to me. But with everyone here expecting so much of me, I figured going to law school was the next best thing. After Mitch though . . ." I pleated a napkin, surprised at how desperately I wanted her to understand. "I realized that life's too short to waste trying to fulfill other people's expectations. So I joined the police force in Washington, D.C., right after I got out of law school."

She smiled and shook her head in wonder. "Well, bless your time. You went after your dream. I'm proud of you, but proudest of all for that."

She approved. Relieved, I played up the positives I'd lived through, downplaying the negatives, and said nothing about the shooting and the fact that once I'd used up all my vacation leave, I would resign and the dream would be over. We talked straight through the morning and most of the afternoon, through cookie baking, lunch, and dinner, bringing one another up to date. I'd begun to sag when she said, "One last thing and then I've got to change and get on over to the church. Remember the tune I used to hum to you when you had trouble sleeping?"

It came back in a rush, at once completely familiar, even though I hadn't heard it in years. "You said your mother had taught it to you."

"It goes back generations. Well, we were at a clinic in Gambia and I heard a young mother crooning it to her baby. There I was, thousands of miles from home, hearing words and all. I couldn't believe it."

"In Gambia?" I wasn't even sure where it was.

"Folks from her village had been singing it to their babies for years and years. It's a good chance that's where my people came from."

I had forgotten Nunna's passion to trace her ancestors. Seeing the joy in her face, I felt my scales begin to tip. It was time to relinquish any resentment of her absence. She'd gained so much that I had to be happy for her. Besides, I had her back now.

"I'm glad you went," I said. "I really am."

Her smile was radiant with gratitude. "Thank you, baby. I can't tell how much that means. Let me up from this table." She pushed herself to her feet. "I hate to leave you on your lonesome your first evening home, but this meeting is important."

"I'll be fine," I assured her. "I heard about the mall. Isn't there anything the congregation can do?"

Nunna gazed out the back door, her eyes on New Bethel. "We doubt it. The problem is the land doesn't belong to the church. It's Ingram family land."

"Ingram? I don't understand."

"Roman Ingram's great-great-grandfather fancied himself a preacher. He bought the property, built himself a church, and let his congregation use the extra land as a cemetery. The family's gone along with the arrangement ever since. Roman, though, doesn't give a fig about history and tradition. And the money the Waverly company's offering him . . ."

"Any possibility that the congregation could raise enough to match that offer, given the time?"

She snorted. "In the hundred years that would take, we'd all be dead. If Waverly stuck to the original plan of eight stores, there'd be no problem; the school property would be enough. But they're planning to widen the highway outside town and when other companies got wind of it, they wanted in. So now they need another few acres and the only space left is the church property and the cemetery."

"Has anyone checked the state or county laws about this kind of thing? In lots of places, the graves are the property of the heirs, no matter who owns the land. If that's true here, nobody can touch those gravesites without the permission of the heirs. Waverly would have to contact each and every one of you."

"Oh, they've done that. Practically everybody has signed and agreed to have their folks moved over to

Lincoln Grove Cemetery in Sellerton. That's thirty-five miles away! I don't drive anymore. I'd have to depend on other folk to get me there so I could put flowers on Mama's grave and make sure it's properly tended. It would be a hardship for me and a half dozen others. So we're holding out." She took a deep breath. "We're up against it, that's for sure. Let me go change." Shoulders slumping a bit, she left the room. For the first time since I'd arrived, she almost looked her age.

"What kind of meeting is this?" I asked when she returned, resplendent in a dress of orchid and blue.

"We're just troubleshooting. Somebody's been digging around back there, and we're hoping we can hire one of the Taney boys to stand guard at night."

"How about I go with you?"

She hesitated, then squared her shoulders. "Listen, baby. I want you to stay out of this. This is our fight."

"Since when is your fight not mine?" I asked, injured at being excluded even though I wouldn't be around.

"Since you became an officer of the law, that's when. It's better you don't get involved."

It was the most logical time to tell her of my decision to resign from the police force but I didn't like the direction this was taking. "What's my being a cop got to do with anything?"

She retrieved the basket packed with cookies and stopped at the back door, looking out across the way.

"That's my family back there. Africa strengthened my connection to them in a way nothing else could. Mama and Grandma and Granddaddy scrimped and saved their pennies and nickels for years to buy their plots. They paid for the right to be buried in that ground, and by God, that's where they're going to stay."

"I hope so, too, Nunna, but—"

She cut me off. "I don't want you in it, Leigh Ann. We aren't going to win against Waverly. Folks like us never do. But I am here to tell you that I will shoot the first son of a bitch that touches my Mama's grave. And it would break your heart to be the one who had to turn me in." She opened the screen door with a bang and was gone.

3

"*Just like the* good old days, huh?" Sheryl said. "The operative word being *old.*"

"I don't care. This was just what I needed."

I'd used Wednesday to get my clothes from the Outer Banks and Thursday to help Nunna with routine maintenance. It was now Friday, the first time Sheryl and I had been able to spend time together. We sat in the swings on the playground beside Sunrise Township School, watching twilight's color show begin in the sky beyond the mountains. Having spent the last couple of hours in an orgy of "Whatever happened to?" and "Remember when?" we were in danger of running out of topics having nothing to do with the subject Sheryl was determined to avoid: the outlet mall. Still, it was no accident that we'd wound up on the property the mall would displace. We'd whiled away many a recess and late afternoon here, jumping rope, playing hopscotch and jacks, or just sitting and giggling about the objects of our current bout of puppy love. Instead of evoking the nostalgia we'd anticipated, however, the sight of the old school had put us both in a navy blue funk.

Even though classes had ended barely a week before, there was an air of abandonment about the redbrick building, as if it knew that now after fifty-some Septembers, the shrill voices of six- to thirteen-year-olds would never reverberate in its halls again. And it seemed smaller than I remembered, as if it had shrunk with age. The playground was in sad shape, the asphalt scarred with cracks. The equipment showed hard use and I wondered how many fannies had contributed to the sheen at the center of the sliding board.

Still, I had to admit that the location, where Main Street ended in a cul-de-sac, would be perfect for the mall. Beyond the west side of the fenced-in playground was the cemetery, and out of sight because of the trees, New Bethel Baptist Church.

"If you really do quit your job, is there chance you'll move back here?" Sheryl asked. "At least, into the area? You'd like Asheville."

"Maybe so, but the two places I know I could begin working immediately are both in D.C. I might even try for a P.I. license. Duck swears that as much as I chafe under all the rules and regulations, I'd be happier as a private investigator."

She eyed me with suspicion. "That's the third or fourth time you've mentioned that name. So who's this Duck, anyway?"

"Ladies."

I jumped, so startled at hearing a man's voice that I almost fell out of the swing. Leaping to my feet, I

swiveled around, knees flexed, my hand reaching
for the baton that usually dangled from my waist.
That I recognized the newcomer and he presented
no danger was a relief, but the fact that I'd allowed
someone to slip up behind me without my being
aware of his approach drove home how easily I'd
begun to shed the caution with which I'd lived for
the last six years. I should have heard him coming.
A dusty black-and-white police car, vintage 1975
or 1976, in mint condition, sat beyond the fenced-
in playground. It had not been there a minute
before.

As for the man himself, he looked not one day
older than the last time I'd seen him and I was sure,
even being generous, that he had to be approaching
seventy. Mr. Nehemiah Sheriff, officially the chief of
police but rarely called Chief Sheriff, the title repre-
senting a bit of overkill since he was the town's one
and only representative of the law. He had the job
because no one else had ever been particularly
interested; in the old days there was little need for a
police presence, except for weekend donnybrooks at
the Roadhouse on the edge of town and the occasional domestic disturbance.

I'm not even sure he was salaried. He supplied his
own weapon and uniform and the town picked up
the tab for gas and repairs to the car he used. When
he wasn't playing cop, he was a farmer on one of the
small family spreads on the outskirts of town.
Farmer or lawman, he was respected and considered fair in his dealings with residents. I'd always
liked the solemn manner he adopted with kids, listening to them as if their childish prattling was not
only important but made perfect sense.

Sheryl fanned herself. "Mr. Sheriff, you scared us to death!"

"Sorry. I didn't go to do that. Just fixin' to check the school while I'm waitin' for the Rowlands and Hiz Honor. Them windows yonder make mighty fine targets for a slingshot or air rifle. Now, let me see," he said to me, rocking from heel to toe. He removed his cap to expose baby-fine pewter gray hair. His skin was like parchment, finely wrinkled and yellowing with age. "It's been a spell, but I'll have your name in a minute. You were one of my crossing guards. Leigh. Leigh Ann. Miss Nunna's girl."

I smiled, rolling with it. "That's right. How have you been, Mr. Sheriff?"

"Tolerable. Glad to see you back. How's Miss Nunna?"

"Doing well, thank you."

"Good. Tell her I was asking after her." He replaced his cap, slate gray eyes boring into mine. "Reaching for your nightstick just then, were you?"

I felt the blood rush into my cheeks. "Yes, sir, I was. You startled me."

"Thought so. Recognized the move. So you're one of us now. Where?"

I looped one arm around the chain of the swing, undecided about revealing my planned defection from the ranks. "Washington, D.C."

His only reaction was a slight widening of his eyes. "That must keep you pretty busy."

"It's never dull."

He gave me a tight-lipped smile. "Ain't that just the way? And the fact that you didn't stop by to let me know you were in my jurisdiction means that you're here for the reunion and nothing else, right?"

Proper protocol if I were on police business, but I wasn't and wondered why he thought it necessary to remind me in the first place. "Of course. I'm on vacation."

He tilted his head back, as if peering at me through bifocals. "When'd you get here? Tuesday, wasn't it?"

I smiled, message received. This was his town and not much got by him. "That's right."

"Just thought your neighbors might have asked for a little help to catch whoever's been monkeying around in the cemetery."

Belatedly I picked up on the tension he emanated.

"Wait a minute, I haven't heard about anything happening in the cemetery," Sheryl protested.

He gave her a steely look. "The point is, I have. Somebody's been digging around over there. Nothing's been disturbed, no gravestones or anything, just a couple of inches of topsoil and grass, uglying up the place."

"Mr. Taney perhaps," Sheryl suggested. The Taneys had been caretakers of the cemetery for years.

"Taney says no. So now some folk claim the Waverly people are pulling a fast one, taking soil samples and doing perc tests and such."

"At night?" I asked. Why was he so uptight about it? "That doesn't make a lick of sense."

"No'm, it don't. Yet and still I'm hearing this and that from this side of town, grumblings that y'all's sacred ground is being desecrated and I ought to put a stop to it. Like I haven't been doing my job and all. I do the best I can with what I got, which is just me. I want to make it clear I wouldn't take kindly to an outsider being brought into my town to do any extercurricular poking around."

"Leigh Ann's no outsider," Sheryl said, hackles rising.

Enough was enough. "I'm here for the reunion, Chief," I said. "And to see Nunna. But for your information, when my vacation's over, I'll be turning in my resignation, and before you ask, I'm not looking for a job on any other force either. Is that clear enough for you?"

He flushed, his eyes cold and steady. I held his gaze, refusing to be outstared.

"Well, then," he said finally, and hitched up his trousers. "Just checkin'. Mind you, nobody's seen a thing in that cemetery, except perhaps Hannibal."

Another shot across my bow. Hannibal, Nunna warned me, had been raising Cain after dark for the past week, barking his head off and scrambling over the fence, perhaps in pursuit of the phantom digger. He'd awakened me two of the three nights I'd been here.

"We're sorry about that, Mr. Sheriff. Someone complained?"

"Mentioned in passin' is more like it. And I've seen him on the prowl around these parts. Thing is, that ain't like him. He's a homebody. So maybe you—or Miss Nunna—have gone out to see what he's fussin' about and maybe spotted something unusual?"

He was fishing and we both knew it. "I've gone after him twice and the only things I saw were neighborhood cats. I figure he's protecting Chester's territory."

Mr. Sheriff looked thoughtful. "Might be. He does have a curious relationship with that fee-line. Y'all better chain him good, especially when they start tearin' down the school. Don't want him hurt. Well,

I'll move on. Sheryl Lynn, remind your mother that one of her brake lights is out, please, ma'am."

"I'll be sure and do that. 'Night, Mr. Sheriff." Sheryl glared at his back, then began to giggle.

I watched him until he'd disappeared around the far side of the school. "What is your problem?" I asked her, irritated that she seemed to find him a subject of ridicule.

Her giggles became outright hoots of laughter. "He actually thought you might be moving in on his job! Folks have been saying it's time he retired. Maybe it's gotten back to him and he doesn't like it. He takes himself damned seriously for someone who doesn't do diddly-squat. Wonder what he'd have done if his name wasn't Sheriff."

"I wouldn't make the mistake of underestimating him," I said, rising to his defense in spite of my annoyance at his suspicions. "Here he is, the only lawman in a town of . . . what? . . . twenty-four, twenty-five hundred tops, and he recognized that I was reaching for my baton."

"Probably saw it on TV. Well, looka here." Sheryl nodded toward the parking lot where a yacht-long Mercedes was easing to a stop and, behind it, a pickup. Two men in short sleeves and khaki pants got out of the truck and, clipboard in hands, wandered toward the school. The door of the Mercedes opened and the driver stepped from behind the wheel, a tall, distinguished man, graying at the temples, casually dressed in light blue seersucker and highly polished loafers. His passenger was the same classy woman who'd come into the diner with the toddler. Out of uniform this evening, in a dark blue blouse, ankle-length denim skirt, and blue thong sandals. Expensive blue thong sandals.

It was the backseat passenger, however, who snagged my interest. Thirty to forty years of age, five-eleven, medium build, black hair, brown eyes, skin the color of rye toast. Blue-and-white polo shirt, jeans, and high-top athletic shoes. *Very* nice pecs and biceps. He reminded me of Duck, but I couldn't figure out why. Spotting us, he waved and came toward the playground gate, his companions trailing him.

"Sheryl, who is that?" I said out of the side of my mouth.

"You haven't met him yet? That's Monty Sturgis, the mayor."

I swiveled around to stare at her. "Of Sunrise?"

She grinned. "Ain't that a kick in the head? Hi, Monty, Mrs. Rowland, Mr. Rowland," she called and got out of the swing. "If you're looking for Mr. Sheriff, he's around on the other side of the school. Checking the windows or something."

"Thanks, Sher." The mayor stepped aside to let the Rowlands precede him through the entrance of the playground. "We'll give him a few minutes with the surveyors. This," he said, his hand extended, "must be Leigh Warren. Montgomery Sturgis—Monty to my friends. My dad's been talking about you for three days."

I shook his hand and made appropriate noises. I should have made the connection and hadn't, for which there was no excuse. His father, Nunna's friend, was a handsome old man and, except for a slightly darker complexion, his son looked just like him. Wide, thickly lashed eyes, long straight nose, a full bottom lip, even white teeth. And both had smiles that would soften pig iron. Just like Duck.

"Have you met Charles and Claire Rowland?" he asked.

Charles Rowland gave me a distracted smile, his slightly protruding eyes warming for a tenth of a second. "Ms. Warren," he said. He'd make a dynamite ventriloquist. His lips never moved. It was fascinating. His contribution made, he turned to face the school and seemed to disappear into some other dimension. Whatever he had on his mind had his full attention.

Claire Rowland chuckled. "You'll have to forgive Charles. He's building the mall in his imagination right now." She slid an arm through Sheryl's. "This young woman and I go back a long way, Monty, but Leigh Ann probably doesn't remember me. I taught eighth grade her last year here at S.T."

Suddenly it clicked. Miss Peete, Sheryl's home-room teacher. Again I followed protocol, said the expected things, praying my face didn't betray how shocked I was. A member of one of the neediest (and seediest) families in town, Claire Peete had come a long way. I remembered the excitement when she'd returned to teach, the ink still wet on her sheepskin. With every other breath, Mrs. Totten used her as an example of what we could achieve if we applied ourselves. If they'd made that big a deal of her coming back to teach, God knows how high a pedestal she was on as the wife of the man who'd be building the mall.

"How's Miss Nunna?" Claire asked.

"She's well, thank you." I knew the reason for the question.

She glanced at her husband, then placed a hand on my arm, her expression earnest. "I'm sorry things have turned out this way, with people so upset. I was in San Francisco when the idea to add on to the original design came up. I don't have a vote in the firm, but Charles does ask my opinion. If he had, I'd have told him the extension would cause problems. The environmental impact of that many more stores, for one, to say nothing of the emotional chaos using New Bethel and the cemetery would cause. Unfortunately, by the time I got back, it was too late to stop it. So I've done the only thing I can to ease the situation. We've—"

"Claire." Her husband snapped to attention, his tone a warning.

"I want Miss Nunna to know," she said. "Tell her, Leigh Ann, that Waverly Associates has agreed to purchase a prime section of Garden of Peace and to relocate everyone buried in New Bethel's cemetery."

"Do-Jesus!" Sheryl plopped down in the swing.

Monty wheeled around, his features taut. "Listen, it's a magnanimous gesture, and we don't want to steal their thunder by blabbing the news before it's announced at the town meeting week after next. So please keep it under your hats and ask Miss Nunna to do the same."

"You don't have to worry about me," Sheryl said, emphatically. "This little bombshell has left me speechless."

I nodded. "Ditto." The Garden of Peace Cemetery was northeast of town and, unless things had changed in my absence, it was the resting place of departed eastsiders and no one else. I wondered what the reaction of their survivors would be. Who knows? They might feel that the mall was worth it. Whether Nunna would was another story. I'd let her find out with everyone else. It just might be enough to placate her.

"There's the chief," Claire said, spotting the lawman as he rounded the school with the men from the pickup in tow.

"And there's Hannibal." Sheryl pointed at the fence separating the playground from the cemetery. "He's busted out again. Looks like he's been raiding somebody's garbage. Better send him home before Mr. Sheriff sees him."

Hannibal sat pressed against the chain link fence, watching us attentively, a remnant of a green trash bag dangling from his mouth.

"Go home!" I called to him. He grinned at me, tail a-wag, but didn't budge.

"I think they're waiting for us over there," Claire said. "Give me a minute, Leigh Ann, and I'll distract the chief so you can shoo the dog home. I'll see you two at the Sunday interfaith service for Estelle, right? Let's go, Charles honey." She swept away without waiting for an answer from us, her husband trailing in her wake with an indulgent smile.

Estelle. Claire had risen high, indeed. I'd never heard anyone call Mrs. Totton by her first name. Good as her word, however, when Claire reached the lawman, she took his arm and turned him so that his back was to us. I hurried to the fence, reached over, and tugged the shred of plastic from Hannibal's jaws.

"Big dummy. Go home," I said, in an official tone. He rolled his eyes, gave a halfhearted wag, and sauntered off.

"How do you feel about the mall?" Monty was asking Sheryl when I returned to the swings. It was something I'd wondered myself. For all the griping she'd done, I still didn't know.

She examined the toes of her running shoes. "Honest? I have to be for it, Monty. It'll mean jobs, in construction, sales, an extra shift at the mill. Without jobs, all the young people will have to keep leaving to find work. So as much as I hate to see the school and New Bethel go . . ."

"Score one for our side," Monty responded. "And I'm serious about sitting on the news about Waverly's plans. It's only fair that they be given the chance to announce it themselves. Don't blow this. Nice meeting you, Leigh. Hope to see you again soon." He hurried away to join the others. He had a nice tush, just right for tight-fitting jeans.

Sheryl poked me in the side. "Stop drooling."

"Why?" After a bit of reconnaissance, I headed for the jungle gym, where I could sit on top and watch the group without being obvious about it. "What's his story? Where'd he come from and how'd he get to be mayor?" Monty seemed like a nice guy juggling a peck of hot potatoes.

Not that I wasn't interested, but after a certain point my mind wandered as Sheryl rattled on about the Sturgis family, who'd emigrated to Chicago long before I'd come to live with Nunna. At the moment I was distracted, having found another reason the mayor reminded me of Duck. They had the same loose-hipped stride and trim backside.

Dillon Upshur Kennedy. Duck. On his way to full recovery, he'd come back to work about the time I'd put in for annual leave. I'd avoided him before I left and would continue to. He'd called the day before, while I'd been grocery shopping for Nunna, and I had yet to get back to him. I didn't have the strength to argue with him about my decision to leave the force. And argue we would, eventually. He was one of the reasons I planned to quit. But I wasn't ready to discuss it with him or anyone else, and wanted no reminder of him or the whole ordeal.

Claire and company, along with the sun, had long since disappeared when Sheryl and I finally ran out of steam. It was dark now, the lights at each corner of the playground affording the only illumination.

"This was fun," she said, as we climbed down from the jungle gym, "but it was sure hard on the backside. Swear to God I've got splinters in my butt. Look, girl, I've got to pick up some barbecue for Mom, so I'm heading back up Main. You'd better hop the fence and take that damned dog home."

"What?" I could barely see him but he was precisely where he'd been before.

"He never really left until Mr. Sheriff and the rest did and then he came back ten minutes later. You aren't scared to cut through the cemetery, are you?"

It was a silly question and she knew it. The cemetery had been as much a playground to me as the school's. "Of course not. Tell your folks I said hello and I'll see you tomorrow."

"You bet. We'll shop till we drop. *Ciao.*" She sprinted out to the street and disappeared in the dark. Sheryl never walked anywhere.

"Come on, mutt," I said to the dog and scaled the fence, which was not as easy as I remembered.

Hannibal welcomed me with a slurp across the back of my leg, then started off toward home, the only part of him visible in the darkness the white tip of his tail. This was my second trip through the cemetery. I'd meandered along its paths the day before, filled with sadness that it would have to be sacrificed in the name of progress. It was an oasis of serenity behind the houses on Sunset, with massive trees that pre-dated the church itself, and strategically placed park benches where one could rest in the shade. It had also been known as a lovers' lane of sorts; those benches came in handy for other than just sitting.

The section of the cemetery closest to the school was the oldest and contained only five formal grave markers. Since most of the people buried here were former slaves whose families couldn't afford tomb-stones, their plots had originally been marked by bits of colored glass or stones. Little of that remained now; over the years, as rain washed them away, they'd been replaced with large whitewashed rocks or small planters. From spring to late fall this part of the cemetery was alive with flowers. But I hadn't noticed any evidence of extracurricular digging. I might check the next day out of curiosity. It was probably a lot of fuss about nothing.

Hannibal trotted on ahead of me and disappeared, hopefully, heading for Nunna's backyard. Hers wasn't the only one affording access to the cemetery; practically all the homes on Sunset with fences at the rear had gates like hers or gaps in their shrubbery. For some it was simply a shortcut to New Bethel, but for most it represented continuity. Beyond their gates were their ancestors, family. I couldn't imagine what it would be like for them when it was gone.

As I reached the fork in the path where I would turn right to get to Nunna's gate, Hannibal, growling like a motorboat, came streaking past me, running hell-for-leather in the direction we'd just left. I swore and sprinted after him, calling his name. Fortunately I didn't have far to go to catch up with him. I found him, still growling, peeking from behind one of the more substantial trees, focused off into the darkness, where a barely detectable figure walked swiftly toward Main.

"Lookit, dog," I said, "this is not your property. People cut through here all the time and the only person with the right to bitch about it is Mr. Ingram. So come on."

It took a damn sight more convincing than that to get him to leave, but after a while, probably sick of my whining, he left and went on home without me. When I arrived, he was busy rearranging the evidence of his earlier invasion of someone's garbage can, now scattered around the base of the back steps.

"Nunna's gonna skin you," I told him and spent the next several minutes picking up as many of the remnants of the trash bag as I could. Then, even though it was relatively early, I locked up and put on pajamas. Nunna would be gone overnight. New Bethel's choir was participating in a two-day gospel workshop in Winston-Salem, so she wouldn't be back until tomorrow evening. I glanced at yesterday's message saying Duck had called, considered phoning to get it over with, chickened out, and went on to bed with a book.

The dream caught up with me sometime during the deepest part of the night and started as it usually did, with my exit from the cruiser onto streets completely devoid of light. Fog swirled around my feet and followed me as I crossed the sidewalk to the entrance to the Cheswick Arms apartments. Inside was a fog-shrouded hallway and a parade of tightly closed doors that seemed to stretch beyond the horizon, like an M. C. Escher eye-teaser. At the end of that hallway, the image jumping toward me, then away, then toward me again was the scene I dreaded: Duck sitting, his back against an apartment door, his legs splayed, the hole in his chest spurting blood like a fire hydrant opened on a hot summer day. Standing over him was the kid, his hands around a small cannon pointed directly at me. I waited to die—again.

He fired—again. I saw the flare, watched the bullet exit the barrel and float lazily toward me. It would seem the easiest thing in the world to step to one side or the other, given the speed with which it approached, but I couldn't move, couldn't yell, couldn't even breathe. The bullet kept coming and I waited for the usual sound it made as it whistled through the air. The dream changed a little from one rerun to the next, so I wasn't particularly surprised when the bullet growled rather than whistled. Then it barked, one short, throaty woof, and I woke up, my nightclothes damp with perspiration. Chester, with whom I'd lost the battle for my pillow, was awake, too, ears on alert. He jumped from the bed and ran out.

Hannibal sounded again, and I got up and went to the window. The light beside the back door cast a feeble amber haze in a circle around the steps. Halfway up the gate, something small and white moved like a pendulum, swinging from side to side—Hannibal's tail, as he struggled to climb over the top. Built low to the ground, he wasn't having an easy time of it, his short legs scrambling for purchase against the chain links.

"Damn it," I muttered, grabbed my terry cloth robe and in thong sandals, hurried to the back door, where Chester waited on hind legs, pawing at the doorknob. There must be another cat on the prowl.

Chester streaked out and across the yard, gliding over the fence with typical feline grace and, spurred by the cat's success, Hannibal hurled himself over the gate and melted into the darkness. I waffled for perhaps thirty seconds, then dug into the junk drawer and found the flashlight. A sturdy leash dangled from a hook beside the door and I grabbed it on my way out. Nunna was already in trouble with some of her neighbors because of her stand against the mall. If Hannibal and Chester ganged up to mangle someone's cat, they'd both be on their way to the pound and Nunna's name would be mud. Looking out into the darkness, I wished I had my service revolver. It was the first time I'd missed it.

I heard Hannibal before I saw him, growling, snarling, as he paced back and forth around the same tree at which he'd stopped earlier in the evening.

"Hannibal, damn it, come on. Cats aren't in your diet." He ignored me and loped over to a nearby concrete bench to burrow under it. I aimed the flashlight at him and saw that he was digging double time, grass flying from beneath his feet—and pieces of a green trash bag. I offered a silent apology for having accused him of raiding someone's garbage. It had obviously been left under the bench, and he'd reacted as any self-respecting canine who'd found edible treasure. He backed out from under the bench, a bone in his mouth, rushed back to the tree, and began to bury his find.

Terrific. Not that it wasn't an appropriate place for it, but I doubted that Mr. Taney would appreciate it. Mr. Sheriff, however, would. Here was the explanation for the mysterious digs he'd found. There was nothing I could do to stop the mutt, but perhaps, if I removed the trash bag, he would follow me home. It was after midnight and I was not anxious to stay out in the chilly early morning air. Nights in the mountains could get downright frigid.

Kneeling before the bench, I played the light under it and frowned. The trash bag hadn't been stuffed beneath the bench, it had been buried, the soil disturbed from one end to the other, in spots more than a foot deep, the dog's claw marks plainly visible. In a second, he was back again, digging as if for gold. Then, bracing on all fours, he began tugging at the bag, releasing a peculiar odor into the fresh mountain air. It was musty, rank, thoroughly unpleasant.

"That's enough, Hannibal," I said, and grabbed his collar. Growling, he pulled for all he was worth as I struggled to secure the leash. It occurred to me he couldn't be pulling plastic; it would have shredded in his teeth. Flashlight in action again, I strained to see. It was fabric, dark, firmly anchored beneath the soil, and when it finally tore free, it sent him hurtling backward onto his behind. He dropped it and returned to the excavation, rooting until he'd unearthed the next available bone.

I picked up the piece of fabric and examined it under the flashlight. It was damp, faded and rent by doggy fangs but there was little doubt that it was part of a denim collar, the initials embroidered on the tip barely legible now. I felt a chill unrelated to the ambient temperature, turned on Hannibal, saw the bone he was struggling to untangle from a snarl of fabric and yanked hard on the chain. He yelped in pain but came out from under the bench, resisting as I towed him toward his beloved tree. It took some doing, but I managed to wrap the chain around the trunk and fashion an awkward knot. He tried to pull away but the chain held fast and he worked out his frustrations by rearranging the soil over the deposit under the tree.

I'd have given anything to walk away and go back to the house, but I couldn't, not after getting a glimpse of the object exposed by the tug-of-war with the fabric. On hands and knees, I examined it in the glare of the flashlight. The denim itself was still too firmly entrenched for me to remove it. The best I could do was to try to rip it to free the bone. Even then, I wasn't entirely successful, but I'd exposed enough to be sure that my eyes hadn't deceived me. It was what I'd thought, what I'd feared: the lower jaw of a human skull.

I plopped down on the damp grass, gasping as if the air had thinned. After a couple of minutes, my mind began to function. For one fleeting moment, a nanosecond really, I'd thought that Hannibal had managed to violate some poor soul's grave. Some of them were unmarked and it was entirely possible that the groundskeeper had inadvertently placed a bench atop it. No go. This was the oldest section of the cemetery; these bodies had been resting in peace for over a hundred years, and poor folk or not, they'd been placed in pine boxes, not twentieth century trash bags. And for damn sure they would not have been buried wearing a denim shirt designed by Valentino.

It was the first time I'd ever seen Mr. Sheriff out of uniform. About the same size as Barney Fife (which we'd called him as kids—out of his hearing, of course), he was always starched and pressed, the creases in his slacks so sharp you could slice salami on them. That night, however, he'd simply pulled a pair of jeans over his pajamas bottoms and hadn't even bothered to camouflage his top, to which he'd pinned his badge. His eyes had the puffy appearance of someone who'd been yanked out of a deep sleep and his hair stood up in wispy gray horns.

Behind him in the doorway was Doc Webster, Sunrise's only physician, looking older than the Gutenberg Bible. I began to wonder if there was something in the town's water that acted as a preservative. I could have sworn that Doc was past retirement long before I'd left for college, yet here he was, black bag in hand, and I wasn't sure why.

"Thanks for coming so quickly," I said, ushering them in, "but you didn't have to bring Doc Webster."

Mr. Sheriff gazed at me as if my pilot light had gone out. "If somebody's up and died back yonder . . . You're sure he's gone? No pulse or respiration?"

"Whoever it was is way past that, Mr. Sheriff."

"Then I need Doc here to pronounce him dead. He ain't much of a medical examiner but he's the only one we got. Can't tell you how much I enjoyed rousting the old bastard out of bed, too. Who is it out there?"

"There's no way to tell. I didn't say someone had died, Mr. Sheriff, I said I'd found a body, as in remains."

"Remains," Mr. Sheriff repeated. "As in bones. In the cemetery."

"That's right."

He scratched his head. "Well, I guess I have to ask what the hell else you'd expect to find in a cemetery."

Doc Webster cleared his throat. "Don't mind him, Leigh Ann—by the way, welcome home. Nehemiah doesn't shift into third until around seven in the morning. Why don't you start at the beginning? Neem, be a good boy now and pay attention." These two had been friends since Genesis and it showed, even at this hour.

I launched into my narrative, keeping it concise and unemotional. It would be a relief to dump it in his lap, go back to bed, and play uninvolved civilian again. I'd thought I was leaving this stage of my life behind me.

"You're positive the fool dog hasn't opened someone's grave?" Mr. Sheriff said.

Out of respect for his position, I forced myself to

remain civil. "I'm sure. It's nowhere near six feet under and there's no coffin of any kind. In fact . . . Never mind. You'll see for yourself."

"Hell, there's bound to be a rational explanation for it, but I'm too damned sleepy to think of one. Let's go. Hannibal chained up?"

"Locked in the bathroom." I hadn't been sure how deep his territorial streak ran and decided to take no chances. If he got loose and bit the chief, he'd be sniffing cyanide before the sun came up. Retrieving the flashlight again, I led them out to the site and retreated to Hannibal's tree, hoping it would telegraph the end of my involvement. I heard movement overhead, looked up, and found Chester perched on a limb, watching us intently.

Mr. Sheriff dropped to his knees and swept the beam of his big lantern across the debris beneath the bench. "Leigh Ann, can you find me a stick? A twelve-incher ought to be good enough. Pull it off a tree if you have to."

Shit. I didn't want to help. I didn't want to be involved in any way. If I'd been thinking, I'd have gone on back to the house as soon as I'd pointed out the bench. But I hadn't, so, obediently, I snapped a twig from the tree and stripped it of its leaves. Poking gingerly, Mr. Sheriff tried to push the plastic back far enough to see its contents more clearly. He shook his head, grunted, then sat back on his haunches.

"I apologize, Leigh Ann. I was hoping like hell this was somebody's idea of a Halloween joke, like a plastic skeleton or something and you'd fallen for it eight months late, but I don't think so. Web, take a look at this."

Doc groaned. "Aw, Jesus. I get down there and you'll have to lease a crane to get me up again. Give me a hand, here."

No doubt Mr. Sheriff could have and would have, considering how little trouble he'd had lowering himself to his knees, but I simply couldn't stand there and do nothing. I held Doc's arm as he went down, his joints creaking like dried-out leather. Rather than kneeling, however, he took one look and stretched out prone.

"I'll be switched," he mumbled. "Can't say who it is, Neem, but I can damned sure pronounce him dead. I could tell a bit more if you'd rip that plastic so I could see better."

I started to protest and clamped my mouth closed. This was not my show.

"Uh-uh. I won't do that," the chief said firmly. "We can't be sure what we've got exactly, so until we do . . ."

I was relieved. All my instincts labeled this a crime scene and I hated to see it compromised any more than Hannibal already had. "You might want to look at this spot, too," I suggested. "Hannibal's been rooting them from under the bench and burying them over here."

Mr. Sheriff hopped to his feet. "He's been a damn busy dog. He may be our phantom digger, only . . . Well, we'll see. Web, come on, you old coot." He helped Doc up and the two converged on Hannibal's treasure trove. Chester moved down a branch as Mr. Sheriff, using one hand, gently brushed aside a little of the hound's handiwork. Distributed under it was a wealth of bones of all sizes.

The chief blew dirt away from a particularly

chunky one. "What part of the body did this come from?"

Doc peered at it. "An ankle, since what you've got there is a ham hock. Whereas this"—he indicated a smaller short bone—"is part of a finger. By God, here's the scaphoid!"

"English, damn it!" the chief snapped.

"Part of the wrist."

"How long you figure these have been buried?"

Doc shook his head. "Can't tell you that. This needs one of those forensic experts. The only thing I can attest to is that some of these bones are human and that they've been here a while. Several years, I'd say."

"But not a hundred or more?" I asked, and considered belting myself in the mouth.

"Couldn't swear to it but I wouldn't think so."

"Old fart," Mr. Sheriff grumbled. "A lot of use you are." He stood up and brushed himself off. "Leigh Ann, can I use your phone, please, ma'am? Gotta call my sons."

"Certainly."

"Think you can stand watch here until I get back?" he asked Doc. "I won't be long, but I don't want any critters disturbing things and I damn sure don't trust that cat up there."

"Then stop yammering and get on with it." Doc moved to a nearby bench and lowered himself onto it.

"The phone's in the kitchen," I told Mr. Sheriff, "beside the refrigerator."

"I thank you. Back directly." He hurried toward the house, looking small and fragile in his impromptu uniform, precipitating in me a surge of affection and sympathy for him. Like him, I wasn't sure what he had either, but I was sure it would mean trouble of some sort.

Doc heaved his black bag up onto the bench. "Let's see. I've practiced in Sunrise and environs for the past forty-some years. Brought a lot of young'uns into this world and held the hands of many as they left it. But this is the first time I've been around for anything like this. 'Fraid it's going to stir up another hornets' nest, though."

I agreed with him, but I wondered if we had the same kind of hornets in mind. "How do you mean?"

"Well, first the experts will give us a profile of that poor soul and tell us how long he—or she's—been dead so we can home in on who it was by the process of elimination. That's when things will get nasty. The family that shelled out hard-earned money for a proper burial will sue the mortician, as well they should. Then everyone else he served in Sunrise will begin to wonder if their loved one's in the three-thousand-dollar model they paid for or a Hefty bag somewhere. We'll be exhuming bodies until the year 2000." He stopped. "And there goes that blasted mall. This just might hold things up long enough for the Waverly folks to change their minds."

I doubted they would. Besides, if they really came through with their intention to ferry everyone buried here over to Garden of Peace, that would clear up any questions about who was in coffins and who wasn't. Since I'd promised Monty Sturgis I'd keep my mouth shut about the developers' plans, I couldn't ease Doc Webster's concerns in that direction.

Mr. Sheriff returned, all business now. "Web, here's my car keys. You're gonna have to drive yourself home. My sons are on their way with a sleeping bag for me and drop cloths and stakes to cover both these spots for the night. First thing tomorrow we'll excavate the whole shebang and send it to the county lab for . . . whatever."

"First thing tomorrow is about three hours from now," Doc said, levered himself off the bench, and took the keys. "The office doesn't open until noon, so I'll be back, and don't you start without me."

"Then don't be late. Leigh Ann, I'd appreciate it if you'd walk him back to the car. He's not as steady on his pins as he used to be."

"Will you be all right here by yourself?" I asked.

"I'll be fine. No different than camping out. You turn in and I'll see you in the morning."

I escorted Doc to the street, waited until he'd driven away, then locked up again. Chester was still out, but this night that's where he'd stay. I slipped back between the sheets and settled down, thinking I had news for Mr. Sheriff. See me in the morning? Like hell he would. I was out of it. Out.

I slept more fitfully than usual and threw in the towel as the sky lost its opaque quality. I kicked Hannibal out of the john, fed him, and then chained him within an inch of his life in the backyard. By dawn, I'd fixed breakfast and, feeling guilty that I'd left the chief to his own devices back there, fixed some for him as well. He greeted the mug of coffee with the same appreciation as a drowning man would a life raft. Then Doc showed up and I took a mug to him. I went back into the house, shut the door, opened it again to admit a very indignant pussycat, and bribed his forgiveness with a can of tuna and liver.

I knew to the minute when the excavation began; Hannibal started raising hell. After about a half hour of his booming basso, the phone rang. The neighbors were calling and I was hard-pressed to know how to respond. I was not going to tell anyone about the body, yet when I explained that there was some sort of activity in the cemetery, everyone jumped to the wrong conclusion. Those for the mall sang hallelujah and assumed that Waverly personnel were on the job doing something or other. Those "agin it" blew their tops since the agreement was that no work of any kind would be done until after Reunion Week. All I could say was that it had nothing to do with the outlet mall, which served to arouse their curiosity that much more.

By the time Monty called, I was about to take the phone off the hook. "What the hell is going on over there?" he demanded, sounding much put-upon. "I'm being accused of all sorts of treachery and don't even know why. I can't leave the hospital right now—"

"Hospital? Are you sick?"

"No. Oh, I see what you mean. I'm the hospital administrator at McKiver Memorial. Since you seem to be the common denominator with everyone who's phoned me so far—your name keeps coming up—I figured I'd better call you. What's happening in the cemetery?"

As he was an official of the town, I felt free to tell him. "I haven't been back there since they started digging, so I can't say how far along they are," I added. "But that's what they're doing."

"A body? In a trash bag?" He sounded overwhelmed. "Oh, my God. I wonder who the poor devil is and what kind of monkey wrench this will throw into things. Look, Leigh, I'm really in a bind and can't leave right now. Would you mind going out there to see what's what and calling me back?"

I shook my head so hard my teeth rattled. "No way. When I called Mr. Sheriff it became an official investigation. I need to butt out and am happy to do it. I'm sure he'll report to you when he can."

"But—"

"Gotta go," I said, cutting him off. "Someone's at the door. Sorry I couldn't help." I hit the disconnect button, the lie leaving a bad taste in my mouth. But I was determined not to get involved, not for him or anyone else.

I almost jumped for joy when the doorbell rang ten seconds later. I hadn't lied after all. I opened it to find Doc Webster, mug in hand, looking disheveled and fatigued. "It was a long walk to go all the way around to the front, but I decided I wouldn't put myself in harm's way," he said. "Your dog's practically frothing at the mouth. Just wondered if there's any coffee left."

I invited him in and gave him a refill. Rather than leaving, however, he slumped into a chair. I was torn, wanting and not wanting to hear. "How much longer will they be?" I asked. It was from about as oblique an angle as I could approach the subject.

He sighed and scrubbed his fingers across his face. "Lord knows it's going to be a while. Nehemiah's got professional help from the county. They've laid things out in a grid, almost like an archeological dig, sieving that soil as if they're panning for gold. He's writing down every detail and filling in a sketch of the site. Never knew he could be so exacting. Guess all those summer courses he took in criminology and such are paying off."

I'd forgotten that the chief used to disappear every summer when I was in high school. "How much has he found so far?"

"A right smart. The remains had been triple-bagged, so the contents stood up pretty well until Hannibal got to them. There may be some bones missing. Smaller ones like you saw—"

I let out a squawk and stood straight up. An image had flashed onto my retinas—Chester atop the refrigerator, Nunna wresting the bone from under his midsection. Lifting the top from Nunna's trash can, I dumped the contents in the sink. The bone she'd fished out from under Chester's tummy was still there in the bottom. I found a newspaper and spread it on the table. Cradling the bone in a napkin, I placed it in front of Doc.

He scrutinized it. "Well, that's one less missing. How'd it get in your trash?"

"Don't ask. Excuse me a minute." Nunna had mentioned that there might be bones all over the house. After three days of living with the cat, I had become familiar with several of his favorite spots, one of which was under my bed. I grabbed the flashlight and the broom, rushed into the bedroom, and dropped on all fours. Shoved up toward the headboard, well out of reach of a vacuum cleaner, was a small collection of cat toys, a bottle top, one earring, and bones. Queasy at the very real possibility that I'd been sleeping over pieces of someone, I maneuvered everything out from under with the broom, collected the bones, and took them into the kitchen.

Doc, nodding a little, snapped awake. "More?"

I placed them on the table without comment and left. There were a couple of other spots to check. At the finish, I'd gathered five bones and one desiccated mouse Nunna would never have been able to get to. I flushed the mouse down the toilet and deposited the remainder in front of Doc. There were now two small piles on the table.

"These are definite possibilities," he said, pointing to the ones on the left. "I'm pretty sure the rest are garbage, but we'd better keep them until we're sure. Any chance Hannibal's got some stashed in the yard?"

I'd already thought of that. "I do not grow bones," Nunna had remarked that first morning. "Be right back," I told Doc, went outside, and flinched at the scene beyond the chain link fence. There were too many trees between me and the excavation site for me to see it clearly. I wouldn't have had an unobstructed view in any case. It looked as if half the town from both sides of Main were gathered back there, completely ringing the dig. The ubiquitous yellow tape used to mark off crime scenes was the only thing holding them back, that and a couple of six-foot-plus Leggett County cops eyeing the perimeter for any signs of trespassers.

Turning my back on the whole group, I did as thorough a search of the yard as I could and came up empty until I noticed that Hannibal had not moved since I'd been out. He sat at the base of the steps with what I could swear was a sly gleam in his eyes. I sat on the ground beside him and slowly lowered my head until I could see beneath the steps. There it was, Hannibal's warehouse for bones. I gritted my teeth and did what I had to do, slithering on my belly to raid his cache. Most I was sure were old and nonhuman. One of them, however, sent shivers up my spine.

I was backing out from under, fanny to the wind, when I heard Mr. Sheriff's voice.

"Leigh Ann, what the hell are you doing under there?"

I rolled over and sat up. "Collecting bones." I held up the newspaper in which I'd rolled them, then noticed the sizable evidence bag he was holding. "What's that?" I asked.

"The skull. I want Doc to see it before I send it to the lab. He still in there?"

"In the kitchen."

This time Doc was snoring, his nose to the ceiling. "Well, if that ain't the most disgustin' sight I've ever seen," Mr. Sheriff said loudly. "Wake up, Web!"

Doc's head came down with a jerk and he glared at his friend. "I wasn't asleep, just resting my eyes. Great guns, Leigh Ann! You look like you've been mining dirt."

"I have. Found these under the back steps." I handed him my loot.

"Take a look at this first." Opening the evidence bag, the chief held it so the doctor could see in. "You remember anybody dying from a wound like that?"

Doc whistled. "God almighty. All right if I take it out?"

Mr. Sheriff glanced at me, then shrugged. "Can't do any more harm than's already been done."

Handling it as if it were made of eggshell, Doc

removed the skull. It reminded me of a shrunken head one of the guys, a notorious practical joker, slipped into my desk one day, except that this one was full-sized and minus the lower jaw that had set this whole scenario in motion. Lifeless curly black hair sprouted in splotches from the pate. The skin left appeared hard and leathery. When Doc turned it around, I understood his reaction. Clearly a third of the back of the skull was missing, the jagged edges suggesting that it was not the result of anything Hannibal or any other animal might have inflicted.

"Lost a lot of bone fragments when we moved it," the chief said. "They're in the bottom of the bag, tagged and labeled. Would you say a wound of that sort could be the cause of death?"

"It most certainly could. It would take one hell of a blow to do that much damage." He scratched the stubble graying his cheeks. "Swear to God, Neem, I don't remember anybody dying of a wound like this. I'll have to check my records, but nobody comes to mind."

"And as far as we know, nobody's up and disappeared," the chief said, "not since I've been on the job. So who the hell is this? And how'd he wind up out there? In a garbage bag, at that."

I'd already noted something neither of them had mentioned. The hair was definitely that of a Caucasian. Unable to keep it to myself, I said as much.

Mr. Sheriff nodded. "She's right. I don't like this. I don't like this at all."

Suddenly, I became aware that Hannibal was woofing his head off, explained when someone knocked at the back door. I opened it for one of the long-legged county cops who'd been working crowd control. He saw Mr. Sheriff and accepted my invitation to come in.

"Sorry to interrupt, Daddy," he said. "Just wanted you to know Mr. Taney's here. Him and his sons are setting up a canopy and he's got some screening to enclose the whole area. You need me and Roscoe for anything else?"

The chief thought about it, and shook his head. "Reckon not. You remember Leigh Ann Warren? Leigh Ann, this is my son, Josh."

He gave me a smile that was downright shy as I shook his hand. He had to be at least six-four. How had Mr. Sheriff begotten a son that tall?

"You and Roscoe go on home and try to get some sleep. They work the three to midnight shift," he said, for my benefit. "The county lets me use them when I need extra help. Put all the evidence bags in the trunk of my car and I'll run it over to the lab directly."

"Yes, sir, Daddy. Nice meeting you, Miss Leigh Ann."

I recoiled in shock. It was the first time I'd been addressed in such a manner and it was a rude reminder that Josh, who looked to be in his early to mid-twenties, considered me his elder. I was, but hell, not that much elderer.

He left and his father elbowed Doc Webster in the ribs. "Take a look at the stuff Leigh Ann gave you so I can bag it and hit the road. After I leave the coroner's office, I gotta find the Rowlands and set up a meeting with the Waverly folk. They ain't gonna like it but nobody's doing any bulldozing or anything else until we make sure we don't have any other nameless corpses stashed back there. Hurry up, Web. I'm so tired my butt's dragging. And give me back my damn pen so I can label the batch Leigh Ann found."

"*My* pen, you mean." Doc handed it over, then returned the skull to its container. "Let's see what we got here," he mumbled and unrolled the newspaper. I waited, holding my breath. He picked up the long one that had made me shiver and laid it on top of the bag containing the skull. It had broken. With the jagged ends, and dried remnants of skin and sinew still clinging to it, it was not a pleasant sight. The smell didn't do much for the appetite either. "Yup," Doc said. "Part of the femur. They can use it to get an idea of his height. Weight, too, probably." He peered at the broken end, frowned and his face turned a pasty gray.

"Web, you all right?" Mr. Sheriff peered at him fretfully.

The doctor stared at the bone. "Can't be," he muttered. "It's impossible."

"What's impossible?" The chief pulled up a chair and sat down. "Stop being dramatic and tell me what the hell's going on!"

Without responding, Doc Webster snatched the evidence bag containing the skull from Mr. Sheriff's hand and opened it again. After staring at it several seconds, he slumped back, shook his head, shook it again. "Nehemiah, I think I know who this is."

"Who?" the chief asked.

"It's this femur." He picked it up, turned the broken end toward Mr. Sheriff. "See those in there? It means the leg was shattered so badly that the only way to repair it was with pins. I had an X ray of this leg. May still have it somewhere." He struggled to his feet. "I'm sure it's the same leg. But it can't be!"

"Goddamn it, Web, it can't be who?"

Doc Webster turned, shaking his head. "I'm not gonna say until I'm sure, Neem. Give me a day or two to look through my dead files. Can't hurt to wait. If I'm wrong, there's no harm done."

Mr. Sheriff peered at him. "And if you're right? For once in your life, speak plain, Web."

"What you have here is a death under mighty mysterious circumstances."

"Hell, I already knew that. Tell me something I don't."

Doc sat silently for so long, I wondered if he intended to answer. "If I'm right, this won't be your only one."

Mr. Sheriff's eyes narrowed. "You mean there's somebody else in a bag out yonder?"

"No. I expect the other one's over in Garden of Peace." Sagging in his chair, he scrubbed long fingers across his mouth and gazed up at his friend with haunted eyes. "And if you think the mall's split this town apart, just wait 'til I find that X ray. Things are gonna get damned ugly. Neem, I gotta tell you, I think we've lived too long."

5

Sunday morning's interfaith service, the first in the town's history, was held behind the picnic grounds in the hollow normally used for softball games. The day was glorious, the setting awe-inspiring. Our mountains, rich with summer green foliage, soared above us. They could be intimidating in winter but their June visages were benign, with a timelessness about them, a reminder of our short-lived existence as opposed to their permanence.

I was in for a pleasant surprise when at the end of the service Claire Rowland left her seat beside her husband and mounted the dais to sing in a rich contralto of near-professional quality. After her rendition of "Amazing Grace," announced as Mrs. Totton's favorite hymn, there wasn't a dry eye in the house. Mrs. Totton, seated front row center, rose and threw kisses at the singers—pure corn but the crowd of several hundred loved it. Charles Rowland beamed, ever the proud spouse.

After the service, Nunna got a grip on my arm that meant I was not to leave her for a second. I was officially on display and all the friends who had been tut-tutting about what an ungrateful brat I was for not visiting as soon as she returned were now to be served Crow Amandine. Trying my damnedest to be philosophical about it—face it, it was the least I could do for Nunna—I greeted her old friends and mine, offering an edited version of why it had taken me two months to get here, so that Charlotte's treachery would remain a family secret. I also steeled myself for a barrage of questions about the events in the cemetery, but Nunna's imposing presence must have squelched that; for the first dozen or so encounters, no one mentioned it.

Then Sybil Allen, a neighbor one street over from Nunna, squeezed to the front of the group around us. Something about her had always made me uneasy as a kid and within two seconds I remembered why. An expert at going for the jugular with a Teflon-coated stiletto, she oohed and aahed over me, patted my cheek and gazed in mock sympathy at Nunna. "Such a shame," she said. Her beady eyes flitted between us like a fly undecided about where to light. "All that money spent on your education and you wind up directin' traffic and writin' tickets. Couldn't pass the lawyer's exam, I reckon?"

I detected steam escaping from Nunna's ears and tucked my arm in hers, squeezing her hand to keep her quiet. "Passed it with flying colors," I said. "Joining the police force was a deliberate choice, Miss Sybil, one I'll never regret."

She sniffed. "Well, there's no accounting for taste.

But it seems to me that crime being what it is in Washington, you'd have enough to do up yonder without coming down here and making us look bad."

"Excuse me?"

"I mean, you and that bag of bones of yours."

I took umbrage at the possessive turn of phrase, but before I could protest, an elderly knight rode to my defense.

"Now, Sybil." Mr. Sturgis, Monty's father, had joined us. "How does that skeleton make anybody look bad?"

Mrs. Allen's glare would have sent a rattler backing into its hole. "Don't play dumb with me, Walter Lee Sturgis. I was out there yesterday morning and I got eyes. The fact that half that skeleton's head's been blown away means somebody musta killed him, right? And it was found in the colored cemetery so what else are people gonna think but that one of us did it?"

"Just a minute, Miss Sybil," I said, unsettled that her chain of logic, as insulting as it was, might have some validity to those listening. I had to pull her fangs before she could distribute any more of her toxic opinions. "Granted, part of the skull was missing, but there may be any number of reasons for that—Hannibal, for one. But if you're sure the damage is the result of a gunshot, you should talk to Mr. Sheriff. Let me find him for you. He's here somewhere." On tiptoe, I looked around.

She backed up, stepping on the foot of the woman behind her. "I didn't say it was, no sucha thing. Somebody said that's what it looked like. I don't know nothing about it, nothing a'tall."

"Sorry to hear it." Mr. Sturgis impaled her with his

gaze. "It sure sounded as if you could clear this thing up for everybody once and for all."

"Well, I can't and don't go telling Mr. Sheriff I can, either. Spreading rumors about a poor widow woman. Ought to be ashamed of yourself, Walter Lee." She scurried away, her eyes averted, but there was no way she could miss the amused smiles she was leaving in her wake.

"I wish I could say that maybe she'll think twice before she opens her mouth," Mr. Sturgis said, "but it would be wishful thinking. Can I offer you ladies a lift home?"

Something about Nunna's expression alerted me that a bit of finesse might be called for. I launched into some fancy footwork. "I drove, thanks, but if it's no trouble, I'd appreciate it if you dropped Nunna off for me. I have an errand to run."

"What?" Nunna asked, putting me on the spot.

"I'm thinking of going over to Asheville to see if I can find a copy of the *Washington Post*. How about on my way back I stop at Fred's for some ice cream for dinner?"

She allowed as how that was a fine idea, and after a protracted discussion about which flavors—plural—I should get, left on her friend's arm. It was a sweet picture and I wondered how much my presence might be interfering with their courtship—all the more reason for me to leave at the end of the week. There'd be a reunion every day—tomorrow for those who'd attended Sunrise Township School between 1940 and 1950, Tuesday for the 1951 through 1960 and so on. I'd been a student during the seventies and a graduate of the class of 1980, so my reunion wasn't scheduled until Thursday. Since

I'd promised Nunna I'd stay for the picnic and the closing ceremony on Saturday, I was stuck until then. All I had to do was to find things to do that would keep me from underfoot. She had never been married and Mr. Sturgis was a sweetie. I wanted this for her. Perhaps it would blunt the loss of the cemetery.

"Good morning."

Enter the younger Sturgis. Monty smiled down at me. At the moment I couldn't see his rear and he still looked good, like a walking Smirnoff ad, the successful executive in a navy pin-striped suit.

"How about a ride?" he asked.

"No, thanks. My car's here somewhere. It'll probably take me the rest of the morning to find it."

"I'll help," he offered. "I asked because I'm the one who needs the ride. My father seems to have left me high and dry. He's sharp as a tack most of the time, but when he's around Miss Nunna his brain turns to oatmeal. Does the effect she has on him run in the family?"

"She doesn't turn my brain into oatmeal, if that's what you mean," I responded. "If you're asking does her brand of witchcraft run in her family, I don't know. We aren't related. I'm over this way—I think." I nodded toward the easternmost parking area.

Cupping my elbow gallantly, he escorted me across the grass. "I thought you were Miss Nunna's niece or something."

I was surprised his father hadn't told him. "No relation at all. Just a stray she came across and took home with her. She's good at that, thank heaven."

He glanced at me. "I assume you're being flippant about yourself. As for her taking in strays, that's the

God's honest truth. I thought sure she was in for trouble when she dognapped Hannibal, but nothing happened."

"It was not dognapping," I protested, then processed the implication. "Are you saying you know whose he was?"

"Oh, yeah. Nehemiah's. Hopped out the back of his pickup on Main Street and wandered off."

I stopped. "He's Mr. Sheriff's dog?"

"Yes, ma'am. Hannibal—that's not his name, of course—is one of four Nehemiah had, and a favorite. Still, Nehemiah knows the dog will have a good home, and he figures it might help make up for the cemetery problem, so he's letting sleeping . . . Never mind, you get the picture."

No wonder Hannibal had glued himself to the fence the day before; he'd recognized his former owner.

"Don't tell Miss Nunna, though," Monty added. "I think she'd be embarrassed."

I laughed. "The hell she would. The dog was loose and to Nunna that meant he was ownerless. If Mr. Sheriff had come to get him, Nunna would have insisted she be paid for however long she'd given the rascal room and board. And Mr. Sheriff would have gotten the point—keep the damned dog on a leash."

Monty chuckled. "A hard woman. I'm not sure my father knows what he's up against. That's a nice change. My Mom, God love her, was a pushover."

It was nice to know he approved, not that it would have mattered to Nunna one way or another.

After a fifteen minute search, we located my car. Moving it, however, was another story. People had parked with no regard for whether they were blocking others and I was pinned in, front, rear, port, star-board, and going nowhere; you couldn't get a paper clip between my car and the one on the right. This was not good. The sun, edging toward its zenith, would turn the interior of my car into an oven before long. I could imagine myself getting in and breaking into a sweat. My dress, a pricey linen two-piece the color of goldenrod, would be soaked two minutes later and shortly thereafter it would be Wrinkle City.

"Looks like you'll have to find another ride," I told Monty, opening my door and slipping in just long enough to roll down all the windows.

"I'm in no hurry." He shrugged out of his jacket, folded it and reaching in, laid it across the rear seat. Then, long legs crossed at the ankles and arms folded, he leaned back against the trunk of my car. "I came by Miss Nunna's yesterday, but you were out."

So he was the persistent S.O.B. who'd kept ring-ing the bell. "Uh-huh, out cold. When Doc and Mr. Sheriff left, I took the phone off the hook and went to bed."

"That early?"

"You bet. I didn't get much sleep the night before."

"Because of the body? That surprises me. All things considered, I'd have thought you'd be hard-ened to that kind of thing by now."

"All what things considered?" I felt my hackles rising.

"Your being a . . . what's the politically correct term? Policewoman? Policeperson?"

"How about police officer? And contrary to popu-lar opinion, it is possible to walk the streets of the

District of Columbia without tripping over a body on every other block."

He leveled a measuring gaze at me. "It seems I've touched a nerve. I'm sorry. But hell, since I've already put my foot in it, I can usually guess the type of work a person does within a minute or two. I'd never have tabbed you as a police officer."

"And I'd never have tabbed you as a mayor," I countered with malice aforethought.

"*Touché.*" He sighed. "This is not going well. Let's start over. Or should I get my jacket and hoof it back to town?"

Maybe he wouldn't be a total loss after all. Besides, since the cars in front of and beside me were easing away, I had less excuse to tell him to take a hike. "So far your luck's holding," I said, "but I wouldn't push it any farther."

"Yes, ma'am." He opened my door for me, his eyes dancing with humor. Once in the passenger seat, he buckled up and, without thinking, checked to be sure my belt was securely fastened. "Sorry. Force of habit. Once a dad, always a dad."

This was news. "How many kids?"

"Two—a girl nine and a boy eleven. They're with their mother in Chicago and spend summers and the odd holiday with me. They'll be here next month."

"Hmm." I backed out of the space, narrowly missing a pair of teens so engrossed in each other that they were oblivious to traffic. "Between serving as mayor, dealing with the Waverly folks, and being a father to your kids, you're going to be a very busy man."

He chuckled. "Don't forget my job at the hospital. By the end of the summer, they'll be checking me in as a patient. Tell me something," he said, as I wove my way between pedestrians intent on hogging any right-of-way. "How do you see so much evil and misery—not just see it but wind up in the middle of it yourself—without letting it affect you? How do you retain your equilibrium?"

I hadn't but wasn't ready to admit it to him. "It ain't easy," I said.

"I know. That's why I'm administering a staff instead of administering to patients. I'm way too long on empathy. A patient suffers, I suffer. A death would devastate me. But I'm good at my job. I look at someone like Doc Webster and wonder how he's held up so long. Glad he has. What would this town have done without him?"

"Buried a lot of people a lot sooner. Which reminds me, I need to find him. He left his pen at Nunna's." I scanned the crowd of pedestrians playing Hit-Me-I-Dare-You and the vehicles whose drivers looked as if they'd like to oblige. No Voyager. "It's a really old fountain pen. I know he'll want it back."

"You'll never find him in this mob. Dad and I saw him getting out of his van at Mr. Sheriff's place. Considering how late we were, by the time he got here he had to be stuck at the back. But he'd also be parked at the back, too, with nobody blocking him in, so he's probably gone already. By the way, what's this about him thinking he has an X ray of the body you found? Would that be accepted as positive identification?"

I did not want to discuss it. "It might, if it turns out to be the only thing to go on. Dental records would be even better. Can we talk about something else?"

"We could," he said, turning sideways in his seat, "and I hope we'll have occasion to at some point—that's not a line, either—but at the moment, I need as much information from as many different sources as I can get and you're one of them. How long would you say it had been there?"

"I have no idea. And don't ask me to guess because I can't. It's not one of my areas of expertise." We'd finally reached the exit of the picnic grounds. Edging between strollers with strollers, don't-give-a-damn teens on foot, and vehicular traffic that had taken earlier exits was like squeezing between raindrops. I concentrated on bullying my way into the stream of traffic and searched my mental files of small talk for a change of subject. "It occurs to me that I don't know where you live."

"Main and Twilight. About the skull. What was your impression of its condition?"

His persistence was annoying. "It was badly damaged, which you must have known or you wouldn't have asked."

His lips tightened. "Don't play games, Leigh. Was the person murdered?"

I was getting pissed. The sooner we got to Twilight Road the better. "How do I know? Possibly. Possibly not."

"It doesn't make sense." He slumped in the seat. "I've been in the area for ten years, and in Sunrise for the last four. Nobody's disappeared. We've had more than our share of funerals but this is a typical small town. We all know each others' business and we've known the cause of every single one of those deaths. Who the hell could this be? And how'd he wind up in our cemetery?"

I saw his point, and as I poked along and finally turned onto Main, realized that I agreed with him. The possibility of a stranger wandering through was unlikely, since there was only one way in and out of town. As dead a place as Sunrise was, the arrival of an unfamiliar car or a strange face amounted to an occasion.

"No one's died of a bad fall?" I asked, relaxing now that traffic flowed smoothly.

"Ted Euker fell off the roof of his barn and broke his neck but his head was intact. There've been a couple of traffic fatalities, both of them eastsiders, and we saw them buried. Right here," he said, pointing. After a second, I realized he was indicating where I should let him out. The old Riley home. "Dad's not here yet. Look, Leigh, I've got a favor to ask."

A caution light went on in my brain. "Ask."

"Will you keep me apprised of what's happening? Not that Nehemiah won't, but you may have a different slant on—"

"Hold it." I slammed the gearshift into park and engaged the emergency brake. "I hate to repeat myself, but I told you yesterday, I'm out of the loop. This is Mr. Sheriff's case, his job. He's the law in this town. He's under no obligation to let me know what's going on and that's fine with me."

"But you could—"

"No." I had to straighten this out once and for all. "Effective week after next I will no longer be an officer of the law and Mr. Sheriff knows that. I've seen as much as I want of the worst side of human nature and I'm getting out before it poisons me any more than it already has. Okay, I found a body and there's no way to change that. But who it is, what happened to him or her, that's not my problem. I want nothing more to do with it. Is that clear enough for you?"

He'd opened the door halfway. Releasing his seat belt, he scanned my features. I waited, assuming I'd probably alienated him, which pinched a little but not enough to make me change my mind.

"Okay, lady," he said finally. He got out, closed the door, then leaned down to look in. "It's funny. I've heard a lot about you since you arrived, from Dad and Nehemiah and Mrs. Totton. And—"

"Mrs. Totton?"

"Especially from her, and they've all spoken highly of you. Not one of them mentioned the fact that you're a quitter."

It stung, precisely as it was meant to do. But I'd been called a damned sight worse. I released the emergency brake, a warning for him to move. He took the hint. "You have a good day, hear?" I said at my chirpiest, and pulled away, watching him in my rearview mirror watching me. Lord, he was so fine! Pity.

No longer in the mood for the *Washington Post*, or anything else that would remind me of D.C., I headed for the diner and the ice cream for dessert. Approaching the corner of Main on which it sat, I spotted Claire Rowland crossing the intersection and was almost on her before I realized it was Maudine, not Claire. Not that they looked that much alike, but they were the same general type—taller than average, blond, and built like brick outhouses. With Claire's money and budget for clothes, Maudine would be damned attractive. I was surprised at not having realized it that first day. Perhaps her working clothes—and attitude—had masked it. Today, however, in a full-skirted periwinkle dress and matching sandals, her hair swirled into an elaborate chignon atop her head, she was drop-dead gorgeous and going to waste in this town.

I pulled up in front of the diner and got out. "Did you walk all the way back from the service? I could have given you a lift."

She turned, startled. "Oh, hi, Leigh Ann. I didn't mind. It's a nice day for a walk."

I wasn't convinced she meant it. In fact, she seemed rather subdued. "Maudine, is something wrong?"

"It shows, huh?" She made a face. "Well, it should. I'm purely pissed at my brother."

"Maurice? What'd he do?"

"He didn't show, that's what. Sent him a ticket and everything. Got Jimmy Worszik to drive me to the airport last night, waited, and he never showed. The bastard. Mama's fit to be tied."

"And you're hurt."

Her lips tightened. "Damn right I'm hurt. I paid for that thing myself and it was a nonrefundable ticket. I was so sure . . ." She frowned. "Christ almighty. Fred must be burning dish towels again. He does it so often, you'd think the damned things were on the menu. I'd better get in there." She hurried toward the door and I followed, surprised that I hadn't noticed the odor myself. It appeared that along with the job, I was also shedding my powers of observation.

"Fred!" Maudine called.

"What?" Fred, a Mr. Clean look-alike, stuck his shiny pate around the kitchen door and whistled.

"God a'mighty, Maudine, we got to arrange for you to wear your Sunday-go-to-meeting clothes every day of the week. The way you look, the customers'll be flocking in here just to get a peek."

She blushed American Beauty rose. "Thanks. Did Maurice call?"

"Phone hasn't rung at all. Sorry, honey."

"That asshole. Just wait. By the way, what have you been burning back there?"

Fred's rubbery features assumed an indignant cant. "I ain't burned a thing. Hey, Leigh Ann."

"Morning, Fred. The air's clear in here, Maudine," I said, and backed out onto the street. The odor was stronger this time, but it was difficult to tell from which direction it was coming. I peered in the window of Myrtle's Hair Care next door and detected nothing suspicious there or in Fiedler's Clip Joint beyond.

"I'll check the stores on the other side," Maudine called as I hurried the length of the block, stopping long enough for a two-second peek into darkened windows. Everything looked normal and the farther down the row I went, the less pervasive the burning smell seemed to be. Traffic had increased and cars slowed, their passengers watching us curiously.

I'd reached the end of the block and was about to cross to the next row of shops when I heard Maudine.

"Leigh Ann, over here!" She'd made it to the middle of the block and stood, her nose against the windows of a narrow store with no sign above the front.

I angled back toward her and almost got my clock cleaned dashing in front of a primer-daubed pickup. "Sorry," I yelled over the driver's curses and hit the curb unscathed. Maudine was right. The smell was stronger on this side. "See anything?" I asked.

"I'm not sure."

Her uncertainty was justified; the interior was barely visible behind partially closed blinds. The ones at the door didn't quite fit, leaving a gap of perhaps an inch and a half on either side. The view wasn't that much better—a battered couch and the end of a coffee table stacked with magazines. I switched to the other side. From this vantage, I could see the edge of a desk and beyond it a closed door.

"What kind of store is this?" I asked.

"It's Doc's office. He moved here a while back. See anything?"

"No, but . . ." I hurried to the feed store next door, sniffed. The odor was nowhere nearly as strong. "We'd better report this, Maudine. If we're wrong, no harm done."

She grabbed my forearm. "Did you hear something? From inside. A bumping noise?"

I hadn't, but plastered my face against the glass again. Wisps of smoke slithered from under the door of Doc's inner office. "Go. Get the fire department, Maudine. Hurry."

"I'm gone," she said, yanking off her sandals and tossing them aside. "Please, Leigh Ann, check around back and make sure Doc's car's not there." Hand raised to stop traffic, an entirely unnecessary gesture, given the attention she was attracting, she pelted across the street in her stocking feet and hit the door of the diner at full speed.

I seriously doubted Doc was anywhere around. He wouldn't have office hours on Sunday, certainly not this one. The schedule of activities we'd received this morning showed an after-service brunch for Mrs. Totton at the Methodist church and, if I remembered correctly, Doc was a pillar of St. Matthews. He was bound to be there. Still, from the rear I might be able to tell how far the fire had spread.

Taking a cue from Maudine, I stepped out of my pumps and, carrying them, sprinted toward the end of the block before realizing that if I cut through the launderette, I'd save a few steps and perhaps precious seconds. I startled a young woman cramming diapers into a dryer as I ran straight through, past the machines, and out the back door to the almost empty parking lot. The young mother's station wagon, complete with three infant safety seats, was parked straddling two slots. The second vehicle, a beat-up Voyager two places over, stopped me cold. It was the same van Doc had been driving the day before.

Dropping my shoes, I ran past the van to the door it was parked closest to, the lettering across the solid black metal—Paul Webster, M.D.—marking it as his territory. Smoke wafted from an ancient air conditioner set in the brick wall beside the door. Pulse racing, I hurled my purse through an open window of the Voyager, plotting, planning, praying. Gingerly, I placed two fingers against the door to see how hot it was and nearly jumped out of my skin when it moved under my touch, opening an inch or so. Heat seemed to race out, as if waiting to escape. Smoke followed, slithering around the sill. If Doc was in there . . .

I kicked at the door, wishing I hadn't been so fast

to shed my shoes. It flew open, bumped against something, and recoiled, starting to close again. The interior was a glimpse into hell. The walls were no longer solid. They were alive, moving, dancing, writhing, red-orange with flames. Black smoke billowed toward the ceiling, folding in over itself as it rose.

Panic gripped me around the throat. If I had to choose between facing an armed madman or a room on fire, I'd take the maniac every time. I couldn't remember a time since my parents' deaths when a burning building hadn't reduced me to a quivering blob of ectoplasm. But I heard no sirens, no alarms. Even if Maudine had placed her call, it might be several minutes before all the volunteer fire fighters could be reached. With the distinct possibility that Doc was inside, I had to do something. Me. There was no one else.

"Doc!" I kicked the door again, causing a repeat of its previous performance: it stopped at about three-quarters, blocked by something. I labored to think logically, putting off Show Time as long as I could. If a piece of furniture—a file cabinet, a desk—had been behind the door, it should have hit it with an audible thud. I'd heard nothing. Whatever was behind it was soft, yielding. It was time to stop farting around.

I yanked off the lovely silk scarf I'd borrowed from Nunna and tied it across my mouth and nose. Hiking the skirt up around my thighs, I dropped to my knees, took a deep breath, held it, and crawled over the threshold into my worst nightmare. After less than a foot, I was blind, eyes streaming, nose running. The scarf was a poor filter. I would not be able to hold my breath for long at this rate. The heat and smoke had mass, weight, as solid as the walls had been. Breathing at all would be a trial, if I survived it.

Groping for the edge of the door, I squeezed my eyes closed and forced myself to go a bit farther, terrified that the door might close and trap me in this inferno. I extended my right arm and snaked it around behind the door, touched fabric, muscle, then metal which, once my brain cleared, I recognized as a belt buckle. Doc. Dead or alive, it didn't matter. I had to get him out of there.

Unfortunately, that meant moving around behind the door to get secure enough purchase to drag him out. I took a breath and realized what it must be like to drown. Something hot and solid filled my lungs, triggering a cough reflex that made matters worse, since I could no longer hold my breath. I tried and felt pressure build in my ears as if I'd suppressed a sneeze. I had to cough, had to breathe. I had to stay alive long enough to get us both out.

A crash—a piece of ceiling coming down—supplied the adrenaline I needed. I scuttled around behind the door, got a good grip on Doc's belt, and pulled. His deadweight resisted. As long as I remained on my knees, I wouldn't be able to budge him. If I stood up, the smoke would be even thicker. I wouldn't be able to breathe at all. Trying the middle road, I pushed myself to my feet and squatted, froglike. Found his belt buckle again and tugged. Everything screamed—arms, lungs, head, nose, eyes. I tugged anyway. A year or two passed before I'd towed him from behind the door.

On my knees again, I crawled toward voices barely audible above the crackling and snapping, found

Doc's ankles and pulled, dragging him inch by inch as I backed toward the open door. Hands gripped my upper arms, loosening my hold on my burden. Past coherent thought, I tried to fight them off.

"Damn it, let go, girl! We'll get him!" Whose voice? I didn't know, didn't care. Doc wasn't safe yet.

I felt an arm circle my waist, felt it lift me from the floor, felt movement as I was carried—somewhere. Suddenly the scarf across my face was gone and it was slightly easier to breathe, but the only parts of me that appeared to be working normally were my ears and my tear ducts. Feet scurried around me, a heavy engine growled nearby—a tanker?

"He's out, Leigh Ann. They got him." Maudine.

I scrubbed at my eyes, coughed, coughed again, feeling as if my lungs were being shredded. I had a question and fought for breath to ask it. "Is he alive?" It was my voice but I would never have recognized it. I sounded like a feminine version of Louis Armstrong.

"Yes, honey." Maudine again.

I'd done it. I'd gotten him out. I'd saved his life. It was okay to pass out now. Which I did. Gratefully.

6

I bitched and whined, even considered tears for a second or two. No one paid the slightest attention; I wound up at the hospital anyway, being treated for smoke inhalation. They dressed a couple of abrasions on my palms I hadn't been aware of, and my bruised knees, which were a mess, then tried to ship me upstairs in one of those gowns with the peekaboo backs. I wouldn't go for it. I wanted to check on Doc, find out how he was doing. I wanted to hear how the fire had started, how much damage had been done. Granted, I was tired and sore, but I'd felt worse than that after a game of racquetball with Duck.

Monty and Mr. Sheriff came into the emergency room cubicle one behind the other as if they were riding a tandem bike. "You needn't ask any questions," Monty declared before I could frame the first of many I had, "because we don't know anything yet. We're here to see how you're doing."

"I'm just peachy-keen, thanks," I said, in a foul mood and still a little hoarse. Along with my apprehension at being held captive—hospitals make me hyperventilate—I looked like hell and knew it. My brand-new goldenrod dress was ruined, consigned to the trash, and I'd long since lost faith in my deodorant, with good cause. "No word on Doc at all?"

"When we know, you'll know," Mr. Sheriff said gruffly. "Now hush up and listen, please, ma'am. That was a brave thing you did, Leigh Ann. Foolish, too, but I want to thank you for it. You know how much Web means to everybody so I'm speaking for the whole town. I gotta get back to him. Miss Nunna's on her way with a change of clothes for you so you can go home." With that, he snapped a semiofficial salute, backed out of the cubicle, and bumped into Nunna on her way in carrying an overnight case.

"Honey," she said, trying to free herself of the nurse hanging onto her arm, "I don't give a kitty who gave what order. I am going to see my baby."

"Madam, please, either you leave or I'll have to call security. Visitors aren't allowed back here without—" Seeing Monty, the nurse stopped and turned a bright red. "I tried, Mr. Sturgis, honestly, but this lady insisted—"

"It's okay, Val." Monty awarded her a reassuring nod. "Dr. Prentiss says he's done all the patient will allow him to do and Ms. Layton's here to take her home. Let's get out so she can change." He hustled the nurse from the room and, after a departing smile for me, left himself.

"Leigh Ann." Nunna hugged me, her eyes filling. "Somebody called and told me you'd gone into a raging fire and pulled Doc out all by yourself and were in sad shape. All I could think was I'd just gotten you back and might lose you again, maybe for good. I don't know if I could have survived that. Are you all right? Lord, child, what happened to your eyebrows?"

I fingered them, unaware until this moment that they were missing. "Probably got singed off. I'm fine, Nunna. Cross my heart. And the sooner I get out of here, the better. I'll need a little help changing." I held up my bandaged palms.

"Well, I hope you won't mind leaving in this. I thought they were keeping you." She pulled one of the knee-length nightshirts I slept in. It was fine. I was so anxious to go, I'd have left in my underwear.

Nunna untied the gown they'd given me and began a hands-on examination of all my burns, bumps, and bruises, tsk-tsking. She probed the back of my neck, peered at my head. "You lost some curls on this side," she said, fingering the charred ends and patting them into place. I drew away but not quickly enough. "What was that? Hold still, now!" She parted my hair. "My land! You didn't do this today. What happened here, Leigh Ann?"

I debated how to answer her. I could flat-out lie, except I was never very good at it and Nunna could sniff out a fib faster than a hound could pick up a scent.

"I was grazed by a bullet," I said, easing the nightshirt over my head. "Nothing serious."

She lowered herself onto the stool the doctor had used, her features impassive. "Grazed by a bullet. When was this?"

"A couple of months ago. It was no big deal, honestly."

"No big deal. An accident? Or was somebody aim-
ing to kill you?"

"It's history, Nunna. Why don't I tell you about it
tomorrow?"

She rose. "No, not tomorrow. Today, just as soon
as I get your secret-keeping behind back to the
house."

I could tell by the set of her lips that it was bean-
spilling time or there'd be hell to pay. The best I
could hope to do might be some judicious editing.
Perhaps between here and home I could decide
what to strike, what to leave in.

I never got the chance. As we were leaving, Mrs.
Totton, pacing the floor in the waiting room, stopped
us.

"Leigh Ann." Mrs. Totton took my hands and
released them immediately when I winced. "Oh, my
dear, I'm so sorry. I had Claire bring me as soon as I
heard. How are you?"

"Just fine, really. A few bruises, that's about all."

"We've been told otherwise, but I won't press
you." She enveloped me with the warmth of her
gaze. "Is it true you've become a police officer?"

"Yes, ma'am."

"Well, if today's any indication, you must be an
exemplary member of your department. You were
an excellent student and the honor code you wrote
was still in use the day we closed our doors for the
last time. It seems to me, you've fulfilled your
Service to Sunrise. You risked your life. No one
could ask more of you."

She'd touched on the IOU that had kept me away
so long. All the playground equipment had been
donated or paid for by former students, according to

Sheryl, who had returned to S.T. to teach for a year to clear her slate. The school's swimming pool had been a joint STS. Eddie Post, who'd become a C.P.A., had come back to help folks with their taxes free of charge two years running. My STS debt, however, had been unpaid. I'd had nothing practical to offer; the last thing Sunrise had needed was a second officer of the law. Now I was off the hook. I couldn't have been more relieved if someone were paying my bills for a year.

Claire Rowland, who'd been in agitated conversation with the receptionist, joined us. "They won't tell me a thing about Doc," Claire said peevishly, and fanned herself with the small clutch bag that matched her dress, a soft lilac, probably silk, the skirt cascading from a waist so small I envisioned one of those torture chambers with stays and laces hidden under all those gathers. Even her excuse for a hat, intricate circles of fabric about the size of a yarmulka, matched the dress. Someone had kept a lot of silkworms busy for a long time to outfit her, except for her shoes. They, at least, were patent leather with ankle straps, gleaming white, the heels so high they'd have given me a nosebleed. She was stunning, a real head turner, and made me feel even grubbier.

"Poor Web." Mrs. Totten dabbed at her eyes. "This will finish him. At his age, there's no question of him starting over again. All his equipment, his instruments."

Claire wrapped a comforting arm around her shoulders. "We can't be sure how much damage was done. You were in there, Leigh Ann. What do you think?"

"Hard to say. With the walls and ceiling on fire, I can't see how anything could have been saved. But—"

I stopped, distracted at the appearance at the entrance of Josh, Mr. Sheriff's son, an extralarge brown envelope under his arm. He'd been impressive in uniform. In his Sunday best, he was definitely hunk material. Spotting us, he strode over. "You okay, Miss Leigh Ann?"

I sighed. As rotten as I looked and felt, the last thing I needed was a reminder of the generation gap. "Fine, thanks."

"Good. Y'all seen my daddy?"

"He's still in with Doc, but check with the receptionist," Claire advised. "She wouldn't tell me which cubicle Doc's in, or anything else, for that matter. Perhaps she'll tell you."

"Thank you, ma'am." He smiled a farewell and headed for the counter.

"Y'all will have to excuse us," Nunna said. "This child needs to go home."

"We should be leaving, too, Estelle," Claire said. "It's a twenty-minute ride back to Sunrise and the folks at St. Matthews are waiting. We were hoping to get some word about Doc's condition so we'd have something to tell the congregation, but we really can't hang around any longer. How'd you get here, Miss Nunna? Do you need a ride home?" She jiggled her car keys at us.

I looked to Nunna to answer, since I wasn't sure how she'd gotten to the hospital either. All I needed was a lift back to Sunrise and my car, still in front of the diner, and some time alone to prepare for the inquisition to come.

Nunna explained that Monty's father had driven her over and would take us back. Claire and Mrs. Totton left and Nunna parked me in a chair while she went off to find her friend. I sat alone, grateful for a moment of solitude. What would I tell her? No matter from which direction I approached it, the truth was simpler. The whole truth. The shooting, my plans to resign, after which she would try to convince me to move back to Sunrise. At one time I might have jumped at the chance, but not now, not with Mr. Sturgis in the picture. I refused to jeopardize what future they might have together.

Besides, there was my own house to get in order. There were decisions to be made and I'd make them alone, knowing I'd always have her moral support if I needed it. So I'd tell her everything and go on from there. I came out of my brown study and began to take note of my surroundings.

Josh Sheriff paced anxiously outside the double doors of the Emergency wing, never still, jiggling the change in his pockets, straightening his tie or combing his fingers through his hair. I was giving serious consideration to going to look for Nunna when Mr. Sheriff came out of Emergency. Josh grabbed his father's arm, walked him to an unoccupied corner, and, after a very brief conversation, handed over the big brown envelope he'd been carrying.

Mr. Sheriff's expression was difficult to read as he pried up the flap and, without removing the contents, glanced inside. His lips tightened. Sidling over until he was directly under one of the ceiling lamps, he opened the envelope even wider, his head tilted to one side as he peered into it. Slowly his jaw became slack. His mouth formed a circle in shock.

He shook his head, as if to clear it, looked again. Then, very deliberately, he closed the envelope and sealed it with the string on the flap.

Perhaps remembering he was in a public place, he scanned the lounge, but few of those waiting appeared to be paying the slightest attention to him. Inevitably, however, his glance settled on me and our eyes locked and held. After a couple of seconds, he returned the envelope to Josh and, swiveling so that his back was to me, exchanged a few additional words with his son.

"Yes, sir, Daddy." Josh practically saluted and left with a purposeful stride.

Mr. Sheriff stood for a moment, deep in thought, then slowly, as if tired to the bone, went back into the Emergency wing just as Nunna arrived, Mr. Sturgis in tow. Under the impression that I'd been admitted, he'd been upstairs, badgering Information for my room number.

At Nunna's insistence, he ferried us directly to the house, with a promise to see that my car was delivered before the day was over, and was unabashedly disappointed when she failed to invite him in.

"Come over later, if you like," she said, no nonsense brooked. "Leigh Ann and I need some time alone."

He left, abandoning me to Nunna at her most determined.

Giving up on any delaying tactics, I laid it all out for her, all the negative aspects of police work I'd omitted that first day, the stress, the emotional tugs-of-war, the daily encounters with malice. Only then was I ready to relate the events that led up to the shooting and the effect it had had on me. Nunna listened without comment, shaking her head occasion-ally. By the time I'd finished I was exhausted, run-ning on empty.

"So that explains the nightmares," Nunna said, surprising me. I hadn't realized she was aware of them. "It hasn't been an easy life, has it? But tell me again why you're leaving it. Because you had to shoot that boy?"

"No. When you pin on a badge, you accept the fact that one day you might have to use your weapon. And I was lucky. After he fired and the bullet grazed me, he fired again but nothing happened. I didn't know whether he was out of ammunition or the gun had simply misfired but the opportunity arose and I took it. I shot him."

"You didn't kill him, Leigh Ann."

"Well, it wasn't for lack of trying, because I meant to do just that. I looked at Duck sitting there on the floor and that kid became every thief I'd ever had to deal with, every pusher, wife beater, child abuser, rapist, mugger, every piece of garbage I'd soiled my hands with over the last six years. I was an avenger, a female Charles Bronson—"

"Who?"

"—a vigilante intent on wiping him off the face of the earth. One less piece of scum to worry about. Only it turns out I was shooting at a good kid who delivered pizzas, a kid who'd been beaten up and robbed three times and had decided that three times was enough. Duck was in street clothes. There was nothing to identify him as a cop. When the kid saw him running up the hall behind him, he jumped to the wrong conclusion and shot him."

"Poor child."

I wasn't sure whether the reference was to the kid or to Duck, decided I might rest easier not knowing, and went on. "Then I came barreling through the door and he figured I was Duck's backup. When he shot at me, as far as he was concerned he was still defending himself."

"And you were defending yourself. I think you're judging yourself too harshly, Leigh Ann."

"No, I'm not." For a moment I tasted the rage I'd felt when I thought Duck was dead. "The only thing on my mind was blowing his fu"—I caught myself—"blowing his brains out. I looked at that kid and saw all the bastards I'd dealt with. I'd had enough and I shot him."

"Well, you're only human, honey. Of course you were angry."

"But the anger's still there, Nunna. My first day back on regular duty, I was dangerous. Made an arrest for disorderly conduct and was a second away from unadulterated police brutality. If my backup hadn't arrived when he did . . . " I drew in a deep breath, still shaken at how close to the edge I'd been. "I want out, Nunna. I don't give a damn anymore. I'm sick of dealing with garbage, sick of taking care of other people's problems. When you become callous about the victims and vindictive with the perpetrators, it's time to find another line of work. There's a friend from law school who's offered me a place with his firm anytime I want it, and another one who'd like to hire me as an investigator. I'm not sure which I'll take yet. All I know is that it's time to turn in my badge."

Nunna set her rocker in motion. "Why did you become a police officer to begin with, baby?"

"I wanted to help people." It sounded so inane.

"Have you?"

"I guess so. But I'm tired of the people I'm trying to protect thinking of me as the enemy."

"That can't be true of all of them," Nunna said with reproach.

"It sure as hell seemed like it sometimes. As of two months ago, they're dead on target. If I stay on the job any longer, I'll be their enemy right enough, a bad cop. That's why I'm quitting."

"Hhmph." Nunna moved to the bedroom door and stopped, hands on her hips. "Walter Lee uses a phrase that usually makes me cringe but it's just right for this. What you've just handed me, and yourself, Leigh Ann, is a load of bullshit."

"Nunna!" Not that I hadn't heard her swear before, but this was completely out of character.

"If you've become so callous and unfeeling, if you don't give a damn anymore, why'd you risk your life today? As terrified of fire as you've been all your life? Why'd you go into that building? Explain that to me."

"I didn't think—well, not much, anyway."

"Exactly. You didn't have to, because way down deep you still care. And don't think I haven't noticed that you didn't say a word about feeling you'd let your partner down."

"He's not my partner. He's—" How could I explain my relationship with Duck?

"He's just a friend," I finished, hoping that would satisfy Nunna.

"A friend. Uh-huh," she said, and I knew it had not. "We may have been apart for many a year, but I know you. Guilt is eating you alive, guilt that you didn't go in with Duck, guilt that you might have been able to avoid shooting that young man, although I don't see how, under the circumstances. Guilt is whispering in your ear that you're a failure, untrustworthy, unfit for duty. And you're listening to every word. *That's* your trouble."

I had no response. She was right.

"I'm going to start dinner. You try to get some rest and think about what I've said. I'll back you in whatever you decide to do, you know that, baby. If you want to come home to stay, the door's open. But it's about time you stopped lying to yourself, Leigh Ann Warren. I know you. And you are not a quitter."

That word again, I thought, as she closed the door behind her. Okay, she was right about the guilt trip. If I'd gone in with Duck as he'd asked, things might have happened differently—how I'd never know, but the possibility would always hang over my head like the sword of Damocles. In a way, saving Doc Webster's life made up a little for having let Duck down. But she was wrong about the rest. I was tired of wallowing in the muck of other people's problems, the detritus of other people's misdeeds. I was tired of feeling as if the work I did made no difference, that things were not improving. And I had to get away from Duck. I wanted out.

I played hermit the rest of that day, letting Nunna field the dozen or so calls to inquire about my health and marvel about what I'd done. I slept, a deep dreamless sleep for the first time in two months. I assumed that coming clean to Nunna had acted as a detergent of sorts, relieving me of a good deal of the soot and ashes in which I'd covered myself since the shooting.

I was completely prepared to play possum the next day as well, only the lady of the house would have none of it. She rolled me out of bed just before noon, changed my dressings, helped me get clothes on, and dragged me to the table for brunch. Beside my plate was a stack of messages.

"Those are calls from yesterday I thought you might want to return," Nunna said. "If the phone rings today, you answer it. I've had all I can take of playing secretary."

I flipped through them weeding out the wheat from the chaff—former classmates, most of whom I hadn't seen since graduation from Central High, a few of Nunna's friends, and two from Mrs. Totton, one from the evening before and another taken a half hour before marked "Urgent." I suspected it was this second call from Mrs. T. that had ended my communion with my virginal couch.

I put the whole stack aside. My classmates wouldn't be going anywhere. They, like me, were stuck in town until our Thursday reunion. Nunna's friends I'd tackle after brunch. I did try to reach Mrs. Totton and breathed a sigh of relief when I got a busy signal. Twice. After stuffing myself unashamedly with Nunna's cooking, I called the hospital for news of Doc and ran into a brick wall. Unless I was a member of his immediate family, they were not at liberty to discuss his condition.

I started down the next most logical route and tried to reach Monty, then Mr. Sheriff. Nothing. Monty was out of the office and so was the chief. I considered walking over to Main to check out Doc's office, remembered what it had been like in that back room, and decided to forget the whole business. I returned most of the remaining calls, tried Mrs. Totton again, and after fifteen minutes and five attempts, gave up, raided Nunna's stash of mysteries, and settled down with Dick Francis and Karen Kijewski.

Then Sheryl showed up, shrieking, "Miss Nunna wouldn't let me bother you yesterday and early this morning, but I've waited as long as I could. I just came from Main Street and got a look at poor Doc Webster's office, so I had to come see for myself that you're all right. Girl, you are *crazy!* You could have been killed in there!"

That effectively destroyed the peace and quiet that had characterized the afternoon and I spent the next half hour describing what had happened in the minute detail she demanded. According to her, Doc's office was a colossal mess.

The subject had been rehashed a couple of times and mercifully exhausted when the doorbell rang. Mr. Sheriff. I was so glad to see him, I'd have yanked him inside had my palms been in any condition to withstand the pressure.

"Come on in," I said, opening the door. "I tried to reach you earlier, but no one answered. Have a seat."

He shook his head, his expression grim. "Thank you, I won't. Aft'noon, Sheryl, Miss Nunna," he said in greeting. Nunna had appeared from the kitchen. "I thought it was only proper that I be the one to tell you, Leigh Ann. Web died this morning."

"Oh, no." I collapsed into the nearest chair. Nunna moved behind me and stood, rubbing my arms. Sheryl, her rich brown skin drained of blood, disappeared toward my bedroom and returned with a box of tissues which she crammed into my hand. Then she sank to the floor as if her legs had given out and began to blubber. Dry-eyed and beyond tears, I passed the box back to her.

It had never occurred to me that he wouldn't survive. Or perhaps complete rejection of the possibility was easier to handle. The news hit hard, devastating me. I was utterly overwhelmed with a sense of loss, and again, failure. I hadn't saved him after all. I'd been too late.

"No, you weren't," Mr. Sheriff said sharply, and I realized I'd said it aloud. "The fire didn't kill him. Didn't help him none, but it didn't kill him. He died of a head wound, was probably already brain-dead when you pulled him out, according to the doctors. He was just so damned stubborn, his heart kept on pumping until a couple of hours ago. Reckon a piece of ceiling hit him or something."

I shook my head violently. "It didn't start falling until I'd pulled him almost to the door. Perhaps the smoke got to him and he hit something going down. Do you know how the fire started yet?"

"Irv Maxwell's doing the investigating. He's there now. Maybe he'll be able to tell me something before the day's over. The coroner's inquest is scheduled for Wednesday morning at nine o'clock. They'll need you to testify."

"Oh, God." This was another facet of my life I'd be glad to leave behind me. I hated court appearances of any kind. Most of the time, they wasted mine, what with postponements and defendants who didn't show up. This would be different and I'd be there, but I dreaded it.

Mr. Sheriff fidgeted a moment, then took a deep breath. "Leigh Ann, I know you're upset but, well, I'd be obliged if you'd come go with me over to Miz Totton's."

"What for?"

He didn't respond immediately, shifting his weight from one foot to the other. It was obvious he wasn't happy at having to make the request. "I'd just as soon she told you. I'll drive you over."

Nunna perched on the arm of my chair and cradled my shoulders. "Nehemiah, it'll have to wait. Leigh Ann's in no condition to go anywhere. Maybe later this evening."

"If it were just me, I'd say this evening would be fine. But you know how that little woman can be when she's got her mind set on something."

In other words, she'd directed him not to come back without me. For a second or so, my mulishness came to the fore. Mrs. T. might be in a position to order a command appearance from him and others in Sunrise, but I was not one of them. Unfortunately, my curiosity overrode the stubborn streak. What could she want? What was so bloody important that she couldn't wait?

"Let me wash my face," I said. "But I'm not changing clothes." I was in shorts and a Minnie Mouse T-shirt. I'd go as is or not at all.

"Then I'm coming, too," Nunna said and glared at Mr. Sheriff, daring him to object. He sighed. Obviously he'd had more than his share of pigheaded women for one day and there were still nine hours to go.

°   °   °

Mrs. Totton's house was a pseudo-Victorian with gin-gerbread galore, and a brick-topped driveway lead-ing to a two-car garage. Curtains at the front window twitched as Mr. Sheriff stopped halfway up the drive. By the time we'd climbed the steps to the porch, Mrs. Totton had opened the door and stood waiting.

Nunna's gasp of surprise was audible. Somehow I managed to suppress my own when I saw our hostess up close. She looked awful, her eyes bloodshot, her face drawn and taut. She had aged ten years literally overnight.

"Leigh Ann, Nunnally, thank you for coming," she said, leading us into a living room chockablock with upholstered furniture on clawed feet, antimacassars across their arms and back, as well as every flat sur-face available. The curtains were pulled together, blocking the afternoon sunlight. The room felt close, stifling.

"You're here. Good." Claire Rowland swept into the room carrying a silver tray with silver-rimmed glasses of iced tea. She was in teal blue today, every-thing matching, from the combs securing her hair above her ears to the toes of her T-straps. "Oh," she said, surprised at seeing Nunna. "I'll get another glass."

Nunna, taking the proffered seat, shook her head. "Not for me, thank you. I've had all the caffeine I'm allowed already."

"Lemonade then," Claire said and disappeared.

Mrs. Totton waited until the swinging door had closed behind her. "I'm sorry about Claire, Nehe-miah," she said, her voice low. "She and Charles are staying here this week. He's gone over to Raleigh, but she saw how distraught I was and refused to leave me alone. She's kept me sane this morning. I could ask her to excuse herself, but—"

"You want her to stay, she stays," Mr. Sheriff said. "It's your house, 'Stelle."

The nickname startled me and brought a bit of color to Mrs. Totton's cheeks as well. "I'm sure we can count on her discretion. For Lord's sake, sit down, man."

Mr. Sheriff refused a chair and posted himself in the arched doorway at parade rest, feet apart, hands clasped behind his back.

Claire returned and made a big deal of passing around the refreshments. "There. Now that everyone's been served, I'll get out from underfoot. Estelle, if I can't convince you to skip the Forties Reunion, at least let me come back and run you over there. What time shall I pick you up? Nobody'll say a word if you're a little late."

"It's almost time to be there, isn't it?" Mrs. Totton's hand shook as she massaged her forehead. "You might as well stay, Claire. Nehemiah," she said, giving him the floor.

He cleared his throat and glued his focus to the toes of his boots. "Leigh Ann, there's a couple of things Estelle thinks you should know. Web found the X ray he thought he had."

"Ah." Suddenly the little scene I'd witnessed in the lounge outside the Emergency wing made sense.

"He left it inside my screen door sometime yestiddy, I don't know when."

"Before the service at the picnic grounds," I told him. "Monty and his father saw his van in your driveway."

The chief swallowed hard and wiped his eyes.

"That old buzzard. Anyhow, nobody noticed the thing until Josh went by the house after the fire. He brought it to me."

"So whose X ray was it?" Claire asked breathily.

Mr. Sheriff glanced at his hostess. "Daniel Totton, Junior."

Mrs. Totton sat back, her eyes closed tightly, her pallor and drawn visage explained.

"Estelle's son?" Claire looked at Mr. Sheriff in confusion.

My gaze flew to the mantel, where a row of ornately framed photographs filled the entire length of it. The center one, larger than the rest, set off a series of images in my memory—a gorgeous boy several years older than we were. Thick dark hair. Deep-set blue bedroom eyes. On the short side with a muscular frame, and a slight limp. Of course, the pins in his leg. I had a vague memory of Nunna writing me about his death.

Nunna straightened in her chair. "It couldn't be, Nehemiah."

"Well, it is. I sent it over to the county medical examiner yesterday, and according to him, it is a picture of the leg bone you seen, Leigh Ann. The bone and the X ray, they match."

"Then the X ray was mislabeled," Claire said firmly. "Danny wrecked his car out on Old Post Road . . . what? . . . over ten years ago?"

"It will be twelve years next month," Mrs. Totton intoned.

"See? I was right. I came to his funeral. He's buried in Garden of Peace. You know that, Mr. Sheriff. You were there, too. Everybody was there."

He nodded. "Yes, ma'am, I was. And until I saw

that X ray I thought Danny was, too. Too badly burned to be recognized. Sorry, 'Stelle. But definitely there."

"Excuse me," I interrupted. "Positive identification was made, wasn't it?"

"Of course." From his tone, I knew I'd insulted the chief. "We may live in the sticks, but we do know enough to use dental records. Johnny Boothe was his dentist and he pulled the files for us himself. According to them, the boy who died in that car was Danny Totton."

"A closed coffin service?"

"Yes." Mrs. Totton sat up straight. "But I had Harry Grace open the casket just before the funeral because I wanted Danny buried with the things he prized most after his car. That was his wrestling trophy and his class ring. I saw the body in that coffin." She stopped, her mouth twisting with pain. "I saw the body. And from the minute the lid was lowered and sealed until his grave was filled in, which I stayed to watch, it was never out of my sight. There was no opportunity for anyone to remove his body unless they dug him up later and why would they do that?"

Claire sniffed. "I hope you take a close look at every mortuary within a ten-mile radius, chief. It wouldn't be the first time one of them tried to get away with burying someone on the cheap."

"You got any particular funeral parlor in mind?" the chief asked sternly, calling her bluff.

"No, but there have been cases where bodies have turned up in cardboard boxes when they were supposed to have been buried in expensive coffins, and you know it, chief."

Doc had proposed a similar theory that night in the cemetery. The memory of him at the kitchen table, snoring contentedly, caused a tightness in my chest. I'd really liked that old man. Yet I couldn't imagine any mortician recycling a coffin once it had been buried.

"Well, I'll be looking into it," Mr. Sheriff said, "because the body in New Bethel's cemetery—and the coroner says it's practically all there, very little missing—has Danny's legs, or one of them."

"There's still the possibility Mrs. Rowland's right," I said. "Doc's X ray may have the wrong name on it."

The chief shook his head. "Wasn't him that put the name on it. The X ray was taken at the hospital in Charlotte where 'Stelle sent the boy to get his leg fixed after he wrecked his motorbike. The name is part of the picture, not just stuck on, and the envelope it was in came straight from the hospital. We can't blame this on Web."

As intrigued as I was by the mystery, I was also becoming more and more ill at ease. They were telling me far more than I wanted to know. I was ready to go home. Nunna must have sensed it.

"Mrs. Totton," she said, "I can't tell you how sorry I am about all this. It must be awful for you. But what did you want Leigh Ann for?"

Mrs. Totton rose, getting to her feet as if moving at all took great effort. She crossed to the mantel and removed the center photograph, her hand unsteady as she traced the line of her son's chin. "Nehemiah and I are arranging to have the grave opened and a second autopsy performed to settle this once and for all. I *know* what they'll find. I remember looking down at what was left of my boy and thinking how unfair death had been to him. Took his life, his soul, his heft—the chest and arms he'd worked so hard to develop for wrestling. There just didn't seem to be as much of him. Now I know why. Dental records or no, that wasn't my boy."

Even allowing for the possibility that she was right, she still hadn't answered Nunna's question: why was I here?

"Nehemiah has made it plain that investigating Web's death is his highest priority and I can understand that. As much as I loved Web, he's not *my* highest priority. My son is. The person in my boy's coffin is a murderer. He killed my Danny."

"Mrs. Totton," I began, appalled.

"Danny loved that car more than anything! He never allowed anyone else to drive it, not his lady friends, his buddies, not even me. If someone else was behind that wheel when it went over the embankment, he was there because Danny was dead. They'd have had to kill him to get it. That's how possessive he was about that . . . that thing!"

Claire, looking very uneasy, nodded. "Estelle's not exaggerating. When Danny was in the car, he wasn't limping, you see. Behind the wheel he could be faster than anyone or anything else out there, powerful, in control. His attachment to his car was, well, unhealthy. You know that's true," she said, on the defensive when Mrs. Totton looked daggers at her.

"What kind of car was it?" I asked. I'd never understood that kind of mania.

"A little red MG. It wasn't new, but he'd worked a year and a half to buy it. He was so proud of it," Mrs. Totton said, her voice sinking to a whisper.

"And drove it like he was signing up for the Indy

500," Mr. Sheriff added. "Same way he drove the motorbike, flat out all the time."

"Be that as it may, my point is he would never willingly give it up." Mrs. Totton replaced the photo. "I want to know who killed him to get it. I also want the names of the people who've known his secret all these years, the ones who allowed me to bury my son's murderer in my family plot while my son's body was left to the mercy of the elements and roaming dogs and cats!" An involuntary shudder wracked her small frame and her eyes filled with tears.

"Estelle," Claire began, shoving a tissue into her hands, "don't you think that's reaching a bit?"

"Reaching?" Mrs. Totton snapped. "Yes, indeed, reaching for the truth. It's the least I can do for my son. I want the name of my son's murderer and of those who could have spoken up when it no longer mattered because both men were dead. *I want those names!* And I want you to get them for me, Leigh Ann."

"What? Me?" I shot out of my chair. "I'm sorry, Mrs. Totton, but no. Mr. Sheriff has his sons and the whole of the county force at his disposal. It's his job and he should be the one to conduct the investigation or to bring in help from the county or the state, if he feels he needs it."

"Thank you," he said with gusto.

"I don't want the rest of the county or the state meddling in our business." Her chin lifted, her lips forming an ugly slash, which I remembered clearly was a very bad sign. "This is a Sunrise affair, and I want to keep it in the family."

"Fine," I said. "Mr. Sheriff and his sons, they're family. I'm sure they're more than qualified."

"And you," Mrs. Totton said, "are too. You're a member of a police force in a city where murder is commonplace."

I put off defense of my city for another day and stuck to the point. "No matter what you think, Mrs. Totton, you don't actually know a murder was committed. Besides, I didn't work Homicide." Just Public Relations, Vice, Juvie Hall, and jail, which had been quite enough.

"But you've surely had some experience. Isn't it the uniformed officer who winds up performing the drudgery? Can you honestly tell me you've never participated in a homicide investigation?"

"No, but it was precisely what you described, drudgery—searching an alley with ten others for clues, knocking on doors, asking questions, but then turning everything over to the Homicide division. That's all. I'm sorry, Mrs. Totton. You said yesterday I've done my Service to Sunrise. I've paid my debt. I will not do it."

"You must."

I was becoming pissed and didn't care who knew it. "My name is not Virgil Tibbs, Mrs. Totton."

"Who?" Nunna said. Clearly *In the Heat of the Night* meant nothing to her.

"You can not force me to be part of this investigation if I don't want to be, and I don't. Mr. Sheriff, if you'll take us home, please."

I was already on my feet and held out my hand to help Nunna to hers. She didn't budge and my heart sank.

"Leigh Ann," she said, "why don't you sleep on it? You could be a big help to Nehemiah."

It was silly but I felt betrayed. It never occurred to

me that she wouldn't back me up. That she hadn't made no difference; I'd said no and I meant it.

Suddenly the room seemed so close, so stifling that I couldn't breathe. I had to go. I moved to the doorway.

"Mrs. Totton, I'm very sorry you may have to bury your son again. You have my deepest sympathy. And I'm sorry to turn you down, but I have to. Mrs. Rowland." I nodded a farewell to Claire, whose sympathetic smile appeared to be the only one I'd get. Nunna gazed at me, her expression a mix of sadness and consternation, but made no move to rise. "I'd be grateful if you'd drive Nunna back, Mr. Sheriff. I prefer to walk."

"Sure thing." With a courtly hand on my elbow, he escorted me to the door and opened it for me. "I 'preciate what you done, Leigh Ann," he said softly. "There's not many would say no to 'Stelle. She'll come around, though. You did the right thing."

"I know I did. Good luck, Mr. Sheriff," I said, offering my hand, momentarily forgetting the state of my scratched-up palms. He took it and, as if sealing a deal, gave it a firm shake. It hurt like hell. But at we least understood one another. I took great comfort in that. There was a lot to be said for being a member of our fraternity. I would miss that when I left but, by damn, it would be the only thing I'd miss.

7

I'd jogged back to Nunna's fully intending to pack. As soon as she came home, I meant to say good-bye and head east for the shore again. Granted, Nunna considered my reasons for quitting my job a lot of horse hockey, but she'd also said she'd back me in whatever I decided to do. I'd assumed that support would extend to my refusal to become involved in this. I was under no obligation to help and in no emotional condition to do it if I'd wanted to. Which I didn't. For the immediate future, the only problems I wanted to solve were my own. If Nunna felt otherwise strongly enough, it was time for me to leave.

I did toss a couple of things into my bag, then inexplicably exhausted, ran out of steam and stretched out across the bed to wait for her. I awoke the next morning in the clothes I'd worn the day before, the spread folded over my body, and Chester across my feet, snoring noisily. No nightmare for the third night in a row. Just dreams. I could get used to that.

Lifting my head, I saw Nunna in the doorway and realized that her voice, part of a dream already fading from memory, had awakened me.

"Mornin', baby," she said, and crossed to raise the shades. "You slept so hard I almost checked your pulse to make sure you were alive. How're you feeling?"

"Okay. What time is it?"

"A little past eight. Coffee's on the stove. I'm running late, so you'll have to get your own breakfast."

I wriggled my feet from under the cat, and blinking my eyes into focus, sat up. She was dressed in deep purple slacks and a pale lavender tunic top. I'd never seen her in pants before. "Where are you going?"

"Over to New Bethel. Vacation Bible School started yesterday. I stayed home for you, but there are ten kiddies waiting for me today. You'd think after almost forty-five years of teaching first grade I'd have had enough of it. I'd go back to work this minute, if they'd let me."

"You still miss it?" I asked.

"Oh, yes, ma'am. I miss being useful, being needed. What I'll do when New Bethel's gone . . . No Sunday School to teach, no Vacation Bible School." She shrugged. "Oh, well. Are you leaving?" She nodded toward my weekender standing open in the corner.

"I'm considering it."

Sliding her hands under the cat, she moved him over so that she could sit at the foot of the bed, then fingered the tufts of the chenille spread. "I'm sorry about yesterday, baby. I was wrong. It just seemed to me that seeing how sick in spirit you are, feeling betwixt and between, and seeing Mrs. Totton, hurtin' and as low as she'll probably ever be, I thought that maybe helping her would be the salve you needed to heal your wounds. But you're a grown woman. It's up to you to mix your own salve, use it the way you see fit, when you see fit, and I have to shut my mouth and let you do it." She got up and smoothed her tunic. "I'll leave you to think about that. I hope you'll still be here when I get back. It would hurt me to my heart to know I'd driven you away."

I still hadn't made up my mind to stay, but I had to clear the air in case I did leave. "If I go, Nunna, it won't be because of you. Don't forget, I didn't know you were here and came anyway, looking for something."

"What?"

"Peace, I guess. A place I remembered as warm and neighborly and quiet. Instead I found the same kind of ugliness I was trying to get away from. So if I leave, it'll be because Sunrise let me down, not you."

"No place is perfect, Leigh Ann."

"I know. I'm not looking for Utopia, Nunna, just some place that'll let me feel better about myself than I do now."

She leaned over and folded her arms around me. "What you need to do is some housecleaning in here," she said, patting my chest. "Then it won't matter where you are on the outside. Now. The reason I woke you, I made an appointment for you at Myrtle's beauty parlor for nine-thirty, so you can get your hair evened up."

I checked the clock. "I guess I can make it. How

long have they been doing our hair?" I'd never been in the salon. Years ago it was understood that their clientele was restricted to eastsiders. Miss Juanita Broadwater and her daughter, Tanya, took care of us black folks on her enclosed back porch, the smell of frying hair and stinky permanents hanging heavy in the air.

"Ever since Juanita retired and Myrtle realized how many heads Juanita's daughter would be doing a week. She offered Tanya a chair in the shop. Soon any of the ladies would take us. Now, let me run." She pecked me on the cheek, her gaze darting toward my luggage, and left quickly.

I wallowed in bed for another ten minutes or so, feeling better for having talked things out with her. At least now she understood. The more I thought about it, the more I leaned toward starting for the shore today and coming back Saturday for the big picnic. If enough people attended, I might be able to avoid Mrs. Totton. Remembering the walking iceberg she could become when one of her students did something to displease her, I did not look forward to running into her. How old do you have to be, I wondered, before you finally grow up?

"Land sakes!" Myrtle, thin as a cattail, tsk-tsked over my hair. Her own, baby-fine and somewhere between August auburn and October orange, was anchored in a haphazard topknot, threatening to escape its moorings any second. "This is gonna be a real challenge. Tanya, come look at this."

There was a good thirty percent more of Tanya Broadwater than when I'd last seen her and she'd

possessed ample proportions back then. Regardless, she looked much the same, a heavyweight
Diana Ross—huge eyes and a two-hundred-watt
smile. "Hey, Leigh Ann. You really did a number
on yourself, didn't you? Whatcha gonna do to her,
Myrtle?"

Myrtle fingered my hair and spun me around in
the chair, peering intently. "Clip, shampoo, condition her within an inch of her life, and clip some
more. We'll decide what else from there." She
picked up the scissors and squinted at me, the tip of
her tongue peeking from the corner of her mouth.

"Oh, Lord." Tanya grinned. "Put up the sign, y'all.
Genius at Work. Leigh Ann, girl, you are in for it."
Giggling, she went back to her station.

I decided to adopt the same attitude I do when
boarding a plane. I gave it up. My fate was in
Myrtle's hands. Closing my eyes, I relaxed, tuning in
to the conversations around me. There wasn't an
empty chair in the place, so the room throbbed with
a cross between ribaldry and rumor. The sounds and
smells were at once so familiar I might well have
been in the salon I used in D.C. By the time Myrtle
had finished the first leg of her clip-a-thon, I'd
learned more about the state of affairs in Sunrise
than I had in the week I'd been back, just listening
to snippets.

After my shampoo, conditioning, a stint under the
dryer, and a thorough rinsing, I was back in my chair,
blown dry again and trying to ignore the click of the
scissors, when from the station behind me, Tanya
said, "Look, Myrtle. Yonder comes some more."

The clicking ceased. The salon quieted, the only
sound the burr of dryers. Curious as to what could

bring the place to a dead stop, I opened my eyes. "Is something wrong?"

Myrtle nodded toward the window. Since her station was nearest the door, I had an unobstructed view of the activities outside, something I'd regretted when I'd arrived. Doc's office was directly in my line of vision and I'd pointedly avoided looking beyond the shop window. Now I couldn't turn away.

Across the street, two little girls, no more than five or six, both blond and very thin, knelt at his door carrying bunches of flowers, obviously handpicked. Mesmerized, I watched as they appeared to debate the best place to put their tributes. Others had been there before them. Hand-drawn cards were taped to the plywood covering the door. Clutches of wildflowers, single roses, peonies, and others I couldn't identify lay along the sidewalk in front of the office. None had the polished presentation of a florist's handiwork.

"That started yesterday." Myrtle leaned against the back of my chair. "A few grown folk but mostly kids, one after the other. They loved that old man. He's the only doctor they've known. Gave 'em their baby shots, dosed 'em through mumps, measles, chicken pox. They're having a rough time with this."

As if she'd heard, the smaller of the two girls dropped her flowers and began to sob, her shoulders shaking, her narrow chest heaving. The other one tried to console her, patting her awkwardly. After a few minutes, they crossed the street and moved out of sight.

The scene set the tone for the remainder of the time it took for Myrtle to finish. Doc's life and career were rehashed with genuine affection, the tales of his acts of generosity and sacrifice folding one over the other while I struggled with my anger that my last image of him would always be the inert figure I'd tugged from behind his door.

"I don't know what this town's gonna do without Doc Webster," Myrtle said. "His wife is a marvel. Won't hear of them putting off anything planned for Reunion Week. Says Doc wouldn't want it. She's thinkin' about havin' the service on Saturday morning."

"Saturday? Wouldn't next Monday be better?" I asked. "People might feel funny about leaving the funeral and going right to a picnic."

"That's exactly what she wants folks to do. She says if Doc had died next week or last, folks would be comin' back to the house after the buryin' to eat. This way, they can go on to the picnic and celebrate his life as part of the reunion 'stead of snifflin' over his death. There. I'm done. Take a look."

Everyone agreed, as I admired myself in the mirror and slipped a tip into Myrtle's hand, that I did indeed look "chick," a description that took a second for me to translate. My curls were a good deal shorter, but not nearly as short as I'd expected, given the amount of snipping I'd heard. They were feathered and layered, framing my face in a way that gave me a gamine air and lopped off a few years. It was cute. I was surprised and pleased.

"Couldn't have done a better job myself," Tanya said, evidently high praise, because Myrtle pinked up with pleasure.

She escorted me outside with a last pat at the nape of my neck and a twist of a curl above my ear.

"I didn't want to say anything in there," she said softly. "I hear the body you found might be Mrs. Totton's son. That true?"

Unprepared for the question, I hesitated, evidently long enough for Myrtle to draw her own conclusion. "Well." She folded her arms across her chest. "There is a God." She reared back, arms folded under her breasts. "I went to see him buried that first time, but I'll be damned if I'm goin' back for the second. I ain't that much of a hippercrit." Without further explanation, she went back into the shop.

I stood for a moment, wondering about the boy who'd evoked that kind of reaction. Then, spotting one of Nunna's friends ferrying her grandchild toward Doc's, both carrying bouquets of white flowers, I forgot about Danny Totton and Myrtle. I stopped in front of Fred's and watched while they placed the bouquets along the curb, heads lowered, the preschooler with his hands clasped in an attitude of prayer.

"Doesn't that just break your heart?" Maudine, holding the door of the diner open, stepped outside. I hadn't seen her since the fire. "How're you doing? I've been worried about you. You didn't look so hot when they took you away Sunday. I wanted to go with you, but they didn't have room for me in the ambulance."

A vague memory surfaced, Maudine's teary voice pleading with someone. I felt bad that I'd been so self-involved since then that I hadn't thought to call or come by to check on her. Acting on impulse, I grabbed her and hugged her. "You done good, Maudine. You saved my bacon. If those guys hadn't gotten there when they did, Doc and I would have been French fried."

When I released her, her eyes had filled, her hands shaking. "God, Leigh Ann, I was so scared! I went looking for you around back and the door was open, everything blazin' like hell and I could hear you coughin' in there. I wanted to go in, but I just couldn't! I'm so ashamed!"

"That's dumb. I'm used to risking my neck. You did exactly the right thing. Thank you."

"Yeah. I just wish . . . Oh, well." She pushed a stray lock off her forehead, her gaze straying to the pedestrians strolling by. Inexplicably, her face drained of color. "I'd better get on inside," she said breathlessly and began backing toward the diner. "A group of folks from the Fifties are having a nostalgia party in here tonight and we're up to our elbows in hamburgers and chili dogs."

I glanced back, wondering at her reaction. Across the street in front of Doc's, a woman, her hair a flaming red, stood with a teenager, reading the cards stuck on the door. There were a few other faces I didn't recognize, reunion folks, no doubt, and a few others I did, but nothing out of the ordinary.

Then what she'd said registered—chili dogs—and without warning, I began to salivate. "Got any hot dogs to spare?" I asked, following her in. "Suddenly I'm starving."

"Come on in. I'll make it myself." I waited while a half dozen teenagers spilled out of the diner, giggling and poking one another. Maudine scowled at their backs. "Thank God they're gone. Took 'em an hour and a half to eat. I guarantee you they left a mess and no tip. Chili dog coming up. And if Fred says one word to me about using one stinking little weenie, I'll deck him."

"Hey, I don't want to cause any trouble," I said, heading for my favorite stool. The diner was empty now except for someone in the back booth, face obscured by the morning paper. "How about a ham and cheese on rye?"

"Sure. What do you want on it? Lettuce and—"

"Maudine!" Fred bellowed from the kitchen. "You workin' today or what?"

She dealt the counter a vicious open-handed slap and stormed toward the kitchen door. "What the hell you mean, am I working? One more smart remark from you and you can chop those goddamned onions by yourself!"

"Jesus! I'm sorry, okay?" Fred peered around the door. "Take a break or something. You've been as tetchous as a grass widder all morning." With a shrug for my benefit, he disappeared.

"Maudine. Hey, is something wrong?" I asked, settling my backside onto the orange cushion.

After a deep breath, she went to the kitchen door and pushed it open. "Sorry, Fred. I'll be with you in a minute." Returning, she began constructing my sandwich, clearly working on automatic pilot.

"Come on, Maudine. What's wrong?"

She stopped, her head lowered. "Oh, God. Maurice is in jail, Leigh Ann."

I stopped thinking about my stomach. "For what?"

"Here." She reached into the pocket of her apron and handed me a letter. "We got this yesterday. Ignore his spelling. Maurice . . . well, he wasn't much for spelling."

I wiped my fingers and unfolded it carefully. It

had been typed on a Stone Age machine, from the looks of it.

Dear Mama and Maudine,

My frend from Children of Hope came to see me and brung me the ticket you sent. He says I have to tell you the truth. I am in jail. I been here nine year because I did a terrible thing and somebody died. It was an acident but he still dead. They put me here for life, but Steve my cell mate say that don't mean I can't get out if I do good behavor. It not so bad but I miss you and Mama an awful lot.

It hurts me that I brung shame on the famly. Im not even going to tell you where this jail is because I dont want you to see me in here. If they let me out on paroll some time I will try and come home, but maybe not sense you cant leave the state when you on paroll. But dont worry about me I am fine. I hope to see you and Mama some day. I love you.

Maurice

I folded the letter and returned it to her, trying to think of something helpful to say. Nothing came. I fell back on, "Maudine, I'm so sorry. Is there anything I can do?"

She put it back in her pocket. "Not unless you've got some way to find out which prison he's in. I figure it's in Colorado because that's where Children of Hope's home base is supposed to be. I can't see somebody from the commune going but so far to take him the ticket."

"Where in Colorado? The commune, I mean?"

"The only address I ever had was a post office box in Denver. That's where I sent the ticket."

"What about the postmark on this letter?" I asked.

"The same—Denver. But Information doesn't have a listing for Children of Hope. If they're into poverty, they may not have a phone. Even if they did, who would I ask for? Maurice didn't mention his friend's name." She sniffled and reached for a napkin to wipe her nose. "Mama doesn't know. I can't decide whether to tell her or not."

"That's a tough call," I said.

"I just can't believe it. Maurice would never hurt anyone, and he's just dumb enough to get his ass framed for something he didn't do. But what can I do about it? Nothing."

She finished my sandwich and passed it to me. I nibbled at it, but my appetite was gone. Perhaps I wasn't as desensitized to other people's pain as I'd thought because I really felt for her and wanted to help. After a second I realized I probably could. I had a friend in Records who could talk a computer into doing everything but diapering a baby.

"Maudine," I said, pushing my plate to one side. "I won't promise any results, but I can call in a couple of favors back at work and ask someone to run a check to see if they can find out anything about Maurice."

Her lips parted. "You . . . you'd do that for me? Why?"

"Why not? I owe you. Like I say, I'm not guaranteeing anything, but I'm willing. It just depends on whether you really want to know."

"I do!" She grabbed my hands. I didn't wince. They were definitely better. "He's my twin, Leigh Ann! It's been so hard with him gone, sending one stinkin' postcard a year. I'd really appreciate you

trying. If there's ever anything I can do for you, anything . . ."

"I'll let you know when the time comes," I said,
and went to the phone at the front of the diner, fingers crossed that this wasn't one of Carrie's days off.
Not only was Carrie there, she answered the phone
and damned near ruptured my eardrum. "Leigh!
Girl, where the hell have you been?"

"North Carolina. How's it going, Carrie?"

"Like always. When are you coming back?"

"I'm not sure," I said, aware of Maudine trying to
look as if she wasn't listening. "Next week, maybe.
Look, it's payback time."

"Uh-oh. How much do you need? I can wire you
fifty, tops."

"I don't need money. Here's the problem." I ran it
down for her, filling in what little Maudine had been
able to tell me.

"What's his middle name, date of birth, and Social
Security number?"

I tossed the question to Maudine.

"Alan," she said, coming from behind the counter.
"Born July 19, 1961. I don't know about any Social
Security number. When he left, he didn't have one."
She stood beside me, gnawing at her bottom lip.

I smiled reassurance and passed along the information. "What do you think?" I asked Carrie.

"I think I'm off the hook, is what I think. Shall I
call you back or what?"

"I'll call you." I debated a second and gave up.
"Carrie, how's Duck?"

Silence hummed at me and a seed of panic took
root in my gut. "Physically," she said finally, "at about
eighty-five percent and pawing the ground to get

back onto the streets. He's fine as long as no one asks him about you. I get the impression he's a tad pissed at you."

That was good news. If he was pissed, he still cared. I might not work with him again, but I didn't want to lose him as a friend. "Tell him I'll call him soon, honest. Gotta go. Thanks, Carrie."

"Your mama," she replied, her usual farewell.

I hung up. "There, it's done."

"Maudine." Fred, looking as if he might be putting his life on the line, stepped from the kitchen but kept one hand on the door in case, I assumed, he had to beat a hasty retreat. "I really do need help back here."

She sighed, playing havoc with the buttons on the bodice of her uniform. "Okay, Fred, I'm coming. Mr. Sturgis, can I get you anything else?"

I turned as Monty lowered his newspaper. "Morning, Leigh. Thanks, Maudine. I'm fine."

"The hell he is," she said to me, barely above a whisper. "He's real low, Leigh Ann. I mean snake-belly low. Why don't you go talk to him, cheer him up? And I'm serious. If there's ever anything I can do for you . . ."

"Go," I said. "I'll track you down as soon as I know anything." She left with what was probably her first smile of the day.

I debated what if anything to say to Monty and decided to stick to my stool and my sandwich, since I doubted he had any interest in talking to me. I was wrong.

He folded the newspaper and got up, leaving some money on the table. Maudine was right about his condition. His eyes were bloodshot, lines of fatigue etched around his mouth.

"Monty, what's the problem?" I asked.

He gazed at me. "I like your hair."

"Thanks, but I hope that's not the problem."

"No. It's not." He leaned back. "I'm not free to talk about it, Leigh Ann. If you have a chance, give Nehemiah a call." He looked at his watch. "I'd better get moving. Before I go, though, I owe you an apology."

"For?" I thought I knew, but I wanted to hear it.

"For that crap I laid on you on Sunday. I was out of line. Only you know what's going on in your life, and whether the decision you've made is the right one for you. I admire you for sticking to your guns."

I'd just as soon he'd chosen some other cliché, but I appreciated the sentiment. "Thanks, Monty. Maybe one of these days I'll fill you in on . . . everything."

"I'd like to hear it. I realize you're in transition, going from one stage of your life to some other, but I hope you won't rule out Sunrise as a possibility. It's in transition, too. If we ever get past the troubles of the moment and get the mall built, the personality of the town will change drastically. I'm determined to see that it changes for the better, because I'm here for the duration."

"You like this town that much?"

"I was born here. I love Chicago, too, but not like this. This is home. Think about relocating, Leigh Ann. We need new blood. You'd be good for Sunrise."

It was a nice compliment and made up for Sunday. "I'm flattered, Monty, but I'm just not ready to make a commitment."

"I'll accept that, but it doesn't mean I'll stop hoping. Gotta go. See you later."

"Okay." I gave up on the sandwich. "Maudine," I called. "I'll be in touch. And I'm leaving the money on the counter."

"Keep it," Fred's voice responded. "It's on the house. Y'all come back, hear?"

"Fred's good people," Monty said, walking with me outdoors.

Things seemed to have worsened in the short time I'd been inside, the tableau in front of Doc's every bit as disturbing as the one I'd witnessed earlier, only with a different feel to it. A faded blue station wagon was parked at the curb, blinkers winking, the door of the driver's side hanging open. Sylvester Hodges, husband of one of Nunna's oldest friends, stood outside the car, shaking his fist at a pair of white men, the younger in a mill uniform, the elder in the faded overalls of a farmer. At Mr. Hodges's side, his granddaughter, Markita, tears streaming, tugged at his arm, as if trying to tow him back to the car.

"What the hell," Monty muttered, and started across the street.

"I thought better of you, Wiley Grimm," Mr. Hodges was saying with heat. "Figured you were a pretty good man. Fair, don't ya know. Then you say something like that to my grandbaby."

Mr. Grimm, his expression matching his name, stood his ground. "Didn't say it to her, no sucha thing!" he responded loudly. "I was talkin' to my boy here. Didn't think she could hear me."

"How the hell could she not hear you, loud as you are. You got a lotta nerve, talking that way around a baby. Ain't none of this her fault and you had no call to—"

"Hey, hey, hey!" Monty shouted, stepping between

them. I followed, hoping I wouldn't have to play cop. "Calm down, Mr. Hodges," Monty ordered forcefully. "You, too, Mr. Grimm. What's going on, anyway?"

"Nothing, Mr. Sturgis," the younger man said. "Come on, Poppa."

"I'll tell you what's going on." Mr. Hodges reached down to put an arm around his granddaughter's shoulder. "I stopped so the child here could put a card on Doc's door and this dumb son of a bitch come saying that nobody colored had any right to be putting anything here, since one of us had probably set the fire that got Doc killed. Grimm's drunk—"

"No sucha thing."

"—and deaf as a post and talks loud, so the child heard him. She comes back to the car asking what does being colored mean. I tell her and she starts bawling because she figured Grimm was saying she'd killed Doc."

Mr. Grimm tugged at a snow-white forelock and rocked back and forth, none too steady on his feet. "Well, that ain't what I meant."

"Just what did you mean?" Monty asked softly, his eyes hard as marble, then repeated the question with enough volume for the old man to hear him.

Grimm's jaw, stippled with a graying five o'clock shadow, jutted pugnaciously. "Whoever did this"— he tilted his head toward the boarded up door— "was trying to keep Doc from findin' that X ray. Ever'body knows that. And whoever buried that body had to be colored or they'd have been noticed. It's y'all's cemetery, ain't it? So anybody with any sense a'tall's gotta figger that something's rotten on the dark side of Main. One of you-uns is responsible for everything and I say it ain't fittin' to have y'all puttin' up cards and such. Somebody knows something, mark my words."

"Not me, Mr. Grimm," Markita cried. "Honest! I didn't even know I was colored! I liked Dr. Webster!"

Mr. Grimm's face turned a mottled red with embarrassment. "I didn't mean you, little miss. It's the rest of 'em, I'm talkin' about."

"The rest of *us*, you mean," Monty said pointedly. "I live on the dark side of Main, as you so colorfully put it."

Hands shoved deep in his pockets, the old man nodded. "If the shoe fits."

"Damn it, Poppa, come on," his son said. "Sorry about this, Mr. Sturgis. He don't mean it. It's the liquor talking." Grabbing his father by the X at the back of his overalls, the young man led him away.

Markita watched the retreat, then looked down at the card in her hand. "I didn't do nothin'," she wailed. "And I don't want to be colored neither." She crumpled the card into a wad and, sobbing, ran back to climb into the station wagon.

I'd seen two children reduced to tears today, the first with confusion and grief at her loss, the second with grief, guilt that there was no need for her to assume, and self-hatred because of the color of her skin. Why was it that when the adults behaved like assholes, it was the children who felt the pain?

Until now Sunrisers had coexisted. Everyone on one side knew everyone on the other, because most had worked at Sundler's Lumber Mill, the town's major employer. They might stop and chat while shopping on Main Street but the interaction stopped there. There'd been little or no socializing between

east and west when I'd lived in Sunrise, but I'd gotten the impression that had changed a little. I had
never, however, seen this kind of racial acrimony
here.

Monty stood staring at the station wagon and the
Grimms' departing figures. "I don't believe this," he
said softly. "My God, what's happening to my town?"

Mr. Sheriff's farm, smack up against Garden of
Peace Cemetery and in the shadow of Old Bluenose
Mountain, was a surprise, larger than I'd expected.
The house, a rambling gray two-story, sat off the
road in a hollow with an impressive vegetable garden in the front and side yards. Beyond the house, a
barn snuggled in the waning heat of a setting sun.
Off to the left, up a rise, several horses dozed in the
shade of big oak trees.

Three sizable tail waggers, dead ringers for
Hannibal, served as combination doorbell and alarm
system. They sounded off as soon as I turned onto
the graveled driveway and ran to meet the car, trot-
ting along beside me until I stopped at the right of
the house where the chief's car was parked in a
turnaround.

I eyed the hounds, trying to get a handle on their
moods. Just because Hannibal was no man-eater was
no guarantee his relatives were as easygoing.
Reassured by the energetic swish of their tails and
dopey tongue-lolling grins, I talked dog to them and
got out slowly. They circled me, sniffing, and after
scratching behind an ear or two, I started for the
house. As I approached the porch, the front screen
opened and the female counterpart of the chief—

gray-haired, lean, and wiry—stuck her head out, her eyes immediately wary.

"Good evening," I said, and to put her at ease pdq, gave her my name.

"Well, evening yourself, Leigh Ann." She came out with a genuine smile, wiping her hands on her apron. "I'm pleased you stopped by. Lord knows I've heard enough about you in the past few days."

"I imagine you have. Sorry to come without calling, but Miss Connie said I might be able to find him here." I'd opted for an edited version. What the town clerk/police dispatcher had actually said was, "He's out to the house. Goes home for supper and whatever else he can get from Dora, if you take my meaning." Constance Oberman was notorious for her lack of tact and earthy sense of humor. Since she was staring eighty in the face, she maintained she could say what she damn well pleased and anybody who didn't like it could go to hell.

"There isn't any trouble in town, is there?" Mrs. Sheriff asked. "He's had enough bad news for one day."

"No, nothing's wrong. He and Doc were haggling over this fountain pen last Saturday," I said, citing the excuse I'd lucked up on as a credible reason for coming. "I wasn't sure which of them it belonged to, and whether I should take it to Mrs. Webster or not. I thought I'd leave it with the chief."

"Oh, my Lord, that pen." Her eyes became misty. "They won it in some contest they entered together when they were in grade school. They've been fighting over it ever since, borrowing it back and forth. He'll want to keep it, I'm sure. Come on in. I just want to warn you that he's a lousy patient. If he growls at you, pay him no mind."

"Patient?" I said, following her in.

"Who's that?" The chief sat in a recliner, his right foot propped on a hassock. Encasing his foot was a clean white cast, his little pink toes protruding from the end.

"Mr. Sheriff! What happened?"

"Damn horse stepped on it," he said morosely. "Broke two bones. Doctor says I've gotta stay off my feet a couple of days. Of all times for it to happen."

"Have a seat," his wife said. "Can I offer you something? Lemonade?"

"No, thank you. Mr. Sheriff, I'm so sorry. Monty didn't mention this when I saw him this morning."

"Because it happened this afternoon. Before I forget it, the coroner's inquest is tomorrow at nine. They'll want your statement."

Damn. The court appearance, another onerous chore I thought I'd left behind. "I'll be there. Before I forget it, I brought you this." I handed him the fountain pen. He fondled it and I could swear his eyes began to water.

"Thank you, Leigh Ann. This means a lot to me." He rubbed the barrel with a thumb. "Doc was murdered, Leigh Ann," he said, his voice hoarse. "Blunt force trauma. Somebody hit him, caught him on the temple. Fractured his skull, penetrated his brain, and made a mess. The M.E. says he's not sure yet what the murder weapon was. Something on the small side, like a ball peen hammer. The wound was only about the size of a dime. Murdered, Leigh Ann. That generous old duffer who spent every day of his life looking after our people, half the time for free.

He deserved better than that, goddamn it. He deserved better than that."

I couldn't speak, couldn't do anything. It had never crossed my mind that the head wound hadn't resulted from a fall. The same rage I'd felt in that hallway two months ago flared through me with the speed of a flash fire. If I'd been the Hulk, I'd have turned a bilious green.

He hadn't been our doctor. Westsiders had gone to Dr. Welcome, one of our own who'd died, according to Sheryl, a couple of years ago. Yet Doc had seemed one of our own, too. It was not uncommon for him to show up at a Sunday morning service at New Bethel, or any special program, especially if kids were involved. He never missed a funeral and the few occasions I remembered that qualified as catastrophes—house fires, deaths in the family—he was among the first to start a clothes or furniture drive, the first to see if help was needed with the funeral. He had seemed color-blind in the best sense of the term.

"Mr. Sheriff, I'm so sorry."

"I've told you that much. You might as well know the rest. Web's back door had been jimmied, file cabinet, too. There were patients' files all over the floor. Edna Nance, his nurse, says he only had a dozen or so X rays, all current. He kept dead files in a storage room in his garage."

Dead files. An appropriate name for them.

"And the fire was no accident. Maybe it was set as insurance because whoever it was hadn't found what they were looking for and figured burning everything would take care of it. Or, depending on when Web got there—he'd forgotten his glasses—to cover up the fact that they'd laid his head open. There's a murderer in my town," the chief said. "A cold-blooded murderer. In *my* town!" He raised his fist as if to pound the arm of his chair, held it aloft for several seconds, then with great deliberation, lowered it, the strain of retaining his composure evident in the muscle flexing at the base of his jaw. "And here I am, laid up."

"Well, if it's only for a couple of days, that's not long. How do you feel?" I asked.

"Like a damn fool, is how. And there's nothing worse than being at Dora's mercy. Maybe I'll shoot myself," he finished, the picture of misery.

"Oh, cut it out, Nehemiah," Mrs. Sheriff said. "You'll survive. So will Sunrise. School's closed, so you don't have to worry about packs of urchins crossing Main. If there's an emergency, the boys can take care of it, or the county. In fact, why don't you let the county take over everything?" She loaded that with meaning. "If that foot's to heal properly, you can't do the kind of running around you'd need to."

"But I can," I said quietly. "I'm willing to help for as long as I'm here."

"You are? How long will that be?" the chief asked.

"Until Sunday."

"This is Tuesday. Evening, at that."

"Granted, it doesn't give me a lot of time, but I'll do what I can to help out."

"You sure, Leigh Ann?" he asked. "It might be dangerous. If 'Stelle's right and her boy was murdered, we've got two on our hands. There's nothing to say the bastard won't kill a third time to keep from being found."

I hadn't thought of that. But at least for now, I was still a cop. "It comes with the territory. Just remember, Mr. Sheriff, I've only played a peripheral role when it comes to homicide investigations. You'll need forensics experts to go over Doc's office to see—"

"Already done. Started Monday morning. Finished today."

That stopped me for a moment until I realized that they must have been parked behind the office. I'd only seen the front today. "Good. As soon as you feel up to it, we'll talk, so you can tell me what you want me to do. I'm not a hot dog out to solve this on my own. If I have any ideas, I'll run them past you first. I'll also check in with you every step of the way."

He began to perk up. "Well, then. My boys will help as much as they can, but for the most part, it's gonna be just you and me. Mainly you."

"I'll do the best I can. That's all I can promise."

"Can't ask more than that. And I thank you. I can't turn loose of this yet and give it to the county. I just can't. I owe it to Web to try. As soon as they hand me the final report on Web's office, I can get to work on the case from that end of things. Until then, we can do a little of this and that to keep 'Stelle from going off the deep end. Dora, bring out the lemonade. We got work to do."

I was in mild shock. I hadn't known I was going to volunteer until I'd opened my mouth to say I would. At least the chief had gone along with it and seemed comfortable with the arrangement. And, as I headed back to Nunna's, I realized that on the whole I felt okay about things, too. In fact, I felt fine, better than I had in nine long weeks.

*   *   *

That didn't last long. Duck called after dinner. I was swallowing the last of my favorite, apple cobbler, when the phone rang. I picked it up without thinking and immediately regretted it.

"What gives, babe?" he asked abruptly. The sound of his voice made my stomach contract. It was not your casual hey-what's-happening? kind of greeting.

"Duck. Hi. How're you doing?"

"Is that polite chitchat or are you really interested?"

I sat down. This would be rough going. Not only was he pissed at me, he was hurt. I could hear it in his voice. "I'm interested, Duck. Really."

"You could have fooled me. I was on P.O.D. for two months, and didn't see you once."

"That's not true."

"My apologies. They did tell me you practically moved into my hospital room the first few days. Unfortunately, I don't remember much about it. Then just as soon as my mind began to clear, you disappeared and didn't come back."

"Well, don't forget, I was on Police Officer Down leave myself. Doctor's visits, clearing up things about the shooting, that kind of thing. And I called you every day—"

"That I remember. 'Hey, Duck, how ya doing? Really? Glad to hear it. Gotta run. I'll talk to you tomorrow.' I go home and do you come by? Uh-uh. I get flowers from you twice and those thirty-second phone conversations. The only way I could find out how you were really doing was to check in with Brimmer and Carrie and a couple of others. I come back to work on limited duty and what happens? You split and head south. What's going on, Leigh?"

Nunna stuck her head in the door and I mouthed "Duck" to her. She waggled her brows like Groucho Marx and went back into the kitchen. "I needed a change of scene, that's all," I explained. "I had to put some distance between myself and the job."

"And me, from the looks of it." A deep sigh rang in my ears. "Leigh, I'm really sorry about the way things went down. I tried my damnedest not to pass out so I could at least warn you if you came into the building. I'd have shot the kid to protect you, but I could barely breathe, much less draw my weapon. You can't blame me for what happened. That isn't fair."

"Blame you?" The thought had never crossed my mind. "Why should I?"

"Because I insisted that you ride along with me instead of dropping you off at home first."

"That's dumb. I don't blame you, honestly, Duck. It was just one of those things, as the song says. Occupational hazard."

"Then there's nothing wrong between us? I haven't blown seven years of friendship?"

He hadn't. I had. "We're fine, Duck. The problem's with me, not us. I needed to get away and do some thinking about what I want and where I go from here."

"Oh." There was a long silence. "Should I be worried by the fact that Grady Breslow has tried to reach you every day this week?"

Damn. Duck knew Grady, knew that I'd worked as a law clerk for him while I'd waited to find out if my application to the police force had been accepted.

He'd asked me to join his law firm just last week. "The only thing you should be worried about is how soon you'll be a hundred percent again. As for me, whatever I decide, I'll let you know, okay?"

"I don't like the sound of that, babe. Come on back. We'll go down to the waterfront, tie on bibs, eat a couple of lobsters, and just talk."

I wondered how many times over the years we'd done that when either of us was troubled about something, or just plain fed up. It was our brand of crisis management and it had always worked. Not this time, however. Duck wasn't an avenue to the solution. Duck was a major part of the problem.

"I can't," I said. "I've made a commitment to someone—"

"Who?"

"A friend who lost an argument with a horse. I have to stay until at least Sunday."

"Male or female?" he demanded.

"The horse?"

"Don't be funny. And what kind of commitment? A date?"

"He's a cop, Duck. I don't date cops, remember?"

"Oh, yeah. Right."

"There's no need to be sarcastic. Besides he's been married longer than I am old, he's white, and seventy if he's a day."

"Big deal. You didn't answer my question. What kind of commitment?"

"Just something I'm helping him with. I've got to go, Duck. I'll talk to you this weekend."

"No. I don't think so, babe." The line went dead.

I stared at the phone, surprised. He'd been pissed. Now he was mad. Once on Duck's shit list, you rarely

got off. Perhaps it was better this way. No more
dread at the thought of breaking off our relationship
when I got back to D.C. The relationship would end
now. Yes, this was better all the way around. So why
did I feel so damned rotten?

"You're gonna do *what?*" Sheryl set the iron down
on the board with a thunk that sent the sheers she'd
been working on slithering off onto the floor.

I picked up the panel and handed it to her. "Help
Mr. Sheriff. We probably won't get much done
before I have to leave, but at least I'll have made a
contribution of some sort."

"Are you crazy?" she demanded. "Seriously, have
you lost your mind? Stay out of it, Leigh Ann. This is
white folks' shit. Let them clean it up."

"Ooh, Mommy, what you said!" Jill, Sheryl's eight-
year-old, had been standing in the doorway where
her mother couldn't have seen her. Popping into the
kitchen, she grinned with scandalized delight. She'd
be able to look down at Sheryl before long. Her dad,
Jim, was six-four and, from all appearances, she was
going to be tall, too.

"What are you doing in here? Out!" Sheryl
pointed toward the back door. "Now, Jillie. Go out
and play with your brother."

"He went with Grandaddy and Grandma to the
store. Besides, I'm watching TV."

"No, you aren't. You're in here getting on my last
nerve and it's too nice an evening for you to be
cooped up in the house. Scram."

Jill's bottom lip shot out. "There's nothing to do
outside. It's boring. "

"Then go count lightning bugs or something. I want to talk to your Aunt Leigh in private, and I want you out from underfoot. Go on, Jillie. Don't let me have to tell you again."

She stomped out, muttering, "Can't never do nothing. I wish we were home." The screen door slammed shut.

"My God, you'd think being bored was worse than death and taxes." Sheryl closed the kitchen door and locked it, turned off the iron, and sat down at the table. "Look, girl, you've been gone a long time. Sure, some things have changed. Our mayor is black, we can get our hair done at Miss Myrtle's and the Clip Joint, even go to St. Matthew's and First Presbyterian if we want to. But that's it. We still live on this side of Main Street and Lord help the nigger who thinks he can move to the other side with impunity."

"What's your point, Sheryl?" I asked, surprised at the direction this had taken.

"My point is that we mind our business, they mind theirs, and nobody's cage gets rattled. Whatever happened to Danny Totton is their business, not ours."

"Even though he was found in our cemetery," I interjected.

"Even though. That's one of the advantages they have that we don't. They can go anywhere they want in this town, our neighborhoods included. Their kids used to make out in that cemetery. I've stumbled across many a pale ass humpin' away in the moonlight back there, and I'm talkin' Caucasian-pale, not just high-yaller. Lord knows how many babies that grew up on the east side were conceived behind

New Bethel. So the fact that Danny was in our cemetery don't mean doodly-squat. He ain't our problem," she concluded, emphasizing each word.

I waffled for perhaps a sixteenth of a second, then made a decision. She'd find out sooner or later anyhow. "Doc was murdered, Sheryl."

"No! Oh, my Lord. How?"

"Somebody bashed his brains in," I said, going for shock value, since so far she hadn't reacted as I'd thought she would to my helping Mr. Sheriff. "It's possible they were simply trying to knock him out. Whether they meant to kill him or not, he died, so now it's murder."

"But why? It doesn't make any sense."

"If you haven't heard, you're the only one in town who hasn't. Someone rifled his files, probably trying to find the X ray before he did."

"And he walked in on them?"

"Or they walked in on him, and whacked him to put him out of operation while they went through the files. Whichever, it's still murder—and arson. The fire was intentionally set."

"It still doesn't make any sense."

"It does if you figure someone was trying to keep us from putting a name to that body I found. That body, and the one in Danny's grave and Doc's death, they're all connected."

"And all white folks' business," she said, recovering quickly. "I thought the world of Doc Webster, and if some of Doc's friends at the mill get likkered up enough, the son of a bitch who killed that darling old man stands a good chance of getting himself lynched before he goes to trial. But it'll be a white son of a bitch dangling from that tree, not one of us.

Let the white folks catch him, Leigh Ann. It's got nothing to do with us."

"Nothing to do . . . ?" This was the last thing I'd expected from her. "How can you say that?"

"Easy!" she snapped. "If it had been one of us in that damned trash bag, or one of us with our brains bashed in, do you think there's a single livin' ass on the other side of town who'd give a flying fuck about it? Not on your life! Stay out of it. How many times do I have to say it? *It ain't our problem!*"

I couldn't believe it. "I did come to the right house, didn't I? You are the former Sheryl Anderson, daughter of William and Grace Anderson, right? Jesus, girl, I remember our first day at Central High when you threatened to kick the shit out of some airhead from Pendletown if she made one more smart remark about Sunrise. You were this town's head cheerleader. Why the hundred-and-eighty-degree turnaround?"

She got up and returned to the ironing board. "Things change, that's all."

"What things?" I persisted. "What happened to you, Sheryl?"

"Life," she said, her expression shutting me out. "I grew up. You'd be well advised to do the same."

"I thought I had. I guess, seeing how you feel, I'd be wasting my breath if I asked for your help, since you were still living here when Danny—or who-ever—died in the car."

"Damned straight, you'd be wasting breath," she said, and attacked the sheer panel with renewed vigor. It was a toss-up as to which contained the most steam, the iron or the ironer.

I let myself out finally, disappointed and dumbfounded. Something had happened to Sheryl. Her bitterness and anger were new components of her personality, acquired in the years since I'd left. One thing for sure: she wasn't the person I remembered, just as this was not the same town I'd left. I didn't know Sheryl anymore and I didn't know Sunrise at all.

8

"*I can't tell you* how relieved I am that you changed your mind."

Mrs. Totton smiled at me across her silver coffee service. Her color was better this morning, her blue eyes bright and alive. I wasn't. I'd been up past two last night going over the material Mr. Sheriff had passed along to me and the notes I'd made during the briefing he'd insisted on before allowing his wife to help him into bed. Then I'd gotten up earlier than necessary in order to get my thoughts together for the inquest, another waste of good sack time. Fortunately my testimony had lasted only ten minutes or so and the inquest less than twenty, with the expected finding: death due to blunt force trauma at the hands of person or persons unknown.

I am not a morning person and with a scant (for me) five hours of sleep, I wasn't operating on all cylinders. I prayed the coffee Mrs. T was pouring for me might stimulate my gray matter. Wouldn't you know, the damned stuff was decaffeinated. I sipped, ladylike, and pretended to enjoy it while Claire Rowland watched me with amused eyes. I wasn't fooling her. I'd felt fairly ambivalent about her until then, but from that moment on, she was okay in my book. She was in mauve today, head to toe. I wondered if she had all her shoes dyed to match.

"We're sorry to get you over here so early," she said, "but the classes from the Sixties will have Estelle tied up all day. As it is, we don't have much time. We were due at a brunch a half hour ago."

My stomach rumbled. I'd had to skip breakfast.

"That can wait." Mrs. Totton's tone consigned the brunch to the inconsequential. "How can we help you, Leigh Ann?"

Glancing at my barely legible notes, I outlined the direction the chief and I would pursue. Josh Sheriff wouldn't be of much help; he was on special assignment with the county until further notice, but Roscoe, whom I had yet to meet, was going over the accident report again. The chief was chafing at the length of time it was taking to receive all the results from the crime scene technicians. Until he had it, he had to delay his own investigation of the murder of his friend. In the interim he'd be trying to locate Dr. Boothe, the dentist who'd supplied Danny's dental record for identification, while I tackled the question of his movements the day he was killed.

"I don't remember your son very well," I told her. "He was far enough ahead of me in Sunrise Township that he was just another big kid and he had graduated from Central by the time I got there."

"He didn't go to Central," she corrected me. "I sent him to Veronna Military Academy. He thought he wanted to be career army like his father, even though he had little memory of him; Daniel was killed in the early days of Vietnam. I thought attending Veronna would get him off to a good start."

"Did it?"

"Unfortunately, no. Danny was . . ." She glanced over her shoulder at the photo on the mantel, her expression softening. "Danny found academy life confining. The truth is he had an artist's temperament, preferred to do things when the spirit moved him. So his sophomore year I sent him to Chelton Hall, a private school in upstate New York that gave him the freedom he needed to thrive. He did well there."

Uh-huh. I stifled a yawn and forced myself to think clearly. If she was leaving soon, I had to use the time wisely. "Mrs. Totton, I'd like to become acquainted with the person Danny was the summer he . . . died—his interests, how he spent his time, who his friends were. Was he living here with you?"

"Oh, yes. You must understand, Leigh Ann. I was almost forty when he was born, a miracle Daniel and I thought would never happen. After his father was killed and there were just the two of us, the older he got, the more protective of me Danny became. He could have moved out, of course, but decided to stay here with me, until he married. As for his interests, that's simple. He was consumed by his art. That and his car."

"His art?"

Mrs. Totton blinked, her lips pinching closed. I had the impression that this was a subject she'd hoped to avoid. "He was a very gifted painter," she said, with a glance at her watch.

Claire looked startled. Evidently she hadn't known.

It was news to me, of course. I found it odd that the walls of the living room were devoid of any kind of artwork. Perhaps the reminder was too painful for his mother.

"He spent his days in his studio, painting," Mrs. Totton said, "so the car was a means of escape. He'd just drive around the countryside for hours after dinner, come back energized, ready to paint again until he dropped from exhaustion. His friends? He had lots of them—people were drawn to him. No one close, though. He didn't seem to need them."

"Does that include girlfriends?"

"Oh, yes. He dated, but said he wasn't ready for a serious relationship. I'm sorry, that's all I can tell you. It isn't very much, is it?"

It sure as hell wasn't. But any picture Mrs. Totton gave me might not be completely reliable anyway, tinted with the colors supplied by her memory and the love of a mother for her child.

"He really was a very giving person," Claire said, as if to help out. "A gentleman, with a keen sense of civic duty. He was the leader of the Boys' Club for several years. And he tutored kids who were having trouble with basic skills. He even stood in for Mr. Haggerty, the janitor at Sunrise Township, when the poor man broke his hip and was off work for so long. Refused to take any money for it, so the school could continue to pay Mr. Haggerty."

Except for the revelation about Danny's artistic ability, I'd heard variations on Claire's assessment of his character the evening before, talking to Mrs. Sheriff after the chief had gone to bed, and later to Nunna and the members of the Sunrise Society, the civic organization responsible for planning the Saturday picnic. An integrated group sitting in Nunna's living room! I'd almost dropped with shock when I walked in on that. I rubbed my forehead, realizing that my mind was wandering.

"There's only one way for you to get to know my son," Mrs. Totton said. I sensed a change in her attitude, a steely resolve. "Come with me, Leigh Ann." She rose abruptly, grabbed her purse, and, without looking back, marched across the living room and up the steps. Claire stared after her, openly curious. She started to rise, then changed her mind and sat down again.

Mrs. Totton had already reached the second floor landing when I caught up with her. She continued to the end of the hall and up another flight of stairs to what had to be the attic and a closed door. She fished a set of keys from her purse and unlocked it, hesitating for a fraction of a second before opening it and standing just inside. She looked back at me, apparently all the invitation I'd get.

I climbed the last couple of steps and moved into the attic. It had been her son's studio and was now a shrine. I doubted a single thing had been touched in the twelve years since Danny had died, except perhaps for cleaning. The close, musty smell I'd have expected was absent and there wasn't a single dust mote dancing in the light streaming through the four windows.

It was one long, uninterrupted space. Linoleum covered the floor. An easy chair sat at the end opposite the door, alongside a footlocker covered with a fringed dresser scarf. The only other furniture was a stool in front of an easel supporting a blank canvas, and a five-drawer tool chest, one drawer open to expose tubes of paint perfectly aligned. Stacked against the walls along both sides of the room were finished works of all sizes, dozens and dozens of them. Mrs. Totton had not exaggerated when she said Danny was talented. His paintings were damned good.

"May I?" I asked. Mrs. Totton acquiesced with a nod. I circled the room, occasionally kneeling for a closer look as I passed the stacked paintings. There were a few landscapes, views of Sunrise and the surrounding area, and a half dozen still lifes. The remainder were nudes, some clearly imitative. I recognized several variations on *September Morn*, and Raphael's reclining ladies. They were only fair, rather static and flat. The others, in his own emerging style, were arresting, vibrating with energy.

"They're remarkable," I said, when I'd completed the circuit. "What a loss. It's such a shame."

Mrs. Totton, who hadn't moved by her station at the door, burst into tears. Kicking myself for not realizing how close to the edge she'd been, I comforted her as best I could, which amounted to a lot of back-patting. After a minute, she went into the purse again for a handkerchief and began to pull herself together.

"Forgive me," she said, wiping her eyes. "I've never opened this room to anyone before. You're the first to see Danny's work since he died. I was especially concerned about . . . well, the nudes. Sunrise is so provincial. I couldn't be sure what people would think. And to have you react so positively . . ."

"There's no other way to react," I assured her. "He really was talented. Did he use live models?"

"Not as far as I know. He painted during the day while I was at school, so it's possible, of course. He'd have had to sneak them past the neighbors. They'd assume . . . Well, you can guess what they'd think. The model would be an outsider, though. No Sunrise girl would agree to pose nude, especially in this house."

If he'd painted without a model, I was even more impressed, considering how young he was. "The energy in his strokes tells me a lot about him," I said, since she seemed to need more.

"Does it really, Leigh Ann?" She peered at me earnestly. "Would it help if you were able to spend as much time as you needed to look around up here?"

I hadn't expected the question, but since she'd asked, it was as good a time as any to outline precisely what I needed. "Yes, it would, but it would be even more helpful if I could see his bedroom, scan the kinds of books he read, look at how he arranged his clothes in the closet. It sounds awful but I need to invade his privacy, Mrs. Totton, to fill in as rounded a picture as I can of your son."

I really didn't think she'd go for it. She agonized over it for several very long minutes and I waited, prepared for rejection. Perhaps Claire's call from downstairs to remind her of the time forced her decision.

"Very well, Leigh Ann. You are an officer of the law, and if I can't trust a policewoman who's also the student who wrote our school's honor code, I can't trust anyone. Do what you must."

I hid my surprise and relief behind a nod of agreement and was about to ask when I should come back when she said, "Danny's bedroom is the one in the back just below us. Everything's exactly as he left it. Close this door securely when you've finished."

I couldn't believe it. It never occurred to me that she'd give me this kind of carte blanche. "Thank you, Mrs. Totton." It was addressed to her back. She was on her way down the steps, one hand over her mouth as if to stifle the urge to retract her permission.

It was chancy, but I had one more question for her. "Is there a picture of Danny you could lend me for a while? I'll get it back to you in a few days."

She thought about it. "Take any but the largest from the mantel in the living room. I won't part with that one. And thank you again, Leigh Ann. I can't tell you how much . . ." She didn't bother to finish, just covered her mouth again and disappeared from view.

I didn't move, listening for sounds of their departure before I began an inch-by-inch examination of the attic. At the end of it, I was still impressed by Danny's talent and even more intrigued about whether or not he'd used models. As far as I could tell, he'd concentrated on the figures of six different women, four white, two black, none of whom I recognized. I wouldn't have in any case; either their faces were averted or their backs were turned. In most the poses were very relaxed: bending at the waist as if examining their toes, stretching languorously, or showering. In others, while the pictures were not that different, there was a tension in their poses that bothered me. I couldn't put my finger on why. I had the feeling that I was missing something, so much so that I went back to Nunna's to retrieve my camera. After pulling out those paintings that troubled me more than others, I photographed them, praying there was someplace I could get the film developed as quickly as possible. Otherwise, the attic revealed nothing extraordinary.

Downstairs was just as frustrating. Danny's bedroom was immaculate, the contents of his closet and dresser drawers organized with clothing and underwear hanging or stacked neatly. He had more denim outfits than a Levi's warehouse. The names on the flaps of the breast pockets and back pocket of the jeans, however, were Italian, like the one on the body in New Bethel's cemetery. In fact, the quality of Danny's clothes made me wonder where he'd gotten the money to pay for them. On Monday Mrs. Totton had said he'd worked and saved the money to buy the MG, yet this morning she hadn't mentioned his having a paying job. Perhaps he'd found buyers for some of his paintings. I scribbled a reminder to ask.

As I stood in the doorway for one last look around, something Duck once said to me popped into my head. "If you really need to know more about a person, babe, cop a peek at his bedroom. Bedrooms tell all." God, I would miss him. More often than not, Duck was right about such things, in which case I had better pay more attention to the room's complete lack of character. If, as Mrs. Totton had said, it was exactly as he'd left it, why were there no indications of his interests or clues to his personality? There were no paintings on his walls, no photographs, no high school or college paraphernalia. His mother had said he'd been proud of his wrestling trophy, so much so that she'd placed it in the coffin. Why, then, were there no

photos of him with his wrestling team, none of him
in uniform?

I'd found no books of any kind, nor magazines. No
address book, no diary or journal, no receipts or
records that he'd sold any paintings or had held
down a job. Danny Totton was a cipher, as blank a
canvas as the one upstairs on his easel, and that did
not make sense. Unless it was intentional. But why
hide all clues about himself?

In the living room, I scanned the photos on the
mantel. They were a pictorial record of his life from
infancy to adulthood, a young man who looked very
much like the handsome soldier holding his son on
his shoulder in a snapshot taken when Danny was a
toddler. The same thick curly hair, mesmerizing blue
bedroom eyes, square jaw, even white teeth. I finally
selected the photo in which Danny appeared the
oldest, placing it under the back cover of the lined
pad I'd borrowed from Nunna's Bible school supplies.

It was approaching eleven when I left the Totton
house, my stomach rumbling like a diesel engine. If
I didn't eat something soon, I wouldn't be able to
concentrate on anything other than how hungry I
was. And it was past time to talk to Maudine about
her brother. I made a beeline for Fred's and ordered
a Superduper hamburger with all the trimmings
from him, since Maudine already had her hands full
with two booths of teenagers and one of preschoolers. While I waited, I headed for the public phone
up front to report in.

"How're you feeling?" I asked Mr. Sheriff.

"You don't want to know. How'd it go with 'Stelle?"

I gave him a thumbnail sketch of my search, after

he'd recovered from the shock of learning how cooperative she'd been. He was in for more shocks.

"Nudes?" he squawked. "As in nekkid women? Painted under 'Stelle's roof? My Gawd, who'd have thought it. I'd like to see them myself."

I told him he'd have the opportunity as soon as the film was developed, and asked where I could take it.

"Asheville, on your way to see Johnny Boothe, Danny's dentist. There's bound to be plenty of one-hour developing places there. Dora was right. He lives up there in a ritzy-snitzy retirement community. Fills in for the resident dentist once a week during the summer and goes down to Hilton Head for the winter. Didn't get to talk to him long, but he says he'll be at home until this evening. You can catch him anytime before then."

I told him I'd leave for Asheville as soon I'd eaten. "Anything else?" Maudine was taking the burgers off the grill. I had to go.

"Well, the medical examiner's balking about identifying the latest body as Totton's. That leg bone's definitely his and belongs to the skeleton it was buried with, but the M.E. says he can't ignore the fact that Totton's dental records don't match the New Bethel corpse and do match the body we got out of Garden of Peace yesterday."

"Think somebody murdered them both and switched heads to confuse things?" I asked, tongue in cheek, as Maudine slapped a slice of Bermuda onion on top of the lettuce and tomato.

The chief took me seriously. "Couldn't have. The Garden of Peace body was burned to a crisp but the skull was still attached to the spine. Ask Johnny if he has a line on Alice Youngman. She was his assistant, took care of his files. She pulled them before his appointments and put them back afterward. Wouldn't let him touch them otherwise. She's the one we need to find. She left some years back and gave Johnny and Sunrise the back of her hand. Haven't heard from her since. Oh, hell, here comes Dora with some soup. I need something I can chew, not slurp. Call me again when you can, hear?"

I hung up. There was no point in responding to a dial tone.

I settled on my favorite stool and dug into the burger waiting for me. I'd finished it, tomato and pickle juice dripping from my fingers, before Maudine had a break. It required guts; the preschoolers were finger-painting with ketchup on the table of their booth.

I made a sudden decision to verify the message Carrie had left for me, before I talked to Maudine. "How about fizzing me up another soda? I want to check in with Carrie and then we can talk."

"Pepsi okay?" She was practically panting with anticipation.

"Fine. Go easy on the ice. I'm thirstier than I am hot."

"You've got it." She rushed away, her face flushed.

Carrie picked up the phone right away. "Didn't you get my message?" she asked.

"Yeah, but I wanted to make sure you hadn't come up with something else."

"Ix-nay. Maurice Alan Fletcher. That's what you said, right? I came up empty. I logged onto every database we got. There is no Maurice Alan Fletcher in any state or federal prison in these United States.

There are no warrants on him, no records of any kind."

"You're sure, Carrie. He said he was serving a life sentence, has been in for nine years."

"Well, he might have managed to get himself arrested, tried, and jailed under an alias. Find out what it is, and I'll find him."

"Okay, okay." Carrie knew her business. I had no other option but to take her word for it. I plastered on my poker face as Maudine came to the phone, handed me the soda, and left quickly. "Do me one last favor," I said to Carrie, once Maudine was out of earshot, "and you have the loan of my leather skirt anytime you want it. See what you can find out about a group called the Children of Hope, based in Colorado somewhere."

She cackled. "Hot damn! Send me your keys so I can get into your closet. You mentioned them when you called before and somebody's been working on it ever since. I can tell you right now they were based in California, not Colorado, and they went belly-up years ago. Rumors of brainwashing, that kind of shit. The way things go, some of them may have gone off and started a new group, but there's nothing on record. Maybe I can tell you more tomorrow."

"You're okay, Carrie," I said, kissing my skirt good-bye. Her hips would stretch it out of shape; I'd never be able to wear it again. "Talk at you later."

"Uh-huh." She hung up and I started back toward the counter, entertaining an unpleasant possibility.

Maudine met me halfway. "What'd she say?" she asked, unable to hold it in any longer. "Let's sit right here." She took the soda from my hand and set it on the table of the frontmost booth. "Oh. Straw." She zipped over to the counter, slapped the straw dispenser, and came back. "Now, where's Maurice?" Her eyes were wide and bright.

I hated to burst her bubble but I had to. "I don't know where he is, Maudine, just where he's not, and that's in jail. Carrie pulled out all the stops. He has no record anywhere. The only thing she could suggest was that he might be using another name."

It was difficult watching her stricken face. She slumped back against the bench and shook her head. "He'd never get away with it. Maurice was . . . well, he had a really low IQ. He might make up a name, but five minutes later he'd forget it. Oh, God." She looked around in confusion. "Not in jail? I should be relieved, but I'm not. Maurice, goddamn it, where are you?"

And why, I asked myself for the tenth time, would he make up such a whopper to explain why he couldn't come back to Sunrise? Unless. It would be the tenth time since I'd gotten Carrie's message that I'd butted up against that word. Was Maurice the John Doe in Danny Totton's grave?

"When did he leave town, Maudine?" I asked.

"July 3 of '82. There was a really bad storm that night. Messed up the town and ruined the plans for the Fourth." She lowered her hands, her face still a mask of despair. "I was relieved he was gone. Maurice was terrified of thunderstorms."

July 3. Danny Totton's wrecked car had been found a couple of days later.

"Did he fly to Colorado?"

Her eyes crinkled in confusion. "Oh. No. When he left here he was moving to Charlotte. Mrs. Rowland—

she was still plain old Claire Peete then—had found this place, sort of a shelter, where they teach the disabled a marketable skill. Maurice was good with his hands, building things. He was going to learn cabinetry."

Something didn't compute. "Why'd he leave on July 3? Wouldn't the shelter be closed on the Fourth?"

"It was, but . . ." She scooted over to the corner of the booth. "We didn't have a car, so he had to catch the commuter bus to Asheville. From there he took one to Charlotte. The commuter bus doesn't run on holidays, so he left on the third. He wanted to be in Charlotte to see the fireworks." Her mouth formed a sad, heartbreaker of a smile. "Twenty-one years old and he'd never seen fireworks. He stayed in a Y that night and the next, and reported to the shelter on the fifth. The last time I saw him he was waiting out on the highway for the five-thirty bus."

It was unlikely we'd be able to confirm that Maurice had caught that bus, not after twelve years.

"How the hell did he get from Charlotte to Colorado?"

"It's hard to explain. When we were little, we lived next door to a monastery over in Grainton. The priests were very nice to us and Maurice worshiped them. He decided he wanted to be a priest, even though we weren't Catholic. Mama was having none of that, so he finally decided he'd be satisfied doing the Lord's work whether he wore one of those collars or not. He was forever hopping the bus to go to revivals and that's where he met someone from Children of Hope. They told him they were building a commune in Colorado and would welcome anyone who knew one end of a hammer from the other and wanted to dedicate their lives to doing good works— right up Maurice's alley. Boom! He was gone."

"Just like that."

"Just like that. He never thought things out, he just did them."

"Did he come back here first?"

She shook her head, upended the salt shaker, and let the salt run out to form a tiny mountain. "That's what hurt. He wrote us once after he got to the shelter, a postcard with a cartoon on the back and a smiley face on the front. All he said was he'd gotten there okay and liked it. Then nothing for weeks. Finally he calls from Denver, explaining about the recruiter and all."

I felt some of the tension leave my shoulders, relieved that I could shelve my suspicion about Maurice's whereabouts.

"This guy was driving back to Colorado the next day," Maudine continued, "and riding with him was the only way Maurice was going to get there, so he couldn't come home first. He hasn't been back since, just the postcards once a year. He seemed happy and Lord knows there wasn't anything for him here." She sighed. "I just don't get it. Maurice has never been a liar. So why this? Oh, God. What will I tell Mama?"

I couldn't help her with that. "That isn't all, Maudine. Carrie says the Children of Hope threw in the towel ten years ago, and their home base was in California, not Colorado."

"What? But—"

An eardrum-piercing squeal from the finger-painters interrupted her and brought Maudine to her feet. "I can't stand it any longer. Let me go kick those young'uns out of here. It'll take me half an hour to clean that table. Ashley Jean! Robert Lewis, y'all quit that! Where's your mama, anyway?"

She read the kids the riot act and shooed them out, returning to the cash register with dollar bills and change stained with ketchup. "Damn it, look at this. It's gonna gunk up everything in the till. God, I'm so sick of this." She sorted the money, placed it where it belonged, and slammed the till closed, tears in her eyes.

"Hey," I said. "Be cool. There's got to be a logical explanation for everything." I just wasn't sure what it was. "There's a possibility a splinter group started a new organization. Carrie says she'll keep looking and I'll check in with her tomorrow."

She wiped her eyes. "I don't know what to think. It's bad enough worrying about Mama without worrying about Maurice, too. I really appreciate what you've done, though. If there's ever anything I can do for you, anything."

A light bulb lit up my brain. "There is something. Mr. Sheriff is laid up for a few days, so I'm trying to help him work out exactly what happened across the street last Sunday and how it's related to the body I found."

She went pale, her eyes fixed on me. "The one they think is Danny Totton, you mean."

I nodded, intrigued by her reaction. But then it had been Maudine who'd consigned Sunrise to the toilet that first day. She'd also mentioned the skeletons in the closets. Was one of them Mrs. Totton's son's? "I'd like to pick your brain since you were around when Danny died."

"I don't know anything about that," she said quickly.

"I didn't mean to imply you do. But you did know him, which is more than I can say. Anything you remember about him would help. Who was around that summer? Mrs. Totton says he had lots of friends and girlfriends, but no one close. I find that hard to believe."

"Believe it." Her eyes changed, hardened, then changed again. "If I say no," she asked, her voice becoming husky, "does that mean you won't ask your friend to follow up on what happened to the Children of Hope?"

"This isn't tit for tat, Maudine. Whatever Carrie tells me, I'll tell you. I don't need an answer from you this very minute. Why don't I check with you when I get back from Asheville?" I could afford to wait that long for her response. At least she, unlike Sheryl, was on the fence about it.

She nodded. "Thanks, Leigh Ann. You're the only person who ever went out of her way to do anything for me. I . . . Never mind. Maybe I'll see you later."

"Hope so," I said, paid for my lunch, and left. Maudine knew something, I was sure. I tucked away the image of her face when I'd asked for her help and shifted mental gears. It was time to focus on John Boothe, D.D.S., and whatever he could tell me.

Mr. Sheriff had described this retirement community as ritzy-snitzy, accounted for by the presence of a doorman/concierge/front desk attendant. The lobby had couches and easy chairs, a monster television and more ferns and rubber plants than a South American rain forest.

I didn't remember Dr. Boothe until he answered

the door of his mid-rise apartment. He'd been the only dentist in Sunrise, but Nunna had always taken me to Miss Sue Walker's son, who practiced in Merriam. Only now, seeing Dr. Boothe's ruddy complexion, did I recall why: he was an alcoholic. Nunna had given him credit for doing his drinking after hours, but woe be unto him who had an emergency once the office was closed. If you were smart, you grinned and bore it until the next morning, when he was sober again.

"Come in, come in," he said expansively, closing the door behind me and waving me toward a white leather sofa. "Have a seat."

The apartment was simply furnished with pieces of no-fuss Scandinavian design against white walls, the only color supplied by a Persian rug, throw pillows, and mobs of flowering plants.

"Leigh Ann Warren. Should I remember you?" He squinted at me, adjusting his bifocals.

"Not necessarily. I am Nunnally Layton's foster daughter."

"Ah. Yes." He nodded, dislodging heavy white hair which flopped into his face. He combed it in place with his fingers. "Seems to me I heard she went to Africa. Missionary work or something."

"That's right. She's back in Sunrise now."

"Is that so? It's good to hear about folks you used to know. You could have knocked me over with a feather when Nehemiah called this morning. I remember when . . ."

I let him waste the next fifteen minutes asking questions about this one and that, half of which I couldn't answer. Even when I explained that I'd only been back in Sunrise a little over a week, he seemed to think that had been more than enough time to have taken the census.

When I'd had enough, I brought things to a halt as gently as I could. "Did Mr. Sheriff explain why I'm here?"

He scratched his chin. "Well, no, not really. He said he'd leave that to you. What's the problem?"

As I launched into the explanation, I began to wish that the chief had done it for me. The dentist was completely unprepared for the news of Doc Webster's death. He did not take it well; in fact, he stepped out onto the balcony to wipe his eyes and blow his nose.

He was unapologetic when he returned. "Web and I went back a long ways. He was a good man. Funeral on Saturday, you said? We'll be there. I interrupted your train of thought. Go on. What's this got to do with me again?"

I continued my narrative with the discovery of the body and its subsequent identification via Doc's X ray, then touched on the matter of the dental records.

"Danny Totton? Estelle's boy?" He got up from his recliner, paced to the balcony door and back. "How the hell could that be? I pulled his chart myself. I'll admit I was a two-fisted drinker back then and I was probably pissed to the eyeballs when Ted Euker called, but I can spell. We only had two Tottons in town and two in our files. I know good and damned well I pulled the right chart."

"This one," I said, placing the file Mr. Sheriff had supplied me on the coffee table.

He sat down beside me, adjusted his glasses. "Damned right," he said, voice ringing with righteousness as he jammed a finger atop the name clearly typed at the top of the chart.

The apartment door opened and a middle-aged woman entered hurriedly, scowling. "Boothe, please! I could hear you cussin' from the elevator. Pipe down. And who's this?"

She was probably twenty years younger than Dr. Boothe, her features softening in middle age, her ebony hair streaked with silver. Her body, however, looked forty years younger. She was in fantastic shape, a perfect size eight or something equally petite and disgusting, her waist so small and trim she could probably wear a rubber band for a belt. She obviously worked to stay that way if her electric blue bodysuit, matching tights, and athletic shoes were any indication.

Dr. Boothe rose with a besotted smile, the first time I'd seen one that matched the definition. He took a roundabout route via "Don't you remember Nunnally, etc.?" before getting around to telling her my name and completely neglecting to tell me hers.

Smiling, she shook her head. "He's hopeless. I'm his wife, Alice. I remember you now. You popped Junior Heckenrood in the mouth and loosened a tooth."

"Jesus. I'd forgotten that." Something told me I had found the missing Alice Youngman.

"Sit down, Allie," Dr. Boothe directed. "Wait'll you hear this." He saved me the trouble of going through it again, breaking the news about Doc to her as gently as he could, letting her recover before continuing with great storytelling panache, climaxing by waving the copy of the chart triumphantly.

"Well, if that doesn't beat all," she said. "You mean Mrs. Totton buried somebody else? The poor woman.

But who could it have been? I don't remember any-one else coming up missing. Let me see that." She took the chart and scanned it.

I was surprised they could tell anything from look-ing at it. It was a copy of a copy of a copy of the origi-nal chart—the standard drawing of the upper and lower jaw with notations that made no sense to me and a series of faded squares, the X rays. "Danny Totton," she muttered. "Prettiest teeth I'd . . ." Her voice trailed off. "Gimme," she said, snatching her husband's glasses off his face and using them as a magnifier. After a minute, she looked up at me. "Danny Totton. Black hair, blue eyes. Muscular build, right?"

"I'd say so, but maybe this will help." I flipped open Nunna's steno pad and slid the photo across to her.

She glanced at it, nodding. "That's the boy I remember. Perfect teeth, perfect manners, on the surface anyway. And this," she said, stabbing with one long, lacquered fingernail, "is not his chart."

9

"*What the* hell *do you mean,* it's not his chart?" Dr. Boothe bellowed.

"Keep your voice down, buster." There was steel in his wife's voice. She slid the photo and the charts back in his direction. "Look at his smile," she ordered. "The child could have been a model for a Colgate commercial. Now look at these X rays. There's a gap between the upper incisors and the canine teeth you could drive a semi through. Honestly, Boothe! How could you have made a mistake like that?"

Dr. Boothe huffed and puffed, his hair flopping in all directions. "His name's on the chart! If it's the wrong name, whose fault is that? Eh?"

She snatched it from him again, her face going pale. Staring at it closely, she gasped. "I didn't type this! I didn't!" she repeated, on the defensive. "We had an IBM Selectric, with the ball. I used a Courier 10 pitch. Pica. Ten characters to the inch. I—Wait a minute." Rushing out of the room, she returned at a trot with a ruler and placed it under the typed name. "I'm right! This is an elite font. Twelve characters to the inch. Somebody bastardized this chart!"

Alice Youngman Boothe was incensed. Her territory had been invaded, her professional honor besmirched. She fumed and paced for five minutes before calming down and excusing herself to go wash her face, having literally railed up a sweat. Her husband appeared unaffected by it. He sat, lost in thought.

I'd been so mesmerized by her performance that it was only after it was over that I remembered the second chart. I slid it from the envelope. "This is a copy of the impressions taken from the body in New Bethel's cemetery. Would you say these more closely matched Danny's teeth? Even if all you had to go on was the smile in this picture?"

He looked them over carefully. "Yes, ma'am. He was very fortunate. He'd inherited his father's teeth, not Estelle's. Perfectly aligned, no problems when his third molars erupted, and the only patient I had with no dental caries. You done?" he asked, as Mrs. Boothe returned and collapsed dramatically in the recliner, completely wrung out. He picked up the bastardized chart and passed it to her. She eyed it with repulsion and refused to take it. "How about using your brain for something constructive instead of raising sand?" her husband said. "I remember these teeth. I just can't remember whose mouth they were in. Do you?"

Still a little huffy, she gazed at it, then shook her head. "I'll have to think about it."

"She's got a phenomenal memory," Dr. Boothe

said, with obvious pride. "It'll come to her. Wait. You'll see."

"Okay." I considered running Maurice's name up the flagpole to see if she'd salute, but saw no point. He'd called Maudine from Colorado so he was alive somewhere. I just hoped that Mrs. Boothe would come up with something before I had to leave. "Do you have any idea how the change of name on the chart could have happened? Wasn't the office locked at night?"

"Of course," Alice responded, sounding miffed that I'd think otherwise. "Not that there was much to steal, but there were a couple of people who were mad enough at Boothe to trash his office."

"Why?"

She grinned with pure wickedness. "My beloved husband used to have a fondness for the grape."

"Corn," he corrected her.

"Whatever. A couple of patients were in too much pain to put up with it overnight. They knew better—Boothe's drinking was no secret—but they insisted they were willing to have him take care of the problem right then and there. Boothe came in drunk as a skunk and pulled the wrong teeth."

"Once I realized it, I pulled the right ones, didn't I?" he asked aggrieved. "And the ones I extracted were going to have to come out anyway. Why the hell did those people put up with me so long? Anyway, to answer your question, we locked the office when we left. No one could have gotten to the files."

"Were they locked up, too?

"What for? They probably should have been, but they weren't. We figured the deadbolt on the door was enough."

"Wait a minute, Boothe." Alice leaned forward, elbows on her knees. "What about after the storm of '82? Half the town was wide open, including the office. It was days before Stan could get a replacement door."

"What happened to the door?" I asked.

"Wind blew it in. It was a mess. Glass all over the place."

I was sorry now I'd missed it. I'd been in Chicago with Nunna. The people renting the house had written her about the storm. It had uprooted a third of Sunrise's trees. One had come down in her backyard, demolishing the utility shed.

"But that's the only time in all the years we were there that the office was more or less open," Alice said.

Dr. Boothe frowned. "Allie, isn't that the same storm that probably caused Danny's—or whoever it was—accident? Found him two days after the storm."

The accident report had indeed blamed the inclement weather, because there were no indications that the driver had been speeding.

"Excuse me," I said, interrupting Alice in the middle of an oral inventory of the chaos the storm had caused. Something had just occurred to me and it was ask now or forever hold my peace. Getting a word in edgewise with these two was a challenge. "Was there much damage in New Bethel's cemetery?"

"Both cemeteries," Dr. Boothe said. "Fallen trees destroyed a lot of tombstones in Garden of Peace."

"I see." Several theories had popped into my head like jack-in-the-boxes, but I needed time and quiet to toss them around and I'd get neither here. "Before I forget it, Mrs. Boothe, what did you mean when you said Danny had perfect manners on the surface?"

"Is that what I said? I'm not sure what I meant, but you couldn't fault his home training. He was always polite, purposefully so, especially to women. I think he fancied himself a lady-killer. You know how some men make you feel they're undressing you with their eyes? That was Danny. With younger women it was probably very effective. It didn't work with me. One, I was too old and two, all I was interested in was his teeth."

I saw no point in telling her that he was probably doing precisely what she described, undressing her in his mind, sizing her up as a potential nude in his next painting. "No luck yet remembering whose dental chart that might be?" I asked her, in case she'd forgotton that the question was still hanging.

"What? No, I'm still thinking about it, though."

Unfortunately, I'd gotten an itch to leave. It didn't happen often, a sudden saturation with my surroundings precipitating a strong desire to get the hell away from wherever I was and go home. I'd had it that night waiting for Duck to come back. I had it now. Everything I'd learned in the last twenty-four hours, beginning with Mr. Sheriff's revelation that Doc had been murdered, had set up a racket in my mind. I literally couldn't hear myself think.

I gathered all the materials, slid them back into their appropriate envelopes and files, and began a departure that I sensed would take a while. Either these two didn't have guests very often or they loved me to death. Whichever, it was another forty-five

minutes before I managed to escape, my ears ringing. The Boothes were nonstop yakkers. I locked
myself in the car and made sure the radio was off
before I started the engine. Had it been on, I'd have
gone straight through the roof of the car.

I swung by the Quick Pix and paid for the prints
I'd dropped off, flipping through them before stash-
ing them in my bag. None I'd photographed resembled Alice Boothe, but I was willing to bet she was
the subject of more than one painting stacked in the
attic. I would go through them again if I ever got the
chance, but for the moment the prints in my purse
interested me the most. They deserved quiet and
unhurried contemplation. I was pleased with them;
I'd done a good job. Even on film, their effect was
the same. They bugged me. Why?

I still hadn't come up with an answer when I
glanced in my rearview mirror and did a double take.
Because traffic was light on this stretch of the two-
lane highway that ran past the turnoff to Sunrise, I
hadn't been paying much attention to what was
behind me. I could swear that I'd seen the old gray
pickup now following at a respectable distance when
I'd traveled this route on the way to Asheville.

One side of my brain served up a perfectly logical
explanation. Truck farmers were a common sight in
this area; a good many lived in Sunrise and ferried
their produce to nearby towns, so there was no reason to think that being in front of this particular one
twice in a day was anything other than a fluke. It was
the other side of my brain that shouted louder.

Truck farmers lit out first thing in the morning. I'd
left at noon. I'd driven all the way to Asheville and
Leisure Lakes—where I realized now I'd seen the

same damned pickup, or one just like it, parked on the far side of the lot when I left the Boothes. It had stuck out like a sore thumb, surrounded by Mercedeses, Continentals, and Caddys galore. Was this son of a bitch tailing me?

I increased my speed by ten miles an hour. So did the truck. I slowed to the speed limit. So did the truck, but there was nothing unusual about that. I was being paranoid. I might have continued to believe that had I not looked up a minute or so later to see the pickup filling my back window. It was almost on me and showed no signs of slowing. I forced myself to stay cool and maintain my speed to find out if the driver was in a hurry and my nose was being tweaked by the gods of coincidence, or whether there was something else going on here. When he tapped my rear bumper instead of his horn, I had my answer.

My car might look like a heap on the outside but it was what was under the hood that counted and I hadn't stinted on horsepower and routine maintenance, since occasionally I'd had to use the car on the job. I was roughly three miles from my turnoff with nothing in front of me as far as I could see.

I floored the accelerator. My Chevy took off like the proverbial bat. In a matter of seconds, I was nudging eighty-five. I checked the mirror. The pickup was trying its best, oily smoke gushing from its tail pipe as it sped up. With a mental nod of gratitude to the Police Academy for the behind-the-wheel training I'd received, I settled down for a bit of serious driving. There'd be no problem as long as the road ahead was clear. If, however, I came up behind some law-abiding citizen honoring the forty-mile-an-hour speed limit, things would get damned interesting.

The pickup tried, I'll give him credit for that. There was no way he could catch me. He could, however, see me when I turned off toward Sunrise; most roads snaked their way through these mountains, but this was one of the few straight shots in the area. There was nothing I could do about that. If the pickup chose to follow me, I'd at least be on familiar territory.

I made the turn onto Sunrise Road on three wheels and saw immediately that my luck was holding. About an eighth of a mile ahead, parked on the shoulder facing me was a county cruiser, a tall, well-built officer beside it checking a rear tire. He heard me coming, wheeled around, reached in, and hit his chase lights. He needn't have; I finessed my brakes and came to a halt at his side—Roscoe Sheriff. He had his brother by an inch, but I suspected he was the younger. He glared at me in disapproval.

"You're Miss Leigh Ann, right? I realize you're helping my dad, but—"

"Yeah, yeah, I was speeding," I said, before he could finish. "Hold on a minute." I turned, looking back. The sound of the pickup's laboring engine was audible, even from this distance. It careened onto Sunrise Road, spotted us and laid down an inch of rubber coming to a halt. Gears ground and complained as the driver shifted into reverse. He backed up to the turn, maneuvered the vehicle around, and sped off the way he had come.

"What the hell?" Roscoe asked.

"Whoever that was tailed me all the way to Asheville and back, then played kissy-face with my bumper until I took off and left him in my dust. Did you recognize the truck?" I got out to check for damage—minor. One insignificant dent.

"There are two or three locals with pickups that color," Roscoe said. "What'd the driver look like? Did you get a license number?"

"I was a little busy. And the cab was too high for me to see him."

He removed his mike from the dashboard. "Looked like a Ford. About how old?"

"Hard to tell. Seventy-something. "

He nodded and called it in. "No tag number available. Traveling south on Whit Road. Needs a muffler." The dispatcher squawked something in return and he signed off. "I don't mean to insult you," he said, "you being a professional and all, but are you a hunnert percent sure he tailed you to Asheville? Reason I ask, sometimes the farm kids are out larking in their daddy's truck and pull stunts like that bumper-bumping, usually on a friend's car though."

I leaned against the trunk and thought about it. I really couldn't swear under oath that it was the same pickup behind me when I'd left. I'd noticed the one in the Boothes' parking lot only because it was in such upscale company, but swear to its make and color? Gray or white? I was almost certain on both counts but there was a lot of room between almost certain and hand-on-the-Bible-I-do.

"I'm not as sure as I'd like to be," I said, "so I'll table the accusation that I was followed—for now. If you manage to find them, though, I will take them to the mat about that bumper business. It's dangerous and I don't play that."

He nodded, taking me seriously. "We don't either.

If I didn't have this leak, I'd be after him now myself. Where are you on your way to, in case somebody catches him?"

I wasn't sure. I had the move-arounds, adrenaline still pumping, so I wasn't ready to go back to Nunna's. Too quiet. "Your house first, then the diner."

"If there's something you want me to pass along to Daddy, I can save you the trip. I've got to go home and pick up another tire, save my spare."

"Great." I recounted the morning's revelations. "Mrs. Boothe, who by the way is the Alice Young-man your father wanted to find, is supposed to call your dad if and when she remembers who that first chart belongs to. Also, ask him how many people know I'm helping him. If that jackass was following me, it might pin down who was driving that pickup."

He winced. "I hate to tell you, Miss Leigh Ann, but pert near half the town knows by now. Lots of folks have dropped by to see how Daddy's doing. Plus me and my brother might have mentioned it to a couple of friends."

Terrific. Half the town.

"Tell him I'll be by later. I want to catch Maudine before she gets off."

"Oh. Glad you mentioned her," he said, replacing the valve cap on the tire. "It reminded me. If her brother's coming back for Reunion Week, you ought to talk to him. He knew Danny Totton 'bout as well as anybody."

"Danny and Maurice? Seems to me they wouldn't have much in common."

"Well, they really didn't." He scratched his nose just the way his father did when he was deep in thought. "It's not like they were buddies or anything.

More like slave and master. Maurice was Danny's shadow, followed him around like a puppy. Old as he was, he even came to our Boys' Club meetings because Danny was the leader."

Twelve years ago Danny was twenty-four and Maurice a couple of years younger. That was a trifle old. The Boys' Club, like the Girls', let you in when you went to first grade and kicked you out once you graduated from high school.

"Danny treated him like dirt," Roscoe said. "Made fun of him because he had a hard time catching on to things. Used to tease him, saying he might as well be a priest since he didn't have a girlfriend."

So he'd known about Maurice's leanings toward the religious life. "How did Maurice react to crap like that?"

"He'd just smile. The only time I saw him get mad was when Danny said something really nasty about his mother. Maurice was a nice guy. All the kids liked him. But Maurice mad was scary. Danny walked on eggs after that, until he found out Maurice was leaving. Ragged him something fierce the last meeting Maurice came to. I'll never forget it. We're out there in the dark behind S.T.'s gym trying to finish the float and Danny's talking about Maurice like a dog, right to his face. Kept calling him stupid, saying it was a wonder he knew day from night. He'd have never done it if he hadn't known Maurice would be gone from then on."

The floats. I'd forgotten that. Sunrise couldn't afford fireworks, so we'd made do with homemade floats in a Fourth of July parade down the length of Main Street. I was a little tired, so it was a moment before I figured out the part of that speech I should be paying attention to. "Hold it, Roscoe. What do you mean, you were out there in the dark?"

"Mrs. Euker was a club mother. She hadn't bought enough crepe paper streamers to decorate the truck bed. By the time she found some and drove back to Sunrise with it, it was dark. It was fun, though. She and Miss Peete—Rowland now—and my mom put together a picnic for us while we waited. Didn't finish the float until after midnight and spent the night in the gym."

After midnight. Yet Maureen said her brother was to have caught the five-thirty bus. "You're sure Maurice was there that late?"

"Positive. Danny conned him into staying to help us decorate. Kept saying stuff like 'You scratch my back, dummy, I scratch yours.' It's a night none of us will forget because of that whopper of a storm that came up early the next morning. Tore every bit of crepe paper off the float. That's the only year I remember we didn't have a parade."

Well, well, well. This was an avenue I'd have to pursue. I got back in the car, waited while Roscoe turned the cruiser around, then followed him back toward town in case his tire went completely flat and he needed a ride. At least that was the plan until I reached the Welcome to Sunrise sign and saw something that stopped me. Roscoe waved and went on.

In the time I'd been gone, a second sign had been added. This one filled the billboard at the town limits, replacing the faded and tattered invitation to try an Orange Crush, an ad that had been there since my kid days. Coming Soon! the sign shouted. Waverly Mall, Main Street in Sunrise! Outlet Shopping at Its Finest! Clothing! Linens! Hosiery!

Shoes! Fine China and Glassware! Groceries! Watch This Space!

Beneath all that was a drawing of the proposed mall. I'm not sure what I had expected, but it certainly wasn't what I saw. With only sixteen stores to be housed, I had envisioned a one-story strip mall stretching from the cul-de-sac where Sunrise Township now stood to some point in New Bethel's cemetery. Waverly's rendering was quite different. The largest store, which bore the name of a local chain, served as the anchor in a semicircular building around the cul-de-sac. It resembled a rustic cabin with glandular trouble. Lots of timber— Sundler's Mill would be working double shifts again. There was something familiar about it; perhaps it was a variation of one of its stores in another city. The remaining fifteen shops, which would extend from the department store onto a good half of New Bethel's property, were arranged in two stories, the upper floor accessed by ramps positioned along the front of the edifice in a big *X*, like crossbeams. Again lots of timber. This section, too, despite its unusual configuration, had a rustic flavor about it. They looked nothing like the stores on Main yet retained an old-fashioned feel to them. I focused on the department store, wondering where I might have seen its cousin. Atlanta, perhaps, or Hilton Head? I couldn't pin it down.

It seemed to me, however, that Charles Rowland and his Waverly Associates were being damned presumptuous. They hadn't broken ground yet, hadn't even razed the school, to say nothing of winning over the remaining New Bethel holdouts. Perhaps it was a warning that, regardless, they would prevail.

The sign as much as announced to all and sundry
that little people like Nunna didn't matter. In the
end, they probably wouldn't, but the company might
have had the decency not to say so. Such arrogance
got me steamed, which translated into a heavy foot
after I pulled away. I was speeding again when I
zipped by a pedestrian whose identity didn't register
until after I'd passed him. Mr. Taney, New Bethel's
groundskeeper.

I stopped and backed up, waiting for him. He
squinted at the car warily as he came abreast and
stopped. "Need a ride, Mr. Taney?" I asked.

"No'm," he said politely. "Don't really need it, but
I sure would 'preciate one."

"Hop in," I told him, leaning over to unlock the
passenger door. "Where are you going?"

"Cemetery." Where else? his intonation inquired.
He got in, secured the seat belt, and sat back as if he
were riding in a Rolls Royce.

Obliging him would mean backtracking to the diner,
but I didn't mind. I'd always liked Mr. Taney. As he
would soon be losing two sources of his livelihood—
he'd also been custodian at Sunrise Township—I felt
he deserved a bit of pampering.

He was an odd duck, short, stocky, with a rolling
gait, his skin a deep, deep brown from years of expo-
sure to the sun. His face, framed by close-cropped
gray hair, was round, full and boyish, belying his
years; he was at least as old as Nunna. His expression
contributed to his boyishness. The mouths of all the
Taneys turned up at the corners in a permanent
smile. Unfortunately a stranger might interpret it to
mean that the Taneys didn't have both oars in the
water. True, none had college educations, but I'd

met many an idiot PhD with barely a tenth of the
Taneys' storehouse of common sense. I considered it
a stroke of luck that I'd run into him. I could test
one of the theories that had occurred to me at the
Boothes'.

"Mr. Taney, the big storm back in July of '82. How
much damage was done?"

He grunted. "Left a proper mess. Took off roofs,
tore up trees by the roots, old ones, too. Couple of
'em fell on headstones, knocked 'em over, broke 'em
to pieces. Took a slap year 'fore the cemetery looked
halfway decent again."

"How soon after the storm were the trees removed?" I asked.

"Went right to work on it the next day. Hadn't
even stopped raining. My boy Norman drove the
tractor over, brought some chains with him. Pulled
'em out quick as that."

"And how long after were the holes filled in?"

Mr. Taney was a slow talker, another reason people underestimated him. He took his time before
responding. "Another couple of days, maybe." He
turned and looked at me, his eyes full of seventy-
plus years of wisdom. "Funny thing, though. There
was one hole didn't need near the amount of fillin' in
I thought it would. Only reason I remember is that
the tree that came out of it was a big ol' live oak my
granddaddy had planted. I sorta took that one personal when we lost it. So what I did, I filled it in the
rest of the way and after it had settled and all, put
the bench on it our family had bought for the cemetery. Seemed like the proper thing to do."

"And that's where I found the body," I said. It was
not posed as a question.

"Yes'm. Didn't 'preciate it, the place being used thataway. Wasn't a fit thing to do. Hear tell it was Mrs. Totton's boy."

I pulled up at the open gate of the cemetery. "It looks more and more like it by the minute, Mr. Taney."

"And the white folks are saying one of us put him there 'cause it's our piece of land. Makes me mad, as many times as their young'uns snuck through this here gate after dark and used our cemetery like it was their bedroom."

An echo of Sheryl's accusation. "Did you ever see Danny Totton over here?"

"Yes'm, saw him cutting through on his way who knows where. Saw him goin' at it with his lady friends a time or two, too. He was a mean one, liked to play rough, treat 'em like dogs. See him on the street, though, and butter wouldn't melt in his mouth."

This was news. No wonder he didn't have a steady girl. How the hell could he paint such warm and sensitive nudes if he was a woman beater? "Mrs. Totton's son? You're certain?"

"Yes, ma'am. Liked to make them cry, he did."

"Did you recognize any of his girlfriends?" One of them might have killed him in self-defense.

"No'm, can't say I did. All I know is they were white. It ain't a Christian thing to say, but whoever buried him gave him a fittin' shroud. They put garbage in a garbage bag. Well, I got me some weeds to pull. Thank you kindly for the ride, Leigh Ann."

I'm sure I told him he was welcome, but I don't remember saying it. I was approaching overload, having learned too much in a short period of time.

Danny Totton was more of an enigma than I'd antic-ipated. His mother certainly hadn't known him very well. Or perhaps she'd worn maternal blinders. There was also the possibility that he was simply a damned fine actor when he wanted to be. Whichever, I'd grown to dislike him. Anyone who'd make fun of someone's desire to follow the life of a religious zealot was a jerk, and any man who got his jollies beating up his girlfriends was an asshole. I was beginning to agree with Mr. Taney. Garbage bags may not have been good enough for Danny Totton. But the question still remained: How had he died and who had put him in the bags to begin with?

Maudine appeared to have been waiting for me, her nose practically glued to Fred's front window. She moved away from it when she saw me and opened the door. "Hi. Just getting back from Asheville?"

"Uh-huh, and I need to talk to you."

"I need to talk to you," she said solemnly. "Dolly, I'm off now, okay?"

Dolly Whisnant, Fred's wife, matched her name, big as a minute and a half, with short curly reddish hair going gray, and a Milky Way's worth of freckles on a Kewpie doll face.

"Hey, Leigh Ann," she called from the grill. "You're looking good. Take Maudine out of here if you need to. I can handle things."

"We can't leave," Maudine said. "Fred wants to talk to you, too. He'll be out in a minute. We might as well take the front booth again. Much more of this and we can consider it ours."

I slid in, wondering how Fred figured into the picture. "Well, while we're alone," I said, "I want to ask you something. You told me that the last time you saw Maurice, he was waiting for the commuter bus, right?"

She sat down and pushed the ketchup bottle and the salt and pepper shakers out of the way. "Right. I walked with him all the way out to Whit Road, then came back to town, crying my eyes out. I knew how much I was going to miss him."

"And he was to catch the five-thirty bus to Asheville?"

"Right."

"Maurice was in Sunrise until after midnight, helping the Boys' Club decorate their float for the Fourth of July parade."

Her jaw sagged. "He—he couldn't have been."

"He was. Roscoe Sheriff remembers him being there. Why didn't you mention that Maurice used to pal around with Danny?"

"Pal around, my ass." Her eyes snapped with indignation. "Danny took advantage of him, used Maurice like a fuckin' doormat."

"Howdy." Fred, his bald pate gleaming with perspiration, plopped down beside Maudine. "What are we talking about?"

"How Danny used to wipe his feet all over Maurice," she responded, still steaming. "Leigh Ann says Maurice didn't catch the bus for Charlotte. He showed up at the Boys' Club meeting that night."

"So? He eventually got where he was going, didn't he? Away from here and I hate to say it, Maudie, m'love, but I for one was glad to see him go."

"Why?" I asked. From the look on her face, it was news to Maudine, too.

"Because he was never going to get what he wanted from Danny Totton."

"Which was?"

"Driving lessons."

"What?" Maudine was incredulous.

Fred removed a handkerchief from his back pocket and scrubbed at his head. "It was a secret. Remember that raggedy old Datsun Rafe McCrory had sitting in his yard? He told Maurice that if he'd learn to drive and get his license, he could use it."

"For what?" Maudine demanded. "This town's so small, you can walk anywhere you need to go."

"Not if you're crippled up with arthritis," Fred said, his voice gentle. "He hated that your mama couldn't get to Sunday services. She could walk to church on her good days, but how many of them did she have, even back then? He wanted to be able to take her."

Maudine lowered her head, tears dribbling down her cheeks. "I could have taught him. Why didn't he ask me?"

"He wanted it to be a surprise. Claire Peete tried to help him with the written exam he'd have to take. He'd come in here in the afternoons with copies he'd made on the machine at school and practice filling them out. Danny promised to teach him to drive a stick shift."

"Oh, Lord," Maudine moaned. "He'd have stripped the gears clean. He and coordination were complete strangers. Hell, he didn't walk until he was three."

"Be that as it may, Danny had promised him and used it to get Maurice to do anything he needed done, like cleaning up at Sunrise Township at night while Danny took the credit for being such a good guy for saving old man Haggerty's job for him."

"You're kidding," Maudine said.

"The hell I am. I don't know who he thought he was fooling. Danny was the only janitor I ever saw go to work carrying a briefcase. Maurice said he'd shut himself up in a room and read until all the cleaning was done. Maurice ran errands, did anything he was asked, waiting faithfully for that slimy bastard to teach him to drive."

"Which he never did," I said.

"In his beloved MG? I hope to tell ya."

"When did Maurice realize Danny would never make good on his promise?" I asked.

"Hard to say. It's been a long time. It was before Claire Peete told him about the opening at the shelter, I do remember that."

"Was he angry about it?"

Fred scratched an ear. "More like confused. He didn't understand someone making a promise they never intended to keep." He looked at me, his eyes narrowing. "So if you're thinking he got so mad that he killed Danny Totton, forget it."

"You . . . you don't suspect Maurice, do you?" Maudine asked, fear arcing from her eyes. "He wouldn't! I swear on my life, he wouldn't! Maurice never got mad about anything!"

"That's not what I heard," I said, breaking it to her gently. "As I understand it, Danny said something unpleasant about your mother once and Maurice got mad enough to scare Danny into good behavior for a while. And for whatever reason, Danny was being particularly vicious that last night at the Boys' Club meeting. I have to wonder if Danny pushed him an inch too far, got in one last dig—perhaps something about your mother, perhaps not—and Maurice flipped. I can't think of any other reason he'd invent such a far-out excuse to justify not coming back to Sunrise."

Maudine shook her head violently. "No. It looks bad, I know, but he didn't do it. I swear he didn't."

"Do you know who did?" I asked very, very softly.

She froze. "What makes you think I'd know?"

"Something you said to me a week ago about the skeletons in Sunrise's closets. Remember?"

Her cheeks flared a deep crimson. "It had nothing to do with any of this. I give you my word." She swallowed, placed a hand with shaking fingers over her mouth. I hoped like hell she wasn't about to throw up all over me and was immensely relieved when she clasped her hands in her lap, her eyes averted. "I detested Danny Totton so much that, terrific as you've been about trying to find Maurice for me, I was going to tell you I wouldn't help you. I changed my mind. I'll do anything rather than have you think my brother is a killer."

"I'm with Maudie," Fred said. "That boy would die before he'd break that commandment. What I came out here to tell you, though, Leigh Ann, is that if you're looking for folks with reason enough to kill Danny Totton, you've got a town full of them this week."

"Excuse me?"

"He pulled the wool over the eyes of the older people, could charm women especially into simpering idiots. The younger ones knew him for what he was—mean, spiteful, and as evil as they come. Your problem's going to be finding anyone who'll say one bad word about him because of his mother. She's done so much for so many kids, helped send so many of them to college, that everyone feels they still owe her. They won't want to see her hurt."

"She might be hurt," I said, "but Doc was killed, Fred. Murdered, hit with a blunt instrument. The fire was set to cover it up."

"No!" They both stared at me, horrified.

"So I'm sorry if Mrs. Totton has to find out what a sleazeball her son was. We're looking for someone who may have murdered three people. That takes precedence over her feelings."

The phone rang. Fred leaned back, extended one long arm and picked it up. "Fred's Diner. Talk to me." After a second, he grinned. "The chief says I need to learn some telephone manners. It's my damn phone, ain't it? Here. He wants you. Dolly's looking pissed. I'd better get back to the kitchen." He patted me on the shoulder in farewell, and went back to work.

"What's up, Mr. Sheriff?"

"I just got a call from the medical examiner's office. He's threatening to bill Sunrise for overtime since they've got three bodies of ours over there. One of his hotshot assistants noticed something suspicious about the body in the MG. Guess what? Somebody hit that boy before he went over the bluff. With a car, I mean. He was already dead when the car crashed."

"Didn't the coroner notice it the first time?"

"What coroner? They knew whose car it was, knew nobody but Danny ever drove it. Maybe if Web had been in town he might have done an autopsy, but he wasn't. They took the remains straight to MacLawton's Funeral Home. Euker called Johnny Boothe for the dental chart that MacLawton used to verify that it was Danny Totton. As for the New Bethel body, well, you saw it. Somebody made a mess of the back of his head, with something big and heavy."

"God."

"And." The chief paused. "This is a sticky one. Alice Youngman—I mean, Boothe—just called. She's come up with a name for that dental chart, the one Johnny thought was Totton's. I think she's right. So does Dora. I'm gonna need your help getting the proof, though."

"Why? Whose does she think it was?"

"Maurice Fletcher's."

I arranged my features with as noncommittal an expression as I could manage, then slid out of the booth to stand up, since the cord was being stretched to its maximum and Maudine was sitting not three feet away, fingering her brother's letter.

I hadn't mentioned my conversations with Maudine or the call I'd made on her behalf. There'd been no reason to. Now there was. "There are a couple of other things you need to know. Why don't I drop by in a few minutes?"

"Fine. Maudine still there?"

"Yes."

"Good. Ask her for the best picture of Maurice she's got. We found a couple Dora took at Boys' Club meetings, but school shots would be better. They always show the kids grinning like idiots and we need to see his smile. I told the medical examiner I'd get it to him first thing tomorrow. Can you handle that?"

"Not without explaining why," I said, uncomfortable at holding this conversation with her so nearby.

"Bring her along. I'll tell her."

He hung up and I stood there, the phone still glued to my ear. I wanted Alice Boothe to be wrong. If she wasn't, there were several angles I'd better consider, the first being the feasibility of Maudine as a suspect. The temptation to ask her to account for her whereabouts the night Danny Totton was killed required a massive dose of restraint; that was Mr. Sheriff's job. And I had only her word that she hadn't seen Maurice again after she'd left him at the bus stop on Whit Road.

I tried this theory and that, but it wouldn't work. I simply couldn't believe Maudine would kill her brother. Danny was another matter. She'd made no bones about how she felt about him. If she'd found out her brother had been the victim of a hit-and-run and Danny had been responsible for it, she might have killed Danny in grief and rage. I had no idea how Maurice had wound up in the car when it went over the bluff, but if Maudine knew, with the odds against anyone discovering that it had been Maurice in the MG instead of Danny, she might have kept quiet and allowed her brother to have the dandiest funeral this town had seen in years. Lord knows she and her mother would never be able to do better. All she'd have to do then was to get rid of Danny's body and the storm provided her with the perfect place— another cemetery. Under those circumstances, rather than see him dug up and replanted now, and have her mother bear the shame of what her daughter had done, she might have killed Doc. Just because I'd seen her coming from the direction of the picnic grounds was no proof she'd been at the interfaith service. And hiding the fact that her twin was dead would be easy, since he was supposed to have left town that night anyway. What if Maudine had been sending the postcards to herself?

There were a lot of questions left, but it could have happened that way.

"I have to go," I said, sitting down again. "Maudine, when was it you talked to Maurice again? On the phone, I mean."

She made a face. "I haven't. He called Mama after he went out to Colorado. I blame that religious bunch. He hooked up with them and just abandoned his family. I'm not gonna forgive him for that. And I could kill him for calling when I wasn't there. That was before we bought the phone with volume control. Mama probably missed half of what he said. Why couldn't he have waited until I was home from work? Now this shit about being in jail so it'll look like he has a good reason for not showing up." She threw her head back, tears standing in her eyes. "Damn it, how could Maurice just flat out desert me like this?"

I stepped back, trying to decide what I thought. The anguish in Maudine's eyes seemed real, the pain of what she saw as her twin's abandonment convincing. But a phone call to a woman hard-of-hearing? Postcards once a year that she could have written to herself? Either Maudine Fletcher was one damned fine actress or someone had been yanking her chain for the last twelve years.

10

"What took y'all so long?" the chief grumbled from his recliner. He fidgeted, trying to get comfortable, a sock pulled over his cast. The dogs pranced around his chair, excited that company had arrived.

"My fault," I said, taking a seat on the couch at Mr. Sheriff's left. It was a nice room, contemporary country, short on flounces, long on unfussy upholstered furniture with lots of throw pillows and rag rugs. "We stopped at Maudine's and got the postcards Maurice sent and some samples of his schoolwork. I figured if Mrs. Fletcher's anything like Nunna, she'd have kept papers or reports, something, and she had." I passed them across to him. "And I convinced Maudine you should see this." I gave him the letter.

"I don't understand." Maudine perched on the edge of a bentwood rocker and refused Mrs. Sheriff's offer of lemonade. "Will somebody please tell me what's going on?"

"In a minute, Maudine. I 'preciate your coming. Just need to ask you a couple of questions. Relax and have something to drink."

"No, thank you. That letter of Maurice's doesn't mean anything, Mr. Sheriff. Leigh Ann had someone check for me, and he's not in jail. What's going on? Why'd you want all this stuff? All's he's done is lie about where he is."

The chief, scanning the letter, raised a hand to silence her. "Nobody's accused him of anything, Maudine."

Mrs. Sheriff placed tall, frosted glasses of lemonade on the coffee table. "Just in case," she said, left, and returned with a plate of chocolate chip cookies. Maudine, her anxiety rising, managed a tight smile of thanks, but didn't touch them.

The chief finished the letter. "When'd you get this?"

"It came Monday."

"Still have the envelope?"

"Yes, sir. Why?"

"If you don't mind, please, ma'am, I'd like to hold on to this letter and the envelope, soon's you can get it to us."

"When can I have them back?"

He hedged. "I'm not sure. There's a chance you won't even want 'em. Look, Maudine, I'm gonna ask you to be patient a minute longer while I look through these things. Then I'll explain."

"Have a cookie," Mrs. Sheriff said, shoving the plate under Maudine's nose. "Fresh out of the oven. How's your mother doing? We miss seeing her at church."

Looking thoroughly frustrated, Maudine removed

a cookie from the plate and held it. "She has good days and bad. She misses church, too."

"Well, pastor'll be bringing her communion come Sunday. And the Ladies' Auxiliary has her on the list of shut-ins to visit." Mrs. Sheriff rattled on, evidently trying to fill the silence while her husband compared the handwriting on the documents. He took his time, to such an extent that even I was getting itchy.

Finally he picked up the school pictures of Maurice. Maudine and her twin shared the same coloring; his hair was thick and blond, his skin as fair as hers, his eyes as wide, but a slightly darker blue. The resemblance, I remembered, once I saw the photos, ended there. Maudine had inherited her father's height. Maurice was stocky and several inches shorter. There was a worldliness about Maudine that her twin would never attain, not in a million years, whereas her brother's smile was a clue to his personality; it had all the sweet innocence of a baby's. It also clearly showed the gaps between his incisors and canine teeth.

Mr. Sheriff sighed, and arranged the material she'd supplied in a neat pile on his lap. "Maudine, your brother left town July 3 of 1982, right?"

"Yes, sir." She sat up straight, knees and ankles together, hands clasped in her lap.

"And since that night, he hasn't been back. That surprises me, seeing how crazy he was about y'all's mama. But I reckon he calls often?"

"No, sir, he doesn't." She cleared her throat. "It's that religious bunch he joined. They must make you give up everything from your past life. That's the only reason I can figure he wouldn't even get in touch by phone, except for the one time."

"When was that?"

Maudine looked at me, alarm in her eyes. She knew it wasn't a coincidence that the chief had asked the same questions I had. "A couple of months after he left town, when he moved out to Colorado. I didn't talk to him, Mama did."

"Uh-huh." He tugged his nose. "Maudine, I'm between a rock and a hard place here. I've got some news that under ordinary circumstances would have to wait until we were sure about it. But I've had to ask Delilah Fuller to do something for me and—"

"Dr. Dooley's receptionist?"

"Right. Good at her job, but she talks too much. Couldn't keep her mouth closed if you wired her jaw shut. She's bound to blab to somebody and sooner or later it'll get around. She's digging through the old dental records that Johnny Boothe passed along to Dooley to see if Maurice's is still there, his or Danny Totton's. And one of my boys will be raiding Web's garage to find your brother's medical file. Ain't no easy way to say it but flat out, Maudine. The fact is it's looking more and more like the person buried in Danny Totton's grave was your brother."

Whatever she'd been expecting, it wasn't this. Her face went blank with astonishment, her expression clearing her in my book as nothing else could have. "No. That's impossible. I mean, you've got his postcards and his letter right there. He's alive."

"I don't think so, Maudine. I want you to listen to me real close. There's a good possibility that the dental chart that was used to identify the body in Danny Totton's car was Maurice's. Somebody did a damn good job of erasing your brother's name and substituting Danny's. They may even have put Maurice's name on Danny's dental chart as a just-in-case. But I trust Web's files and, according to them, the body Leigh Ann found is Estelle Totton's son. I'm getting surer by the minute that Maurice was the one who died in that accident and somebody—probably the same somebody who changed the dental chart—has been sending those postcards to make you and your mama think he was still alive. The writing is close, I'll say that, and we'll get a handwriting expert to look at them, but I'd bet this farm Maurice didn't send them. I'm pretty sure your brother's been dead all these years."

"No." Maudine shook her head and covered her ears. "No. You're wrong. I know my brother's writing when I see it. Those postcards are from him."

"Well, I hope I'm wrong, but I don't think I am. I'll get these to the lab first thing tomorrow, along with the pictures of Maurice and anything Delilah and Roscoe find. Don't know how long it'll—"

"No! Maurice is alive. It couldn't have been him in that car because he didn't know how to drive. All right, my brother wasn't the smartest person in the world, but even he wouldn't have been dumb enough to try to drive that MG. On Old Post Road, too, snaky as it is?" Jumping to her feet, she stood over him. "I see what's happening here, Mr. Sheriff. Time for Sunrise to fuck over the Fletchers again, right? Somebody killed Danny Totton and you need a patsy to pin the blame on. Maurice is off somewhere and can't defend himself, so he gets the brass ring? I don't think so. Y'all got away with screwing me, but I'll be damned if I'll let you do it to my brother!"

Mr. Sheriff shifted in his chair. "What are you talking about, girl?"

"Don't play dumb with me. You and Mr. Euker and your badges, protectors of the law. Protectors, my ass! There are certain people in this town gets y'all's protection and Lord help the rest of us poor suckers. Not this time, Chief Sheriff! Not this time! Give me my stuff!" She snatched the postcards and photos from his lap, ran to the door, and stormed out. The dogs, barking with excitement, followed her.

"What the hell was that all about?" Mr. Sheriff asked. "Teddy Euker's been dead nine years. Fool fell off the roof of his barn and broke his neck."

His wife, who'd remained silent so far, went to the door and whistled for the dogs. "But Teddy stood in for you five or six summers while you took those courses. That was . . . what?. . . fourteen, fifteen years ago?"

"Has to be," I said. "I was still in high school and I remember Mr. Euker parking behind the billboard waiting for speeders." I stopped, probing my memory. "That's also about the time Maudine dropped out of school. The rumor was she was pregnant."

"By Teddy Euker?" Mr. Sheriff gaped at me.

"I never heard who the father was supposed to be. I do know that Maudine's very bitter about something. My first day here she said that Sunrise had several skeletons in its closet, and implied that there was some sort of corruption or cover-up going on."

"In *my* town? What the hell?"

"Well, she's right, isn't she?" Mrs. Sheriff said. "Or Web would be sitting at our dining room table playing Pitty-Pat with us." The dogs returned, so she sat down again and pulled some knitting from a cloth bag beside her chair. "If there was no cover-up, we wouldn't have the wrong name on that poor child's dental chart. So get down off your high horse, Nehemiah. The girl's right."

"Maudine knows something, Mr. Sheriff," I said. "Whether it's related to this is anybody's guess, but she's been harboring a grudge against Sunrise for a long time."

Mrs. Sheriff looked thoughtful. "Well, something certainly happened to her. She was so bright, as motivated as they came. Set up Totton's Tutors on her own initiative to help students who were having trouble, probably because of Maurice's problems. I was faculty adviser for the TTs the first two years, so I knew her pretty well."

I was stunned, since I'd been a member of the TTs myself. I hadn't realized that the group had been Maudine's idea. And didn't remember until this moment that the chief's wife had taught at Central.

"Her senior year," Mrs. Sheriff continued, "she was a different girl, surly, staying to herself, doing sloppy schoolwork. One day she got up and walked out of a class and didn't come back. Then she disappeared from town for a long time, so she may have been pregnant. Probably went somewhere to have her baby. Showed up again and worked at the mill for a while, then went back to Central, graduated, and moved away. Whatever happened to her over that summer really changed her. She hasn't been the same since."

"How far did Maurice get in school?" I asked, out of curiosity.

She looked embarrassed. "He made it to Central

and shouldn't have. He was so sweet and tried so hard, all his teachers at Sunrise Township bumped him to the next grade. If we'd had special education in this area, he might have survived. He finally gave up his first year there. Maurice went through practically every tutor in the club."

"And any one of them would be familiar with his writing," her husband said. "We need a list of everybody who worked with him. Maudine might remember. And Connie's got the questionnaires the reunion committee sent out. I'll put her to work checking to see who's got the kind of job where they travel a lot and could mail those postcards. We need to get those things back from Maudine," he added. "If that body is Maurice's, those postcards are evidence. I'd rather not do it, but I'll get a search warrant if I need to."

I got up. "Let me talk to her first. She could be a great help, if she'll cooperate."

The chief snorted. "If she's smart, she will. She's got to know she's a suspect, too. Considering how bad Danny treated her brother, she had the motive. I doubt she killed her twin, but if she knew he was dead, I wouldn't put it past her to cover it up, for her mother's sake. And she could have killed Doc."

"I don't believe that for a minute," Mrs. Sheriff said.

"I don't either now," I seconded her. "If she'd been sending the postcards and that letter, she wouldn't have asked me to try to find out which jail he was in."

Mr. Sheriff wasn't ready to dismiss the idea. "Maybe, maybe not. Let me know one way or t'other what she says. By the way, most of the boys at that Boys' Club meeting the night of the storm are in town this week, so I'll get on the phone with them, ask to see if anyone remembers anything that might help. They spent the night at the school, bunked in the gym. One of them might have seen Danny or Maurice leave. Why don't you stop by for breakfast and I'll bring you up to date."

"Assuming they remember anything," Mrs. Sheriff said. "I don't. Claire and Rachel Euker don't either. You're welcome to come in any case, Leigh Ann."

The Seventies had scheduled a brunch at eleven, but if I ate sparingly here, I could enjoy the midday meal, too. In the evening, there'd be a dance in S.T.'s gym. Both would include people who were in school with Danny Totton.

"Thanks. I'll be here. Let me fill you in on a couple of other things I found out today and then I'd better see if I can find Maudine." I passed along Mr. Taney's revelation about the hole in which Danny Totton's body had been found, and told him how I thought our perpetrator had been able to alter the dental chart.

"By God, I'd forgotten what that storm did to Main Street," the chief said. "I didn't get here until later that week."

"It looks as if the storm was an accomplice in all this," I pointed out. "It provided the hole the body was buried in and opened up Dr. Boothe's office. The fact that this guy was smart enough to take advantage of the circumstances says a lot. Maurice doesn't fit that profile. Besides, the car crashed sometime during the storm. Maurice was already dead when Mr. Taney's son removed the fallen tree. So the question becomes who hit Maurice and put him in that car?"

Mr. Sheriff shot me a pleased smile. "Smart thinking. It's a shame you're packing it in. You're good at this."

Thanks to Duck and the tidbits of experience he'd passed along to me over the years. "I just wish I had more time."

"Don't worry about it. You've given me one hell of a jump start and I'm grateful. Better get moving. Maudine's got long legs. She may be back to Main Street by now."

"Leigh Ann." Mrs. Sheriff rose and walked with me to the door. "Tell her that there are people who care about her. That child's not alone and I want her to know that."

I promised I would, but suspected Maudine wouldn't be interested. Whatever this town had done to her had left an open, festering wound, and Mrs. Sheriff's kind words were nowhere near strong enough to heal it.

The only reason I spotted her was that out of habit I glanced to my right as I pulled out of the Sheriffs' driveway. The orange fabric of her uniform against the lush green of the lawn and the white tombstones would have been hard to miss. The gates of Garden of Peace were open but, rather than driving in, I left the car on the shoulder of the road and walked in. Maudine sat, knees drawn up, head bent, at the base of the tallest grave marker, a rectangular column with a cherub atop it, by far the most ostentatious of the tombstones. Even without the engraving, I would have suspected it was Danny Totton's resting place—or was supposed to have been. A gaping hole was all that was left now.

I didn't hear her crying until I was almost on her. I topped, not certain whether I should intrude. These were sobs from deep in the gut, the sound of oss, loneliness, agony. It reminded me of the way he little blond girl had cried for Doc. Those wrenching sobs told me one thing for sure: Maudine new that what Mr. Sheriff had told her was true. Her brother was dead.

I stood for several minutes and waited until she appeared to be gearing down. Unsure what kind of eception I'd get, I approached slowly. She must ave heard me or perhaps sensed my presence; she looked up and stared at me, her eyes red, the lids swollen. Angry red splotches marked her cheeks where her fists had supported her head. Wordlessly, he averted her face.

"Mind if I sit?" I asked. She shrugged, and I lowred myself beside her. I'm not a handkerchief carier, but I did have a few Kleenexes, which I dug out nd placed in her hand. She nodded her thanks and pressed them against her eyes. I glanced around for he photos and postcards but didn't see them. If she'd ipped them up and tossed them, we were in trouble.

I spent several moments discarding a dozen inanies before giving up and expressing what I felt. Maudine, I'm sorry. If there'd been any way to prepare you beforehand, I would have, but I simply couldn't without spilling the beans altogether. It might have been kinder if I had, but I wanted Mr. Sheriff to see Maurice's pictures first, just in case hey didn't match the X rays on the dental chart. There's still a possibility we're wrong."

She shook her head. "No, you aren't. I had a feeling all along that something wasn't right. Maurice wouldn't have stayed away all this time without call-ing. He'd have phoned and wouldn't have bothered writing at all. His handwriting and spelling were awful; he never wrote anything unless he just had to. And the one and only time he did call, to tell us that he was in Colorado, he called home? Uh-uh. He'd know I wouldn't be there and that Mama's hearing was so bad she might not even catch who it was. It didn't make sense. Now it does."

"It wasn't Maurice."

"I know. It's so awful, Leigh Ann," she wailed. "My brother, my *twin*, is dead and all I can feel is relief because it means he didn't turn his back on me. He didn't abandon us for the Children of Hope." Another round of tears began and I slipped an arm around her. She must have needed the touch of another human because she turned and cried her heart out, her face buried against my shoulder.

This time it didn't take as long for her to recover. Wiping her eyes and nose, she leaned back against the tombstone, exhausted. "But he didn't kill any-body, Leigh Ann. My brother was no murderer and I'm not going to let them pin that on him."

"We don't think he did anything," I assured her, "except perhaps witness who killed Danny Totton."

"He was definitely murdered?"

"'Fraid so. Maurice did come back that night, Maudine. He was at the school, helping to decorate the float. If he saw what happened to Danny, he was in danger." I hesitated, but she had to know. "There's something Mr. Sheriff didn't get to tell you before you left, Maudine. Maurice was already dead when the MG went over. His injuries indicate that he was hit by a car beforehand, probably the MG."

"Oh, God. How can they be sure?"

"That's not my bailiwick. All I can tell you is what ᵗe medical examiner said to Mr. Sheriff. It may be a ᵗhile before they determine who died first, Maurice ᵗ Danny. If it was Danny, considering the condition ᶠ his skull, the murderer needed a reasonable ᵡplanation for his death and after the crash he had , a body that had gone off Old Post Road in Danny's ᵃr. Then he got rid of Danny's body, let everyone ᵗink that Maurice was Danny, and made it appear ᵗat Maurice was still alive somewhere."

"The bastard." Slowly she turned to look at me. "He ᵢlled Maurice, too. Oh, God." Her head dropped to ᵉr chest.

"The first hurdle is positive identification of ᴹaurice's body, which is why Mr. Sheriff needs the ᵗings I asked you to bring along. What do you say? ᵂill you let him have them back?"

She nodded and reached into the bodice of her ᵘniform. "Here."

"Thank you." I took them and slipped them into ᵐy bag. "There's something else you can do, if you ᵂill. You started Totton's Tutors, right?"

"My Service to Sunrise," she said, the acid back in ᵉr voice. "I was so sure I'd get one of those scholar-ᵗhips that I figured I'd be taking care of my STS ᵉarly. I could leave this hick town and never have to ᵒme back."

"The point is, whoever sent the postcards knew ᴹaurice's writing well enough to fake it. It may have ᵉen someone who tutored him."

She turned to look at me, her eyes boring into ᵐine. "You're right. But, Jesus, there were so many ᵒf them. I'll try to make a list, but it's been so long."

"Try anyway. And listen, Maudine. It's obvious something happened that soured you on Sunrise, something to do with Mr. Euker and the skeletons in the closet you mentioned last week. It's also obvious you think Mr. Sheriff knows what happened. You're wrong. He was floored by what you said. Do you want to talk about it? Does it have anything to do with all this?"

She shook her head once. "No. And it wouldn't do any good anyway. It's too late and it won't change anything." She stood up and brushed off her rear. "You mind taking me home? I'll get started on the list of tutors tonight. Come by the diner tomorrow morning and pick it up."

"You aren't going to the Seventies brunch?"

"No. That's for families. Maybe I'll drop by the dance tomorrow night. I haven't made up my mind yet."

I decided I'd give it one more try. "Maudine, don't you think it's time you let go of whatever's eating you? Mrs. Sheriff asked me to tell you that there are people in town who really care about you, that you aren't alone."

She stared at me. Without further comment, she skirted the open grave without looking down and headed toward the gate.

I stopped at the chief's house long enough to drop off the postcards and photos, then drove Maudine back to her sad little house.

As she got out, she nodded toward a twin of her house across the street, a small, squat four-room place, vacant now, the porch posts listing dangerously to starboard. It hadn't seen paint in years and the floor of the porch sagged like a spavined horse

"Who'd ever believe that's where Claire Rowland was brought up? An outhouse in the back and junked cars out front. There's a lot to be said for marrying well. If I sound jealous, I am. It got her out of Sunrise and I envy her that."

"Don't forget, she's back."

"And she can leave whenever the hell she feels like it. Leigh Ann, what am I gonna tell Mama?"

I advised her to keep quiet about everything until Maurice's body had been identified—correctly. "Leave her her illusions for another day or two."

"Yeah. Okay." Her shoulders sagged. "See you tomorrow." She started up the cracked sidewalk, then turned and came back. She stared at me for a full thirty seconds before saying, "Keep your eyes open at the brunch tomorrow. Let me know if you see anybody who looks familiar."

"Won't most of them? Half of them are my class-mates."

"Then take a look at the other half. See you." She waved and went on in.

I headed for home. It had been a long day. My head was buzzing with odd facts and annoying ques-tions, and the episode with Maudine had put me through an emotional wringer. All I wanted to do was fill Nunna's old-fashioned tub, soak until I looked like a prune, think about nothing, and feel nothing for a while. I parked on the shoulder in front of the house, too wrung out to wonder about the unfamiliar compact car I had to park behind. If Nunna had company, I hoped she wasn't laboring under the impression that I'd help her entertain. This was an evening for polite excuses. I had an appointment with a bottle of bubble bath.

I opened the screen door, stepped into the living room, and knew my plans for relaxing had just been trashed. Nunna had company, all right. Dillon Upshur Kennedy.

Funny thing about Duck. You don't notice him at first. He's a basic brother, an average-looking guy—average height and weight, medium brown complexion, black hair, brown eyes. He comes off as quiet and unassuming, so if he's in the company of someone more outgoing or a lot better looking, you may not even remember having met him. The next time—after he's reminded you of the first—you notice things you missed before, for instance, that his brows are smooth and sleek, a perfect frame for eyes the color and clarity of topaz, with long, curly lashes, his smile the kind that makes you smile as well. He emanates a warmth that puts you at ease immediately and draws you to him so quickly that you leave thinking of him as a friend you've had for a long time. He in turn is buddy to many but anyone he himself calls a friend is a lucky person. He takes friendships very seriously. The two of us went back a long way, pre-Mitch, in fact. In other words, there was no reason for me to be surprised to see him. I was anyway.

"Duck! What are you doing here?"

He sat on the sofa with Chester draped across his thighs like a ginger-colored lap robe. Gently, he moved him to an adjacent cushion, stood up, and crossed to me. He'd lost weight. "I've come to take you home."

"Excuse me?"

Nothing bugs me more about the guy than his

tendency to do things like that. Not "How about going back with me?" or "Are you ready to go back now?" Uh-uh. "I've come to take you home," as if I had no say about it. Big Brother has spoken. Drives me up the wall. Just as I was about to tell him that, he leaned over and kissed me.

Understand, this was a first, even though we'd been through a lot together. It was Duck who'd kept me from going off the deep end after Mitch, who'd been his best friend, was killed. I'd sat up with him many a night, drinking coffee by the gallon, just listening as he mourned his father's death, his younger sister's downward spiral into alcoholism, his problems with this case and that. He had camped out in my apartment during a particularly vicious bout I'd had with the flu, bringing me orange juice and soup, talking to me until I slept. I'd done the same for him after he'd caught it from me. We'd laughed together, bickered constantly, blown up at one another a time or two. But exchange a kiss? Uh-uh. It had never been that kind of relationship. So I was completely unprepared.

My first reaction, after my surprise, of course, was astonishment at how incredibly soft his lips were. And warm. And gentle. And how they seemed to encourage a response whether the kissee had intended one or not. Mind you, we aren't talking open-mawed, tongue-trysting, eat-you-alive kissing here, but it was still the most downright, capital-E erotic buss on the mouth I'd ever experienced. My erogenous zones went Zow-ee! That shocked me even more than the kiss and brought me to my senses with a snap. I had to get things back on a more comfortable basis pdq.

I stepped away from the embrace just as Nunna swept in from the kitchen with a tray. On it, a pot of coffee, two cups, and a slab of chocolate cake. It was freshly made; the house smelled of baking. Her entry gave me time enough to regain my composure.

She beamed at me. "Hi, baby. Look who's here. Wasn't it nice of him to come check on you? We've been having the nicest chat."

I peered at her with suspicion. Two nice's back-to-back? Her good china? Her best silver coffee service? Duck had done it again. Nunna was his.

"Warren, this lady's cooking puts my mother's to shame," he said, moving toward her. "I asked her to marry me, but she says she's taken."

"This child can sure talk trash. Sit down, honey," Nunna said to him, refusing his offer to relieve her of the tray. She placed it on the coffee table. "Leigh Ann can pour for you. You're sure about the ice cream? All I've got to do is dish it up. French Vanilla, just the thing to go with this cake."

He smiled at her. "No, thanks. After your delicious lamb chops, I barely have room for this. But I'll manage."

Lamb chops. Granted, Nunna needed no excuse to open her refrigerator; she'd feed a busload of tourists if they simply stopped in to ask directions. But she cooked lamb chops with mint jelly for only a favorite few, usually someone she'd known for years. And Duck couldn't have been here all that long.

"Is there any left? Lamb chops, I mean." I wasn't even hungry, not for food, anyway, and it was, again, a childish reaction: jealousy. She hadn't seen me for years and hadn't fed me lamb chops yet.

"Of course, baby. They'll be ready whenever you want to eat." In spite of what she'd said about my serving the coffee, she poured a cup for him herself, pushed the plate of cake toward him, and stood back, arms crossed, waiting.

He took the hint, sat down again, and picked up the fork. Almost delicately, he cut off a corner, ate it, and, with eyes closed, did a creditable impression of Chester, in that he damned near purred. If he'd had whiskers, he'd have licked them clean. "Delicious. No wonder you've put on a pound or two, babe. This lady could cook for God."

A pound or two. I spluttered, too steamed to be articulate.

Having won the expected accolades, Nunna nodded. "Well, then. I'd better get to work on next week's Bible lessons for the kiddies. Leigh Ann, how'd it go today? Has the body been positively identified yet?"

I wasn't sure which body she meant and also wasn't anxious to talk about my current activities in front of Duck, at least not yet. Since he didn't react with surprise, I surmised she'd already told him everything.

"They probably will be by tomorrow," I said, covering both bases, and bodies. "The one found in the car was almost certainly Maurice Fletcher."

"Maurice? Mrs. Fletcher's boy? This will kill her. And poor Maudine. Let me go fix something to take over to them. Another cake perhaps, since I've got to drop one off for Geneva Webster." She glanced from Duck to me. "Are you two going to fight?"

"Yes, ma'am," we said, in chorus.

"I thought so. Just keep it down. Don't want the

neighbors calling Mr. Sheriff to complain about the noise. Leigh Ann, let me know when you're ready to eat. And you, Dillon, finish every crumb of that cake or you'll hear from me."

"I will, Scout's honor." Standing again, he pecked her on the cheek. Another pang of jealousy pierced the armor I was constructing for the wars to come. Nunna smiled, pleased, glanced at me, and left.

"That," I said, as soon as she was out of earshot, "was as disgusting a performance as I've ever seen. Jesus, Duck, how could you take advantage of an old lady like that?"

"I did no such thing. Why didn't you tell me about finding the body? For that matter, why didn't you return my calls? The least I deserve is common courtesy."

He deserved a damned sight more than that, but I wasn't about to tell him so. "How's the chest?" I asked, sitting down in the rocker and pouring myself the other cup.

"Fine. I'm not here to talk about me. What's this bullshit about you quitting when you get back?"

I sighed. Nunna must have talked her head off. He has that effect on people. "It's not bullshit, Duck. I've had it. Burnt out. Nothing left to give to the job—nothing good anyhow. Didn't you hear about me and the disorderly conduct I brought in the day before I took off?"

He nodded. "I know him. The guy's an asshole with an attitude. He probably deserved whatever you gave him."

"No, he didn't," I corrected him. "He was just drunk and raising hell. The way I reacted, you'd have thought he'd beaten someone to death, which is what I was about to do to him. I don't want to be one of those cops brought up on charges of police brutality, Duck. It's time to go play elsewhere."

"Couldn't you have talked it out with me?" he asked quietly. "Okay, I agree you overreacted. But all you have to do is continue counseling, get it out of your system. That's what post-shooting therapy is for, to help you get rid of all the garbage."

I really didn't want the coffee. I pushed it away and decided to let him hear a bit more of the truth. "Duck, I let you down. I can't forgive myself for that."

He gawked at me, incredulity written all over his face. "Let me down? How? You weren't even there."

"Exactly! I could have, should have gone with you."

"It wouldn't have changed a damned thing, might have made things even worse, with two of us. It was stupid of me to come up behind the kid the way I did. I was careless and paid for it."

"How is he? The kid?"

"Fine. He'll be in physical therapy for a while, but that's better than being in a coffin. He's also wallowing in just as much guilt for shooting you as you probably are for shooting him. His parents don't blame you, by the way. They're just thankful you didn't kill him."

I decided to keep my mouth shut, since I hadn't gotten around to telling Duck that had it not been for the pain in my head when I aimed at the kid, he'd be six feet under right now.

"Let's cut to the chase," Duck said, sitting back and stretching. "Your problem is you're running, but not from the job. You're running from me."

"You?"

"Uh-huh. Isn't it about time you admitted you're in love with me so we can get on with things?"

This was my night for spluttering, which I did—again. He'd hit too close to home. Until the shooting, I'd kept Duck locked in a niche labeled Big Brother, even though he was two years younger. No other relationship with him was feasible. I didn't date fellow officers. It simply added stress to an already stressful situation. Besides, after Mitch, I'd decided it was too risky to lose my heart to a man in danger of losing his life every day. No matter what I did from now on, Duck was a cop and always would be. He loved it. So whatever my future held, it would not include Dillon Upshur Kennedy. It was time to lie and burst his bubble.

"Duck, listen to me, okay? I love you, yes, but I'm not in love with you. Honest."

"Sure you are. Now that I've brought it to your attention, you'll realize I'm right. If you don't mind, I'd appreciate it if you'd get around to admitting it fairly soon. I'm tired of waiting, babe. Sure, I dig older women, but you're dangerously close to my cutoff point, age-wise. And your biological clock is ticking louder than Big Ben."

His intent was to rile me. This was the familiar pattern and I reacted as I invariably did. I lost it. "You arrogant, egotistical son of a bitch! I wouldn't have you on a silver plate. A card-carrying tomcat like you, who's bedded every D.C. Metropolitan Police employee in a skirt, civilian or uniform? Not on your life! Your problem is you haven't been able to add me to that list. I'm ruining your record. Sorry, buddy. In love with you? Not on your life, thank you. So cut the bullshit."

"It's not bullshit," he said calmly. "And my reputation for conquests is vastly overrated. All told, there've been three, okay? You may not be in love with me—which by the way, I don't believe—but I am crazy over you. I've been waiting for you since Mitch died. Since before he died, actually. He knew it."

My mouth dropped open. "What?"

"I met you first, remember? He was my best friend, so when you fell for him instead of me, I stepped into the background. But he died knowing that he didn't have to worry about you because I was waiting in the wings. And when I woke up in the hospital a couple of months ago, I realized it was time to stop playing second fiddle to a ghost. I'm here to state my intentions. I lost you to Mitch for a while. I could have lost you for good in that hallway. This black man wants you to know he ain't losin' you again, babe. Life's too damned short."

I was flabbergasted. I had no idea he'd been carrying a torch all these years. And his resolve about the two of us scared me silly. Duck had more than a trace of pit bull in his blood, and I had neither the emotional energy nor the physical stamina to handle him at the moment. I retreated, as usual.

"I'm beat, Duck, so let's drop it. I'm not changing my mind about quitting. I've had it with fighting crime. We fought and I lost."

"Which, of course, is why you're doing what you are now, right?" He chuckled. "Jesus, you are so full of it. Okay, we'll talk about us later. And we will talk about us. So tell me about your case. There aren't enough bodies in D.C.? You've got to come down here and dig up more?"

It would be a relief to change the subject. Besides,

he'd make a good sounding board. Since he wasn't involved, he might see something we were missing. "How much time do you have?" I asked.

"I told you I'm here to take you home. If you insist on staying until Sunday, that's how much time I have. Miss Nunna says I'm welcome. Face it, babe, I'm not going away. So start at the beginning."

I gave in for the time being. Duck's head is so hard it should be added to the chart of elements. But I had to admit it would be damned comforting to have him around. In fact, almost like old times.

11

"*Right pleased to* meet you, Mr. Kennedy," the chief said. He met us at the door on crutches and appeared to be pretty adept with them.

I still hadn't figured out how Duck had talked me into bringing him along. It didn't really matter; he would be heading north once we left the Sheriffs'. It had taken a lot of wheeling, but he'd agreed to leave and give me some space.

"Call me Duck, sir," he said with a special warmth he reserved for members of the brotherhood. "I hope you don't mind me crashing your breakfast like this."

"Not at all. We're used to feeding extras. Roscoe! Josh! Come meet Leigh Ann's friend, Duck." The morning routine must have allowed for one and only one call to the table. The younger Sheriffs sounded like a herd of bison coming down the steps, their expressions curious, expectant. "He works undercover on the Washington, D.C., police force," the chief elaborated.

Swear to God, from the reverence with which they greeted him you'd have thought Duck was a member of the F.B.I. or the Secret Service. I noticed they didn't call him Mr. Duck, yet I was still Miss Leigh Ann. Maybe they were just being polite instead of being respectful to their elders. Somehow it made me feel better.

The meal was incredible. The last time I'd seen that much food was at a Redskins' Boosters breakfast. Even Duck, who can eat his weight just snacking during a break, gawked at the spread. Evidently it was daily fare here; the Sheriff boys showed no surprise at seeing steak, ham, scrapple, hotcakes, eggs, and biscuits on the table.

Eating, however, was not to be the sole activity on the menu this morning. After the blessing had been said and the plates loaded, the chief wasted no time. "You've talked to Duck about the case?" he asked. Duck nodded, his mouth already full. "Good. Don't want him to feel left out. What do you think?"

Duck swallowed. "That somebody got away with murder and if it hadn't been for the proposed mall, your perpetrator would still be thinking his luck was holding."

"Damn right. That blasted mall's been a pain in the butt from the day Claire Rowland brought it up, but we never thought it would cause this kind of trouble. Now. I called to talk to the club members who worked on the float that night, Leigh Ann. The two youngest Euker boys, Cecil and Andy, are the only ones that made it back for Reunion Week. 'Course Teddy Junior's already here. Seems that the other seven

RSVP'd they were coming, then called their folks at the last minute and said they couldn't make it. Anyhow, about that night. Josh and Andy Euker— he's the baby boy—were awake with bellyaches from all the junk they'd eaten. They saw Totton leave the gym, and assumed he was going to the rest room."

"What about Maurice?" I asked.

"He left right after," Roscoe responded. "Josh and I got to talking about it last night and put it together. See, all I remembered was how rotten Danny had been treating Maurice, but Josh knew why. Tell 'em, Josh."

The older brother took a moment to bite into a slab of ham. "The thing is, the bus Maurice was supposed to take never came. He stood out there for hours, then gave up and walked back. He needed a ride to Asheville and he came to the gym to ask Danny to take him."

A perfectly simple explanation that hadn't occurred to any of us. "Danny told him no?" I asked.

"He told him he'd take him when we finished the float. That's why Maurice had to put up with all the crap Danny was handing out. He needed the ride. So when they left, I figured they were on their way to Asheville. I told Mr. Euker that."

"Then why wasn't it in the report I read?" I asked.

The chief looked down the table at me. "A good question. All he put in the report was the time they bedded down in the gym and the fact that Totton was still there at that point in time. Nary a word about Maurice even being there. I got me a feeling."

"Uh-oh." Roscoe grinned. "When Daddy's got a feeling, somebody's in trouble. Who is it this time, Daddy?"

Mr. Sheriff slathered butter between his hotcakes. "Teddy Euker, Jr., for one. He was awfully cagey on the phone last night. Wanted to know why I wanted to know. Damn near pleaded the Fifth and I hadn't accused him of anything."

"I never particularly cared for him," Mrs. Sheriff said, pouring coffee all around. "There's something sly about him."

"Dora's a good judge of character. Anyhow," her husband continued, "then I talked to Cecil Euker, the middle boy. Sounded so nervous I bet he had to change his skivvies when he got off the phone with me."

"Nehemiah!" Mrs. Sheriff exclaimed.

"I know it was a long time ago, but Cecil couldn't seem to remember anything, who-all was there, what y'all were doing, the fact that you spent the night in the gym. All three of those boys are hiding something."

"It's a shame Duck can't talk to them," I said without thinking, then chomped down on my tongue. I'd spent a good part of the previous evening convincing him to leave and I'd just given him all the excuse he needed to stay.

"You good at this kind of thing?" the chief asked.

"Sort of." Duck reached for a biscuit the size of a dessert plate. "People seem to tell me things. I don't know why."

Mr. Sheriff looked to me for confirmation.

"It's the truth," I said, grudgingly. "All he does is talk, doesn't even ask questions. I guess they relax. Sooner or later they slip. He points it out to them and, before long, he's got the whole story."

"Well." The chief fingered his mustache. "Since you'd already planned to keep your ears open during

he brunch and party tonight, Leigh Ann, it would
e the most natural thing in the world to take Duck
long with you. Teddy Junior'll be there. Between
he two of you, maybe you'd come up with some-
hing for me to work with after you're gone."

What could I say? Especially with my foot in my
nouth. Duck glanced at me sidewise, a note of tri-
mph in his eyes. All I could do was glare back. He'd
von this round. Shit.

Vhat with all the running I'd done the day before,
'd forgotten I had nothing to wear to the Thursday
vents. My suitcase was crammed with shorts, hal-
ers, jeans, and T-shirts, de rigueur at the beach but
tterly useless for a dressy occasion. I'd forgotten
ow creative Nunna could be. She went foraging in
er trunks. For the brunch she paired a silky peas-
nt blouse with a flowered silk skirt that must have
ontained a good three yards of fabric. The second
utfit was a royal blue ankle-length dashiki, hand-
mbroidered with gold thread in an intricate pat-
ern around the neck, hem, and full, flowing sleeves.
here was nothing I could do about shoes; my white
hong sandals would have to do. Fortunately, they
vere relatively new and I hadn't worn them on the
each.

I'd been hoping that since Duck had shown up in
hort sleeves and khaki slacks, carrying a duffle bag,
e wouldn't be prepared to attend the reunion activ-
ies either. No such luck. He'd packed a summer-
veight suit, just in case, he told me with a grin. It
vas by no means formal attire, but the brunch and
he dance wouldn't be formal occasions. He'd fit in

fine. In fact, he looked terrific. I gritted my teet
and admitted to another defeat.

I hadn't been all that enthusiastic about this whol
reunion business to begin with, but I'd particularl
dreaded the prospect of the brunch. From my ga
sessions with Sheryl the week before, I knew tha
almost all the friends in our circle were now marrie
and planned to drag husbands and kids to this even
to show them off. Since I had thought I'd be alone,
hadn't been looking forward to the inevitable ques
tions in all their variations: why wasn't I married
when would I be tying the knot; did I really prefer
career to wifehood and motherhood.

Having Duck with me solved one problem: I ha
an escort. Otherwise it made no difference at all;
got the questions anyway. And Duck, the slimy dog
responded, whenever the questions were aske
within his hearing, with a shit-eating grin and th
words, "Whenever she's ready, so am I. Don't kno
what the hell she's waiting for." I could have kille
him. In spite of the annoyance he presented, how
ever, the picture-taking session for the Reunio
Album, and the dreaded receiving line so Mr.
Totton could say hello to everyone, I found, to m
disgust, that I was thoroughly enjoying myself.

It was a real treat to run into friends I hadn't see
since graduation. Only a few had changed beyon
recognition—fortunately, for the better. Tedd
Euker, Junior was one of them. He'd been a clone o
his father when I'd known him—thirty pounds over
weight with sideburns down to his mouth and jean
down to his hipbones. He was now slim and trim, h
hair conservatively cut. Whatever he was doin
these days, he was definitely Establishment.

Sheryl, herding her husband and kids to a table some distance away, shot me a tentative smile. Bearing no grudges, I smiled, waved back, and could sense her relief all the way from the other side of the cafeteria.

I realized as soon as I saw the setup that my original plan to circulate, eavesdrop, even prime the pump with idle comments about Danny/Maurice/Doc, if necessary, would not work. This was a sit-down brunch, eight to a table, seats assigned. The place card next to mine read Dillon U. Kennedy. Nunna's doing, I suspected. The other names were completely unfamiliar. Duck and I would be stuck with strangers from an earlier Seventies class and their kids until the meal was over and the speeches made. Mrs. Totton, Claire and Charles Rowland, and several members of the Sundler family, who owned the mill, occupied a table on a platform, so the speeches were a given.

All things considered, it wasn't bad. The food wasn't either, although I could only pretend to eat; I was still stuffed from the Sheriffs' breakfast. Duck dug in as if he hadn't eaten this month.

The speeches, too, weren't bad, primarily because they were short. Mrs. Totton welcomed "her children," and made only a veiled reference to the topic on everyone's mind, the mystery surrounding her son's death. Our presence, she claimed, had made a very difficult week easier to bear. No one, it appeared, knew quite how to respond. There was a low murmur, then scattered applause.

One of the Sundlers offered a summary of what had happened in the years since we'd left the school, which amounted to not much. Then Claire rose and made a welcome speech, since she'd taught many of us during her tenure at Sunrise Township. There followed a blatant commercial for the mall from her husband, complete with chalkboard-sized illustrations. I still couldn't remember where I'd seen a shopping center like it and didn't realize I was frowning with concentration until Duck leaned over and whispered, "What?" in my ear.

I shook my head. "Nothing."

"Secrets, m'love?" he asked, his tone brimming with seductive suggestion. I rolled my eyes at him and kicked him under the table.

Once the speeches were over, it was milling-around and powder-the-nose time. I didn't move fast enough. The line outside the rest room door ran half the length of the cafeteria.

"I'm going to join the parade," I told Duck. "Be right back." I hurried to get in line before it got any longer. After the juice and coffee at the Sheriffs and the second cup at the brunch, however, waiting, for me, was out of the question. I remembered clearly where the girls' rooms were; I'd been a hall monitor outside the one on the second floor for the whole of the fifth grade. Leaving the line, I prayed the door to the corridor was unlocked, thanked God when it was, and slipped out of the cafeteria. Two other desperate souls had had the same idea; they walked toward the rest room at the end of the hall, their heels clicking against the worn hardwood floors. I didn't know them; one was a tallish redhead, the other a pear-shaped hippy blonde.

"All that worrying for nothing," the blonde said. "I told you she wouldn't come."

Her companion tugged at the hem of her bolero

acket. "I almost wish she had. I'd really like her to meet David, just so she'd know that—" The end of her sentence was lost in the chatter of other voices as they entered the bathroom. This one sounded full, too.

I sprinted toward the stairs and ran up to the second floor, fingers crossed that I'd find at least one unoccupied stall. The corridor was empty and permeated with an air of desolation. I tried a couple of classroom doors as I passed. They were locked, which was just as well. I didn't have time to go browsing.

The girls' room was empty and dim thanks to its frosted windows. I hit the light switch first, the door of the nearest stall next. Much relieved a minute later, I had pulled up the under layer, and was pulling down the outer one when the lights went out. Puzzled, I swore, flushed, flipped back the bolt of the door, and pushed. It didn't open. I slammed a hand against it. It wouldn't budge. It wasn't until the toilet had completed flushing that I heard the sound of breathing on the other side of the door. I froze.

"Listen, bitch," a voice whispered huskily. "This is your last warning. Keep meddling in ancient history and that's precisely what you'll be. History!"

Heart rapping, I dropped to my knees to look under the door and caught a glimpse of dark slacks and the sole of a black shoe as it darted out into the hall. I pushed at the door again. It opened wide, hitting the adjacent stall. It was no more than a second before I yanked open the bathroom door and, back against the wall, peeked out into the corridor. Empty. Silent. Either the whisperer had zipped down the steps or had ducked into an unlocked classroom.

I moved to the stairwell and looked over the railing. Nothing. I had to make a choice: check the nearest classrooms for the bastard or take my fanny back downstairs where there'd be safety in numbers. I opted for the latter. Nunnally Layton had not raised a fool.

In the cafeteria, Duck was not where I'd left him. The place was still swarming and it took me a few minutes to locate him because Sheryl had shanghaied him. Once I knew where he was, I stood out of the way and took a good look at the crowd. There was no hope of recognizing the whisperer; half the males in the place wore dark slacks and shoes. I began edging my way toward Duck, engaged in animated conversation with Jimmy, Sheryl's son.

"There you are." An arm slipped around my waist and I turned to find myself in Claire Rowland's embrace. She was in white today, chiffon, I thought, with white patent leather purse and the same sexy ankle straps she'd worn last Sunday. Her husband, moving to her side, smiled at me with the lower half of his face. His eyes were remote, as if his thoughts were elsewhere. "You look terrific," Claire said. "I love that skirt. Are you enjoying yourself?"

I allowed as how I was. "How's Mrs. Totton holding up? She looks okay, but looks can be deceiving."

"She's fine. How are things going? She asked me to check, since it doesn't look as if she'll get to talk to you privately."

I hesitated. "It would be best if she gives the chief a call. He'll fill her in. Just tell her things are moving fairly rapidly."

"What things?" Claire asked. "The identification of Danny's body? The other one? What?"

"Sweetheart." Charles, tuning in, touched her arm. "You weren't listening. It's Mr. Sheriff's responsibility to release that kind of information. You're putting Miss Warren in an awkward position asking things she can't tell you."

Claire pulled in a deep breath. "I'm sorry, Leigh Ann. It's just that it's so important to Estelle. She's suffered so much already. I want to see this over with for her."

"From what little Miss Warren's said, it looks like that may happen sooner rather than later." Charles wrapped an arm around her shoulder and Claire seemed surprised, as if public displays of affection from him were unusual. "Be patient," he admonished her. "This too shall pass, remember? Then we can get on with what we came here to do, build the mall and revive this little town. What did you think of the presentation?" he asked me.

"It was very well done. The people at my table were certainly impressed. By the way, have you used a similar design on another shopping mall somewhere? It reminds me of one I've seen, but I can't place it."

"Oh, no." He dropped his arm, his eyes coming alive. "This is the first venture of this sort Waverly has attempted. We're trying to branch out. The next time you visit Estelle, have Claire show you the firm's portfolio. Up to now, all we've specialized in are custom-designed homes, a church or two, but mostly motels. Not that we aren't proud of those, too. But this is a test case, so it's important to us that it succeeds."

"Did you tell Miss Nunna about the space in Garden of Peace?" Claire asked, lowering her voice.

"No. I decided it might be better if she heard it from you. It'll be your surprise."

Charles smiled, which did wonders for his long, solemn face. "Thank you. We really do want everyone to realize that we understand their objections and we'll do everything we can to accommodate them. We should circulate now, Claire, gain a few more allies."

"Of course." She squeezed my hand. "You'll be here this evening? See you then." They moved away, Charles glad-handing the first person he met.

I checked for Duck again. He and Jim, Sheryl's husband, were now chatting with one of the Broadwater boys, whose name I couldn't remember. Sheryl and the kids were nowhere in sight, so I started toward Duck, squeezing past the redhead I'd seen out in the hall. With one hand she held firmly to the coattail of a teenage boy and with the other tried to catch the attention of someone on the far side of the cafeteria.

"Come on, Mom," the boy said. "Let me go get him."

"And have you disappear again, too? Can't turn my back on either one of you for a second. I'll give him one more minute to get his point across and then I'm interrupting."

"Geez," the kid whined. He turned in my direction and I saw him head-on. Probably shorter than he'd like to be, and stocky, he was dark, his hair thick with unruly curls that brushed the collar of his white shirt. He looked familiar. "Hey, Mom, there's Jennifer," he said and, waving at someone behind me, smiled. I did a double take that almost gave me whiplash. He had Danny Totton's intensely blue

eyes, Maudine's chiseled features, and Maurice
Fletcher's baby-sweet smile.

I stopped where I stood, too shocked to move.
This had to be the person Maudine had hinted I
should look for. Pulling a two from this place and a
two from that, I did some fast addition and came up
with a very interesting four. Mommy: Maudine.
Daddy: Danny Totton. The age was about right, thirteen, fourteen tops, which would jibe with the time
Maudine left Central High. I began concocting sce-
narios. Maudine, pregnant with Danny Totton's
baby, had to present a genuinely sticky position for
him. She was a bright student with a lot of potential,
but she was also the daughter of the town drunk, a
member of a family the eastsiders considered an
embarrassment, a family with a son whose mental
development had stopped in the fourth grade. Lord
knows Mrs. Totton would have had a different class
of young woman in mind for the mother of her
grandchildren.

Maudine had said flat out that she'd detested
Danny Totton. Had he ditched her? Denied it was
his child? That may have been motive enough to kill
him. But if that was the case, why'd she wait two
years to do it? It was time for Maudine and me to sit
down and have a long heart-to-heart.

I started toward Duck, who saw me coming and
excused himself to meet me halfway. "Hey, babe," he
said in greeting. He nudged me toward the door.
"What can you tell me about that Broadwater character?"

His first name popped into my head. "Tommy?
He was in the class behind mine, just another neighborhood kid. Seemed nice enough. Why?"

He steered me outdoors and around to the playground away from the crowd. "Jim and Broadwater and I were shooting the breeze, talking about baseball, sports in general. Broadwater's a staff photographer for *Sports Today,* that new magazine. Anyhow, Jim—nice guy, by the way—said something about you helping Nehemiah, and asked how things were going. Broadwater just got into town this morning and didn't know what Jim was talking about. I let Jim explain, since I couldn't be sure how much was common knowledge."

"What did he say?" I asked, curious as to what Sheryl might have told him.

"He just gave him the bare bones, no pun intended, explained about the body you found and likelihood that it was the Totton boy. Broadwater sorta gulped and said that wasn't possible, the accident, etc., etc. Then Jim told him about the X ray of Totton's leg, and said he was probably murdered. Broadwater almost had a stroke. He babbled something about having to be someplace and hit the door running."

It didn't make sense. Tommy would have been around nineteen that summer. I couldn't recall the members of his crowd, but it certainly wouldn't have included Danny Totton. Why should he freak over this? I voiced my thoughts to Duck, who crammed his fists into his pants pockets, which meant he was doing some mulling of his own. He jingled his keys for a couple of minutes, another thing he does that drives me up a wall. Just as I was about to deck him, he stopped.

"Any possibility that Broadwater was a member of the Boys' Club?" he asked.

"What boy wasn't? But not when Danny was killed." I explained the age limit. "He'd have still been going the year before, though. Danny was leader then, too. That's three club members whose reactions have been really weird—the Eukers and Tommy."

"And the others ducked out of the reunion at the last minute," Duck continued my train of thought. "Wonder if those guys were up to something fishy and now that you and Nehemiah are digging into what happened to Totton, they're running scared."

Which might account for the scare someone tried to throw into me in the girls' room. I described what had happened upstairs, along with the adventure with the pickup the day before.

Duck's eyes became a smoky topaz, which meant he was a very angry man. "I don't play that," he said softly. "Nobody messes with my stuff."

It was a second before that registered. My temperature shot through the roof. "Your *what*?"

"Leigh Ann!" I turned and saw Nunna marching a group of kindergartners onto the playground—recess time at Bible School. Those little kids were the only thing that saved Dillon Upshur Kennedy. His stuff, indeed!

One of the urchins broke ranks and Nunna grabbed him by the back of his shirt. "Here, baby," she said, waving an envelope at me. "Somebody slipped this under the door for you. How was the brunch?"

"Delicious," Duck responded. He trotted to her side and relieved her of her captive, tucking the kid under one arm. "Where do you want this?" he asked her.

"How about the state penitentiary? Put him on the swings. All right, little people," she called to the others. "Enjoy yourselves. You've got half an hour." They exploded from the line like shrapnel, spraying in all directions.

I evaded them by heading for the fence, with the plain, white envelope addressed to "Lee Ann." Somebody didn't know how to spell my name. Holding it up against the sun revealed something square, perhaps three by three and stiff, like cardboard. Using a door key as a letter opener, I slit it along the short side and let the contents slide out into my hand. It landed facedown, a Polaroid snapshot mounted on cardboard backing. I turned my hand over, letting the photo fall right side up on the envelope. It was a snapshot of Sheryl, nude, standing under a shower, her face lifted as if to welcome the spray. One hand plucked at her long ponytail, which had fallen forward and lay plastered across her right temple.

Wondering who had sent it, I stared at it, uneasy at seeing my friend unclothed. She'd always been very modest about undressing around others. That feeling lasted all of a second. The familiarity of the pose was like a kick in the back of the head. It was a dead ringer for the poses in several of Danny Totton's nudes. Evidently he had used live models by photographing them, then painting from the photo.

So Sheryl had posed for Danny Totton. Despite the evidence in my hand, I couldn't believe it. Even if she'd done it willingly, it still wasn't the kind of thing she'd have wanted known. To give him credit, he'd done a masterful job of masking her identity. I hadn't recognized her as one of his models. The fact remained that if she'd been comfortable enough with Danny to allow him to photograph her in the buff, she knew him a damned sight better than she'd let on. Damn it, she owed me an explanation.

I slid the thing back into the envelope wondering who had sent it just as Duck deserted the kid whose swing he'd been pushing. "What'd you get?" he asked, approaching with a swagger. Seeing my face, he sobered. "What's wrong, babe?"

I'd shown him the photos I'd taken at Mrs. Totton's, and I would eventually let him see this one, but not yet, not until I'd talked to Sheryl. Perhaps it was misplaced loyalty, but I felt I owed it to her. "Remember the time you thought you had evidence that Leo was on the take and you sat on it until you'd confronted him with it?"

"Yeah. So?"

"This may provide a motive, but it's something I have to check out with the subject on a personal basis first. Once I've done that, I'll show it to you and, if I have to, give it to Mr. Sheriff. Okay?"

"Any possibility the subject will cut out on us?"

"None."

Reaching over, he stroked my chin. "Then do what you have to do. I trust your judgment and this is your case, babe."

Something snapped. "I wish to hell you'd stop calling me that!"

He looked startled. "What?"

"Babe. I'm not Paul Bunyan's blue ox and I don't like the way it sounds."

He gazed at me in silence for a moment, then nodded. "Okay, Leigh. But do you know why I've always called you that? Because you were such an innocent when I met you."

"Me? Innocent?"

"Small-town girl, wide-eyed, trusting, a real babe in arms. That's always been the thought behind the name. You've never heard me call you or any other woman baby. 'Babe' was just for you, a term of affection. If it offends you, I apologize. You'll never hear it again."

He was right. I'd never heard him call any of my female coworkers baby or honey and the like when addressing them. Even in the locker room, where denigrating terms for women were common, I could not remember Duck using any of them. I'd misjudged his intent. I was also pretty sure I had hurt him. Before I could figure out what to say, he changed the subject.

"How far is it to the Sheriffs' place, about a mile?" he asked. "I'm going to walk back to talk to Josh and Roscoe. They're as straight-arrow as they come, and if that Boys' Club was up to something, I doubt they were in on it if only because of who their father was. But maybe they'll remember something that didn't seem fishy to them back then."

"It's worth a try," I said, trying to drum up enthusiasm I didn't feel. "Take the Chevy. I'll walk home. See you later."

He nodded and left, after one long, searching look. He was worried, but there was nothing I could do about it. I gave him time enough to get back to the car before I went looking for Sheryl.

Jim was still in the cafeteria in a heated conversation with someone I didn't recognize. Easing up beside him, I touched his elbow. "Excuse me a minute. Where's Sheryl?"

He blinked, shifting gears. "Uh, on her way back

to the house with the kids. Jillie has this thing about using public toilets."

"Okay. Thanks. Go back to your argument."

He did just that and I left, wishing I weren't too dressed up to hop the fence and cut through the cemetery. By the time I'd made it around to Sunset and the end of the block, there was no sign of them. I crossed the street and knocked at the door of the Anderson house.

Sheryl answered, eyes widening with pleasure. "Hi! Come on in."

"I'd better not. Sheryl, I need to talk to you privately. Can you come over to Nunna's for a minute?"

Her smile disappeared. "I haven't changed my mind, Leigh Ann. If that's what you want to talk about, I won't be going anywhere."

I debated how to handle this. Sheryl could out-stubborn a mule. I had to get her alone. "Come out here and close the door," I said softly.

It wasn't what she'd expected. Curious now, she glanced back, checking for the kids, then stepped outside. "Okay, what?"

I decided there was no point in pussyfooting around. I removed the photo and held it up. "Want to tell me about this?"

Her mouth opened, her eyes widening to twice their normal size. Her skin, a rich, dark chocolate took on a gray cast, like a Hershey bar left in a refrigerator too long. "Oh, my God!" she whispered. Then she fell apart.

12

"*Oh, God. Oh, God.*" Sheryl clutched her stomach and bent over double. I caught her as she sank toward the porch floor.

"Hey!" I said, putting ice in my voice to get her attention. "Your kids are inside. Do you want them to see you like this?" She straightened up, breathing deeply, and dropped her arms to her sides. "That's better. Now, Nunna's?" I asked.

The response was a bob of her head. Draping an arm around her shoulder, I walked her across the street and into the house. She collapsed in the recliner, knees to her chin in a fetal position. I removed her shoes and placed them to one side. Something about them set off a ping-ping-ping in my head, but there wasn't time to concentrate on it. I'd expected her to be embarrassed or perhaps defiant, insisting that she'd done nothing to be ashamed of. This reaction seemed a bit extreme. After all, the photograph wasn't exactly pornographic.

"I'm sorry, Sheryl. I hated to do that to you, but I had to. Come on, now. Get it together. We've got to talk before Duck gets back."

She lifted her head, her eyes red and puffy. "Where'd you get it?"

"Someone slipped it under the door. I don't know who."

She groaned. "Oh, Lord. There may be copies of it all over town. What'll I tell Jim?"

"I can't help you with that, but this is the original, if that makes you feel any better. And I'm the only one who's seen it so far. What I do with it depends on what you tell me. Come on, Sher. I don't know how much time we have."

She turned around in the chair. "It was awful, Leigh Ann. I've never told anyone."

Awful? "I don't understand."

"It happened in '81, the weekend after you left for Howard our sophomore year. I was supposed to leave for N.C. State the following Tuesday. Mom was late washing the linen for the altar—it was her turn—so I starched and ironed it. By the time I finished and took it over to New Bethel for her it was dark. I fixed up the altar and left by the back door like always. Somebody socked me, knocked me cold, Leigh Ann. When I came to, I was in the trunk of a car with this bag over my head, and my hands and feet were tied and I'd been gagged."

"What?" I glanced at the photo again, completely baffled.

"He drove for what felt like hours. Then he finally stopped and got me out of the trunk, carrying me like a sack of potatoes. God, I was so scared." She shuddered, remembering.

The tale she was spinning seemed to have little to do with the photo. "Any clue where you were?"

"Uh-uh. He carried me inside a building—I could hear him unlocking doors. I wiggled and kicked but nothing I did seemed to make any difference. He was so strong! He went up some stairs, then down, up and down several times. Then he walked a long way, unlocked another door, carried me in, locked it behind him, and dumped me. Just dropped me on something padded."

"What had he said?" I asked.

"Not a single word. That made it all the more terrifying. He snatched the bag off my head and, goddamn it, that's when I realized I was blindfolded, too. Then he untied my hands and told me if I so much as raised them above my waist, he'd slice me like a rasher of bacon. Those were the first words he said to me."

"What was his voice like?"

"Creepy. Really soft, a husky whisper. That was as scary as if he'd yelled at me. Then he pulled off my T-shirt and bra an inch at a time, as if he was really enjoying it. After that he tied my hands again and untied my ankles long enough to take off my shorts and panties, all the time whispering, whispering, warning me not to try to kick him. I still hear him in my dreams."

I had goose bumps. She was sure as hell convincing. "And you didn't recognize the voice at all?"

"No, except I was sure he wasn't black. Then he said all he wanted to do was take a few pictures, that if I did what I was told, cooperated, he wouldn't hurt me and would take me back to the church when he finished. By that time I was so scared, I'd have walked on water if he'd asked me to." She got up and began to pace in her stocking feet, still shaking. "It was crazy. He positioned me this way and that, then snapped a picture. He stood me up and snapped a few, then laid me back down again and took more. He must have taken thirty or forty pictures. All the time I was begging him to please let me go. He just kept snapping, snapping, snapping."

"Are you sure this didn't happen in a house? This was taken while you were in the shower."

"How do I know? I told you, I was blindfolded," she protested, distracted by my interruption.

I wasn't sure what was happening here. There was no blindfold in the picture.

"Then . . . then the motherfucker raped me, Leigh Ann." Her voice broke and tears streamed down her face again. "I did everything he asked, hoping he'd keep his promise that when he was finished with his kinky picture taking, he'd let me go. The mother-fucker *raped* me instead."

"Oh, Sheryl." I stepped back, mentally, and recon-sidered. I'd been a cop long enough to recognize the truth when I heard it. She wasn't lying. She had been raped. "Honey, I'm so sorry."

"I hated him. I can't tell you much I've hated him, Leigh Ann. And I hated myself for believing the bas-tard, for not fighting back instead of going along with his program."

"What could you have done all trussed up like that?"

"I don't know. Something. Anything. But I didn't, and got screwed, literally, for being a good little girl."

"Was he brutal?"

"All things considered I guess he could have been

a lot rougher. He just forced my knees apart—my ankles were still tied—and raped me. Twice. Didn't even take his clothes off. Thank God it was quick—I mean, he came both times almost as soon as he'd forced his way in. Then he picked me up, carried me back out to the trunk of his car, drove around for a long time, and dumped me, blindfolded and naked as a jaybird, on the back steps of New Bethel."

"What did you do? I mean, how'd you get home?"

"I practically scraped my face raw against a step getting the blindfold off and saw that he'd left my clothes right there on the ground. I used my teeth to get my hands free, untied myself, got dressed, and ran home."

"And you never told anyone? Why?"

She whirled around. "Because the same thing had happened to Darla Michaels the summer before, except she wasn't raped—or if she was, she didn't admit it. She reported it to Mr. Euker and he grilled her something awful. She said by the time he finished, she felt like a fool. She couldn't prove anything."

"But you could have, Sheryl. The guy socked you, right? He had to have left a bruise. And you said he ejaculated twice."

Sheryl was silent for several heartbeats. "I didn't report it because I knew who it was. It was that goddamned Danny Totton. I recognized the sound of his MG. But how would I prove it? Nobody'd ever heard of DNA testing back then. And you and I know that if it came down to my word, a darkie from the dark side of Main, against the word of the crown prince of Sunrise, who were they going to believe?"

Her argument incensed me. "For God's sake,

Sheryl! Since the same thing had happened to Darla, who's as lily white as they come, they'd have had to take you seriously. If nothing else, they'd have started watching Danny."

"I couldn't chance it," Sheryl cried. "I couldn't risk turning Mrs. Totton against me. She's the only reason I got that scholarship from her sorority. All she had to do was pick up the phone and they'd have canceled it. I wouldn't have been able to go back to college! I had to go, Leigh Ann, or I'd have wound up like my parents, working the night shift at Sundler's Mill, coughing up sawdust the rest of my life. I had to make a choice and I made it!" She dropped into the recliner again. "I'll never forgive myself, but I did what I thought I had to do at the time."

I tried to think of something to say and came up empty. The choice she'd made stank, but I had intimate knowledge of the desperation behind that decision. She was right about Mrs. Totton. Sunrise Township's principal could make the worst kind of enemy. One kid had made the mistake of swearing at her back in fourth grade. Not only had she expelled him, but when his father had brushed the lapse off as high spirits, it was rumored that Mrs. Totton had seen to it that he lost his job. A month later the family was gone as if they'd never existed. For most of us Mrs. Totton was the only route out of Sunrise by one means or another.

Precisely because I knew the desperation behind Sheryl's decision, there was a question I had to ask. "Sheryl, where were you the night of the big storm back in '82?"

She stared at me in astonishment. Finally she closed her mouth. "You think I killed Danny? I didn't. I almost wish I had. But the whole family was in Roanoke visiting Aunt Wilma. You can ask Mama and Dad. They'll confirm it."

I nodded. I would indeed confirm it. Sheryl had a first-class motive. I had to be sure she hadn't had the opportunity as well.

"I was glad when we got back and found out Danny had killed himself in that car," she said, no apology in her voice. "I'm even happier now. He got what he deserved. Whoever killed him did me a favor."

"Revenge may be sweet," I said, "but don't forget, that person probably killed Doc, too."

That shut her up for a second. "It didn't solve anything, did it?" she asked sadly, rubbing her forehead. "Just made things worse. Now I have to worry about where that picture came from and how many others he took are floating around this town."

I looked down at it, almost tempted to give it to her. That wouldn't solve anything either. As I examined it again, hoping for some clue as to where it had been taken, it hit me why I had expected one story and had gotten another. She had only glanced at the picture. She hadn't seen it up close.

"Sheryl," I said. "Take a good look at it."

She shook her head. "I can't."

"There's something you missed the first time. Look at it again."

She had to pull in a couple of deep breaths before she could bring herself to reach for it, and another couple before she lowered her eyes. She blinked, brought it closer. "This wasn't taken that night! That's no blindfold, it's my hair! I don't understand! Where was this taken?"

"I don't know. Does that look like your mom's bathroom?"

"Uh-uh. Her tile's pink. This had to be before that night. I had Miss Juanita cut my hair real short the very next day. He played with my hair and I didn't want any reminders of what he'd done. He—or somebody—took pictures of me naked and I didn't even know it? It's been bad enough living with the rape all these years. Now this!"

I took it from her before she got any ideas, like ripping up the thing. "I'll do what I can to see that this doesn't fall into the wrong hands, but I will have to show it to Mr. Sheriff. It's evidence." I didn't say it, but this sneaky-peeking may have been a preamble to the attack on her. "And you will have to tell him what happened. It may not have to go any farther than him, but you will have to tell him. Okay?"

Pain scythed across her face but she nodded.

"Go on home, now. And Sheryl, see a rape counselor or this thing will eat you alive."

She slipped her feet into her shoes and nodded. "Maybe I will. I don't know." She stood up and smoothed her skirt, suddenly hesitant. "Are we still friends, Leigh Ann?"

I hugged her and hoped it would put that fear to rest. "You're my ace-boon-coon," I assured her, and walked her to the door. "See you at the dance tonight."

She sighed. "Yeah. I sure don't feel like going, but Jimmy's looking forward to it. I love him to pieces, Leigh Ann, but swear to God, the man can't dance worth a poot."

I laughed and she perked up a little. She made her way across the street in those ridiculously high heels that added a good three inches to her height. She had the legs for them, but I wondered how long her Achilles tendons would hold out. The ping-ping began in the back of my brain again and I wasted a couple of minutes trying to figure out what it was trying to tell me. When nothing happened, I let it go again. Sooner or later it would resurface. It had to. Something told me it was important. So was the conversation I planned to have with Maudine. I left Nunna's and started for the diner.

It was packed, but no Maudine. Dolly swooped past me with plates of Fredburgers. "Sorry, honey, if you're looking for Maudine, she didn't come in. Called and said her mama took real sick early this morning. Haven't heard from her since. Sure wish you'd check on her, Leigh Ann. She ain't got nobody but us and we're so busy we can't leave."

Damn. Maudine lived toward the outskirts of town. Duck still had the car, so I'd have to walk. I wished I'd changed clothes when I'd had the chance. Sweat stains and silk, if I remembered correctly, were incompatible. And this was Nunna's silk, not mine.

"Problem?" Dolly asked, ferrying a dishpan full of dirty plates from table to kitchen.

"No car. A friend's using mine."

"Oh, the guy with the funny name. I understand he's a real sweetie. Here." She fished into the apron of her pocket. "Take mine—the blue Civic with the ribbon on the aerial. Tell Maudine to let us know if there's anything we can do."

"Dolly, thanks. I'll get it back to you as soon as I can," I promised.

"No hurry. Fred's is here if we need it. Oh. Miss Nunna dropped off a cake this morning for Maudine and Mrs. Fletcher. Over there by the ice-cream cones. Why don't you take it to her, since you're going." She hurried away, dishes clanking.

I got the cake, left, and, thanks to Dolly, made it to the Fletcher home just in time to see an ambulance pulling away from in front of the house, heading back toward Main. I swore, wondering whether to follow it. Even if I did, if Maudine was on her way to the hospital with her mother, the subject I'd intended to discuss with her would have to wait. The cake, too. But hell, the least I could offer, I decided, was moral support.

I pulled over into the yard to try a U-turn on the narrow street and noticed that, in her hurry, Maudine had left the house wide open. They had no screen door. The interior would be full of flies by the time she got back. Leaving the motor running, I got out and ran to the front porch to close up for her and almost missed seeing her sitting in a paint-chipped rocking chair just inside, staring blindly into space. She seemed unaware of my presence, despite the creaking boards, as I crossed to the door.

"Maudine. Do you need a ride to the hospital?"

She didn't move a muscle, didn't answer. I watched her for a second, then went back to the car to shut off the engine and get the cake. She still hadn't moved when I returned. There was a serenity about her that didn't seem appropriate, given the circumstances.

Uninvited, I went in and touched her shoulder. "Maudine."

She came to with a start, looked up at me in confusion. "Leigh Ann. What are you doing here?"

"Dolly told me your mom had been taken ill. I came to bring this cake Nunna made for you and to see if there was anything I could do."

She held my gaze, the serenity of a moment before stealing over her features again. Taking the cake, she held it in her lap. "Thank Miss Nunna for me. That was really sweet of her. You, too. That's one of the things I remember about you," she said. Her voice was wispy, vague. She might have been talking to herself. "You were nice to everyone, treated all the kids the same, no matter which side of town they lived on. Not like some."

I wondered if she was cracking up. "Your mom, Maudine. I can take you to the hospital, if you want."

"No need. Mama's dead," she said, as if softening the blow for me. "Died about an hour ago, trying to hold on until Maurice got here."

"You didn't tell her . . ."

"I kept putting it off. Glad I did now. She's free, Leigh Ann. And so am I. I can finally give this town the back of my hand."

"Where will you go?" I asked, and sat down on a sagging velvet sofa. The room was sparsely furnished with worn pieces, but it was immaculate.

"Back to Charleston, I reckon. It's the only other place I know. And now that Mama's gone and I'll be going soon," she said, leaning forward to place the cake on the blond coffee table, "I can tell you anything you want to know. We never had much and the people in this town always looked down on us because Daddy drank so hard, but Mama, she had a lot of pride. I kept quiet for her. Now it doesn't matter." She sat back, relaxed, at ease, her expression expectant.

I decided to oblige her. "I saw your son at the brunch."

She nodded. "Figured you would. He's a nice-looking kid, isn't he? I let Maisie Chatwell and her husband take him soon's he was born. Hadn't seen him since until day before yesterday when I saw him and Maisie in front of Doc Webster's."

I remembered. "Danny Totton's his father?"

Her eyes glazed over with frost. "Yes."

"What did he do, refuse to acknowledge the child?"

She laughed, a harsh, grating sound. "He didn't dare say it was his. If he had, he'd have been admitting that he'd raped me."

I jerked upright. "You, too?"

Maudine stared at me, her body rigid. "I wasn't the only one?"

Sheryl, Maudine, perhaps Darla. I thought about the six subjects of Danny's paintings and wondered if there were three more rape victims out there to be accounted for. "How'd it happen, Maudine?"

The story she related was almost word for word the one Sheryl had told me, except Maudine had been grabbed leaving Sunrise Township School after an early evening meeting of Totton's Tutors. There were two major differences. Maudine had fought for all she was worth once she realized that the photo session was only the first course. Danny had lost his head and in his anger at her resistance, had forgotten to disguise his voice a couple of times. She'd recognized it, had even called his name, and had been beaten and knocked unconscious. As a result she was out cold during the first sexual assault. The second had occurred in New Bethel's cemetery, after she'd regained consciousness. She'd been beaten again, raped, and left bound and gagged. And had reported the incident to Mr. Euker as soon as she'd gotten home.

"What did he do about it?" I asked.

"He called Danny, had him come to his house, and told him what I'd said. Danny lied his ass off. His story was that he'd been working on a project with the Boys' Club all evening and that two of Mr. Euker's sons would back him up. They did, Cecil and Teddy Junior. Both of them swore Danny had been with them the whole time."

Cecil, who Mr. Sheriff had said sounded panicky on the phone. And Ted Junior, who'd also raised the chief's suspicions. If they had lied for Danny, Ted could have been the phantom whisperer in the girl's john.

"You never told the chief about it?" I asked.

"For what? I figured Mr. Euker did when Mr. Sheriff got back into town. If Mr. Euker didn't believe Danny had done it, why would Mr. Sheriff? Even if they believed me, they wouldn't go up against Mrs. Totton. Nobody would if they had kids in school."

A variation on Sheryl's excuse. "Why didn't you go directly to Mrs. Totton?"

"Oh, sure, and have her turn against me? Danny had an alibi. What did I have? Nothing and nobody. Danny even swore he didn't have a camera."

I hadn't seen one in his room. For the first time it occurred to me that Danny might not have acted alone. "Maudine, are you certain he was the one taking the pictures? Is there any possibility there was someone else in the room?"

She stopped, seemed to consider it. "No. It was

really quiet. I'd have heard anyone else. There was just Danny. I'm sure of it."

He could have borrowed the camera. Josh or Roscoe might remember if any of the members of their troop had one. I glanced around for a phone to call the Sheriffs, then realized the answer had probably been staring me in the face at the brunch. Tommy Broadwater. Duck said he was a professional photographer, and now that I thought of it, he was always taking pictures of special events at New Bethel. He'd seemed a pretty nice guy back in high school. I couldn't imagine him being involved in this kind of caper. Yet when he'd heard what had been going on over the last week, he'd bolted. With that kind of reaction, it wasn't likely he'd left the snapshot of Sheryl. Who had? And for that matter, why?

I smelled collusion. If I was to believe Maudine, two of the members of the Boys' Club had lied for Danny. Had they known why he'd needed an alibi that night? Did they have one for the night Danny and Maurice had died, one that would stand up under scrutiny? They weren't the only ones I needed to ask.

"Maudine, where were you the night Danny Totton was killed?"

"My alibi is on her way to the morgue. I was sitting right where you are, with Mama, hoping to hear from Maurice. I even watched the storm come up. The only other person who could vouch for me is Claire Rowland, but that was way after midnight. I saw her out in her yard when the wind started rising."

"Doing what?"

"Taking in lawn chairs so they wouldn't blow away. I went out on the porch and asked if she needed any help. She might remember it. I don't know. I didn't kill Danny, Leigh Ann. That's not to say I wouldn't have if the chance had come up. But it didn't. And I didn't. Can I ask you something?"

Turnabout was fair play. "Ask."

"Are y'all spending half as much time on Maurice as y'all are on Danny Totton?"

It was a fair question. "I may be wrong, Maudine, but I figure if Mr. Sheriff finds out who killed Danny, he'll know who killed Maurice and Doc. Danny's murder is the key. And for your information, I could swear on a stack of Bibles that Mr. Euker never said a word to the chief about the assault on you and the others. I could tell him now, but it would be better if you did."

She shrugged with indifference. "Sure. Why not?"

"How about right now?"

She thought about it, then pushed herself to her feet. "Sure," she said again. "Why not?"

"I can't hardly believe it," Mr. Sheriff said, stunned to the point of incredulity. "I don't give a good goddamn whether Euker believed it was Totton who raped you or not, he should have made out a formal report. He should have had Web see you that very night. My God, Maudine, no wonder you turned sour."

She eyed him with open suspicion. "You really didn't know?"

He whacked the arm of his chair, his face rutabaga red. "Damn it, girl, I'm the law in this town! Granted, I ain't much, but I've done the best I can by the citizens of Sunrise. Tell me something. How many Saturday nights did I come to your house to quiet down your daddy?"

She stiffened. "Dozens, I guess."

"How many times did I lock him up in the court-house so y'all could have a little peace, for a while, anyways?"

"At least once a month."

"But he was out by Monday morning, wasn't he, so he could punch the clock at the mill on time. I could have charged him, sent him up before Judge Feester, who'd have put his cantankerous behind in the county jail for ninety days at a time without batting an eye. I didn't, because I knew without the check he brought home every Friday—what he didn't drink up—your family would have to go on welfare and your mama couldn't have taken that. Right?"

Tears glistened in Maudine's eyes. "It would have killed her."

"Yes, ma'am. I did what I thought was right under the circumstances. I look after the people under my protection. Do you honestly think I'd have sat back and done nothing if I'd known somebody was out there abducting our womenfolk, taking their pictures naked, and raping them to boot? Do you?"

I was so proud of him. His righteous indignation rang with truth and seeing it, I reached into my purse and extended the envelope with the Polaroid to him. "This is for your eyes only, but because of it, I just found out that Maudine wasn't the only victim."

Mr. Sheriff opened the envelope carefully and pulled out the photo, handling it so that Maudine couldn't see it. He looked at the photo and blanched. "Where'd this come from?"

"Someone slipped it under my door after Duck and I left for your house this morning. I saw several versions of it in watercolor but didn't recognize the subject. According to her, this was taken without her knowledge some time prior to the assault, which took place back in August of '81."

"No." The chief shook his head. "Her, too."

"She didn't report the incident to Mr. Euker because, again, according to her, she knew of someone else who'd been abducted and photographed the summer before. That person had reported it to Mr. Euker and had been subjected to such mistreatment that she let the whole thing drop."

"Lord God," the chief moaned. "I trusted that son of a bitch with my town five summers in a row." He sat breathing like a bellows for a good minute, anger etching deep furrows across his forehead and around his mouth. Finally, he snatched up the phone at his elbow and dialed. "Rachel, this is Nehemiah. Your boys home? Just Cecil? Mind sending him over? There's something I think he might be able to clear up for me." He listened for a second. "I'm right sorry to hear that, but tell him I won't keep him long and he can go right back to his sickbed. Thank you kindly." He hung up. "Ted Junior's not back from the brunch yet. It's just as well. From the way he acted on the phone last night, Cecil's the weakest link. I want to watch his face when he walks in and sees Maudine sitting here. I'm betting this boy's no poker player."

"The slimy little weasel," Maudine muttered.

"Don't say a word," the chief warned her. "Let him jump to his own conclusions."

"Where's Duck?" I asked, wishing he were around for the session to come.

"Him and Josh went looking for Tommy Broadwater. Duck said the way he skedaddled when he
heard about Doc and Danny, Tommy knows something. Maudine, I'm gonna want a statement from
you about that night, every little detail you can
remember. After your mama's funeral will be fine.
And if you need some help planning the service, call
Dora. She'll go with you to the funeral home. Just
tell her when. I know you want something nice for
your mama, but Dora'll see that they don't stick you
with something you can't afford."

"Oh, Mr. Sheriff, I'd be so grateful. I can't tell you
how much I've been dreading . . ." The remainder
was drowned out. Probably for the first time since
her mother had died, Maudine burst into tears, sobbing no doubt for the passing of her mother, twin
brother, and a chapter in her life.

I became aware of a shadow beyond the screen
door: Cecil Euker. I wondered how long he'd been
standing there. Something told me Mr. Sheriff knew
to the second when Cecil had arrived.

"Come on in, boy," he said, before Cecil had a
chance to knock. "Sorry to hear you're feeling puny.
Set yourself down. If everybody cooperates, this
shouldn't take long."

I had to assume that Cecil took after his mother.
Tall and slender with fine brown hair, he had deli-
cate features. He was by no means effeminate, but
he'd have made a gorgeous woman. He took the
chair farthest from the chief, clear hazel eyes
anchored on Maudine, then me. "Ma'am," he said,
bobbing his head in greeting. I figured that included
both of us.

"Cecil," the chief began, "I want you to think back

a ways, back to a summer night in nineteen and eighty. You were . . . what?. . . ten or thereabouts, right?"

"Yes, sir." Cecil frowned, as if confused.

"On this particular night, Miss Maudine there paid your daddy a call. Do you remember that?"

"Yes, sir. I think I do."

"And your daddy asked you and your brother . . . what did he ask you?"

He thought about it, brow furrowed. "Oh. He asked if we'd been with Mr. Danny that evening."

"And y'all said?"

His eyes began to widen as if his memory was clearing. He wet his mouth, leaving his bottom lip glistening. "We said yes."

"And had you? Been with Danny all evening?"

Silence. Cecil fixed his gaze on the chief's nose and concentrated on it for several long, nerve-racking moments. No one moved, letting the silence spin itself out, spiderweb-thin. He cleared his throat, his eyes troubled. "Mr. Sheriff, I'll answer you, but can I ask why you want to know?"

"Sure enough. Miss Maudine says that earlier that night, Danny Totton ambushed her, blindfolded her so she wouldn't see who he was, trussed her up like a chicken ready for slaughter, took pictures of her, beat her up, then raped her. You and your brother were Danny's alibi."

Cecil's color had begun to fade about a quarter of the way through that recitation. Halfway through he was sheet white. By the end of it, he'd turned green. Without warning, he bolted from the room and just made it off the porch before he threw up.

"Guess he really was feeling puny," Mr. Sheriff

said, with complete lack of sympathy. "Dora won't be happy about the way he's fertilizin' her petunias. Y'all just keep still now. See what happens next."

We sat twiddling our thumbs, waiting for Cecil's stomach to settle. He took his time about it. I was a little edgy, since he could just walk away if he wanted to, but he simply stood out on the walkway, framed by Old Bluenose Mountain behind him.

Finally, he stepped onto the lawn, disappearing from view and I jumped to my feet and went to the door. Cecil was on one knee fiddling with something beyond the porch. In a second, he came back around to the walkway, a garden hose in his hand, and hosed off the area he'd soiled.

The chief smiled. "There's hope for that one. He's gonna be all right."

I sat back down with a quick glance at Maudine. She might have been a statue. Except for her respiration and her eyelids, she was completely still, as if she'd left us for some tranquil place inside herself. The chief watched her intently, and I suspected he'd never really looked at her closely before. There seemed a trace of surprise in his eyes.

Cecil moved out of sight again, I assume to replace the garden hose, and shortly, his steps sounded on the porch again. He came back in, cramming a handkerchief in the back pocket of his khaki slacks, beads of water glistening in his hair. The collar of his polo shirt was wet; he must have sprayed his face and head.

"Sorry, sir," he said, his attitude apologetic but with no trace of embarrassment. "I cleaned off the flowers the best I could."

"'Preciate it, son. You feel better now?"

"No, sir, I feel just awful. I'm glad this happened. I'm studying for the ministry and there's no way I could'a climbed into anybody's pulpit with this stain on my soul." He crossed to the couch and stood in front of Maudine. "Miss Maudine, I want to ask your forgiveness. I loved my daddy, but the truth is he was a sinful man. He never told us why he was asking if we'd been with Mr. Danny. If we'd known, we'd never have said what we did."

"Then why did you?" Mr. Sheriff asked. "Why'd you protect him?"

Cecil turned to face him. "You have to understand, sir, we didn't realize that's what we were doing. Far as we were concerned, we were protecting ourselves. I don't know who we were scared of the most, Mr. Danny or our daddy. Our tails were in a crack. We knew that if we didn't lie for Mr. Danny, he'd tell on us and then kill our dog the way he'd killed Mrs. Allen's. If we told the truth, our daddy would probably kill us. Ya see what I mean?"

"What was the truth, Cecil? What was everybody hiding?"

His head drooped, his shoulders sagged. "That we were all Peeping Toms."

The chief leaned to one side, his brows climbing toward his receding hairline. "Peeping Toms? All of you?"

"Not Josh and Roscoe. They didn't know anything about it."

"What about Maurice?" Maudine asked, her voice grating.

"No, ma'am! Not Maurice either." He looked shocked at the very idea. "See, Mr. Danny found a hole in the wall at school between a utility closet and the girls' locker room and their shower. He made it larger and fixed it up so you couldn't tell from their side. But from the time I turned ten until Mr. Danny died, he charged us fifty cents and let us go in the closet and watch them undress and shower."

I clasped my hands in a prayer of thanksgiving that I'd been so terrified of water, I'd never used S.T.'s pool and hadn't learned to swim until I reached college. And only then because I needed the credits to graduate.

"Wait a minute here." Mr. Sheriff scowled. "Y'all watched little girls?"

Cecil's head dropped even lower. "Little girls, big ones, grown ladies, too. The way he set it up, the Boys' Club met at seven. The school's new swimming pool was open to the public every night at eight. After our meeting, we'd leave, then double back and slip into the closet. And watch."

"And take pictures sometimes?" I asked.

"Ma'am?"

His face answered my question. He knew nothing about the photographs. "Never mind. Sorry to interrupt."

"That's all. We didn't mean any harm," he said, earnestly. "We knew it was wrong, but that was half the fun at first. Then, well, it changed, began to feel dirty. So we stopped."

"What changed it?" the chief asked.

Cecil's eyes wandered in our direction, then away. "I don't exactly remember. Maybe it was the look on Mr. Danny's face sometimes when he was watching his favorites." A spasm shook his thin frame.

"Was I one of them?" Maudine asked so softly I could hardly hear her.

He bobbed his head, his face flaming. "Yes, ma'am."

"Who else?" the chief asked.

"I . . . I don't remember. It's been a long time."

"Who else?"

"I only knew about Miss Maudine and the lady who worked for the dentist."

"Alice Youngman."

"Yes, sir, that's her. And Sid Michaels's sister."

"Darla." I supplied the name.

"There was a black lady, too. I've seen her out jogging on Main Street sometimes, but I don't remember her name."

"Describe her." I wanted to be sure.

"She's real short and has long hair and big eyes."

The chief and I shared unspoken confirmation, our eyes meeting.

"I'd always been a little afraid of Mr. Danny before, but I was really scared of him after we found out what he did to Mrs. Allen's dog just because she chased him out of the cemetery one night. I couldn't stop going to the meetings—Dad thought belonging was good for us—but I never went in that closet again."

"So, for the record," Mr. Sheriff said, "you and your brother had not been with Totton that night."

"No, sir. I mean, yes, sir."

"I'll need a statement from you, everything you just told us. Everything. Understand?"

"Yes, sir." Cecil looked stunned. I suspect that until that moment he hadn't been sure he'd be going home ever again.

"I'll also want a statement from your brother, but there's no reason to tell him you talked to us. We'll handle it."

"Thanks, Mr. Sheriff. I can go now?"

The chief nodded.

"I can't tell you how sorry I am, Miss Maudine."
Cecil backed toward the door. "I never believed
all the bad things Dad said about you that night,
and after I found out he was saying them to practically everybody, I never felt the same about him
again."

Suddenly it clicked, the rumors about Maudine in
the letters from Sheryl and a couple of other
friends, to the effect that Maudine had become a
tramp who slept with anyone who zipped his pants
up the front and didn't have to sit down to pee. I felt
Maudine's anger spreading through my mind.
Danny Totton had fouled her body and Mr. Euker
had fouled the only thing she had left: her good
name.

"Well, well, well," Mr. Sheriff said, after Cecil was
gone. "I'll have to think about how to handle this.
Those other ladies may not want to admit what happened to them, but it's important that they do."

"I warned the subject of that snapshot that she'd
have to talk to you."

"Good." He leaned over and scratched his leg
above the cast. "If this ain't one ugly can of
worms. We start out trying to find out who killed
Web, thinking that the same person probably
killed Totton and probably Maurice. Only it turns
out that not only was Totton a Peeping Tom con-
tributing to the deliquency of a passel of minors,
he was also a serial rapist. There's a good chance
somebody's husband or daddy or brother found
out what he'd been up to and beat him to death
over it. Then there's poor Maurice stuck in the

middle of it. The most likely person to cover up the fact that he died about the same time as Totton may be one of his tutors. Maudine's list had a good dozen people, male and female, my wife being one of them. We start out with no suspects at all and now, by God, we've got a whole town full of 'em."

13

"*Mr. Taney left* a message for us to look for him at the dance," Duck said, coming out of the house. "Wow, you look terrific." When I didn't respond, he peered at me, squint-eyed. "What's wrong?"

I sat on the front porch in the swing, dressed like an African princess and feeling like a royal fool. The dashiki was beautiful, exquisite actually, and I didn't think I did it justice. Someone of Nunna's height could pull it off, but I felt overwhelmed by it. Nunna had tried to talk me into wearing a headwrap that matched the dashiki, but I passed on that and raided her jewelry box instead, winding up with ten bangle bracelets, five around each wrist. I wasn't sure how long I'd be able to tolerate them; every time I moved I jangled and clanked like Marley's ghost, and I wasn't in the mood for jangling and clanking.

"Come on, Leigh. Talk to me. What's the problem?" Duck, super fine in the dark jacket and white slacks he'd disappeared earlier to buy, sat down beside me in the swing.

"I'd forgotten why I wanted out of this business," I said. "This afternoon reminded me."

I'd spent a total of a minute and a half on the phone with Darla Michaels Peckham, Myrtle the beautician's daughter, whose hysterical denial that she'd been abducted and raped convinced me that she had been, and a good forty-five minutes with Alice Boothe, who confirmed the assault she'd endured a month before Danny Totton's death. She'd had no clue as to the identity of her assailant.

"I decided not to report it," she explained, "because everybody knew Boothe and I were more than dentist and dental assistant, if you get my meaning. His first wife was still alive—just barely, but still alive. I was afraid his name would be dragged into it, since I'd just spent the evening with him, and I didn't want that to happen. It would have killed Evelyn. So I kept my mouth shut. Then when the storm made such a mess of the office and a tree wiped out my bedroom at home, I took that as a sign and left. I'd had enough of Sunrise."

So had I. Three murders, one of the victims a serial rapist, a cop with highly questionable ethics, and years of cover-ups. And it wasn't over yet, not by a long shot. I hated the thought of leaving Sunrise with the case still open, but I hated the thought of staying in this charged atmosphere even more. And the last place I felt like going was to a dance.

"Don't you ever get so disgusted with how mean and malicious people can be that you want no more of it?" I asked Duck.

"At least once a week. It doesn't last long." He

took my hand and nibbled on a knuckle until I snatched it away. "It's all a matter of perspective. For every thug out there, there's a victim, or one waiting in the wings. If I catch the thugs, I'm not only reducing the number of bad guys on the streets, I'm reducing the number of victims. I'm making a difference, Leigh. *We're* making a difference. How many people can say that about the work they do?"

He was right on an intellectual level, but I was on a different plane, nursing an ailing spirit.

"What's really bugging you?" he asked. "Don't give me the big picture. Break it down into component parts."

It took several moments for me to figure that out, and another few to find the words to vocalize it. "This place is very special to me. It was shelter, a base, when I needed it the most. It bothers me that—"

"That it's not perfect?"

"Give me a break," I grumbled. "I'm not that naive. But this was home, Duck. It never occurred to me I'd find the same kind of carnage and carnage-makers here I thought I'd left. Sure, it's on a smaller scale, but it's the same brand of evil, the same kind of pain. I'm furious at these people. They could have put a stop to the whole business umpteen years ago. The very first woman Danny Totton assaulted could have raised enough hell so that Euker would have had to do something. But she didn't, her family didn't, and Euker didn't. Now here it is fifteen years later and we've got four women raped that we know about, three people dead, and a murderer still running around loose. They *let* it happen. I'm sick of it, Duck. Sick of it."

"Then let's split." He got up, pulled me out of the swing.

"What?"

"Let's go inside, pack our shit, and hit the road. You're right. They deserve whatever happens to them. The place on the Outer Banks is still available and I don't have to be back in D.C. until Monday. We'll swim, eat a lot of seafood, lie out on the beach until we're the color of charcoal, and let this place stew in its own juice. How 'bout it?"

"Are you crazy?" I skirted around him to the other side of the porch. "Just walk away, leave Mr. Sheriff trying to cope by himself when he can't even walk? He's a good man, even better than I thought, but I'll bet he's never had to deal with a murder before. Okay, we've only got a couple of more days to give him, but we can't just cut out on him like that!"

"Then what, my love, are you bitchin' about?" Duck asked softly, and grinned.

I couldn't help it; I hit him. I'd been holding the embroidered clutch Nunna had loaned me and before I knew it I'd hauled off and whacked him upside the head with it. Hurt him, too. I saw him wince. Damn, it felt good.

He blinked a couple of times before the grin reappeared. "See? You must love me or you wouldn't have hit me. Are you ready to go boogie now?"

"You-drive-me-*nuts!*" I said, teeth clenched.

"Lord," Nunna called from inside, "I'll be so glad when you children stop fighting and play nice like you got some sense. Now, kiss and make up."

"The hell I will." I marched down the steps, almost tripping on the hem of the dashiki, adjusted my gait, and kept going. Kiss and make up indeed!

⚬   ⚬   ⚬

The Seventies dance was already in full swing inside Sunrise Township's gym, a Bee Gees song pulsating into the evening air each time the door opened. At the sound of the first note, Duck's butt began to twitch. Among other things, Dillon Upshur Kennedy is a dancing fool. Since the theme for the evening was Disco! Disco! Disco! my boy was in for a good time and so was anyone lucky enough to hit the floor with him.

"Do me a favor," I said, as we approached the door. "Dance with Sheryl, okay?"

He reared back, feigning hurt. "Last night you called me a tomcat. Tonight you treat me like a gigolo. What am I, a plaything you can pass off to your friends?"

I caught the humor in his eyes, and dissolved with laughter. "Why is it so hard to stay mad at you? Come on, you idiot."

He smiled. "That's better. Look, babe, I mean, Leigh, I know it's a cliché, but everything will work out eventually. The point is that when Sunrise needed your help, you gave it. Superwoman you may be, but not even you can solve all its problems. The folks here have to get up off it and do it themselves. And you have to do what's right for you. I know I've been giving you the blues about quitting, but if turning in your badge is what you need to do, do it. I think you'll be making the mistake of your life, but I'm in your corner no matter what you decide to do. Okay?"

I nodded, suddenly dangerously close to tears. Somehow he'd said all the right things, pushed all the right buttons, and it was as if he'd lifted a ton off my shoulders. I hadn't realized that his opinion mattered that much. Giving him up would leave a bigger hole than I'd thought.

Entering the gym was like stepping back twenty years. "Good God," Duck muttered. Spotlights slithered back and forth across the dance floor. Somewhere hidden projectors flashed the front pages of local newspapers against the walls, reminding us of good and bad times—antiwar demonstrations, the launch of Mariner 9, Watergate headlines, Arthur Ashe's Wimbledon title. A surprising number of men wore tight-fitting white suits, à la Travolta, I realized, once I'd rejected my first guess—the KFC's Colonel. There were a couple of tuxedos, a few dinner jackets, but most of the guys were fairly casual. Women were decked out in everything from ball gowns to dresses short enough to qualify as bathing suits. I began to feel less an oddity in my dashiki.

"Hey, they've got food!" Duck's eyes began to glitter. This from a man who'd just demolished two heaping plates at dinner. Refreshments were being served under the basketball hoops, finger food, and fountains cascading a pink liquid which, from the number of people holding cups under the falls, had to be spiked.

Tables and chairs ringed the walls, their tablecloths strewn with remnants of hors d'oeuvres and half-empty cups of punch abandoned to the lure of "Staying Alive." The dance floor was jammed, classmates gyrating with hips switching and elbows flying, inhibitions checked at the door. I suspected some, like me, who felt like complete idiots trying to master today's dance steps, welcomed the opportunity to fall back on routines they remembered from their salad days. Perhaps I would later. At the moment, my lettuce was sadly wilted.

Duck staked a claim at a table by leaving his jacket on the back of one chair. I removed the photo of Sheryl from the clutch, palming it to pass to Duck. We'd brought it on a whim.

"Why don't you hold on to it?" he said. "I'd have to put it in my back pocket and once I start dancing, it might work its way out."

Considering some of the moves I'd seen him make when the spirit hit him, I knew he was right. I slipped it into one of the dashiki's capacious pockets and left Nunna's bag on the other chair.

"This won't be easy," he said above the music.

I had to agree with him. There were several items on the evening's agenda. We'd learned, to our frustration, that the utility closet no longer existed, eliminated when the locker rooms were renovated and enlarged five years before, but Duck wanted to collar Tommy Broadwater, a professional photographer now, to find out what, if anything, he knew about the pictures taken from Danny Totton's cosy little blind downstairs.

We also wanted a look at other sections of the basement. The sterility of Danny's bedroom had always bothered me and his tenure as janitor here could have provided any number of places to store things he would not have wanted his mother to see. Our chances of striking pay dirt after so many years were next to nil, but we had to look. Mr. Taney had agreed to give us a tour of the nether regions once he'd finished helping to set up the gym for the dance. The problem would be finding him and Tommy Broadwater in this mob. We hadn't expected t would be this crowded.

"Well, business before pleasure," Duck said, jiggling to the booming beat. "Let's start circulating. You hunt for your Mr. Taney, since I don't know what he looks like. I'll keep an eye out for Broadwater." Taking my hand, he led me along the outer edge of the dance floor.

I spotted Sheryl and Jim. She had not exaggerated. I had no idea what her husband thought he was doing, but by no stretch of the imagination could it be called dancing. Squeezing Duck's hand, I tilted my head toward them.

Duck slowed, saw them, and looked appalled. "Damn! The boy's gonna give the race a bad name. He's got no rhythm at all."

"That's why I asked you to dance with her," I shouted above the din.

"I would have anyway, but now I consider it my civic duty. Man, that's a shame. Good as she moves? He—"

He stopped because I had, courtesy of a firm grip on my elbow. I glanced back and found myself graced with Monty Sturgis's mesmerizing smile. What he did for a dinner jacket was downright inspirational.

"Care to dance?" he asked, then realized I was not alone. Both guys were immediately on the alert, like a pair of dogs meeting for the first time, circling one another, sniffing.

Amused, I introduced Duck to Monty. "A fellow crimefighter from D.C.," I explained as they shook hands. "And a good friend—most of the time."

"Most of the time?" Monty shot Duck a questioning look.

"We fight a lot." Duck feigned mild exasperation. "She's ornery, stubborn, as mean as they come. A good cop, though, all things considered."

I rose to the bait as I'd been doing from the first day I'd met him. "What's that supposed to mean?"

Monty looked from me to him and back, then nodded, his face relaxing in a smile edged with sadness. "He's got your number, Leigh. Let me tell you, man, if you didn't, I'd be punching every combination possible to get it myself. So. When will you be taking her back to D.C.?"

"Just a damned minute," I squawked, resenting the way I was being discussed as if I weren't there.

"I've got to be back on Monday," Duck said. "She probably won't leave until she's sure Nehemiah can carry on by himself."

If Monty was surprised that Duck had met the chief and was on a first name basis with him, he hid it well. "How're things going?" he asked me, just as the sound of the Bee Gees faded. The dance floor began to clear.

"You tell him," I said to Duck. "I think I see Mr. Taney over there. It's okay," I added. "Monty's the mayor of Sunrise. He's entitled."

"Why don't we step outside?" Monty waved toward the door. "Less racket. But I want one dance with you before the night's over, Leigh." He glanced at Duck in a tacit request for permission.

"Any problems with that, Daddy?" I asked, glaring.

Duck's hands flew up in a gesture of surrender. "Hey, if it's okay with her, it's okay with me. I don't tell her what to do."

"Since when?" I said, and started across the dance floor, Duck's patronizing chuckle ringing in my ears. "Move On Down the Road" from *The Wiz* began. Immediately I was surrounded and had to wiggle my

way to the far wall, dodging flying limbs and jutting
behinds. By the time I could seek sanctuary between
the tables, Mr. Taney had disappeared. I saw,
instead, Thomas Broadwater leaning against the
wall, chatting with a model-thin woman with skin
the color of honey. Tommy was on the make,
doggedly seductive, so I assumed the woman was
not his wife. He leaned close, whispering in her ear,
and she laughed, tossing a mane of ebony hair off a
bony shoulder and walked away, leaving him with a
pained expression for his trouble.

I swooped in on him before he could decide who
his next quarry would be. He'd probably get lucky
before the night was over; he was a hunk, six-two
give or take a quarter inch, smooth, dark chocolate
complexion, and lashes I'd have killed for. Back in
high school, I'd have fainted if he'd looked at me
twice. I wasn't in high school anymore.

"Tommy," I purred, and planted myself in his path
so he couldn't move.

"Hey, it's Leigh Ann"—he took my left hand,
checked for a ring—"Warren. I can't believe you're
unattached. Man, talk about aging like fine wine!
Why don't we go somewhere and talk about whatever comes up."

I could have puked, but opted for a sucker punch
instead. I pulled out the photo of Sheryl and turned
it to face him. "Let's talk about this instead." It was
chancy, but I was doing it with her grudging permission. After studying the quality of the composition of
the picture, Duck was convinced that whoever had
taken it hadn't been your average point-and-shoot
photographer. That meant Tommy. Sheryl had
finally agreed.

Swear to God, his eyes bugged out, and not because of Sheryl's perfect dimensions either. "Wh . . . where'd you get that?"

I returned it to my pocket. "We can do this the easy way, which means you talk to me about the nice little hidey-hole downstairs and the models who didn't know they were modeling," I said, "or we can do it the hard way, which means you can explain it to Mr. Sheriff. Your choice."

"He knows?"

I smiled. "Oh, yes. He knows. Cooperate, and you'll make things easy on yourself. Stonewall and . . ." I let his imagination fill in the blank.

"Shit!" He glanced around, desperation in his eyes, then seemed to deflate. "Okay, okay. Where can we talk?"

We were only a few feet from the exit on the cemetery side of the gym, so I looped my arm in his—just in case he decided to bolt—and walked with him outdoors to what was evidently the smokers' area. Benches and ashtrays were strategically placed along the edge of the walkway. We passed a knot of puffers and took the farthermost bench.

Tommy sat down and leaned over, elbows on his knees. "It seems sleazy now," he began, getting right to the point, "but I swear, Leigh Ann, it didn't feel like that at the time. The way it happened, a bunch of us were sitting around bullshitting about . . . well, you know the kind of lies teenage boys tell."

"How many of us you'd boffed, you mean."

"Yeah. We all knew we were lying, but one guy was awfully convincing."

"No 'one guy' crap," I said. "Be specific, Tommy."

He winced. "Okay. Ted Junior—Euker. He was

talking about which ones he'd done, and his description of the bodies of the girls—and woman—sounded like he'd really seen them nude. So I dared him to prove it. I told him I'd lend him one of my cameras and unless he came back with a picture of his latest with no clothes on, I wasn't going to believe him. He brought back Maudine Fletcher." He lifted his head, remembering. "God, was she built! Anyhow, when I examined the picture closely, I realized it had been taken in the showers right here. I knew good and damned well he hadn't been in there with Maudine, so I went looking for the place he'd snapped it from."

"And found the utility closet."

He groaned. "Hell, if you know about that, then you know about Danny Totton and the others."

"Names, Tommy," I prodded.

He listed a good dozen older boys. "They elected me club photographer. I'd sneak into the closet with them after the meetings, snap away with my Polaroid, and the guys would buy them off me. That helped with expenses. But it was all in fun, Leigh Ann, honest."

Fun. Sure. "How many did Danny Totton buy?"

"None. He had his own camera, would use up three or four rolls of film at a time. But he never showed them around or sold his."

"You developed them for him?"

"Uh-uh. He did them himself, had his own darkroom setup somewhere. Now, Danny." His expression hardened. "That was one slimy motherfucker. He'd sit in the utility closet all evening and when he wasn't taking pictures, he had his fly open, pumping, man."

"I'm supposed to believe the rest of you just watched?"

He hesitated. "Jesus, this is embarrassing. We all did it a couple of times, but I got to tell you, group jerk offs just weren't my thing. I finally stopped going altogether and so did the rest of us. Danny had the room all to himself after then. Well, most of the time, anyway."

He'd left the door ajar purposely, so I kicked it open wide. "And the rest of the time? Who was with him?"

He turned to look at me. "You've got to promise you'll never let on who told you."

"Sorry, I can't do that. For your information, you aren't the only member of the Boys' Club we've talked to. You may simply be confirming information we already have."

He held out for a good thirty seconds. Finally, he said, "Old Man Euker found one of Ted Junior's snapshots and Teddy spilled his guts. Mr. Euker called us all together, demanded any snapshots we had, and scared the shit out of us by reminding us of how certain men in this town would react if they found out what we'd been doing, Maudine's father for one. We'd simply never thought about it. Mean as Mr. Fletcher was, he'd have killed us. Literally. We promised we'd never set foot near that closet again. He said he'd burn the pictures and, as far as he was concerned, that would be the end of it. A few months later, Ted Junior and I found out his daddy was visiting the closet himself, him and Danny in there, zippers down. Ted Junior said that was probably the only way his daddy could get it up, that he treated his mother like dirt and they hadn't slept in the same room in years. He hated his father."

Well. That explained Mr. Euker's behavior toward Darla and Maudine. If he had exposed Danny Totton, he'd have exposed himself as well, no double entendre intended. So Sheryl's picture must have come from the Euker household. Cecil hadn't known about the photo sessions. That left Ted Junior. Or Mrs. Euker.

It also raised the specter of Mr. Euker as the rapist, but that picture wouldn't jell. For one thing, we'd had a nickname for Mr. Euker: The Sniffer. We never knew the reason, perhaps allergies, but Mr. Euker had a habit of sniffing audibly several times a minute. Had he been the rapist, his victims would have had him pegged in no time flat. Short of holding his breath during the whole assault, he would never have been able to pull it off. I was back to Danny acting solo.

"Look, Leigh Ann, somebody's daddy probably killed Danny Totton for the slimeball he was, and I can't say I blame him. But if word gets out about the rest of us and the picture taking . . ." Perspiration glazed his forehead.

"If word gets out it'll be because one of you guys blabbed. Now, put everything you've told me on paper and get it over to Mr. Sheriff's—tonight. He'll be expecting it. One last thing—did you really give Mr. Euker all of your pictures?"

"Are you shitting me?"

Right. I stood up. "Okay, Tommy. This helps a lot. By the way, the Reunion Committee has your current address, so don't get any ideas about running out on us. This is a murder investigation and Mr. Sheriff will subpoena your ass in a minute. Do we understand each other?"

He raised his hands in surrender. "No problem. I want the m.f. caught. Danny deserved what he got. Doc Webster didn't."

Neither did Maurice, I mused, as we strolled back into the gym, where a conga line snaked its way around the perimeter of the dance floor. I saw the Rowlands for the first time and wondered how I'd missed them before. They were both in white. Claire was stunning in a snug-fitting dress with spaghetti straps and layers of iridescent white sequins. Matching shoes, of course, the ankle straps again. When she shimmied in and out of the path of one of the spotlights, the effect was blinding.

I watched for a while, then, out of the corner of my eye, caught an arm waving. Mr. Taney, looking like a teddy bear in a tuxedo, gestured from behind one of the fountains of punch. I held up a finger, hoping he'd understand that I'd be a moment longer. The conga line petered out as the music ended and I sprinted across the floor toward the other exit, just as Duck and Monty stepped back inside, laughing and backslapping like old pals.

Then Roberta Flack's silver-toned voice filled the silence—"The First Time Ever I Saw Your Face." Two bars into the song, the mood in the gym was mellow with romantic promise, a miracle only Roberta could perform in such a short span. The crowd hushed. Unable to resist the magnetic pull of the seductive atmosphere, couples came together and glided out onto the floor. Monty and Duck both moved toward me, their intent obvious. At the last minute, Monty gave way and with a gallant sweep of his arm, let Duck proceed toward me unimpeded.

"Next time, buddy," Duck told him, and gathered me in his arms.

I could count on one hand the number of times I'd danced with Dillon Kennedy. He was such a natural, his moves so polished that I was intimidated. I mean, the man is good. He was just as smooth, I discovered quickly, on slower numbers, guiding me with the slightest pressure at the small of my back.

He pulled me closer. "Come on, Leigh," he said softly, his lips against my ear. "Relax. Just go with the flow and enjoy it."

I didn't tell him but the pep talk wasn't necessary. The combination of the music, his expertise and proximity had already worked all the magic I dared allow. We weren't exactly plastered together but I doubted you could see light between us. I loved the way he fitted against me and the way I fitted against him, as if our molds had been made to match. I loved the feel of his arm around my back, the feel of my fingers entwined with his. It was right, that's all, and for the first time in centuries, certainly since Mitch, I let go, gave it up, however you want to put it. I relaxed and became one with the moment, one with Duck, moving with perfect ease, a partner in every sense of the word.

I didn't know how I'd manage ending our relationship, but I had to do it. After the pain I'd felt when Mitch was killed, I promised myself that never again would I allow anyone to become as important to me as Mitch had been. I had turned a corner in a hallway a couple of months before, seen Duck on the floor, and realized that promise had been broken a long time ago and it was time to admit it.

As much as we fought and bickered, we'd enjoyed

a thoroughly unique platonic relationship. It was Duck I bitched to about the job. It was Duck I talked to about my dates and the few with whom I'd hit the sheets, regretting it later. We could discuss, confess anything to one another. I had loved that, felt secure in that. I'd convinced myself that to add romance to that mixture would be to change it for the worse. It had been safer to keep him crammed in the Big Brother niche. Now that he was out, I'd have to give him up, along with the job.

Around us, others appeared to have succumbed to the lovey-dovey atmosphere. Even the Rowlands looked to be in a romantic mood, Claire smiling up into her husband's face, Charles peering down at her, completely smitten. When the song ended, the deejay must have realized he had a good thing going. "Killing Me Softly" began before I'd had a chance to disconnect from Duck. He pulled me even closer and I felt his lips move against my ear as gently as a hummingbird's kiss. Heat slithered across the nape of my neck and I knew that this dance would have to be our last.

"We need to work our way toward the refreshment table to your left," I said. "Mr. Taney's waiting for us."

I hadn't intentionally set out to destroy the mood, but that did it. Duck nodded, loosening his hold on me. "Can we finish this dance?"

"Sure. By the way, I ran into Tommy Broadwater and bearded him in his den."

"What'd he say?"

We were back on a more familiar footing now and I felt a shark-sized nip of regret as I related the gist of my conversation with Tommy.

"That explains why he panicked this afternoon," he said. "You done good, Warren."

High praise, from Duck anyhow, but for some reason it gave me little pleasure. And now that things were more normal between us, I didn't want to dance anymore. "Come on." I grabbed his hand, towed him toward Mr. Taney, and made hurried introductions.

Mr. Taney made a great show of sizing up Duck, evidently found him satisfactory, and shook his hand. "Just looking out for her," he said. "We got to take care of our own. I got my keys right here. Y'all want to go on downstairs now?"

We allowed as how we most certainly did and followed him to one of the doors that led directly into the school.

"'Fore I forget it, Leigh Ann," Mr. Taney said, unlocking the door to a basement staircase, "did you get that envelope I left for you this morning?"

"*You* left it?" I asked. Duck and I exchanged glances. This was an unexpected development.

"Found it on the ground outside the cafeteria door. I didn't know if you was coming to the brunch, so I slid it under your door. Now, what is it you folks are lookin' for?"

I looked at Duck, uncertain how much to tell Mr. Taney until I remembered his descriptions of Danny Totton's amatory techniques in the cemetery. There was a good chance I was the first person he'd ever mentioned it to. I held an internal debate which lasted until the bottom of the steps.

"Mr. Taney, I'm going to count on your discretion. Remember what you told me about Danny in the cemetery?" His eyes flicked to Duck and back. He nodded. "Well, the situation was worse than you thought. Those women weren't there under their own volition."

"Ma'am?"

"Danny kidnapped them and raped them. So far we know the identity of four of them. There were probably more."

Mr. Taney's shoulders slumped an inch, his face graying. "I didn't know! My hand to God, Leigh Ann, I didn't know that's what was goin' on, or I'd have done something! Oh, my Jesus!"

"It's okay, Mr. Taney." I patted his round cheek. "I'm hoping you'll be able to help us now. Danny stood in for the janitor who broke his leg—"

"Luke Haggerty. I remember that."

"Great. There's a chance he used some place in this basement to develop pictures he took of his victims. We're looking for those snapshots. It's been twelve years, so they may be long gone. But if they're squirreled away down here somewhere, they'll help provide the motive for his murder as well as identify his victims."

"Lawd, this is gonna kill poor Miz Totton. You reckon one of them did him?"

"Maybe, maybe not. Where would be the most logical place for him to set up a darkroom?"

"He would need running water," Duck added. "Some place he could block out the light while he was using the developer."

Mr. Taney unsnapped his bow tie and dropped it in a pocket. "Let's see now. No point in even bothering with this end of the building. The pool's right through yonder." He pointed over his shoulder to the door behind us. "I been in every inch of it and the locker room and showers and Lord knows I ain't seen no dirty pictures nor any place he coulda hid 'em. If they're still hereabouts, they're at t'other end."

"Any sinks down there?" Duck asked.

"There's the water closet next to the room that was the janitor's office back then. It ain't been used since they put in the pool and made a space for the office at this end."

"That sounds promising," Duck said. "Where is it? Understand, we just want to get an idea what we're up against tonight. We'll come back tomorrow to start the serious searching."

"This-a-way. I swear, if this don't beat all. Lawd, Lawd, Lawd."

The basement layout pretty much mirrored the upper floors, a long central hall running the length of the building. There were fewer doors on each side, probably one for each two upstairs. "These is full of old stuff they stopped using," Mr. Taney explained as we passed. "Desks and tables and the like. Nothing wrong with 'em, except they old. They'll bring a nice piece o' change at the auction."

I hadn't known about that. I could just imagine someone bidding for a battered desk and finding it full of pictures of nude women. "When's the auction?" I asked.

"Week after next. Gonna spread all this out on the playground and let folks browse. The rooms on this other side, they're full of old file cabinets, every last drawer jammed with paper. Hope to God them pictures ain't in there or it'll take you a slap month to find 'em. Here we are."

He opened the door to a cavern of a room that

housed the furnace and water heater. A flimsy partition set off a space crammed with boxes of books,
phys ed equipment, dented pots, cracked dishes, an
assortment of effluvia. On the far side of that was yet
another partition, behind which were several desks
and stacked chairs, a folded cot upright in a corner
with draperies tossed across it, a footlocker with
cafeteria receipt pads stacked on it, and a conference room table piled high with all sorts of junk and
rusting tools. "This was Haggerty's office. That door
there's to the water closet."

My eyes were glued to the footlocker. It was a
twin of the one I'd seen in the Tottons' attic. "I'll bet
this was Danny's," I said, removing the receipt
books. "Can we move it under the light?"

Duck grabbed the handle on one end and pulled.
It didn't move. "Damn! What's in this thing?"

Mr. Taney shook his head. "I don't know, but Miz
Totton told me a long time ago not to bother with it,
so she knows it's down here."

"Hmm." Duck shoved back the table to give him
more room, stooped and opened it. "No wonder."
The bottom was neatly packed with bars and flat,
round weights.

"Danny was a wrestler," I explained.

"He was also a drinker." In a pocket in the lid were
several empty liquor bottles cushioned by magazines
rolled around them. Duck peeled one from a Scotch
bottle. The cover left no doubt about its subject matter: hard-core porn. That was all.

Duck tossed the magazine back in, closed the lid
and brushed the dust from his hands. "Next," he
said, and opened the door of Mr. Taney's water
closet. I stepped in behind him, surprised to see that

it was a public toilet much like the ones upstairs, with four stalls and three basins. A metal storage cabinet stood just beside the door, with five deep shelves full of cleaning supplies, the labels faded with age. Mr. Taney stood beside a sink, watching us with bright-eyed curiosity.

"There you are," Duck said, pointing to the bottom shelf stacked with shallow trays and large gallon-sized plastic containers. "Developing equipment." He removed several boxes of dishwashing powder, shoved aside bottles of window cleaner caked with dust. Behind the largest box of powder, tucked well out of sight, was a leather case. "And here's his camera," Duck said, lifting it out. He unsnapped the case. "Thirty-five millimeter, an old one, too." He turned it over to show me the back. A panel of the box the film had come in was taped to the rear. "That means there's still film in it." He passed it to me.

"It's probably no good after all this time," I said.

Duck secured the snaps and looped the strap around his neck. "You'd be surprised. There have been cases where film was developed after twenty years. The pictures came out fine. We'd better give this to Josh or Roscoe to have developed at the county lab, though. God knows who his subjects were."

"This is y'all's business," Mr. Taney said, "but I can't see that boy leaving any dirty pictures in that cabinet, not with the cafeteria staff in and out of here for supplies all the time."

"A good thought," Duck agreed. "If these were his quarters, though, and he did the developing in here, they're probably in this vicinity." He closed the doors of the cabinet. "Well, we'll finish looking tomorrow."

"Can you use me?" Mr. Taney asked. "I can help till I have to pick up the ice sculpture Fred's working on for the Eighties party."

I'd forgotten Fred's talent with an ice pick. The mention of his name set off an interesting little buzz in my head. I closed my eyes to think. Something he'd said. When? Sometimes it felt as if I'd been back in Sunrise for weeks. There'd only been one occasion when we'd exchanged more than a few words and that had been . . . yesterday? Yeah. We'd sat in the front booth with Maudine, talking about Maurice and how Danny had . . . The fog cleared, the memory of Fred's voice coming in loud and strong. "The only janitor I ever saw go to work carrying a briefcase."

I opened my eyes. "Mr. Taney, have you come across a briefcase down here anywhere?"

"Briefcase." He scratched the end of his nose. "Seems to me like I have. Let me think." He slewed his mouth to one side, strolled back into the adjacent space, and stood, looking around.

"Taney!" A voice yelled from the top of the steps. "You down there?"

"Who's that callin' me?" He stuck his head out into the hall.

"Me! Les! The fountain's stopped running again."

"Shoot. Be there directly." He came back, distracted. "What was I lookin' for now?"

"The briefcase," Duck prompted.

"Briefcase. Seen it when I was looking for something to . . ." He checked under the desks, mumbling to himself. From there he squeezed between a stack of chairs and under the conference room table. "Uh-huh. Here it is. Can't reach it without messin' up my jacket."

"I'll get it." Duck slipped off his own jacket and the camera and passed them to me. Mr. Taney backed out of the cramped space and watched as Duck worked his way past the stacked chairs. He disappeared under the table and rose with the briefcase in his hand. My spirits sagged. It was old and bulky like a doctor's bag, with scuffed, scarred brown leather. Not the kind of case I'd imagined Danny carrying.

"Y'all need me anymore?" Mr. Taney asked, putting on his bow tie. "I'd better get up there. People get right ugly when those fountains ain't actin' proper. If y'all would please turn off the lights and pull the doors closed, I'd 'preciate it."

"Thanks, Mr. Taney." I walked with him out to the hall. "I'll let you know if this is the one we're looking for. If it isn't, maybe we can set up a time to meet tomorrow."

"Anything I can do to help. I owe them ladies. Jes' leave a message to the house." He hurried away with his curious, rolling gait.

"This must have been his father's," Duck said, when I joined him in the janitor's quarters again. "The initials are barely legible now, but they're definitely DMT."

"Is it locked?" I asked. It wasn't. "This is too easy," I mumbled as Duck pulled it open. Empty. "I should have known."

He stuck a hand in and felt around. "Wait a sec, Leigh." He removed a key from his pocket and used it to pry around the perimeter of the bottom panel.

After initial resistance, it began to give way. He raised it to reveal a secret compartment three or more inches deep, packed with neatly stacked plastic sleeves punched with three holes to fit into a photo album. Each sleeve held three photographs, six if you placed them back-to-back.

"I'll clear a space," I said, and began removing clutter from the surface of the nearest desk. When I'd finished, Duck, who'd spent the time separating the sleeves, laid them out seven across, four rows deep. There wasn't room for them all; he still had a handful left. The desktop had become a photographic collage of the under-forty female population of Sunrise of twelve years before. Sheryl, Dolly, Myrtle, the Burdette sisters, faces and names I'd forgotten until that moment. They were all shapes and sizes, from bond-paper white to deep dark chocolate, all nude or damned near it.

"Maudine," I said, pointing to one. There was no mistaking her buxom figure.

Duck shook his head, squinting at it. "Uh-uh. That's the Rowland woman."

I picked it up for a closer look. "You're right. The way things go in this place, they may have had the same father. These are all from the shower," I pointed out. "Are there any that were taken somewhere else?"

Duck's response was to flip over the sleeves. At first glance they appeared to be more of the same. "These," he said, pointing to several on the bottom row.

I gasped, my arms pebbling with goose bumps. I recognized the subject only because of her resemblance to her mother, Myrtle, but I certainly felt

Darla's terror. She posed blindfolded and nude, hands and feet bound, reclining on a pale green background I recognized immediately—the draperies now covering the cot in the corner.

"The son of a bitch! Those shots were taken right here. And I swear that position matches one of those nudes I photographed. *That's* what bothered me—the position of the hands! He left the ropes out of the paintings but the hands didn't look natural in them because they were tied!"

Duck's face was grim. "Who's this?" he asked, pointing to a shot of a woman against the same green draperies, her hair dark and curly, her skin a toast brown.

"Goddamn him! That's Ivette Ingram, a really nice girl. Her father owns the land New Bethel's on. She committed suicide our junior year at Central. We never understood why."

Duck removed the photos of Darla and Ivette, stacked the others, and put them aside. Then he spread out the remainder. "Bingo," he said softly.

Bingo indeed. There were still more shower scenes but most of the last batch on the desk were shots taken after the abductions. They were all there, the others, in tortured positions on the green damask draperies. Sheryl, Alice Boothe, Maudine. Blindfolded, bound, in some instances gagged.

"The scumbag," Duck muttered. "This was a sick bastard. I don't know about you, but I've seen enough. Let's get these over to Nehemiah." He crammed them back into the briefcase and tossed the camera in on top of them. "Whoever bashed his skull in did this town a favor. Let's move it."

We went back up, turning off lights and closing

doors as we left. Upstairs the voices of the Carpenters and "Close to You" filled the gym. Romance was in bloom again. The Reunion Week photographer moved through the crowd snapping pictures, the response of his flash attachment an intermittent arc of lightning in counterpoint to the sweep of the follow spots.

Jim and Sheryl crossed our path as we made our way around the edge of the room. Here, at least, Jim appeared to know what he was doing. I gave Sheryl a thumbs-up, and made a mental note to buy white the next time I needed something dressy. The contrast was striking against her dark skin. When we'd gone shopping, she'd blown an hour debating whether to get white pantyhose to wear with her white spikes, or sheer black ones for her black patent leather T-straps. She'd opted for the latter and it looked damned good, better than I'd have imagined. I had voted for the all white.

Suddenly I stopped, my mouth open with shock. Duck, bringing up the rear with the briefcase, bumped into me, treading on my heel.

"What's up, Warren?"

Finally, *finally*, I realized what had been pinging at me, a picture that had meant nothing at the time, but sure as hell did now.

"Leigh?" Duck said, his topaz eyes darkening with concern.

"How late is it? I need to find a phone. Fast."

To his credit, he didn't ask why. "Ask Mr. Taney if there's one you can use."

The sweet little man stopped wrestling with the stopped-up punch fountain long enough to direct me to the phys ed teacher's office. "Here's the key," he said, handing them over. "Just pull the door to when you come out."

I thanked him and sprinted back to the inner sanctum of the gym teachers, past locker rooms that still smelled of sweaty socks. I crossed my fingers that Mrs. Totton was still up and that her memory wouldn't fail me. She answered on the first ring and came through for me like a champ. Her memory for detail was remarkable. I was only sorry I couldn't explain why I was asking.

"Why ever not, Leigh Ann?"

There's no way I was going to tell her on the phone that I thought I knew who had killed her son. I owed it to Mr. Sheriff to run it by him first. I'd also have to prove it and for that I'd need Mrs. Totton's help.

"I'm a night owl," she said. "I rarely get to bed before midnight. Please feel free to stop in tonight. I'll never get to sleep otherwise."

I made no promises except to let her know how late we'd be. I pulled the door closed and headed for the gym, eyeing the shadows as I hurried through the locker rooms. I was edgy, I admit it. The incident in the upstairs john had left its mark. Nobody was going to catch me off guard twice in one day.

"Leigh Ann." Ted Euker, Junior stood blocking the door to the gym.

I stopped, feeling my pulse increase by a factor of two. "Teddy," I responded in kind.

His demeanor was nonthreatening. He was trying for Mr. Cool, but there was uncertainty in his eyes. "If I ask you a couple of things, will you give me straight-up answers?"

"If I can."

"Was it really Danny's body you found in the cemetery?"

I thought about it and, on a hunch that there was something Ted Junior wanted to get off his chest, decided to go for it. "They're ninety-nine percent sure it was."

"Then who was killed in Danny's car?"

I was treading on thin ice here, but my hunch was even stronger. "Maurice Fletcher."

Surprise, surprise, Teddy wasn't. His eyes were bleak. He'd known it all along. "So whoever killed them, especially Danny, probably killed Doc, right?"

Nobody had ever called the boy stupid. "Right, Ted." I let that sink in, then asked, "Want to talk?"

"Yeah, I guess so." He slumped onto one of the benches and sighed. "It was me in the pickup yesterday. And I'm sorry about this morning, too, in the bathroom upstairs. I just wanted to scare you."

"Congratulations. You succeeded. Who were you trying to protect?"

His mouth twitched. "It's complicated. My mom, for one. But Cecil told me he'd talked to you and Mr. Sheriff, so you already know what a rotten S.O.B. my dad was. We really didn't know we were providing Danny an alibi for rape that night. But this is different. I thought I was doing the right thing, keeping quiet about what I knew. I was wrong."

"How so?"

"I was probably the last person who saw Maurice before he died. He told me a couple of things I've been sitting on ever since. But to kill Doc . . . I'm not protecting her any longer."

"Who, Teddy?"

He turned, his eyes full of determination. "Maudine Fletcher."

"Everything okay?" Duck asked, when I joined him.

"I know who did it, Duck." I'd known before the call to Mrs. Totton and Teddy's story confirmed it. Once that piece of the puzzle had been dropped into place, the other one that had been bugging me resurfaced, hung in the ether for a second, then floated down and settled into its niche. "All we have to do is prove it. It's going to ruin so many things. Oh, God, Duck. People are going to hate my guts when this is over."

14

"*There you are.*" Duck came out of the back door and sat down beside me on the steps. "How long have you been out here?"

"Since dawn. Couldn't sleep, so I watched the sun come up over Old Bluenose."

"Which one is that?"

I pointed at the lowest of the three mountains that watched over the town on the east. "The one in the middle. That's actually the local name for it, because the trees at the top are so dark. Around dusk, they look almost navy. But in the morning, the sun shows above it first. The light washes down over the center part of town like, I don't know, a liquid gold waterfall. That's how the town got its name. Sunrise reaches us first."

"Why didn't you wake me? I'd like to have seen it."

I almost had. I'd peeked in at him but he was sound asleep, facedown on top of the covers, arms stretched wide. I'd watched him for several minutes, soothed by the sound of his soft, even breathing. Waking him had seemed cruel; we hadn't gotten to bed until after three. Just because I couldn't sleep was no reason to rouse him.

Hannibal, unaccustomed to companionship at this hour, woofed his delight and climbed the steps to plump his pudgy bottom down between us. Duck scratched him behind one droopy ear, then scratched me behind mine. I hoped to God Hannibal didn't have fleas.

"Wiped out?" he asked.

"More like drained." It was an apt description. The powwow with Mr. Sheriff after we'd left the dance had been tiring enough; the meeting with Mrs. Totton had been just awful. Telling her of her son's true character had been the hardest thing I'd ever had to do. She'd rejected it out of hand at the beginning, and we'd had to show her the photographs and point out the parallels in the paintings Danny had done. Even after six years of police work, I'd never witnessed that kind of pain. In the end she'd believed us. She had no choice.

She'd also been surprisingly cooperative. Whatever his crimes, Danny Totton had been her son. He'd been murdered and she wanted his killer brought to justice. She'd agreed to everything we'd asked of her. Hopefully before too long, it would be over, but life would never be the same for her.

Nunna insisted on making coffee for us before going to Bible School; neither one of us wanted anything more. It was the first time in the seven years I'd known him that I'd seen Duck refuse food. I felt better, knowing I wasn't the only one whose stomach was in knots.

"Reckon there's no other way to handle this, is there?" Nunna said, filling Duck's cup for the second time.

I waved her off when she approached me with the pot. "Not without spreading everyone else's business all over town. Most of it will come out at the trial, but this way we might be able to avoid hurting the others any more than we have to."

"That wicked, wicked child," Nunna said. "His poor mother."

"Talk about your bad seed." Anger suffused Duck's face. "And Euker. He makes me want to throw up."

"Well, at least his wife tried to make up for what he'd done," I pointed out. "It couldn't have been easy for her, holding on to his collection of nude shots until her boys were grown and could take the shock when she exposed him. If she hadn't sent that picture of Sheryl, we'd still be in the starting gate."

"It's just a shame she didn't realize that her sons were already on to their father," Nunna said.

"And she had no idea just how corrupt her husband was. Well, I'll finish this cup. Then we'd better get busy."

"And I'd better get ready for my children," Nunna said, removing her apron. "Thank heaven for Noah. They can entertain themselves drawing the ark and the animals. Y'all be sure and call me at the church if there's anything I can do to help afterwards. I'll be praying for you."

We weren't the ones who'd need it, but I thanked her anyway.

Once we left the house at seven, time seemed to

collapse in on itself. There was a lot to do to turn suspicions into facts—garbage to plow through, phone calls to make, pressure to be applied to get at the truth, film to develop. Noon was on us before we knew it. We arrived at Mrs. Totton's a few minutes late, but with everything on our respective checklists completed.

She opened the door for us with faint blue shadows under her eyes, her skin pallid and tissue paper–thin. She wore an aura of resignation. Whatever battles she'd fought since we saw her last were over. She appeared to have accepted defeat. Overcome by the magnitude of what she'd been through, I folded her in my arms. She seemed so small and frail, the bones of her shoulders so fragile to have held up under so much weight.

"Thank you, Leigh Ann," she said, with a travesty of her usual smile. "I needed that. You don't blame me for . . . for . . ." The rest wouldn't come.

"Of course not. Remember what you used to tell us? Everyone has choices available to them and in the end must accept responsibility for the ones they make. If you really meant that, then you can't blame yourself for what Danny did."

"You're right, of course." She stood a little more erect and, with her head held high, greeted Duck and led us into the living room.

Mr. Sheriff, as fresh as if he'd had eight hours of sleep, was already there, settled in a rocking chair his injured foot propped on a low stool. "Get everything done?" he asked.

"Just barely." Duck placed the material we'd gathered, several large envelopes and a grocery bag, on the chief's lap. "The photographer put up a squawk but we promised to buy a couple of Reunion Week albums so he cooperated. It's all there. Did Roscoe and Josh make it back?"

He nodded, undoing the clasp of the larger envelopes full of proofs. He picked out one, examined it at arm's length, nodded, and put it back. The grocery bag was next. He opened it, looked in, his face hardening with disgust. Closing it again, he said, "Just like you said, Leigh Ann. So everything's ten-four. Now we wait."

We didn't have long. There was a knock at the door and Mrs. Totton went to answer it. A brief, low-pitched conversation ensued, making me wonder whether someone we weren't expecting had shown up. Seconds later, Mrs. Totton ushered Maudine, who wore a stunned expression, into the room. She'd come from work and was still in uniform.

"I've told Maudine that I've been in touch with the funeral home," Mrs. Totton announced, "and have taken care of all the arrangements. Maurice and her mother will be buried side by side in Garden of Peace."

Dazed, Maudine dropped into a chair. "I . . . I don't know what to say."

"It's the least I can do." The subject was closed. "By the way, there are sandwiches, cookies, and iced tea on the sideboard. I assumed you might not have had time to stop for lunch."

"You shouldn'ta put yourself out," the chief said. "I'm not hungry but something to drink would sure hit the spot."

Probably without thinking, Maudine started to rise. Mrs. Totton pushed her back down. "You're here as a guest in my house, not a maid. I'll serve."

Removing the linen napkin covering the tray with precisely cut sandwiches, she placed it on the coffee table in front of Duck, then returned with the tray containing glasses and the pitcher of iced tea. "We'll save the cookies for dessert."

Maudine sat on the edge of her chair, her back ramrod straight, hands in her lap, knees and feet together, like a kid sent to the principal's office for some transgression or other. Her lips were pinched tight, her eyes darting from face to face. She was on uncertain ground, having been given no explanation for her required presence. The Queen Mother had called to ask her to come, a summons she'd have been hard-pressed to ignore, if only out of curiosity.

Mrs. Totton saw to the chief's request, and was filling the other glasses when the front door opened and the Rowlands strolled in, filling the foyer with chatter about the price of wallpaper. The newcomers started toward the stairs, saw us, and hesitated, as if unsure whether to join us. Claire, after an awkward pause, opted for the bright and chirpy approach. Arms full of shopping bags, she stepped into the doorway.

"Afternoon, all. Sorry, Estelle, we didn't realize you had company. There were no cars outside. We won't interrupt. I'll just put your packages in your bedroom, and you can look at them later."

"Have you two had lunch?" Mrs. Totton asked, her voice unsteady.

"Well, no, we really haven't," Charles said, eyeing the sandwich tray.

"Then take a couple of these up with you. And—" She stopped. "I'm being silly. There's no reason you can't stay down here while you eat. Nehemiah's about to give me a progress report." Maudine's startled blue eyes focused on the chief. "You two have as much right to hear it as anyone, considering what you're doing for the town. Unless you'd rather not, of course."

Charles wavered for half a second. "I'd be lying if I said I'm not interested, but I've got a conference call to make and it's important I not miss it."

"To Merriam?" Claire asked, and wrinkled her nose. "That settles it. Wait a minute, sweetie." She dumped her packages into her husband's arms, swept into the room to wrap two sandwich halves in a napkin and take them back to him. "The last thing I want to do is sit up there with my tummy growling and listen to you 'Uh-huh' and 'Uh-uh' for the next fifteen minutes. You go on. I'll fill you in on what you've missed when you come down."

She pecked him on his cheek and came in to sit in the chair beside the chief's. Her calendar must have said baby blue for today's date because that's what she wore, relentlessly, from the tiny enameled earrings in her lobes to the ballerina flats on her feet. "Maudine! Hello," she said, reaching for a sandwich. "I didn't know Fred's delivered."

"I—uh—" Maudine stuttered and rose. "I guess I'd better be going."

"No, no, no." Mrs. Totton waved her back down and shoved a glass of iced tea into her hand. "It's time somebody served you for a change. Maybe you hadn't heard, Claire. Maudine's mother died day before yesterday."

"No, I hadn't." Claire seemed genuinely distressed. "I'm so sorry. Mama will be devastated. They were such good friends."

Maudine mumbled a thank you, took a sip from the glass, and put it down, resuming her former ram-rod posture.

Claire helped herself to half a sandwich and sat back, gazing around expectantly.

"Well, might as well get this show on the road," the chief said. "Let's go over what we already knew about July 3 of '82. The boys finished decorating the float after midnight and bedded down in the gym for the night. But little Andy Euker had an upset stomach and was awake around twelve-thirty when Danny got up and slipped out of the gym. Danny proceeded to abduct a woman he ran into outside. Following the same pattern he'd used before, he tied her up, gagged and blindfolded her, and snuck her downstairs to the janitor's office. Then he stripped her, photographed her, and raped her."

Claire gasped. "Oh, my God! Danny?"

"Then he carried her out to New Bethel's ceme-tery. For some reason, he enjoyed finishing his assaults on some poor soul's grave. But Andy began to feel worse. His sleeping bag was by the door, so he got up and went outside to throw up. He saw Danny come out of the other end of the building carrying something across his shoulder. But it was dark and he couldn't tell what it was."

"My God! This is awful!" Claire looked pale.

"Danny must have forgotten that he'd told Maurice he'd give him a ride into Asheville when the float was finished. Maurice realized Danny had left and went looking for him. He met Andy out back and Andy told him he'd seen Danny going into the ceme-tery. The rain hadn't started up then but the wind and lightning had. Maurice was terrified of storms, and he asked Andy to go with him and show him which way Danny had gone. He needed that ride. That's how Andy Euker came to be with Maurice when they spotted Danny having intercourse with a lady in the cemetery."

Claire shook her head. "What must he have thought? Andy couldn't have been any more than nine or ten."

"Seven," Duck said. "Maurice didn't want him to see what was going on, so he told the boy to go back. Andy didn't argue, but he also didn't do as he was told, either. He hid behind a tree. That's where he was when the wind shifted and he heard the woman scream and saw Danny hit her. Maurice reacted immediately and went to her rescue."

"Bless his heart," Mrs. Totton murmured.

"Andy Euker's statement," Mr. Sheriff said, reading from a sheet he'd removed from yet another envelope. "'Maurice went bananas, yelling his sister's name—'"

"What?" Maudine leaned forward. "*My* name?"

"'—and grabbed Danny by the back of his jacket. He yanked him off of her and hit him with one hell of a haymaker and knocked him cold. Then he went to help his sister. She was stark naked and crying.'"

"It's a lie!" Maudine shouted. "I was home with Mama!"

"Maudine." Mr. Sheriff lowered his head to peer at her. "Either you keep your mouth shut or I will take you off to jail right now. What's it gonna be?"

Her face flared an angry red, but she sat back, gripping the arms of the chair so hard that her knuckles turned white.

"There's a little more," Mr. Sheriff continued. "'I ran back and woke up my brother, Cecil, and told him what had happened. He told me to stay there and he sneaked out. That's all I saw.'" He put that sheet aside and picked up a second. "Now this one here's Cecil Euker's statement. Want to hear it?"

"I would," Mrs. Totton said.

"All right, I'll skip to the part concerns us. 'By the time I got out there, Maudine was by herself, up on the rise near the gate, and all I could see was her back. She was freaking out, crying, on her knees with this big rock in her hands, from one of the graves, I guess, pounding the ground over and over, like you'd kill a snake. Then a car drove up to the gate, moving in jerks like whoever was driving couldn't get out of first gear. It was Danny's MG. Maurice got out and ran back to Maudine. He bent down and I realized there was somebody on the ground in front of her. Maurice said, "He's dead," and started to cry. He said something about getting help and I heard him say Daddy's name and Maudine kept shaking her head no. Finally he pulled away from her and ran out of the cemetery and disappeared in the dark. Maudine just stood there. I figured Maurice had gone to get my dad. I didn't want to be around when he came, so I went back in and faked like I was sleeping.'"

"Oh, Maudine." Claire gazed at her, her eyes brimming. "Nobody will blame you for what you did. It wasn't exactly self-defense, but still it was certainly justifiable."

Maudine started to speak, but a glance from the chief made her change her mind.

"And our final witness," Mr. Sheriff said. "Ted Euker, Junior."

Right on cue, Teddy came in from the kitchen and

stood in the doorway. He looked nervous but determined.

"Tell us your part of the story, son," the chief said.

Teddy cleared his throat. "Mom had sent me to
the gym to get Cecil and Andy because the storm
was getting worse and she wanted them home. Just
as I turned onto Main Street, I see Maurice running hell-for-leather in my direction. So I pull over
and ask him what's wrong. He says he caught
Danny raping a woman in the cemetery, that he hit
him to get him off her, and Danny was dead. He
wouldn't tell me who the woman was, just said he
was on his way to report it to my father. I made him
go over the story again, then realized that if
Maurice had only hit Danny once, Danny was
probably just unconscious. I told him I'd be glad to
check. He said he might not be all that smart, but
he knew dead when he saw it. So I told him to wait
until I picked up my brothers and I'd take him to
Dad. He said he couldn't wait and ran on down
Main."

"Poor Maurice," Mrs. Totton said. "Such a sweet
child."

"I drove on toward the school," Teddy went on.
"Just as I turned into the cul-de-sac, Danny's MG
came barreling from the direction of the cemetery,
turned right, and sped off down Main. I laughed my
head off. There's poor Maurice thinking he killed
Danny when Danny's driving through Sunrise like a
bat out of hell, as usual."

"Danny wasn't dead, after all?" Mrs. Totton asked.

"Yes, he was," the chief said. "That's why when the
wreck was found, Teddy decided not to say anything.
Andy and Cecil had told him what they'd seen.

Teddy got to thinking about it. If Maurice had really hurt Danny and that's why Danny had crashed, Maurice might have to go to jail. He didn't think that was fair, since according to his brothers, Maurice had killed Danny in defense of his sister. Since as far as they knew, Maurice had left town anyhow, he and the boys decided that the least they could do was protect his sister. Right, Teddy?"

"Yes, sir."

Maudine looked as if she was in shock, trying to digest what she'd heard.

Mr. Sheriff slipped the two statements back into the envelope. "When Danny's body turned up in the cemetery last week, they began to rethink things. They hated to think that a sister would kill her brother, and they couldn't figure out how she'd done it. Plus they'd sat on it for so long they were afraid to tell the truth. I had to threaten them with jail terms before they'd open up."

"How," Mrs. Totton asked hoarsely, "did my son wind up buried in New Bethel Cemetery?" Her face was pale, but she appeared to have weathered the narratives fairly calmly.

Duck looked at the chief, who nodded for him to take over. "Since Danny was dead and Maurice had run off, we know of course who was driving the MG. We think she stashed your son's body out of the way and went after Maurice to convince him not to tell what had happened. On the way she decided it would be simpler if he weren't around to tell anyone anything." He glanced at Maudine. "We think she caught up with him on Old Post Road on his way to the Eukers and ran him down. The medical examiner says his injuries are more consistent with someone who'd been struck from behind rather than someone who'd crashed headfirst in a car. If an autopsy had been performed back then, it would have come to light right off."

"Claire convinced me," Mrs. Totton said quietly, "that there was nothing to be gained from having his body damaged any more than it already had. I went along with it."

Maudine sagged and covered her eyes.

"Once she'd hit Maurice," Duck continued, "she realized she had two bodies on her hands. So she put Maurice behind the wheel, put it in gear and aimed it so that it went off the road and crashed four hundred feet below. I think she saw that, from the looks of it, the fire would make a visual identification impossible. Both men were about the same size and, with luck, Maurice would be identified as Danny, which is precisely what happened—with the help of a doctored dental chart."

"Right." The chief bobbed his head. "So Danny died for raping one woman too many, and Maurice died because he came to the rescue of the woman who, in the dark with only occasional flashes of lightning, he thought at first was his sister."

Maudine blinked and stared at Mr. Sheriff.

"I don't understand," Claire said. "If it wasn't Maudine, who was it?"

"The same person who killed Web to keep him from identifying Danny's body. Leigh Ann, there was a question you wanted to ask?"

I'd been so engrossed with the narrative that it was a moment before I realized what Mr. Sheriff meant. "Oh. Yes. Mrs. Rowland, I'm a shoe freak. Everybody else looks at people head to toe. I do it bass-ackward.

I've been fascinated with the way your shoes always match your outfits."

Maudine stared at me as if I'd lost it. Claire's expression was a twin of Maudine's, but she sounded affable enough as she said, "There's this little man back home who'll take any fabric you bring him and dye your shoes to match."

"How clever." I bit my tongue as Duck rolled his eyes at the ceiling. "You know the shoes of yours I really flipped over? These." I reached into the largest of Mr. Sheriff's envelopes, extracted a photograph, and handed it to her.

She looked at it, surprised. "Well, my goodness, where did this come from?" She put her sandwich, as yet unbitten, down on the table and studied the picture.

"The photographer for the Reunion Week album sent Mrs. Totton the proofs of the pictures he's taken so far. He snapped this as the three of you were leaving for the interfaith service. I love those shoes. Lilac's one of my favorite colors."

She smiled, brushing crumbs from her fingertips, something happening behind her eyes. "Mine, too. Lord, I hope he won't waste space in the album with this one. It isn't that good."

"Don't be modest. It's terrific. I was wondering though. When I saw you in the Emergency wing at the hospital, you had on this same dress and hat, but with the white patent leather pumps you were wearing last night at the dance. Why'd you change shoes?"

She held my gaze but I thought I detected a slight change in attitude. "I broke a heel just before the service began and had to hurry back here and change. No great catastrophe, just inconvenient."

"I'm sure. Well, heels can be fixed easily enough. When Mr. Sheriff's finished, could I have a closer look at them? I'd like to see if I can find a pair like them."

Her head tilted to one side, her eyes watchful. "Ohhh. I don't have them anymore. The heel snapped in two. I threw them away, which was stupid. If I'd kept them, I could have taken them back."

"Well, you know Sunrise." The chief's icy voice cut across our inane conversation. "We aim to please." He picked up the grocery bag from beside his chair, reached in, and removed a pair of badly stained high-heeled lilac pumps, both intact.

Claire gasped, but remained composed. "What in the world? Did you think they were mine? I told you, I broke a heel. Where'd you get those awful things? And why?"

"Oh, pardon my manners," the chief said, ignoring her questions. "I didn't introduce you to Dillon Kennedy here. He's a detective with the Washington, D.C. police force. Him and my boy Roscoe and a couple of his trooper buddies spent the morning at the dump, pawing through a ton of garbage to find these shoes. They've gotten so nasty we won't ask you to play Cinderella and try them on. But they're yours all right. And once the lab has had a chance to examine them, it wouldn't surprise me a tap if they found brain tissue on one of these heels. Web's brain tissue. You used the heel as a lethal weapon and killed that harmless old man."

Claire bolted from her chair and spun around to see Roscoe standing at parade rest in the foyer. Swiveling, she darted for the door to the dining room. Josh stepped through it and stood silently. Maudine gawked, mouth open.

"Sit back down," the chief ordered. "Might as well be comfortable while I read you your rights."

Claire retreated to the chair, her mouth an ugly slash across a face the color of boiled shrimp. It didn't go well with all that baby blue. She sat in frigid silence, her eyes narrowed.

"Perhaps you didn't really mean to kill Dr. Webster," Duck said gently. "If that's the case, with a good enough lawyer, you're looking at reduced charges, manslaughter, perhaps. Hit me with that shoe, now, I might bleed a hell of a lot, but I doubt you'd even knock me out. Someone Dr. Webster's age, though, his skull was thin, even thinner at the temple. Did he interrupt you while you were rifling his files? Is that the way it happened?"

Duck and the chief and I were so intent on Claire that we'd forgotten Maudine, who still sat, her mouth open in amazement. She came slowly to her feet. "Of course, it was you! You were helping Maurice with the written part of the driver's license exam. You'd tutored him before. You knew his writing. And you moved your family out to Colorado because of your mother's asthma; she always wrote us about your visits. *You* sent those postcards! You bitch!" Suddenly she launched herself at Claire, her face distorted with rage. "*You* killed my brother! You murdered Maurice!" She drew her arm back and hit Claire with such force that she knocked her over onto Mr. Sheriff. The rocking chair tipped sideways, spilling them both onto the floor, Claire landing on his wounded ankle. The chief howled with pain. Maudine, her fingers ensnared in Claire's hair, fell onto her, going for her throat with the ferocity of a lioness protecting her cubs.

"Do something. Stop them!" Mrs. Totton shrieked and stepped back against the sideboard. Teddy moved to stand next to her, an arm protectively around her shoulder.

"Leigh Ann, see to Daddy!" Roscoe shouted, and waded in to try to separate the two women.

It wasn't easy, as Mr. Sheriff was at the bottom of the pile. He pushed, I pulled, and they rolled off him. He scooted out of the way on his backside, his face white with pain.

Claire clawed at Maudine's hands, raking her fingers with her nails. She was a big woman, but Maudine was bigger, fueled by fury and vengeance. No mistake, she meant to strangle Claire to death. It took Duck, Josh, and Roscoe to break her grip.

Then Charles clattered down the steps and blanched at the scene still playing itself out. "My God, what the hell's going on here? Get away from my wife!" He reached down to grab Duck, when Claire's flailing feet caught him in the groin. He gasped and doubled over onto Duck's back.

Duck, sandwiched between Charles and Maudine, turned his head to look back at me. "Leigh," he said, his teeth clenched, "ya want to give us a little help here?"

I hadn't exactly been idle, having uprighted the rocker. I helped the chief back into it. Once he was settled, I pounced on Charles, twisting his arm behind his back. He came up, his free hand clutching his crotch, and gave me no trouble as I walked him to the sofa. He sat and stayed. By the time I'd managed that, the guys had loosened Maudine's hold on

Claire's throat. Roscoe, the taller of the two brothers, hauled her up and dumped her in the chair she'd left, holding her securely. Duck and Roscoe ministered to Claire, who, despite the angry red marks on her neck and a good deal of coughing and wheezing, croaked a stream of epithets as they helped her from the floor to the couch.

Roscoe cuffed her, just in case. Claire cussed on with such earthy language that Mrs. Totton recoiled in shock. Even her husband gawked at her through his pain as if he'd never seen her before.

"Shut up, Claire!" he shouted at her. He rocked back and forth, pale as cold cream. "You people," he said, gasping, "had better explain your actions this minute or you're looking at a lawsuit that will bankrupt this town. Remove those cuffs immediately!"

"Be quiet, Charles," Mrs. Totton snapped. "Nehemiah, are you all right?"

"I'll live. It's throbbing a little, but it's tolerable."

"It's bullshit, all of it," Claire said. "Danny never touched me. He wouldn't dare. He liked the young ones he could bully and manhandle."

Mrs. Totton stared at her in horror. "You knew about the other girls? You *knew?*"

"She knew," I said. "Darla Michaels told her the whole story." My second call to Darla had penetrated her defenses.

"And you did nothing?" Mrs. Totton asked, incredulous.

"Darla didn't know who her assailant was," I explained. "Perhaps something she said convinced Mrs. Rowland it was Danny, I don't know. But if she had come to you with what she thought was true, would you have believed her?"

Mrs. Totton's eyes were colder than the Antarctic. "We'll never know, will we?"

"I wasn't sure," Claire insisted. "But Danny never touched me. He wouldn't! I was like a big sister to him."

"Well, sir, after raping five women, what did a little incest matter to him?" Mr. Sheriff opened a smaller envelope and tossed the prints from Danny's camera onto the table. Charles picked them up, looked at them, and turned slightly green. His wife averted her eyes, unable to look at them. "Claire, why didn't you tell me?" he asked her. "My God, woman, why didn't you tell me?"

"Let's finish things up," the chief said, wincing a little. "After she wrecked the MG, Claire walked back to the school, only a mile or so, picked up her car, and drove home."

"Wrecked the MG?" Charles looked around in confusion.

"I saw her!" Maudine exclaimed. "It was almost three in the morning. The wind was getting vicious and she was out there in her yard. She said she was putting the lawn furniture away."

"Uh-huh. She was damn lucky. The storm did her a lot of favors. It prevented the car from being found for a couple of days. It felled a giant oak, leaving her a perfect burial plot for Danny. She had to wait a day or so before she buried him proper, but she got it done. The storm also left Boothe's office wide open so she could slip in and change the name on two dental charts, Maurice's and Danny's. Once that was done, she was home free."

"And the last thing she could afford," I said, "was to have Doc Webster put Danny's name to that body. So she killed him, too."

Charles had tuned out in defense of his sanity. The dreamy look in his eyes was a dead giveaway. I wondered what he was building in his mind this time. His wife's mausoleum?

Claire jerked herself into a sitting position. "That is the most ridiculous yarn I've ever heard. If you're stupid enough to pursue this, Mr. Sheriff, my lawyer will rip it to shreds. Then my husband and I will see that this town pays so dearly that the only thing it'll be fit for is a sewer."

"You've already done that, Claire," Mrs. Totton said. She sounded tired, uninterested. She glanced at the tray of sandwiches on the table. "No one's eaten. Perhaps someone would like some cookies instead." She turned around to the remaining tray.

"She killed my brother!" Maudine wailed. "Why? *Why?*"

"Perhaps because of her goals of fifteen years ago," Mrs. Totton said, removing the napkin. She began to rearrange the giant oatmeal cookies. "Claire was determined to marry money and come back so rich someday that everyone who'd called her poor white trash would have to eat their words. She was engaged to Charles when Danny died and was undoubtedly afraid that if Maurice reported what had happened to her, Charles wouldn't marry her. She'd be soiled goods." Suddenly, Teddy, who'd been watching her curiously, blanched, his mouth opening and closing. "Claire made choices in response to the situation and will have to take responsibility for them," Mrs. Totton said. "Isn't that right, Leigh Ann?"

Before I could respond, she turned from the tray with a small silver-colored revolver in her hand.

Teddy dived for cover. Josh and Roscoe reached for their service weapons.

"'Stelle, don't!" Mr. Sheriff cried, trying to lever himself to his feet.

"I must," she said, and shot Claire Peete Rowland dead center in her forehead. Then, before the Sheriff boys could fire, she turned the gun on herself.

15

"*More fried chicken,* Duck?" Nunna peered down the picnic table at his plate, which he'd just emptied for the second time. "And you haven't tried my broccoli and cauliflower salad yet."

Sheryl and I shared a look of amazement. "The man has a black hole for a stomach," I said.

"That's why he and Monty took to one another right off," Mr. Sturgis said. "My boy recognized a fellow trencherman when he saw one."

"I remember when I used to be able to eat like that," Sheryl said wistfully. "I remember when I could do a lot of things I can't anymore. Oh well." Chin propped on her fist, she surveyed the picnic grounds, her enormous eyes flitting from one table to another. "Swear to God, this is so weird. I've never been to a funeral picnic before, much less a combined wake and funeral picnic. It's so hard to believe Mrs. Totton's really gone."

"No point in wasting all the food we'd prepared,"

Nunna said. "And we're celebrating two generous lives, not their deaths. Doctor Webster and Estelle Totton dedicated their lives to the folks in Sunrise."

"What happens now?" Jim asked. "To the town, I mean."

Monty, matching Duck mouthful for mouthful, said, "That's up to Rowland. I figure I'll hold off for a decent interval, let him bury his wife and adjust to life without her, if he can, then let him know we're still interested, if he is. We really need that mall."

"Miss Nunna might not agree with you," Jim said. "My mother-in-law certainly doesn't."

Monty looked down at the end of the table. "That right, Miss Nunna?"

Her expression was unreadable at first. "*If* Mr. Rowland decides to put it up and *if* he keeps his word about moving our people to Garden of Peace, and *if* that means that it's open to all of us from now on, I guess I could go along with it."

"Well, do-Jesus." Mr. Sturgis smiled, his eyes bright and warm on her. "So Monty finally told you."

"I did," I confessed. "After yesterday, I figured it couldn't do any harm, since it probably won't happen anyway."

"We'd best forget the whole thing," Sheryl said. "He's not coming back here. I mean, the whole place has got to remind him of his wife. Seems to me, after all she did, he wouldn't want any reminders."

"You never know." Monty waved a pork chop bone for emphasis. "I get the impression he was committed not just because this was Claire's hometown, but because it was a new type of venture for his firm. He may want to go ahead and follow through."

"It may have been a new venture," I grumbled,

"but it damned sure wasn't a new design. It's just like the Company's Comin' chain he put up all over the west. I stayed at one in Portland. The only difference with the motels is that each cabin stands alone. For the mall he simply stacked them and smooshed them together. That curved A-frame department store for Sunrise's mall and the main building of the motels are just alike. Take a look at the first faked postcard from Maurice. If Maudine had seen that billboard, she'd have recognized it."

"And Claire sent it and the rest," Monty said. "But who called Mrs. Fletcher and pretended to be Maurice?"

"Claire," Duck said. "Her voice is deep for a woman. She'd known Maurice all his life, knew how he talked, and knew his mother was hard-of-hearing. It worked."

"Ugh." Sheryl shuddered. "What kind of mind dreams up a scheme like that?"

"The warped mind of a woman engaged to a rich man she intended to marry no matter what," I said. "Mrs. Totton may have been the way out of Sunrise for most of us, but Claire had done everything right, graduate degree, everything, and was still stuck here teaching. Charles was her ticket out and she wasn't going to let anybody mess that up. All told, she killed three people to get and keep that man."

"Poor Doc." Monty's spirits took a momentary plunge. "Bashed on the head with a woman's spike heel. What a shitty way to die—excuse me, Miss Nunna."

"How'd she set the fire so she'd be back at the worship service before it started burning good?" Mr. Sturgis asked.

"Simple." Duck eyed the desserts. "She soaked a

stack of patients' files and left them on the hot plate. From that point it was just a matter of time. They smoldered a good while before they caught. She returned to Mrs. Totton's, changed shoes, and hurried back to the service in time to sing. Perfect alibi."

Monty sighed and got up. "Well, I'd better go circulate. With Mrs. Totton gone, I sorta feel I should play host. I'll be back for some cobbler, Miss Nunna."

"All right, son." She patted his arm as he passed. "Best I put it away for you now, the way these folks are eating."

Son. Uh-huh. Things were working out fine.

Duck poked me in the side. "Are you as good a cook as Miss Nunna? I've got my standards. Any woman I marry's got to be able to cook."

"Lucky for you that there are plenty of them out there," I said. "As for me, I figure there's a man somewhere who'll appreciate a woman who can rip the cardboard off a microwavable frozen dinner in two seconds flat, and punch in the cooking time without having to look at the keypad."

"Afternoon, everybody."

I turned around backwards on the bench to greet Mr. Sheriff. He looked tired. "Want to sit down?" I asked.

"No'm, I'm just hear to say how-do. Trying to get around to as many as I can, keep folks' spirits up. Miss Nunna, I want to thank you for letting me take up so much of Leigh Ann's time. I figure we'd have solved Web's murder by and by, but I never thought we've have everything wrapped up in a few days time because of a woman's passion for shoes. When are you takin' her home, Duck?"

"Wait a minute," I interrupted. "He isn't taking

me anywhere. I drove my car here. He's the one running up rental car bills. If you're asking when I'm leaving, I'm not sure. Maybe tomorrow morning. Maybe not."

The chief gave Duck a knowledgeable grin. "You're gonna have trouble with this one." He sobered. "I'd like to ask a favor, Leigh Ann."

This warranted a cautious response. "What is it?"

"Maudine's burying her mama and Maurice tomorrow afternoon. She won't lack for a turnout, folks bein' as curious as they are, but I think it would mean a lot to her if you were there."

"Then I'll stay. What about Mrs. Totton's funeral?"

"No service. The letter she left for me laid it all out. She'll be buried beside her boy in their family plot. No preacher, no words over her neither. That's what she wanted, that's what she'll get."

I glanced sidewise at Duck and his eyes met mine. He'd said the same thing about his mother's desire for a monster television a while back.

I had a question for the chief that had kept me awake last night. "Mr. Sheriff, is there anything we could have done to prevent what happened?"

"She felt responsible, Leigh Ann. Danny had already paid for his crimes. She wanted to make sure Claire did, too. Once she'd seen to that, she herself had to pay. That was her code."

It wasn't good enough. "I keep thinking that if she'd known about her grandchild, it might have ended differently," I said.

"Grandchild?" Jim asked. "What grandchild?"

"Later, honey." Sheryl patted her husband's hand.

"She knew," the chief said. "Met the boy at the brunch Thursday but didn't realize he was her grandson until I told her yesterday morning. After she got over the shock, she allowed as how it was best to let sleeping dogs keep on snoozing. Couldn't do anything but harm to tell the boy how he came to be in this world and the kind of man his daddy was. Maudine agrees."

"Leigh Ann." Nunna's eyes warmed me. "None of it was your fault."

"Amen," the chief said. "It ended the only way it could have, so there's no reason for you to feel guilty. If anybody should, it's me. I should have guessed that's what 'Stelle would do." He held my gaze for a second longer than necessary and suddenly I was sure he had known what to expect. He might not have anticipated that it would happen when and where it had, but he'd known it was coming. In allowing it to happen, he'd done what he'd felt was best for the people under his protection, Mrs. Totton included.

"I 'preciate everything you—and Duck—did for me," he said. "You ever need anything, either one of you, just call. And come back to see us, hear?" He swung away on his crutches and headed for the next table.

"You were right about him," Sheryl said, watching his progress. "He's okay. I wish I'd trusted him. Now." She turned to me. "Are you really going back to D.C. and your job?"

"And me?" Duck asked quietly.

I looked down the table at Nunna. She smiled, her eyes telegraphing a message in mother-to-daughter language. She was right. For all the horror of the afternoon before, I was glad I'd been here, glad that, despite the carnage and senseless tragedy, I'd had a hand in exposing the dark side of Sunrise to the light, in revealing the ugliness that had clouded so many lives for so long. I had enjoyed my brief professional association with Mr. Sheriff and his sons, had enjoyed the spice Duck had added to the mix. They had restored my pride in being a cop and my confidence in myself. Whether I went back to the job or not, I felt damned good about myself inside.

I turned to Sheryl. "Let's just say I'm giving it serious consideration, okay?"

Duck grinned. "Hot damn!"

♨ HarperPaperbacks *Mysteries by Mail*

The Weaver's Tale by Kate Sedley
It is the 15th century. A man has been murdered, and the brother of a respected citizen hanged for the crime. Months later, the victim turns up alive—only to be murdered a second time. Who is the killer and how might this all be connected to a nobleman's fancy?

Drift Away by Kerry Tucker
Photojournalist Libby Kincaid learns that her friend Andrea has been murdered by the accused killer she had been defending. Libby goes undercover at Andrea's cutthroat law firm and finds herself in the hot seat as she comes close to a murderer.

Homemade Sin by Kathy Hogan Trocheck
When feisty Callahan Garrity of House Mouse Cleaning Service hears of her cousin's murder, she dons a detective cap and does a job on grease and crime in Atlanta.

Parrot Blues by Judith Van Gieson
A chief suspect in the kidnapping of Neil Hamel's client and her rare macaw has expired. To find out more, Neil enters a dangerous game of bird-smuggling and one-upmanship. So far, the only eyewitnesses are parrots—and they're not talking.

The Trouble with Thin Ice
by Camilla T. Crespi

A bride-to-be, is arrested for a very cold-blooded murder—the week of her wedding. Simona Griffo, a friend who likes to meddle in such matters, starts asking questions. As she puts the pieces together, however, she unwittingly pushes herself onto thin ice.

Hearing Faces by Dotty Sohl

Janet Campbell's neighbor has been brutally killed, and there's no apparent motive in sight. Yet Janet refuses to live in fear. When a second murder strikes the apartment complex , Janet's life turns upside-down. Seeking answers she discovers greedy alliances, deadly secrets, and a vicious killer much too close to home.